Sandhill County Lines

SANDHILL COUNTY LINES

stories

Clay Reynolds

TEXAS TECH UNIVERSITY PRESS

This book is typeset in Dante. The paper used in this book meets the minimum requirements of ANSI / NISO Z39.48-1992 (R1997). ♾

Designed by Lindsay Starr

Library of Congress Cataloging-in-Publication Data
Reynolds, Clay, 1949-
Sandhill County lines : stories / Clay Reynolds.
    p. cm.
Summary: "Sandhill County—Clay Reynolds's Yoknapatawpha—is the setting for nine short stories depicting life in small-town and rural north central Texas, the region that also informs Reynolds's novels, from The vigil and Agatite to his most recent, Threading the needle"—Provided by publisher.
    ISBN-13: 978-0-89672-615-4 (pbk. : alk. paper)
    ISBN-10: 0-89672-615-0 (pbk. : alk. paper) 1. Texas—Fiction. 2. Short stories, American. I. Title.
    PS3568.E8874S26 2007
    813'.54—dc22

                                                                        2007018625

08   09   10   11   12   13   14   15   /   9   8   7   6   5   4   3   2
BK

Texas Tech University Press
Box 41037, Lubbock, Texas 79409-1037 USA
800.832.4042 | ttup@ttu.edu | www.ttup.ttu.edu

For Judy, without whom I'd never hung on nearly this long

.

Contents

Preface

Not long ago, I learned of the death by natural causes of a man I knew as a friend in high school. Although I'd not had any communication whatsoever from him in nearly forty years, the news of his death awakened my own sense of mortality, as such news always does. But a more shocking reaction followed quickly: I realized that even though his name was as familiar to me as anyone's I'd ever known—we were the same age, grew up together; he was one of that close inner circle of friends every child develops, particularly in a small town—I could not "see" his face in my mind. It bothered me.

After a few weeks, the problem moved from nagging to annoying. By coincidence, I had to return to my hometown on a personal errand. It's a four-hour drive, and on the way, the notion that I still couldn't conjure the face of my deceased childhood buddy began to bother me more and more. In spite of the fact that I was in something of a hurry to complete my errand and return, I decided to stop by the public library and to spend a few minutes perusing old high school yearbooks, seeking to restore a countenance to the name of my long-ago friend.

I easily located his "mug shot" in our high school annuals. The youthful and somewhat smart-aleck face that peered into the camera's lens did more than recreate an image to match memory of a name. It also uncorked a veritable flood of other recollections I had of him, of us, during our youth. I also remembered incidents I had long forgotten:

games of kick the can and touch football on his yard, birthday parties, and many long, idle afternoons in the Texas heat. There was also the time he "borrowed" (without my knowledge or permission) my brand-new bicycle and brought it back with a bent fender and broken wheel sprocket, but without apology; and there was the sudden, bitter, and somewhat guilty recollection that the last time we talked, we quarreled over twenty dollars he owed me and never repaid. Of course, I also recalled the time we shared an afternoon playing the first electric guitar either of us had ever seen, and a wild road trip we once made to Wichita Falls to score some alcoholic beverages. We were unsuccessful, but we had an adventure.

I don't know what happened to him after we querulously parted company in that long-ago summer. In truth, I can't say that I've since thought much about him at all. But there was something strange about looking into the grainy black-and-white image of his eighteen-year-old face, a countenance I once more carry handily in my mind's eye, something almost surreal. When I saw it, I instantly understood that in my mind he will always be as he was—at eight, at twelve, at eighteen—for I have no correspondence with him from any later time. He is, in a sense, frozen in place, as, I assume, am I to any number of people from that time and place who possibly have not cast more than an occasional thought my way over all these years.

Another odd thing happened, though, as I sat there in that small-town library and flipped through the pages of those old yearbooks. Time and the urgency to depart dismissed, I found myself wandering through a thicket of long-forgotten faces and names. And like most thickets—at least in West Texas where mesquite passes for trees—it was full of painful thorns and twisted, misshapen limbs that refused to conform themselves into a comforting scene. Each photo recalled a personality, and I was overwhelmed by a wilderness of wonder and impossible questions about what became of them. I know what happened to some, naturally, as my family and what few of them I continue to keep contact with keep me informed. But apart from that comparative handful, I had no knowledge of the fates of most of these people at all. At one time in my life they were, for better or worse, more important to me than any other group of people in the world. I knew all of them—loved some, lusted hopelessly after others, desperately envied or felt superior to many, hated and feared more than a few. A number of them struck me as being people I always planned to get to know better, but somehow never did. And now, nearly a half-century later, I realized that I had utterly forgotten almost all of them, shut them away in a vault of memory that has been rarely if ever opened.

It's a natural thing, of course, to recollect such people and wonder what they became when they grew up, to wonder if they married, divorced, found careers, achieved wealth or went bust, realized their ambitions or found themselves broken and disillusioned. Many I remembered as individuals with firm convictions and sound ideals, the sort of folks who exuded confidence in the rightness of their visions, however wrong they may have been, and the certainty of their beliefs, however erroneous they were ultimately revealed to be. Our generation was brought up to have convictions, to develop them and nurture them, and never to surrender them for caprice. In most ways, I was just like them, and like most of them, surely, I soon found that the world was a far larger and more difficult place than I ever imagined from my small-town, West Texas perspective. Life, I eventually learned, was primarily made up of lies and limitations. Visions, beliefs, convictions, I later discovered, were subject to as much sudden and violent change as the West Texas weather.

At the same time, there was so much that seemed so right in those faces, so self-assured and courageous. Blemishes were, naturally, carefully concealed, and even the candid shots of ourselves going about the all-too-important business of being adolescents seemed to exude a kind of surety about where we were, who we were, and who we were sure we would become. So for several more hours than I truly had time to spend, I found myself flipping those glossy pages and confronting myself as I was, one of many long-forgotten faces and names; and I was constantly stung by how quickly the vitality slips away from a time and place and people, how rapidly it passes away into dusty memory.

———

One dictum writers hear over and over again, particularly from instructors of writing who, often, are not themselves successful writers, is to "write what you know." Most writing students take this to mean that setting, background, details of character and plot are to be drawn exclusively from personal experience or, at the very least, from learned knowledge. They therefore attempt to shape facts into fiction. The result is seldom satisfying. Caught somewhere between memoir and extrapolation, they constantly struggle with compromise, with the difficulty of making the actual shape fit the imaginary mold so they can tell the story they want to tell. Too often, writers respond to a criticism that something is not credible or doesn't work with the protest, "But that's what she really did!" or "That's what he really was like!" Reality always gets in the way when a writer takes the instruction literally, for no fiction can ever be as remarkable as fact, or as incredible. Made-up stories, fictions, should never conform to the reality of memories, however embellished, softened, or sharpened they may have become over time. The facts—what one knows—always get in the way and turn things back onto themselves; and in the end, what comes out usually seems pointless and vague. At the very most, it's anecdotal.

What that imperative clause means, I think, is that a writer should discover what he or she knows in the heart, not the head. It is the emotion that concrete memory evokes that forms the foundation for a story, that shapes a character and creates a fiction that reveals something about what the writer wants to say. This is because what any writer wants to say is something about him- or herself. We are, after all, as individuals, the most fascinating people we know; loathe as we are to admit the conceit, we are desperately eager to share all we know of ourselves with anyone we can find. In a way, writers are like barking dogs, shouting "Look at me, look at me! See what tricks I can do to show you something about myself." Emotions, be they horrendously traumatic or wonderfully endearing, are the core of that revelation, for it's not the facts of any given memory that cause us to recollect it; rather, it's the response such events stimulated in us, the emotive reaction we had that we ultimately want to share. It's as if what our "barking" is really saying is, "See, you feel it the same way I did!"

So, emotions are the bedrock of fiction. They are more powerful than the facts, and many times, it is how we feel about something—in reflection, in retrospect, in rumination—that informs our need to create fictions based on it. In order to do this effectively, a writer needs to distill the given facts, and from that process glean what was truly meaningful, whether it was tragic or joyful, gruesome or hilarious—and recreate it in a way that will provoke in the reader a similar—one hopes identical—reaction. By doing so, in a roundabout way, we come to terms with a recognition of who we truly are.

Not long ago, I wrote the following about my grandfather and my childhood, and a place that no longer exists. It illustrates what I mean:

Punkin Center

The place was called Punkin Center, with an *n* instead of *mp*, but no one imagined that it was original. There were Pumpkin Centers all over the place—even one in the next county over, and I eventually heard of one in Oklahoma, Tennessee, and even Ohio. But in Hardeman County, it was "Punkin Center." I assumed for years it was an aberrant pronunciation, and I was always disappointed to fail to see any pumpkins there, for I associated pumpkins with Halloween candy and Thanksgiving dinner, pleasant and inviting things. But I learned later that the real name was "Punkin Center," named for some guy named "Punkin," who set up the store there years before. That may have been a lie.

It was not the name but the store that made it special. It was located on the southeast corner of a remote crossroads. The roads themselves were arrow-straight and carelessly paved with that curious gray-white concrete associated with old movies and what little remains of the pre–World War II highway system that occasionally can be glimpsed from an interstate overpass. The stripes were fuzzy orange, and the cracked surfaces were streaked with black tar patches half-heartedly applied to cover the potholes, and there was no shoulder, just a bar ditch overflowing with crisp Johnson grass, already seeded out and dying a rattling death in the summer wind. Once, the roads probably came or went somewhere important, but other thoroughfares replaced them long before I was born. Now they were merely country roads, leading nowhere and back, except to Punkin Center. And that was good enough.

The store itself was a kind of everything place, unique in its commonplace identity. On one side were antique gasoline pumps with the mechanical handles that required an attendant to fill a glass tank on top while a bell ticked off the gallons, then allow gravity to run it through a hose into a tank. There was no longer an attendant or a bell. Nor was there gasoline, not since before the war, when coupons were hard to get, good help harder. The driveway was mostly gravel, but it used to be just dirt, mud when it rained. That wasn't much of a worry. In those days in West Texas, it never rained.

There was a long, covered porch that ran the width of the front. On one side it was anchored by a huge chinaberry tree, and on the other by a towering mimosa. They were the only trees worth the name that would grow there. Along the planked floor of the porch, benches and wooden rocking chairs and those rusty old metal lawn chairs with backs like seashells all lined up, facing out to the identical dusty fields beyond. Behind them, and beneath flyspecked sash windows and an array of rusting metal signs advertising tobacco and bread and beverages, was a row of block-ice coolers, and in each was the excuse for the stop, the reason why my grandfather told me we'd go to Punkin Center. "We'll get us a col' drink," he would say; then with me riding shotgun, he'd pilot my grandmother's old Model A from their farmlike house down the brittle white-hot griddle of broken pavement and into the dusty lot of Punkin Center. We'd wait for it to quit dieseling so he could set the brake, then get out and climb up those splintery wooden steps—a threat to barefoot boys—then sit a spell in the shade with a dripping bottle of frigid, sweet liquid confection in our hands, while he looked with rheumy eyes—never shielded by any shade other than his hat or his hand—out over the drought-ruined fields and breathlessly cursed the encroaching mesquite and the "goddamned Republicans" who were responsible, if not for the years of rainless summers, then at least for everything else that was wrong in the universe.

My grandfather was a Yellow Dog Democrat.

Inside the store, there were shadows and smells. Leather and fresh denim, gun oil, grease, and the distinctive odor of mothballs and linseed. The walls were hung with utensils for field and kitchen, and the shelves were stocked with old-fashioned hand tools and cooking gimcracks. In the back, gathering dust in the darkness, were groceries. Nothing fancy. Breakfast cereals hot and cold, bread, flour and meal, canned vegetables and fruits, tins of lard and syrups, crackers and cookies, and one small rack of nickel candy bars—Baby Ruths, Butterfingers, Three Musketeers, Mars Bars, Cherry Mashes, and Zeros—I was forbidden to touch and knew better than to ask for. And there was a dusty display of plastic toys, sacks of soldiers, cowboys and Indians, tiny cars—also unthinkable, "a goddamn waste of money," I'd heard grumbled from a man whose spirit had the admiration of generosity, otherwise. Punkin Center clung to the past that spawned it, refused to give in to the present. Inside that store, it was as if time stopped sometime in the twenties, but the place continued to move forward carrying a grudge against imposed change.

A long counter ran down one side of the store, and on top was a thick roll of brown paper and a spindle of string for wrapping bulky purchases. At one end was a massive cash register that rang with the sharpness of a rifle report when a sale was made. The place was cooled by huge rotating fans, their axles linked by a serpentine leather belt that turned on a stile propelled in endless rotation by a noisy electric motor back in the dusty, shadowy depths, next to the iceboxes where the dairy produce reposed, the only concession to modernity in sight. H-bombs and *Sputnik* were of far less consequence than gone-over cottage cheese. The Russians had given us no harm except for part of the proper name of tumbleweeds (Russian thistle).

I was seven, then eight and nine in those summers. My grandfather had been a horseman, a wrangler, but I never saw him on a mount, and he was a rural mail carrier, but I never saw him carry or even read a letter, although I did watch him hang a sack of mail from a hook, where it would be magically snatched away, another put in its place, by the FW&D Zephyr when the mail car sped by en route to Denver or Fort Worth. The train was a constant in his life, the tracks a horseshoe pitch from the back porch. In spite of the noise, sparks, and violence of its passage, it was somehow comforting in its constancy. Trains meant things were moving, that there was still a world out there somewhere beyond the dusty horizon. That was reassuring, somehow.

My grandfather was a West Texan, and he understood the country and the men who broke their backs on it, and the reasons why it broke them. After securing our cold drinks and making our manners with the Punkin Center storekeeper, who always wore a huge white apron, white shirt, and tie, and who never seemed glad to see anyone, we'd go out and sit on the rusty lawn chairs, joining the men in bleach-faded overalls and blue and brown workshirts starched so stiff you could cut yourself on a crease. They sat, six-ounce Coke and Dr Pepper and 7-Up bottles in leather-callused and liver-spotted hands, sweat-crusted straw hats on their hair-thin heads, heavy, worn brogans stained with the red loam of the cotton fields on their feet. Now and then one would sigh or curse mildly, and once in a while one would roll a cigarette or fire a cheap cigar to match my grandfather's pipe in filling the burgundy wasps' nests and dirt-dobber mounds in the eaves with clouds of gray-blue smoke that doubtlessly reminded some of the myth of thunderstorms. Some worked plugs and expertly spat their amber juice onto the red ant beds that formed large bald circles in the sparse gray gravel of the drive, never soiling the porch, never needing to wipe a drip away from a sunburned chin. Few spoke more than a few words. But what they said resonated: The cotton wasn't going to make again this year, because it needed water they couldn't afford to drill for or pump out, rain they decided they'd never see, and was overrun with Johnson grass, careless weed, milkweed, devil's claw, and thistle. Hoeing was no damned good. The weevils and beetles would get what the sun and wind didn't. The wheat planted last summer had been left in the fields to feed cattle that now were turned out on burned prickly pear and useless mesquite beans in the endless hope that somebody somewhere would declare a war on somebody else so the price of beef would rise once more. A mule was better than a horse for work in the sun, but milkers went sour in hot weather, and there was nothing to do about chickens that wouldn't lay but to eat them. They were too tough to fry, had to be boiled.

And I was barefoot and in short pants, sunburned and bored, and the only kid in sight. I knew better than to talk, to ask for anything, or even to move. My grandfather never scolded me, but I always feared he might. So I sat there nearby and was quietly proud of him who always wore a gray felt Stetson, no matter what the weather, and whose shirt was always white and khakis were always clean, whose boots laced high on his ankle because, he once told me, that's what real cowboys wore—"not those fancy star-studded house slippers you see in the picture shows"—and which were always polished to a high black sheen that matched his Kaywoodie that he kept lit with sulfur-smelling matches. "You ever see a match burn twice?" he'd sometimes ask me. I always denied it. I always got burned. I didn't mind, though. I sat and listened to the grasshoppers and cicadas singing in the August heat, marveled at the occasional coo of a mourning dove, and think of my friends at the swimming pool in town or gathering for somebody's birthday party or watching cartoons on somebody's Philco television, and I tried to work up an envy that wouldn't come any more than it would rain on wishful thinkers. I'd finish my Delaware Punch, hurrying to get it down before it heated to the point where it came to taste like cough medicine, and long for another while I watched my grandfather sitting and smoking and staring out to the sun-baked fields with the men around him, thinking of a time when those crumbling roads out there led to somewhere that they never had the time, the motivation, or the courage to find. Instead, they were here, at Punkin Center, sitting in the shade of a porch, shielded from the crop-killing, soul-draining sun, out of the sand-laced blast furnace of a wind, drinking ice-cold soft drinks into which they sometimes put a handful of peanuts or, if they were bold enough, a dollop of whiskey from a poorly hidden flask, and silently contemplating the injustice of Adam's fall and the vile, utter uselessness of their own brows' sweat.

Punkin Center is gone, now. The store is gone, and so are all the others like it. Places that never knew neon signs and air-conditioning, places that only sold what you needed, never what you wanted, but never tempted you beyond your means. The crossroads there have been widened, topped with modern pavement that is well maintained so it can transport the absentee landlords in their hermetically sealed, air-conditioned, and fully equipped vehicles to and from their holdings and the shiny glass-and-steel malls of the city. Nearly fifty years later, the spot where Punkin Center stood is a blank caliche turnout that leads to a pipe fence gate that opens into a gravel road that meanders off into the choking mesquite—no one would ever guess cotton fields had once been there—toward a natural gas well. The chinaberry and mimosa trees are long gone, choked out by ubiquitous mesquite. There's not a timber or a nail left to remind anyone that there was a time when a store like that offered an oasis in a desert of hopelessness, a community where men driven desperate by drought and bad luck could gather silently and sit wordlessly and think and smoke and sip their lives away without regret, whittling silently on the wood of wonder, not seeking a form to explain fortune, only wearing down time, one long, sharply curled shard after another.

Punkin Center was a port, in a way, and in another way, it was a church, a Gilead with the balm of fellowship. The items it offered for sale were only an excuse to come there. Pick up a box of soda crackers, maybe a sack of pure cane, possibly a package of Brown Mule and fifty cents' worth of ten-penny nails, and four spuds for dinner. Pay for it all with two-dollar bills left over from cookie-jar savings amassed during the war that took a son or a brother, or sent somebody home with a long blank stare in his eyes, one that wouldn't go away, no matter how many sermons he heard, and maybe take that buffalo nickel or mercury dime received in change and, after a moment's thought, drop it on the counter in trade for an ice-sweating bottle of commercially concocted nectar. The beverage wasn't important. Gyp water or day-old coffee would have done, as would cheap whiskey or homemade gin. It wasn't the beverage. It was the company. The store created that. Punkin Center was that. More than an enterprise, an emporium, a commerce, it was a reason to get up that morning, put on a clean shirt, and shave the stubble from a vein-scarred chin, a place to go and try to find a cause, a purpose, and then, to discover it while sitting out there in the relief from a blistering sun, sipping something cold and wet while watching towering dust devils dance across the cracked pavement of roads that led nowhere but to and from Punkin Center.

———

Some might say that by characterizing this afternoon's visit to a remote country store with my grandfather that I had "preserved" it, saved it in some odd way from the oblivion of time and faulty memory. But I don't think so. In the first place, the piece, even though it's based on many, many facts recollected from my youth, is not factual. Punkin Center was a real place, a store, and I did visit it with my grandfather, and we did drive there—often—in my grandmother's old Ford. But on no particular visit did all of the elements described in the piece come together at once. And there are several manufactured "facts" in the piece, as well, lies if you will. I never was a fan, for example, of Delaware Punch—too sweet—but the sentence, I think, reads better with that particular name, as opposed to Dr Pepper or 7-Up, one of which was more likely my beverage of choice. I could have as easily written "Grape Nehi" or "Chocolate Soldier," if my purpose was to stretch invention even more than I did in an effort to tie the event to a specific time and place. But "Delaware Punch" seemed to fit, and I was more comfortable with that minor prevarication.

Made-up facts aside, though, many details of the sketch are actually drawn directly from my memory, even though some of the feelings I express in the sketch are not peculiarly associated with that particular time or that particular place. Rather, they are drawn from my entire childhood experience, the emotions I remember being connected to a more general time and place, to people and events that, in and of themselves, are random and disorganized in the hodgepodge of experience, in the personal encyclopedia of what I know.

What I do know—and what the sketch is really about, I think—is that I admired my grandfather, as do most small boys. I saw him as being different, better somehow, from others. I believed that I had been chosen in some odd way to be proud of him, to emulate him, and to carry the image of him in my heart. As he died when I was still quite young, that image is far more important to me than the reality of him, the fact of him. It is that image and the emotions associated with it that I wanted to shape into a short fiction about people who lived on an agrarian landscape in a time baked by drought and haunted by doubt, a place where resignation vied with determination on a daily basis, where unquestioning commitment could only be sustained by meeting the hardness of life head-on. These, for better or worse, were formative elements to my own character. Those emotions, forged in the harsh remoteness that was West Texas in that time, are mostly what I know, so that's what I wanted to write about. What I know.

As a writer, I think, what I know isn't merely West Texas. What I know—or think I know—is people. It just happens that some of the most interesting people, to me, are West Texans. That doesn't make them different from people anywhere else in most ways, but it does provide a locus, a platform from which knowledgeable fictions can be launched. It also provides me with the opportunity to seek recognition.

———

In the prologue to *Agatite*, my second published novel, I wrote a line about my imaginary county and town. I said it was a place more or less stuck in "a time when hope had promise to bolster it." I was writing, then, about an earlier time than the yearbooks I glossed in my library investigation, a time more closely aligned with Punkin Center, a locale that I've borrowed and enlarged in my fictions. But the phrase came back to me as I turned those pages and felt myself falling helplessly backward into a time and place that existed some fifty-odd years ago. Apart from the youthful and eager faces of my contemporary adolescents, I also saw how many were posing in front of places that no longer existed. The buildings, businesses, and concerns that provided a backdrop for the yearbook photographs are almost all gone, now, some not even well remembered. A few of the houses that provided scenic stages for dressy group portraits have fallen into dereliction, or have been torn down entirely. Some have been victimized by fire, but most others have merely fallen before changing times, new technologies, altering economics. Even the high school building itself is long forgotten, razed to make way for a more modern structure that, today, is itself showing alarming signs of age. Our school, we thought, was huge, solidly old-fashioned and substantial, and it was dear to us, our "alma mater," our "auld lang syne." Now, its image is relegated to a faded color photograph on the library's wall, just as so many places have been filed away as grainy impressions, gradually slipping into the past, gradually being woven into the fabric of memory.

In a way, it's as if my entire history, like the history of all those black-and-white images in those yearbooks, is fading away, as well. Memory alone can't sustain it, because, like any fabric, it wears thin with overuse and is subject to decay. Facts are too easily patched into a quilted collage. Too often, we only remember the names, not the faces, and too often we've forgotten the hopes that we thought were impervious to change so long as there was a promise to bolster them.

All that's left are the emotions; all that matters is the heart.

———

For me, the stories of Sandhill County are like those images. They are my poor effort to preserve the emotions, the hearts, not the facts of a time and place and people I happen to know. There is no attempt here to tell the true stories of those images or to try to sustain their existence by committing them to some prosaic memorial. On the contrary, my stories are fictions, and while they are based on what I know, I maintain that what I know is what I felt—and still feel—for that place and that time and those people. In a sense, these stories are like photographs in a high school annual: snapshots, both candid and posed, of people in a time and place that, however remote and naïve it may have been, was still the center of their universe. As they were the center of that center, their stories become all that much more intense and, I think, that much more true. Like the cores of planets, those people are concealed behind rigid facades until recognition reveals them; whether they boil over, explode, or merely simmer quietly in the vacuum of time and memory depends much more on their integrity than it does on their faithfulness to fact.

The stories in this collection concern different looks at several individual centers, and they display brief recognitions, both quiet and explosive, both comic and tragic, that expose those hidden cores and often force the characters in them to come to terms with who they are and where they are going. In some, such as "A Better Class of People" and "Mexico," I've attempted to show the deeper honesty that lies beneath a surface of image, and to illustrate how we can learn from the folly of others. At the same time, I hope to illustrate how that even in the most dire situations, humor can often provoke the deepest wisdom. In others, like "The Prodigal" and "The Baptism," I've attempted to demonstrate how appealing appearance and blind faith can conceal a terrifying corruption that, often, is only revealed in tragedy and the scars that life leaves.

Most of these stories are, in one way or another, love stories. I think "Etta's Pond" and "A Train to Catch" are stories about propinquity, even after death, and loyalty to what once mattered, even though it is long gone. "Bush League," on the other hand, deals more with the deceiving, fickle nature of anticipated affection and the sadness that comes with the ultimate confrontation with fate. "Dogstar" and "Nickleby" are about compassion of a different sort, of the love of man for beast, particularly when the beast is a man.

Written over a period of about twenty years, these fictions have come to represent something else, not artifacts fixed in time such as photos in a high school yearbook, but evolving testaments to what I know and what I hope I've learned. Accordingly, I have revised most all of them from their original published forms. In some places, I've tried to soften them, and in other places I've tried to give them a sharper edge. As I've matured and am coming more and more to terms with my own mortality—something that seldom occurs to a younger sensibility—I have discovered that the exuberance of youth tends to moderate when the promises that bolster hope tend to be revealed for what they truly are. Now, I see that they were never promises at all, only suggestions of possibilities that, truly, can only be realized through experience, and through the knowledge that recognition and experience offer.

The "lines" of Sandhill County are, then, markers, in a way. Like most county lines, they are imaginary, mere marks on a piece of paper that are chiefly valuable to highway department workers, so they'll know when, exactly, to stop resurfacing a road, or to alcohol merchants, so they'll know where, exactly, it's legal to market their wares. But abstract or not, they exist concretely in the minds of those who live within them, and they're especially real to those who cross them and go elsewhere. What's left behind, person or thing or place, quickly becomes a ghost. It remains fixed in memory as what it was until they return to view how it's changed. So they must rely only on their memories—on what they know—to conjure the emotions and the images that, ultimately, define them.

There are many stories written after the idea of people who can obtain—through purchase or other device—whole different memories. Most of these tales end badly. I think this is because we tend to define ourselves less because of who we are—right now—or who we will be—someday, if all goes well—than in terms of who we have been. We tend to consider the hopes we once had in light of the promises we once believed were genuine; and, most often, if we're honest about it, we laugh or we cry. The point is that we express our emotions when we examine what we know.

I think most of us spend most of our lives trying to forget the bad, the embarrassing or shameful, and recreating the memories of the good, the rewarding, gratifying, self-sustaining, or, at least, the funny. But from time to time, especially when peering into the chronicles of the past through that opaque glass of time, we are sometimes confronted with the whole image, warts and all, and we are forced to look into our cores and admit that, on the whole, things have turned out different from what we expected, after all. Promises and possibilities aside.

We are, in sum, the product of what we have been, and we all come from somewhere. We cannot purchase or manufacture, at least not honestly, new memories, new origins. In fictions, though, we can recall the brighter and sharper elements of our natures, and we can refine them and use them to expose what we hope might be true about ourselves, about the lies and limitations of life, about one another, and learn a great deal in the process. It is how we define ourselves, and, I think, it is what we know.

Sandhill County Lines

A BETTER CLASS OF PEOPLE

Well, me and Earl Watkins and Virgil Hightower was sitting round J.D.'s having our afterwork-on-Friday beers when the whole thing started.

Now, we wasn't looking for no trouble or nothing, though I'd have to allow that it more often found us than didn't, but that was mostly 'cause of Virgil, who could be meaner than homemade sin, specially when he'd had a couple of beers—if you know what I mean—but we was just sitting there. That's what we always did on Fridays after we got off—I mean, hell, you know, "It's Miller Time," and all that—though we seldom or never drank no Miller High Life. But like I say, it was Fridayafterwork when it all started.

We was specially tired this particular Friday in question as we'd been out stringing fence for Old Man Hadnought over to Blind Man's Creek, and it was 'bout as hot as it ever got—hot enough to melt the hinges off a Mescan's stove, Virgil was fond of saying—all day long, so we was specially tired and thirsty, and we'd already drunk 'bout six beers apiece 'fore the sweat stopped dropping off our noses, and we was feeling good and cool, you know.

Anyhow, we was sitting round the table we always sat round, making eyes at Elvira Hotchkiss and her best friend Pearl Hansley, who was entertaining us by getting up ever now and then and sticking quarters into the jukebox and playing Willie Nelson songs, every time giving us a flash of thigh whenever one or the both of 'em'd get up from their table. Virgil was telling some lies 'bout how he'd won a prize for bull-dogging over to the Cowboy Reunion in Snyder two years back, and Earl allowed as how he was planning to sign up for the Santa Rosa next year, maybe in bronc-busting or bull-riding, which was all a lot of dry thunder, since ol' Earl couldn't ride a dead mule without falling off. But we was just blowing off the steam of a week's work, like I say, when in walks these two college kids.

Now, right off that was weird. It's not that J.D.'s was a secret or nothing, though the whole idea of a bar in a dry town wasn't nothing you put on a billboard or nothing. The whole county knew 'bout it. But it was weird that two college boys'd even think of coming in just like they belonged there, paying no nevermind to nobody at all. I mean, it was like the most natural thing in the world for 'em to come sidling up to the bar and ordering up a couple of cold ones, and truth to tell, if I'd been alone, I likely wouldn't of noticed it at all. But like I say, I wasn't alone. I was with Virgil and Earl, and I guess that's what made it seem so weird.

Prob'ly ol' J.D. Crawford, the bartender and owner, was 'bout as sur-prised as us, but he didn't say nothing, just served 'em their drinks, pretty as you please, and stood back and kind of looked at 'em. After a bit, he shook his head and flat-out asked 'em, "Y'all ain't been in here before, have ya?" But they just shook their head and turned their backs on J.D. like he wasn't even there or nothing. Now that wasn't very nice, but I suppose where they was used to drinking—wherever that was—you don't have to talk to the bartender, even if he is the owner, 'less, of course, you want to.

Now, like I say, J.D.'s wasn't no secret or nothing. It was in the back of the ol' Highway Bowling Alley. The bowling part of the bowling alley burned down 'bout ten years ago, everthing but the back room, which was considerable large for a bowling alley. They rebuilt the insides, of course, but they didn't put back in no bowling alley, which was a losing proposition, anyway, or least that's why everybody said Ol' Man Water-ford burned it down in the first place—for the insurance money—though that's a rumor, not a fact—but they put in a grocery store, instead. But when it went bust in a year or so, right after they opened up one of them chain discount outfits over to the other side of town, there wasn't nothing up front but a big ol' empty building.

But in back, right away, J.D. Crawford seen opportunity knock. So he got the mayor and the sheriff and most of the city council to put up the money—or most of it, anyhow—and go in with him to open up J.D.'s. It was a kind of private club and secret watering hole—if you know what I mean—for folks who didn't mind knocking back a drink or two in public, more or less. And for a while, it did real good.

You see, ol' J.D. did it up right. He got some real pretty mirrors for over the back of the bar, and 'bout the only light there was came from some of them beer signs—you know, the kind that flash and show you waterfalls and snowy mountains while they change colors and such. He had a jukebox and a pinball machine and one of them new video games, but there wasn't no dance floor or pool table. J.D. figured he'd be pushing his luck to allow pool-shooting and dancing.

At first, the Baptists and the Campbellites got up on their high horses and raised holy hell 'bout J.D.'s. They threatened to turn everybody in to the Highway Patrol or somebody, but J.D. went down to a couple of their meetings and convinced the preachers that it was probably safer for folks to come out to his place and have their illegal drink than to drive over to Oklahoma and have a *legal* drink and maybe get cut up in one of them river joints and then drive home all bloody and drunk and maybe kill somebody in the bargain. He also told'em—so I heard—that if they was doing their job right in the first place, folks wouldn't want a drink in the second place, and they should look on J.D.'s as a chance to have some bona fide sin right there in town without having to import it from over to Oklahoma.

So the preachers went into a huddle and agreed that they wouldn't say nothing 'bout it if J.D.'d keep the minors out and make sure there wasn't no trouble in the place. And he did. That is, he most always did.

For a while, J.D.'s was for the real snazzy crowd—you know what I mean—lawyers and car dealers and town ranchers and the like. But after a while they started selling booze out to the country club, and business began to slide off. That's when Virgil and Earl and me started coming in, since it was clear as a blue sky that J.D. needed riffraff such as us to keep the place going. By the time of all this, we was 'bout the biggest business he had, 'cept for Super Bowl Sunday or maybe a private party now and again—and when one of them went on, he'd just set us up a keg in the ol' bowling alley, which, like I say, was empty since the grocery store went bust.

Anyhow, for a long time, tourists and strangers'd drive right past the ol' burnt-out sign for the grocery store out front and never know that a regular saloon was operating right here. I mean we'd sit and laugh at'em drying for a taste of something tall and wet besides a lukewarm soda pop from Frank Dryden's Phillips 66 station, riding right past and having to go to Wichita Falls—or damn near it—for a righteous drink while we sat inside blowing the foam off of a frosty cold bottle of suds and relaxing in the twenty thousand bee-tee-yous of ol' J.D.'s air-conditioning. And after a spell, we come to the idea that J.D.'s belonged to us—to our class of people—specially on Fridayafterwork, when all the rich folks was out to the country club and their high-toned bar. And even though it was too early for the usual serious drinking to start, it still wasn't that normal for a couple of college boys to come sashaying in and ordering up beers just like they done it every week. In fact, like I say, it was weird.

I mean, it was sort of a dare, and I doubted serious if Virgil'd let it go. One thing 'bout ol' Virgil was that he always took a dare.

I suppose it was their clothes that got to us most. We was sitting round in smelly ol' work clothes we'd had on most of a week, and while all of us owned cleaner—and better—we'd never thought to of went home and changed or took a bath or nothing—not for a Fridayafterwork in J.D.'s anyhow. If we'd been planning to date up Elvira or Pearl or somebody, that'd been different. But we was working men, and we didn't think we had to apologize to nobody for how we was dressed. But these two kids made us feel all dirty. And I noticed Earl, and even me, too, looking down at our busted, greasy ol' fingernails and kind of shuffling our wore-out ol' boots under the table.

These boys was dressed like they was out playin' tennis or something. They had on these cute little short britches that didn't come down long enough to cover their skinny little knees and these little white socks that barely came up over their ankles. But their shirts was what caught your eye. One of them had on a pink shirt! Can you beat that? A full-grown man—practically—wearing a pink shirt. You know, one of them little short-sleeve kind that only has three buttons, the kind the fancy dudes wear when they go out to the country club for a round of pasture pool so they can pretend they're golfing on the PGA. The other one had on a yellow one just like it, and I suppose that was some better, though I'd have to allow it was only a snake hair's difference between pink and yellow when it come to a grown man wearing it. But to make matters worse, right on the pocket of each shirt was this little ol' pin that sort of caught the light of the beer signs and sparkled in your eye.

But even though they was dressed to play tennis or golf or something, it was obvious to the born blind that they hadn't been doing much of nothing at all. There wasn't no sweat on'em, and, matter of fact, they looked like they was scrubbed up for a church picnic or something. And that just made us feel worse, specially when Elvira and Pearl started sitting up straight and winking and giggling and stuff trying to get their attention by hiking up their skirts a mite and sticking out their chests all over the place.

Well, we watched'em for a bit while they finished their beers and ordered 'nother round, and while ol' J.D. was fishing down in the cooler, ol' Earl jabs Virgil in the ribs and says something real soft-like that I couldn't catch. Then he gets up to go take a whiz.

While Earl's inside the john, Virgil leans his chair back on its hind legs and says to me, "I think we're fixing to whup some ass." He says it real loud, too, so everybody could hear. I seen Elvira and Pearl pull in their chests and adjust their chairs a bit so they could get out of the way when the fur started to fly. But both of'em kept right on giggling and winking and stuff.

Now, I just sip my beer and grin back at Virgil. I didn't know exactly what to 'spect since ol' Virgil just might do anything. He was kind of crazy sometimes. Back in high school, he got into a beef with some guys over to Kirkland, and him and 'bout five other football boys decided to run'em out of town. They run'em as far as the Hoolian cutoff, anyhow, when Virgil turned over his car and rolled it 'bout a hundred times. Three of'em was killed outright, and one lingered on for near a year. You could hear him late at night outside the hospital, so I'm told, screaming and carrying on. It was real spooky, I hear tell. Anyhow, they sent Virgil down to Fort Worth, where they put a steel plate in his head and give him a glass eye. He didn't have a tooth he was born with, neither. From a distance, you couldn't tell nothing was wrong with him just by looking at him—

'cept for the eye, of course—but the whole thing had a powerful effect on his personality. And after a few beers, like I say, he could turn real mean.

Well, one thing Virgil didn't like worth a dog fart was college kids. I knew there was no harm in'em, mostly, but I wasn't 'bout to disabuse Virgil Hightower of the notion that college kids was responsible for all the troubles in the world, specially those that fell to the share of Virgil Hightower—including the trouble in particular Virgil had holding a steady job—for fear he'd take in his mind to stomp a mudhole in my rearend or something. So when he took his usual dislike to college kids, I just grinned like I was doing now, but I don't mind telling you, I was more than a little troubled 'bout what was likely to take place.

Used to be that if a fella had long hair or a beard, ol' Virgil'd rag him just to pick a fight. Most times, Virgil'd whup up on him pretty good, too, 'cause you see, Virgil's 'bout six foot four and must of weighed close on to two fifty or so, and 'cept for some soft spots round his middle, he was solid as a Kenworth truck. His hands was like hammers, and when somebody'd stand up to him, they'd look into that glass eye of his—which was all scratched and cloudy—and start doubting sanity—theirs for standing there and Virgil's in general. I'd seen him fight on more'n one occasion, and generally when all the dust settled, he'd be standing there in the middle of broken bones, blood, and spilt beer and laughing to beat the devil.

He decided he hated college kids back during the Vietnam War when everybody in the country but him seemed to be getting drafted or enlisting or something to go off and fight the gook commies. They wouldn't take him, of course—'cause of the steel plate and glass eye—but he figured that anybody who *could* go and didn't go must be queer, and he set it as his bounden duty to see to it that all the queer draft dodgers and such who was helping to lose the war by going to college and giving aid and comfort to the enemy was personally punished by Virgil Hightower. It just made him mad as a jug full of red ants when he'd run across a college kid.

He always hated longhairs and hippies, too, but by the time I hooked up with him, he'd found out that some of these dudes with ponytails and scraggly clothes was actual war vets, and some of'em was working highway construction and such, and some of'em was even tougher than ol' Virgil was, so he transferred most of his meanness to college kids and left the longhairs and such alone, which was fine with me, since my hair tended to be a touch longish, and I hated to shave regular just 'bout worse than anything. But I wasn't no college kid—that was purely clear—and him and me got to be good friends—or at least as good a friends as Virgil ever got with anybody—and when he said he was going to whup some ass, I figured that whatever I got into by going along with it wouldn't be as bad as what Virgil'd do to me if I tried to get out of it or, worse, tried to stop him.

Pretty soon, Earl comes out of the john, zipping up his pants right in front of Pearl and Elvira, makin'em giggle and squeal like they never seen nothing before—which would of been a outright lie had they said so—and he kind of walks real easy-like up to the bar and the two kids, who was finishing up their second round and ordering up thirds.

"What's that on your titty?" he asks real loud to one of the kids, who I recognize as being named Lambert, pointing at this little ol' pin that was, like I say, sitting on his shirt pocket and glittering in the bar sign lights. Then he turns and winks at Elvira. But Lambert don't say nothing. He just picks up some quarters which J.D. left for change on the bar—real nervous like—and goes over to the jukebox and starts plunkin'em in.

"I said, what's that on your titty, college boy?" Earl asks him again, but Lambert just keeps feeding them quarters into the juke and picking out them bullshit Barry Manilow songs that nobody'd listened to in 'bout a hundred years. Finally, Earl shrugs and goes back over to Elvira and Pearl and tries to feel one of'em up, but I can see he's not going to have no luck.

Now, some folks'd call Earl a good ol' boy from the word go. Others—truth to tell—generally'd call him a asshole, and I'd have to allow as how the second parties'd be closer to the truth. He was pretty friendly with people—'cept when he was round Virgil. Him and Virgil went way back, and he was always trying to impress Virgil some way or 'nother. He had a ol' lady and two ugly kids, but he never hardly was at home. Back in high school, she'd filed rape charges on him when he knocked her up, and the only way he could talk her out of it was to marry her—which he did. Still he thought hisself a ace stud or something, 'cause he was always lying 'bout how much he was getting on the side, and I knew for a fact that other'n his ol' lady—who was ugly as a mud fence and prob'ly outweighed Virgil—that the only exterior loving he ever might of got was whitefaced and shorthorned—if you know what I mean—and he was prob'ly too drunk to remember even that. But he put on a lot, especially, like I say, when Virgil was round.

So, he was over to Elvira and Pearl's table, trying to get a hand down Elvira's blouse and pinching Pearl's butt and such, and Lambert quits fooling round with the juke and goes back over to the bar. Earl and the girls was squabbling and giggling, and Virgil signals J.D. to bring him and me 'nother round.

Now, Earl's basic problems was numerous. He was uglier than God made sin, and he had snaggly ol' teeth and greasy hair and pimples, though he'd never see forty again. And he was short. He claimed he was drafted and got thrown out of the navy 'fore he got to fight, but I heard they got rid of him 'cause he was always getting *into* fights and getting the cowflop stomped out of him and they threw him out 'cause he was crazy—depends on who tells the story—anyhow, he tended to be a real loudmouth and show-off. Like a lot of short guys, he knew he needed to have two things to keep from getting the peewaddle beat out of him a lot, and he had both. One was that he had muscles, lots of 'em. Once, on a bet, he lifted up a full-grown mare right on his back, right off the ground, and I seen him carry two bales of hay, one under each arm, just as a matter of routine. The second thing was a good-sized friend like Virgil to back him up when he got in over his head—which he generally did.

I reckon that all that makes him sound like he was yellow, which I guess he was—muscles, loudmouth, and all—but whether he was or not, I'd never thought that two college boys'd be much of a match for him. And I guess he must of figured the same, 'cause 'bout the time Elvira and Pearl started getting pee-o'd at him, he started back over toward'em.

The main trouble with people like Earl is that they always mean well, but they screw up more often than not, and, in fact, that was what I figured was 'bout to happen. And I 'spect Virgil thought the same, since he just sighed real deep and tired-like when he seen Earl heading that way again.

You see, Earl'd been responsible for the only jail time Virgil'd ever done. They'd been down round Sweetwater several years back, hanging round and doing some fishing and drinking in some honky-tonk, when in walks these two college kids—just like now—and they got into their usual fight after a spell, with Earl getting things rolling, as usual, and Virgil stepping in to mop up. One of the kids got a couple of good swipes in at ol' Virgil 'fore he beat him right through the floor, and then Earl, who was by all accounts drunker than usual, got the bright idea to hang'em.

Or at least to pretend to. I doubt they really intended on hurting them kids any more than they was already hurting, but they got a piece of rope from somewhere, drug'em out behind the honky-tonk, and pretended to string'em up from this mesquite tree.

I heard it was a tiny little ol' tree—more of a bush, really—and I doubt you could of hung a polecat from it, but it scared the absolute virginity out of them kids. One of'em busted loose and took off, and after Virgil and Earl fooled round with the other one for a while—give him some rope burns and the like—they let him go and thought no more 'bout it.

Well, it turned out that the one who got away was the son of a United States Congressman, and in 'bout two hours the whole damn county was crawling with Highway Patrol, FBI men, and Texas Rangers, and they quickgrabbed Virgil and locked him up tight.

Naturally, ol' Earl didn't get caught at all. People like him hardly ever do. He hightailed it as soon as he smelt trouble, and he was home in bed 'fore Virgil got jailhouse breakfast. Poor ol' Virgil was in the hoosegow most of a month 'fore his mama and our sheriff and a whole host of other folks from here went down there and bailed him out and convinced everybody that they was only fooling round with the kids and that Virgil'd been sort of two quarts low on common sense ever since his car wreck and all. So finally, they let him go with a warning not to come back to Sweetwater. Which he didn't.

Anyhow, ol' Virgil went right for Earl soon's he got home, but someway or 'nother, Earl talked him out of killing him right then and there, and by the time I hooked up with'em, they was fond of laughing 'bout the whole thing. Least Earl was. Fact of the matter was that he was particularly proud of bringing it up and reminding Virgil of what a lowlife he was for running out on Virgil and leaving him to face the music all on his lonesome. "Virgil," Earl'd say and reach up and slap him on the back—too damn hard, you ask me—"You just got to start hanging round with a better class of people!" Then he'd laugh. I always noticed, though, that Earl laughed a lot louder and harder than Virgil did.

But other'n that, Earl didn't seem to take no notice of the whole thing, and even though he didn't get into as many fights as he used to, he'd still go off on a tear now and again, and Virgil'd be obliged to back him up.

This time didn't seem no different from any other time at the start. Earl just gets right up eyeball to eyeball with ol' Lambert, who was the smallest of the two—though he still had half a head on Earl—and breathes his snaggly-toothed breath all over him and says, "I think I asked you a by-God question, college boy!" Then he grins real big and throws a wink over our way and takes a long pull off his beer.

Well, Lambert don't say nothing at all. But he gives the other kid, Joe Robert Something, a kind of desperate look out of the corner of his eye and starts to turn round to the bar where his beer is, and Earl pegs him hard with his finger right on his chest where that little pin is sitting on his pocket. "I said, I asked you a question, college boy! Y'all can wink and grin at each other later on."

Lambert still don't say nothing for a second longer, but his mouth starts moving and nothing's coming out. I can see he's scared to death and don't want no fight, and I look down into my beer feeling sort of uncomfortable-like. I mean, it's downright embarrassing to see a man pushed into a fight he don't want.

Now, I don't hardly know Lambert, and I don't know Joe Robert at all, 'cept by first name, of course, mainly 'cause they was from sort of high-class families. I mean, their daddies wasn't no bankers or nothing, but they had enough money to send'em to fancy colleges out in California, which is where they was home from this summer. I figured'em to be a decent sort of folks, even if they did go out to California—one thing Virgil and me generally agreed on was that California was a evil place— 'cause when they was home for the summer they got on at the gyp mill and worked their young tails off. Course, their daddies prob'ly seen to that, so they wouldn't go soft or nothing. Work in a gyp mill is hard work, if you know what I mean. Still, they was better off than we was or ever would be. I mean, hard work or not, class tells.

You see, they didn't act like the rest of us. If memory serves, they never did, even when they was growing up here. Joe Robert, I recollected, played a little football in high school, but he busted up his knee and had to quit. But Lambert never played no ball at all. Fact of the matter was, I remembered when I heard that crappy music he kept playing on the jukebox, he was in the band. The *band* for God's sake! I mean, it was a sorry waste of size and talent for a boy like that to be tooting a horn when he could of been playing ball for his hometown school. Least, that's what Virgil and Earl always said 'bout them queer boys in the band.

I never give the matter much thought one way or 'nother. But I guess if you reason it out for yourself, there might be some kind of advantage in being in the band—that is, 'less you was real good at ball, which most ain't. I mean, you got to figure it's better to ride the band bus to all the games with the cheerleaders and the twirlers and other girls than to ride with a sweaty bunch of guys who was just 'bout to get busted up and stuff in some silly game, after which they'd be too tired to walk, let alone get hold of some ol' gal on a way that'd pay 'em back for all the pain and stuff. And I never told Virgil this, but I guessed there'd be likely more opportunity for queerdom in the locker-room showers than in some damn trumpet section, but I wasn't sure of that my own self, 'cause I wasn't in the band nor played no ball, neither.

Anyhow, when ol' Earl starts poking his dirty finger into Lambert's pocket, I begin to get real uncomfortable. Lambert's mouth is still moving, and Earl just keeps yelling at him so he couldn't hear what he was saying, even if he was saying anything at all, which he wasn't. "I asked you what in the blue-eyed hell this is?" I reckoned Earl'd just poke that little ol' pin right through ol' Lambert's chest if he didn't answer him in a minute.

"It's a pin," Lambert stammers out finally, and Earl starts sputtering and spitting and carrying on something awful.

"Well, what the hell!" Earl shouts right in Lambert's face. "I can *see* it's a pin! What I wanna know is what's it doing there?"

"It's a fra-fra-fraternity pin," Lambert says, and he starts to babble a little bit. He notices, I guess, that ol' Earl don't know a fraternity pin from a lanced boil. Which I don't, neither, so I sort of sit up to hear more. You see, I thought it was a church pin or something.

Lambert tries to get hisself together and go on. "A fra-fraternity . . . ," he says and swallows real hard. "Kind of . . . you know . . . a lodge, like a club—"

"Don't tell me what a goddamn lodge is, you dumb fairy!" Earl is fairly well screaming at Lambert by this time, and ol' J.D.'s starting to get real nervous while he's getting us our beers ready to bring over. I can see that Lambert's 'bout to pee all over hisself, he's so scared. There wasn't no way out for him. No way. Whatever he said to Earl was going to be the wrong thing, now, and Earl was going to hit him one way or 'nother. So it was no surprise to me that he didn't say nothing at all.

Earl reaches down and grabs Lambert's shirt pocket and rips it right off, fraternity pin and all, then yells at him so loud I thought he might bust a vein. "What kind of dumb shit you think I am?"

Now, it was a stupid question. Everybody knew that. Even Earl would of knew it, if he'd thought 'bout it. But he didn't. And nobody 'spected nobody to answer it, not really, and Earl's grinning like a puke-eating dog over to Elvira and Pearl, proud as a new moon over how witty he's being and figuring that he's got Lambert good with that one.

"I don't know. What kind of dumb shit are you?"

It was Joe Robert who says it, and I thought ol' Earl was going to have a stroke. I mean, it gets so quiet in that bar, you could of heard a bug fart. J.D. starts backing down the bar, and Elvira and Pearl start shoving their matches and cigarettes and change and stuff into their purses, 'cause they know that sure as a blue suit hates brown shoes, when Earl gets his wind, there was going to be some kind of fight.

Now, like I say, I don't know much 'bout Joe Robert at all. Mostly he hung round with Lambert when they was home from college, which was kind of queer, I guess, him being a former ballplayer and all, but I reckoned they sort of fell in with each other out there in that California college. And since they was both working at the gyp mill and so on, it was more natural than not for 'em to be friends. He was different from Lambert, though. I mean, ol' Lambert looked for all the world like a scared little ol' puppydog, and if he didn't wet hisself in a minute, I'd of guessed that he was purely dry inside. And while Lambert wasn't soft or nothing, like I say, he wasn't no fighter, neither. You could see that much just by looking at him.

But Joe Robert was different. He don't look scared of Earl at all. In fact, now that I think on it, I'm sort of surprised that he didn't take Earl's head off right then and there when he jerked that pocket off Lambert's shirt. But then again, Virgil's sitting right there, and from the looks of things, he was backing Earl's play.

Like I say, I figure Earl for a pretty good-sized yellow streak someplace, specially 'cause ironass as he often tried to be, he never took on nobody bigger than him, 'less they was all blubbery fat or something, and he often had a chore finding that many ol' boys smaller than him, since he was, like I say, a sawed-off little peckerwood. But Joe Robert wasn't no fatty, and he was built at least as good as Earl was—that was plain through that little ol' shirt of his—and he had a good foot on Earl in height, which meant his reach wasn't too shabby, neither. So it finally dawned on me that Earl'd bit off more than he could swallow.

It must of dawned on Earl, too, 'cause he turns round to us and grins that snaggly-toothed grin of his and asks, "Y'all want some of this half-assed glass of buttermilk?" His voice sounds sort of whispery and strange-like, and I know he's part scared and part madder'n a scalded dog.

Now, I don't know what to do. I don't want to look like I wouldn't stand by ol' Earl in his hour of need and all, but at the same time, I can't see that these two ol' boys had done nothing to hurt nobody in the first place, even if they was in our bar. I mean, we didn't *own* it or nothing, and God knows, J.D. needed the business from anybody who come in, and I can see clear as creek water that Earl started this fight, and he could of just let well enough alone. So I feel real relieved when Virgil belches and says, "Naw. I'm getting too old for this bullshit. You handle'em, Earl."

Well, it would of been reasonable apparent to the dead and buried that Earl can't handle both of'em. I mean, Lambert was pretty much gone to hell by now, but I can see plain as morning that ol' Joe Robert wasn't going to back down a inch, and once he laid into Earl, Lambert might just find some backbone sticking out of the mess I figured was already loaded up in them little ol' tennis britches. The long and the short of it was that Earl was in trouble.

Anyhow, I look over to Virgil to see what he was going to do, but he just signals J.D. to hurry up with our beers, hikes up a leg, breaks wind, leans back. Earl, Lambert, and Joe Robert hadn't moved a eyelash, and I got to say, I seen Earl looking better.

'Bout that time, Elvira and Pearl get all their stuff together and get up like they was going to rabbit out the front door, and Earl jumps on the chance to yell at somebody. You see, it finally come on him that Virgil wasn't going to pull his fat out of the fire, and I can see that like me, he was entertaining some serious doubts 'bout his being able to do it all by hisself. "Y'all just sit your asses the hell down!" he yells at'em, and you could almost hear ol' Elvira's bottom jaw hit the floor at the pure gall he's showing.

"Listen here, you half-growed little pissant," she yells back at him. "You just watch your mouth when you talk to me. I ain't some white trash you just come across."

Now, that was funny—specially when her and Pearl stuck their noses up real high in the air and marched theirselves right into the ladies' john instead of out the front door, like I'm sure they intended—'cause there wasn't many ears in the county hadn't heard one or the other or both of'em being as foul-mouthed as any Wal-Mart Wanda you ever run up on in the toy aisle whaling hell out of her kids.

But the way Earl took it took all the fun right out of it. He don't say nothing back to'em at all. He just starts to sull up. The shape things was taking, I guess he figured he couldn't even lick Elvira in a cussing contest.

Well, one thing 'bout cowards, short cowards in particular, and ol' Earl specially, is that if there's any way they can win a fight by cheating, they will. Like I say, I been round plenty of fights with him and Virgil, and more often than not, I seen him pick up a pool cue, a bottle, or a chair—anything heavy—and crack somebody's skull with it when they wasn't looking. I never said nothing to him nor Virgil 'bout it, 'cause most times it was somebody who was big enough to clean my plow for sure, and I was just as glad to have'em out for the count, if you know what I mean. Still it didn't set right with me to watch it, even in passing, 'cause nothing makes folks madder'n a dirty fighter, even when they was cheating just to keep their own teeth in place.

So when Earl starts swelling up, I can see his brain working, trying to find someway to get a edge on ol' Joe Robert and take him out of the game so he could bat cleanup on Lambert. And I was right. Mostly.

I seen him reach down into his jeans pocket and take something out, all the time trying to hold his temper, and then he makes a fist round it and swings.

It's a real neat, roundhouse kind of punch, and it would of put Joe

Robert's lights out sure—if Earl'd connected with him, that is. Which he didn't. Joe Robert seen it coming and just ducks down in kind of a crouch, pretty as sin on Sunday morning, and Earl runs his fist right into the cinder-block wall on the other side of where Joe Robert's face'd been.

Just 'fore Earl starts yelling, I thought I heard Virgil laugh, real soft-like.

Like I say, Earl's yelling—screaming would be closer to the truth—and he stands up high as his little ol' short legs'll let him, grabs his right hand with his left, and hoots at the moon like he can see it through J.D.'s roof. What was in his hand, I see when it fell on the floor, was a roll of nickels, which I guess he reckoned would coldcock Joe Robert good so he could go to work on Lambert. But it backfired, and I suppose Earl had 'bout four broke fingers for his trouble. I could see, you know, why Virgil thought it was funny. Like I say, nobody likes to see a man fight dirty, even Virgil.

Anyhow, Earl's stretched up and out and yowling like a stomped-on yard cat, but like I say, Joe Robert'd ducked down in a kind of crouch, and while he's down there, he grabs up a fist of just plain ol' air and come up with it like a piston on a Peterbilt.

When he straightens up, his feet was spaced just right to give him leverage, and his knuckles connect with Earl smack dab on the jaw, and he just purely lifts him right up off the floor, like he has a string or something jerking him up from the back of his neck. Earl rises right up, just like that, sort of hangs there a second or two like he's balancing on Joe Robert's fist, then he come down and hit the floor like a load of wet horse turds. I heard the crack of his jaw breaking someplace between his rising and his falling.

Well, ol' J.D., who'd been just coming round the other end of the bar with our beers, stops dead in his tracks, takes one look at Virgil, and hauls ass out the door, dropping our beers in the process. I guess he reckoned there was going to be some kind of mess in a little bit, and he didn't want no part of it. Or he'd went to get the sheriff.

I wished he'd brung us our beers 'fore he hightailed it, though, 'cause they was spinning round and foaming and so forth, and I felt a powerful need of one. I don't think I ever seen a man hit that hard on purpose.

Now, the question on everybody's mind at that point was what Virgil was going to do. Least, know it was on my mind, and I can tell by looking at Joe Robert and Lambert that they wasn't thinking 'bout the senior prom or nothing. The former was standing there rubbing his knuckles and looking down on ol' Earl, who wasn't saying nothing, just laying there and kind of moaning, still holding onto his busted hand. Lambert was also looking down at Earl, and I can see he don't believe what he's seeing. I mean, he was 'bout ten seconds from getting the absolute bug juice stomped out of him, and now the would-be stomper's crying like a new-born calf down on the floor, wallowing round in the tobacco juice and spilt beer and glad for the chance to do so.

Real slow-like, both of 'em raise up their eyes and look over to Virgil and me, and pretty soon I get to feeling real uncomfortable all over again. I decide the best thing to do was join 'em and take a look at Virgil my own self and see whether or not he 'spected me to do anything at all.

That's when Virgil stands up.

Now, when I say Virgil was big, it don't really tell the whole story. He was a by-God giant. His shoulders was most all of three foot across, and his arms hung down so his hands could almost touch his knees. And I 'spect to them boys, he looked even bigger than that. I mean, I reckon they figured him to be just a tad smaller than one of them big ol' office buildings down to Dallas.

Anyhow, Virgil belches, tips his Cat hat back on his half-bald ol' head, and sighs real loud while he shakes his head and rubs his whiskery ol' chin. I mean, if you ever seen anybody scared, it was them two college boys. Let's face it, it was one thing to take out Earl, 'cause strong as he might of been, he wasn't big, and he wasn't mean, and without Virgil round, like I say, he didn't have no reputation to speak of at all.

But you didn't have to live your whole life in this town to know 'bout Virgil. Hell, I'd only been here 'bout two hours myself 'fore I come up on somebody who wanted to bend my ear 'bout how Virgil's hit a ol' boy up to Pampa so hard he bled from the ears, or how he'd punched out 'nother ol' boy's pickup so hard he put a dent in it just 'cause he didn't like the color. So he had some kind of reputation, if you know what I mean, and you can bet your Saturday off that them boys was feeling some panic. In fact, they was actually shaking as he commenced to walk over towards them.

Virgil just moves real slow over to where they was still standing over Earl, who was whimpering and crying real soft-like. I reckoned he was hurting pretty bad, 'cause he wasn't doing what he generally did—which was to start yelling at Virgil to "git'em" or nothing. I see that Joe Robert wasn't in too good a shape, neither. I could tell even in the dim red light of the beer signs that his hand was busted up some, too, and it was prob'ly swelling, so he wasn't going to have no kind of punch left, even if it would of made any difference against a man the size of Virgil. Which it wouldn't.

But I got to hand it to him. He wasn't backing down a inch. No sir. He tries to make some kind of fist out of them swole-up knuckles and just stands there, waiting for Virgil to get up to him.

Now, that's where ol' Lambert come up and surprised me. I suspect he surprised hisself some, too. 'Bout the time ol' Virgil gets over to where they was standing—Earl all the time still down on the floor, don't you know—that skinny little ol' kid reaches out and pushes Joe Robert back. He doubles up his pitiful little ol' horn-tooting fists and tries to look Virgil straight in the eye, or at least as straight as you can look a man in the eye when he's a good six inches taller than you and only has one good eye to boot.

I figure as sure as there's preaching on Sunday, Lambert was going to die. Or least of all, he was going to wish he was dead. I mean, all Virgil had to do was reach out and pop him up side the head, and he's going down like a gut-shot goose. But I guess he knew that, and I guess he didn't much care. He seen what he had to do, and no matter how much it hurt, he was going to do her. He was showing some class, and he didn't move a twitch. Scared as he was, I guess, he couldn't let Joe Robert take all the punishment he figured Virgil was 'bout to deal out.

Now, it seemed to me that he'd been a whole lot better off if it'd been the other way round. I mean, by rights, it should of been him who took out ol' Earl, and Joe Robert would of been left for Virgil. Not that even Joe Robert had much of a chance against a man like Virgil, neither, but at least it would of balanced out a bit better. But there ol' Lambert stood, and it was too late to do anything but grin and bear it, which he did, 'cause he knew, just like me and Joe Robert knew, that Virgil was 'bout to hit him so hard he'd hurt his mama's memory.

I'm getting real nervous and feeling kind of puny my own self, truth to tell. I mean, here's my best friend, Earl, my working buddy, with a busted jaw and hand, slobbering round on the floor like a runover rabbit, and I was sitting there sucking on a empty beer and watching everthing like it was on TV or something. But I couldn't see what there was else for me to do. I mean, it was already two to one, but you got to count Virgil 'bout four times, so the odds was more'n balanced in his favor in the first place. And I wasn't too keen on the idea of getting messed up in all this in the second place. You see, I all of a sudden recollected that ol' J.D. kept him a .38-caliber hogleg out to his trailer house, which was parked 'bout a hundred yards over to the other side of the highway. And even if he'd forgot 'bout it and had went for the sheriff, I guessed things didn't look all that good for anybody standing up when he got back. I mean, you could call what I figured was 'bout to happen a fight if you want to, but by rights and counts, I'd call it a killing, pure and simple. And it was going to commence just as soon as Virgil let go with one of them pile drivers he called fists.

But Virgil didn't hit nobody. He just stands there looking at them two boys, who was sweating threepenny nails by now, watching Lambert, who had them skinny little fists all doubled up, ready to die for his friend, and down at Earl who now was trying to climb up the side of the bar.

"See what you done?" Virgil asks.

'Bout that time, I see Elvira and Pearl sneaking out of the ladies' john, and they give me a look that says, "What-the-hell's going on? Then they see Virgil standing there in front of Earl and them boys, and they hustle their tails back inside and slam the door. I guess it was obvious. Least, it seemed so to me.

"I said, see what you done?" Virgil asks again, but them two kids don't say nothing. I guess they figured they'd already answered one question too many in J.D.'s that night and planned to just keep their mouths shut and take what was coming like men. Anyhow, they just stand there, and ol' Virgil starts shaking his head.

Now, I'm getting real interested in the goings-on, since Virgil don't have no threat in his voice at all, not what I seen 'bout a hundred times before when he was trying to egg some stupid hard-lick into throwing the first punch. Then, all of a sudden, he yells, "See?"

"We see," Lambert says in a sort of choking voice, clearing his throat a little bit, but not dropping them fists. I swear, that boy was doing his dead-level best to sound tough, just like he's up to whatever Virgil was 'bout to do to him, which he wasn't.

"You made J.D. spill my beer," Virgil says, and he reaches down, real casual-like, and just picks up ol' Earl by the back of his shirt with one big ol' hand. I mean, he just lifts him up off the floor like he was a baby puppydog and kind of shakes him. All of a sudden it dawns on me that he wasn't talking to them boys, at all.

He was talking to Earl.

He shakes him again, and Earl squeals like a ruptured shoat. "These college kids seen what you done, you stupid son of a bitch," Virgil says. Then he looks over his shoulder to me with his one good eye. And I swear—he winks at me!

I can see that Lambert finally glommed onto what was happening, and he looks like the Second Coming has just been announced. I swear, he nearly faints dead away, he was swooning so much when Virgil turns away from him, and he looks sort of sick-like to see ol' Earl dangling out to the end of Virgil's arm like a bag of cowchips or something.

"You think we can finish that fence by our ownselves?" Virgil asks me.

I just nod and don't say nothing. Then I look down at my empty beer. I feel downright embarrassed for Earl, if you know what I mean.

Then Virgil drops Earl down on the floor, making him holler out loud again, and he just stands there looking them two boys over, up and down. Then he turns and starts to walk away.

I hear somebody say, "Well, I'll be go to hell," real soft-like, and I see Elvira and Pearl standing by the ladies' john door. I mean, they was almost crying. It was like the end of a era, if you know what I'm talking 'bout.

All of a sudden, Virgil stops, and I figure he heard'em, but I was wrong. Elvira and Pearl quickjump back inside the ladies john, and'em two kids prob'ly loaded their drawers if they hadn't done so before. They actually jumped off the floor when they seen him spin around. Virgil might of been a big'un, but he could move fast, I can tell you.

He goes back over to where Earl was lying and crying, mewing like a newborn kittycat, don't you know, and reaches down and grabs him up by his greasy ol' hair, yanking back his head real painful-like. I bet it hurt more than his hand and jaw put together. "Earl," Virgil says real gentle-like, "you just gotta start hanging round with a better class of people." Then he drops him again and leaves right out the front door without 'nother look left nor right.

Well, I tell you what, I don't know what to do. I take a breath, which felt like 'bout the first one I ever took, and I watch them college boys slump down by the bar next to Earl, who, I guess, had passed right on out cold. Elvira comes out with Pearl, and they go back to their table like nothing had happened at all, and after a minute or two, them college boys sort of got theirselves together and scraped round to find that pocket with the fraternity pin on it that Earl had ripped off, then they sort of slunk out the door. And, 'cept for Earl, who was still passed out on the floor, everthing looked just like it did before. Only it wasn't like it was before, and it never could be again.

After a bit, ol' J.D. come roaring in, and sure enough, he had that rusty ol' pistol out and was waving it round like a crazy loon till he figured out there wasn't nobody to shoot with it. He checked on Earl to make sure he was still breathing, then he finally got round to cleaning up the spilt beer and brung me 'nother, which I drunk real slow-like. I mean, I figured this was 'bout my last beer in ol' J.D.'s for a long time. Which it was.

Pretty soon, ol' Earl come to, and he sort of crawls and limps out the door without giving me so much as a look. But I don't feel too sorry for him, don't you know, since I guessed he's had it coming for a long time and just finally got it. Which he did.

And I figured I didn't want to hang round with ol' Virgil much no more, neither, and I didn't want nothing to do with ol' Elvira and Pearl, who was now giving me the eye, since they figured there wasn't nobody else in the place and it was getting late. Which it was.

You see, I figured things'd went 'bout as far as they could go in one direction that Fridayafterwork, and even though I didn't think that much more of them college boys than I did 'fore all this happened, I guess I learned something. And I decided I better start looking for a better class of people my ownself. Which I did.

MEXICO

Curly Hughes sat on the tailgate of his GMC pickup, smoked a cigarette, sipped a lukewarm beer, and watched Elwood Hays use a two-foot length of telephone cable to beat the absolute living shit out of Charlie Donahue. Since the two combatants were lodge brothers and very close friends, Curly had promised Charlie he would stop the fight before Elwood got seriously hurt, but things had been going on for nearly ten minutes now, and it didn't look like Charlie was going to get in another lick. He'd thrown the first punch, of course, but that was the last time he'd touched Elwood at all. Elwood had touched him, though, and he kept right on touching him, and every time that piece of phone cable came down on Charlie's back and side, Curly thought it might be the last time Charlie would get up.

Elwood needed a good licking, Curly thought. It was a shame he wasn't getting it.

"Are you goin' to come over here an' help me or not?" Charlie called between blows from the phone cable. "You're s'posed to be my friend."

Curly took another sip of beer and thought the matter over. Elwood had been screwing Charlie's wife, Louise, while he worked the swing out at the gyp mill for the past six months. Rumor was that Charlie's newest kid—his third—was Elwood's, too, but word around the lodge was that the kid might belong to any number of good old boys who had paid Louise a visit while Charlie was earning double time during the past several years.

Louise was a lot younger than Charlie and still a looker, even if she did have three kids. Lately, Curly had thought quite a bit about her himself.

Elwood didn't say anything, but he was huffing and puffing and swinging at Charlie with wide arches that showed the sweat stains under his arms, even though they were just getting over a norther and it was chilly. They were both forty pounds overweight, and they had both been drinking for several hours. It should have been an even match, except Elwood had the cable on him when they got started.

He started working the cable on Charlie's head, and Curly tossed the beer bottle into a cardboard box in the pickup's bed and slid down. He found an axe handle under the toolbox and pulled it out. It was muddy in J.D.'s parking lot, and the joint's neon-sign lights reflected prettily in the puddles. He stepped carefully to keep from getting his boots messed up.

"Elwood, you 'bout had enough?" Curly asked. He rolled up his sleeves and walked around a big puddle over by the two men. Charlie was down in the mud and whimpering, trying to keep the cable from hitting him in the face again.

Elwood paused and looked at Curly. "Huh?" he asked.

Curly stepped up, squared off, and swung the handle around from the right. Elwood received the blow solidly on the back of his head and dropped like a box of rocks. He didn't get up.

"Why in hell didn't you do that a while ago?" Charlie demanded. He climbed to his feet and began trying to wipe the mud off his jeans. Blood streamed from his nose and also from two or three mean cuts on his face and hands. "That son of a bitch damn near beat me to death."

"You looked like you might of got him on the run any minute there," Curly said. He glanced down at Elwood, who was still out cold. "I told you to hit him on the jaw. He's got a glass jaw."

"Well," Charlie found his cap and began slapping wet gravel off of it, "I didn't get much of a chance. Where'n hell he get that pipe?"

"Guess he had it in his truck," Curly said. "An' it wasn't a pipe. It was a telephone cable. He works for the telephone company."

"Yeah, well, it felt like a pipe. But his truck's way over yonder." Charlie pointed out vaguely toward the end of the parking lot where Elwood's green Ford Supercab was parked in the fog. "He didn't have time to go get it. Had it with him. Like to knocked my teeth out." He stuck two fingers into his mouth and worked them around. When he spit, it was bloody in the neon reflections. "Man don't walk around with a pipe in his pants."

"Well, you were in there telling God an' half the world what you were going to do when you saw him. Guess somebody warned him, an' he was just drunk enough to go get it."

Charlie inspected Elwood's form. He was still out cold. "He screwed Louise. We had a fight last night, an' she told me."

Curly didn't respond. He went back to the pickup's cab and found two more beers. "We goin' to go to Mexico or not?" he asked.

"I don't know." Charlie limped over. He fingered his torso in search of broken bones. Curly opened his beer and handed the other to Charlie. "I might be all busted up. I'm hurtin' too much to tell."

"Goddamnit, you said we was goin'," Curly said. "You said you had the money. I sure don't. You got two days off. 'Sides, we promised Jackpot."

Jackpot was also a close friend, and a lodge brother. He used to ride bulls on the international circuit, but he got too old and too busted up. He was now retired, but he didn't have any pension.

"Why can't he get laid round here like everybody else does? Why we got to go all the way to Mexico?" Charlie demanded.

"'Cause he stutters. An' he's so ugly, there's not a whore in Dallas *or* Fort Worth that'd touch him. Not one he can afford, anyhow."

Charlie looked down at his ruined clothes. "I got to go home an' change. That son of a bitch broke my nose."

"Well, then, let's do it."

Charlie stood still for a moment, bent one leg up from the knee to see if it still worked, and nodded. Curly lit a cigarette and started around to the other side of the cab. "Say, you want to take him with us?" Charlie pointed at Elwood.

"We're already taking Jackpot," Curly said. "Can't get more'n three in the cab. Goddamn Highway Patrol's sure to pull us over we get four in there."

"Yeah, but Elwood was plannin' to go," Charlie argued. "If we hadn't got into a fight, we'd already be halfway there. He was wantin' to go."

Curly stepped gingerly over to Elwood's slumped form. "We could throw him in the back, I guess," he said. "But you take him. I don't want to mess up my shirt."

Charlie limped over and hefted Elwood's dead weight. Curly finally had to help, but he kept Elwood's muddy boots out at arm's length while they dumped him into the bed and slammed the tailgate shut.

"Think he'll be all right?" Charlie wondered when they pulled out into the highway lane.

"Get him a blanket from your place," Curly suggested. "That'll keep him warm."

"Listen, you fat, no 'count son of a bitch, you think you're goin' to go runnin' all over the goddamn country an' leavin' me here with the kids again, you got 'nother think comin'," Louise screeched at Charlie when he stomped past her into their twelve-by-forty mobile home. He ignored her and started peeling the wet, muddy, and bloody clothes from his body, leaving them where they fell. "You're s'posed to fix the dispose-all this weekend. Toilets is stopped up, too. That'un of the kids won't quit runnin'. You ain't goin' nowhere."

She suddenly realized he was not alone, shaded her eyes, although it was pitch beyond the spill of light from the doorway, and sweetened her tone. "Oh! Hi, Curly, Jackpot. Y'all come on in here. Watch them steps. They're rotten." She turned and yelled back toward the hallway, "That's somethin' else his royal highness was s'posed to take care of this weekend."

"Hi, L-L-Louise," Jackpot said, removing his hat and twisting it in his hands. Curly just nodded and lit a cigarette as he came into the room and sat down on a barstool at the counter. Two kids were taking apart a stuffed animal in front of a country-rock video that blared out of a console color TV in the corner. In the back, where Charlie was banging around, the baby squalled.

"Why don't you pick that baby up?" Louise yelled. She moved behind the counter and picked up a cigarette she had left burning in an ashtray, took a drag, and blew a stray lock of hair away from her pretty blue eyes with the smoke. "He needs changin'," she sighed. "Charlie'd rather have a tooth pulled'n change a dirty diaper."

She had on a nearly transparent white blouse tied in a knot beneath small, firm breasts. She wore no bra, and her nipples were tiny, pink buttons beneath the cloth. Long, dark hair spun down both sides of her face and laced across her shoulders. Her exposed tummy was flat, tight, in spite of having an eight-month-old baby and two other children besides. Curly remembered that she had the biggest collection of home workout videotapes in town, or so Charlie bragged. Her jeans were tight around firm tubes of thigh.

"Where the hell's my good shirt?" Charlie bellowed over the baby's crying. "The one with the purple flowers on it?"

"Up yours," Louise yelled back. Then she turned a warm smile on her guests. "Y'all want some coffee or a beer or somethin'?" Curly remembered that she had been a waitress at a truck stop out on 287 when she and Charlie met.

"D-D-D-Don't go to no t-t-trouble," Jackpot said. He flopped his long form down on the floor and started tickling the kids, who melted into a squirming mass of squeals and screams.

"I could use a beer," Curly said. He always liked to watch Louise bend over into the refrigerator while she fished around for the bottles, which really wasn't necessary, since the whole bottom two shelves were solidly stocked with beer. She had a nice rear end, he thought. It was her best feature.

He was enjoying the show when Charlie stormed into the room. He had put on clean jeans, but he hadn't found the shirt. His huge white belly flopped out over the belt buckle. His navel looked like a hairy badger hole, and bruises from Elwood's cable were already purpling across his back and sides.

"Goddamnit, Louise," he yelled. "Seems like the least you could do is keep my shirts clean." He started digging through a plastic laundry basket in the corner.

"Wash your own goddamn shirts," she squawked back at him. "I got better things to do." Then she set the beer bottle on the counter in front of Curly. Sweat rolled down it when it hit the humidity of the room. Her nails were long and bright red. "I ain't your slave," she finished softly and with a new smile for Curly. "You sure you don't want a beer, Jackpot?" Her blue eyes never left Curly's.

"Well, l-l-long's you're servin'," Jackpot said painfully. One of the children had him down on the floor and was trying to bite his hand. The other was jumping up and down on his skinny stomach. "These k-k-kids get b-b-bigger every time I see'em. They're h-h-h-harder to handle'n a gr-gr-green Brahma."

"Yeah, well, they're a handful," Louise called absently from inside the refrigerator. Curly was sure she gave her bottom an extra wiggle or two just for his benefit. "But I got me a new day-care center," she said as she turned and produced another bottle. "They'll be over there every afternoon from two to six," she said. Her voice softened, and her smile was directed again at Curly. "Two to six," she repeated when she twisted off the top.

Jackpot kicked the kids off of him just as one landed a deep kick to his groin. He had a sick grin on his face when he limped over and took the beer with no comment. His face was bright red.

"Give her more goddamn time to watch soap operas an' paint her goddamn toenails," Charlie grumbled. He pulled a ball of wrinkles from the basket, sniffed it, and nodded. When he pulled it on and stretched it over his stomach, the creases magically smoothed out into a bright western shirt with huge purple roses above the yoke. "Spends more time on the floor stretched out in front of the TV'n she does in the kitchen. Ain't had nothin' to eat round here that wasn't froze or boiled in a year."

"Charlie," she said, her blue eyes growing large with alarm as she studied him, "what in God's name happened to your face? Looks like you took on a whole bale of bobbed-wire."

"That son of a bitch Elwood Hays come at me with a pipe," Charlie explained over his shoulder. He disappeared down the hall again.

"That right?" Louise asked Curly. Her face showed a confusion of shock and satisfaction.

He nodded. "'Cept it wasn't a pipe. It was a phone cable."

She looked doubtfully at the plastic line running from the telephone to the jack in the wall. "Phone cable?"

"It's r-r-rubber-lined glass. T-T-T-Two inches thick," Jackpot explained. "I got hit up side the h-h-head with one of them once. N-N-Nigger boy du-done it over in Hou-Houston at the r-r-r-rodeo. Put my d-d-d-dick in the du-dirt, I can tell you. Got my wallet an' my c-car ke-ke-keys 'fore I could see straight. I can't see how ol' Ch-Ch-Ch-Charlie's walkin' round."

"How's Elwood?" Louise asked both of them. "He okay?" There was concern in her voice, but not much.

"I guess he's okay," Charlie said. He came around the counter and went to the refrigerator. He had a pink afghan in his hands. "Curly here dropped him with a poleaxe just as he was 'bout to put my lights out for good. Ain't that right, Curly?"

Curly said nothing and sipped his beer.

"You had a fight with Elwood, too?" she asked, her eyes narrowing. "What'd y'all do, gang up on him?"

"Hell, no," Charlie said. He dragged a cooler out from beside the refrigerator and started emptying ice trays into it. "I walked up and asked him if he'd been over here sniffin' your crotch, like you said he had, an' he just come up an' hit me with that pipe."

"I never said any such a thing!"

"Did, too. Standin' right over there. You said he'd took you 'to the limits of satisfaction.' Don't that beat all?" Charlie looked at Curly and Jackpot for sympathy. "Man's wife talkin' to him like that. It's them god-damn TV talk shows that does it."

Jackpot nodded wisely.

"Well, I was mad," Louise said. "I might of said anything."

"Well, he didn't deny it," Charlie said. He tossed the empty trays into the sink, then dumped the remains of the ice maker's bucket into the cooler as well. "An' I was just gettin' a mudhole stomped in my ass when Curly here jumped up an' knocked him down. That was all. We was defending your honor."

She looked from Curly to Jackpot to Charlie. "That right?" A grin cornered her mouth up at one end. She was so cute, Curly couldn't stand it. He looked at his bottle and read the label.

"You still drivin' for Woodrow's Wholesale Gas?" she asked Curly.

He shook his head. "Quit this mornin'."

She licked her lips. "You need to come by for a cup of coffee sometime."

Curly felt suddenly too warm and reread the label. Two to six, he thought.

"I wa-wa-wasn't there," Jackpot said. "They co-come for me after it was over. Get me 'nother bu-beer, Ch-Ch-Charlie."

Charlie obliged and then began shoving the better part of a case of bottles into the cooler.

"So where's he at, now?" Louise asked. Her painted fingertips bracketed her bare midriff and she cocked a hip.

"Back of my truck," Curly said. "He's still out."

She flew out the door.

"Kids, y'all be good for your mama," Charlie ordered casually as he closed the cooler and hefted it up onto the counter. One of them was urinating into a large pot with a dead plant in it. The other was back to work on the stuffed animal. Clouds of cotton swirled around the room in front of the TV. "Here." Charlie handed the afghan to Jackpot. "We can cover him up with this."

"He's sleepin' like a baby," Louise said as she pushed past them on her way back inside. "He's got him a goose egg on the back of his noggin, but I guess you didn't hurt him none. Where you goin' with my afghan?"

Charlie had the cooler and was already outside. "Mexico. We got to cover him up so he don't freeze," he said. "Grab some tater chips, Curly."

"Not with Aunt Harriet's afghan you don't," Louise yelled. "It was the last thing she did for me was make that afghan." She disappeared down the hall as Curly followed Jackpot outside.

Curly found two jumbo bags of chips on top of the refrigerator. A bottle of hot sauce was on the shelf next to the sink. He took that, too.

Charlie opened Curly's pickup and put the cooler on the floorboard. Jackpot stood uncertainly next to the truck bed with the afghan in his hands. "Let's go," Charlie yelled. "Shotgun!"

"I already cu-cu-called 'shotgun,' g-goddamnit," Jackpot yelled. Then he offered, "Let's tr-tr-tr-trade off."

"All I know is I'm drivin'," Curly said.

"Here." Louise emerged with a ragged yellow comforter in her hands. "Use this. We got it when we had to bring that sideboard home from Mama's."

"Goddamn sideboard like to give me a hernia," Charlie said, holding open the door. "Throw it on him, an' get in. It's startin' to rain."

Jackpot made the exchange and dumped the comforter over Elwood, then he climbed in the middle.

"You *ain't* goin', Charlie," Louise yelled. "I told you that you ain't runnin' off an' leavin' me every time you get a weekend."

"We'll be back on Sunday," Charlie hollered back and shut the door. "If you get a chance, why don't you take the Chevy in for a tune-up. It's runnin' ragged."

"Goddamnit, Charlie, I'm tellin' you, you better not go!"

"Well, you can just stand there an' tell it to the taillights of this here truck," he said lightly. "'Cause I'm goin'. I work goddamn hard, an' I need my rest an' relaxation."

"You're just goin' down there to consort with Mescan whores," she accused.

"Well, least they give me peace," he said softly. "One way or another," he chuckled. "Be back on Sunday," he called louder. "Tell the kids I'll bring'em a pretty."

"Well, I won't be here," she threatened. "I mean it! I'm goin' to Mama's."

"That'll last till the water boils," he grumbled and opened a beer. "Sunday," he called as Curly started the truck and began to back out. "An' don't forget 'bout the Chevy."

"I mean it!" she called angrily. "If you go, you can just as well stay gone." Then she dropped her tone to a lower, sweeter pitch. "Good to see you again, Curly," she said. "You don't be a stranger, hear?" One hand escaped the afghan and curled a strand of hair around a red nail.

They were at a rest stop a hundred twenty-five miles south of town before Charlie realized he'd left his wallet in his other pants.

———

"You re-re-reckon Elwood's got any mu-mu-mu-money on him?" Jackpot asked. It was seven in the morning, and they sat at the International Bridge in Laredo and contemplated the border. Jackpot looked older and uglier than ever, Curly thought. His graying red hair stuck out in five directions at once, and he was so skinny, it was a wonder he could keep his trousers up.

Curly lit a cigarette and looked through the rear glass. Elwood's dark form was humped under the comforter. "It'd be the first time," he admitted.

Charlie slumped against the door, sound asleep. They had finished off all the beer they had, and they couldn't buy any more before eight o'clock in the States or until they crossed the border into Mexico.

"Well, ju-ju-ju-just how in hell we goin' to get our horns c-c-c-clipped, if we don't have the pr-pr-price?" Jackpot moaned.

"We ain't here to get *our* horns clipped," Curly pointed out. "We're here to get *your* horns clipped, an' it don't look like we got the price of more'n a trim."

The trips to Mexico had originally been Jackpot's idea. He was so ugly, so skinny, that he couldn't even get one of the honky-tonk retreads over in Oklahoma to dance with him, let alone give him a tumble, even if he had the courage to talk to one of them, which he didn't. His stutter accentuated his natural shyness to the point of aggravation. The infrequent trips to Mexico were his only chance to satisfy what he called his "nu-nu-natural urges," and since he had been picked up for DWI five or six times, he couldn't drive anymore and relied on Curly or some other friend to provide transportation. He didn't have enough money to buy a car, anyway.

"Ch-Ch-Charlie owes me a hundred dollars," Jackpot whined. "For puttin' that gr-gravel down in his du-du-driveway. He said he'd p-p-p-pay me when we got here to keep me from bu-bu-bu-blowin' it back home."

"Well, Charlie's money's still 'back home,' so I guess you won't be 'bu-bu-bu-blowin' it' here, either." Curly was angry.

"Ain't you g-g-got any mu-money?"

"I got eighteen dollars, an' you got twelve," Curly said. "We're out of beer, an' we ain't ate nothin' but potato chips all night."

"You got a cr-cr-credit c-c-c-card," Jackpot accused.

"That'll do for food an' gas," Curly sighed, "but it won't buy what you want."

"Thought you wanted it, too," Jackpot said.

Curly didn't answer. He usually did indulge himself on these trips. It was harmless fun, he thought. Besides, he had come to like Mexico. It was warm, sunny, relaxed, homey. He could really kick back there and be somebody he never could be back home. Propane truck drivers don't get much respect, which was why he had quit.

This time, though, he couldn't get his mind off Louise, off her blue eyes and perky little tits and flat little belly, off her cute little bottom swishing from side to side while she found the beers in the refrigerator. Somehow the prospect of a Mexican girl didn't grab him right at the moment. And he was suddenly tired.

"I'd be glad to chip in my money," he said. "I can live without it. But we still ain't got enough."

"Well, shit," Jackpot said. "Shit, shit, shit." He was almost crying.

"I know a place," Charlie muttered. He was waking up and stretched as best he could inside the cab. "Two dollars'll do. You may come home with the blisterin' drips, but it'll do the job."

"Well, let's gu-gu-go," Jackpot said. "Let's j-just go."

Curly dropped the shifter and eased the truck into the bridge lane.

"What 'bout ol' Elwood?" Charlie looked behind them into the bed.

"Let him sleep," Curly said. "Mescans won't care. I know I sure don't."

———

The row of buildings on Nuevo Laredo's southwest side looked as if they hadn't changed since Houston whipped Santa Anna. The streets were dusty chugholes, and there were no curbs or lights. Some buildings still had hitching posts in front of them. Crumbling Spanish imperial architecture fronted the dirtiest series of shops, houses, bars, and brothels Curly had ever seen. This wasn't the neighborhood they usually visited, and it worried him a little. He parked the pickup in an alley, and they piled out. Charlie pissed on the side of a building while a scrawny dog barked at them and two doe-eyed children looked on. Curly and Jackpot inspected Elwood.

"You 'wake?" Curly asked Elwood, but he only groaned and rolled over.

"Lemme 'lone," he grumbled when Jackpot also prodded him. "Got me a headache. Just take me home. I'm cold."

"He don't nu-nu-know where he is," Jackpot said. "R-R-R-Reckon we ought to haul him out? Get a du-du-drink or two in him?"

"Let him be," Charlie offered. "He's not hurtin' nobody." He pulled the comforter up to cover Elwood's head and then tucked it under his feet. "Looks like a load of manure," he said. "Not even Mescans'll steal shit."

They sauntered around the corner and drifted into the first door marked "Cantina" they found.

Even though it was now bright daylight outside, the inside of the cantina was dark and smoky. A few swarthy men sat around tables or rested their heads on folded arms behind piles of bottles and glasses. Two women dressed in see-through black lace nightgowns and spiked heels lounged next to the bar. They looked sleepy and tired. The bartender glowered at the newcomers as they took a table.

"Cervezas. Tres," Curly yelled, and the publican's frown melted to a disinterested look as he pulled three Carta Blancas from a cooler and handed them to the girls. They shrugged off their weariness and brought over the beers. Curly paid them three dollars and tipped them another.

"You from Tejas?" one of them asked. "College boys?"

"No, we're not no goddamn college boys," Charlie said in an outrush of a belch. "We're just horny gringos. How much?"

They looked from one to the other and then back down to Charlie. "Twenty bucks, American," the one who spoke first said. "That's for straight up. Anything fancy costs you more."

"Twenty bucks!" Charlie boomed. "Chica, you didn't get twenty bucks when you was a virgin in the donkey show. Two dollars is the price, 'less y'all are sellin' somethin' you're not showin'." He put one finger on a nostril of his battered nose and made a loud sniffing noise.

Curly looked at the two girls while they tried to decide how to accept the fat American's insult and proposition. One was about sixteen and so thin she almost didn't have breasts. Acne scars ran down both cheeks, and her eyes were too close together. The one who was doing the talking was meatier and had big tits, and her complexion was clear, but she wasn't much older. Neither was particularly appealing.

"You're kiddin' me," she said. "Two dollars went out with black-and-white TV. You want me to be nice, you pay the whole damn price," she rhymed.

"Must of been some ol' boys from South Dallas down here." Charlie jabbed Jackpot in the ribs.

"Fifteen, straight up. Bottom line. And no nose candy," she bargained.

"We'll think 'bout it," he said. "Get us three more beers."

They stalked off and Curly studied their naked hips undulating beneath the thin fabric. All he could think about was Louise, and it made him surly. Normally, they were in better joints than this one. "We'll go find someplace else," he promised. He wanted to go to another cantina he knew, a place where the morning sun was warming on a bright patio and the beer was colder. The girls were prettier there, too.

"They're all ru-ru-right," Jackpot urged. "If we can g-g-get them to cu-come down, then they're f-f-f-fine. Either of them."

"You got the taste of a mongrel dog," Charlie said. "We can do better than that."

"Not for f-fifteen d-d-dollars, we can't," Jackpot whined. "An' for tu-tu-tu-two times, that's all we g-g-got."

"Less the beers," Curly added. "I don't think they take MasterCard here."

The girls came back with new bottles. Curly peeled off four more dollars. The beer was extra expensive here, like the girls.

Charlie got up and hefted his crotch. "I'm goin' on a scout," he said. "See what else there is round here." He took the bottle and left.

"Give me your cash," Curly said. Jackpot obliged.

With Charlie gone, the girls came back. One sat on each of their laps and began kissing their necks and feeling their crotches. Curly took over the negotiations while Jackpot grinned and blushed.

"Ten dollars, straight up, two times," he said to the girl on Jackpot's lap. She was the fat one, and she was doing a good job on the lanky cowboy. His narrow, ugly face contorted in pleasure as she ran her hands down into his shirt. She seemed to like him.

The girl looked into Curly's face, then nodded, rose, accepted the bills, and led Jackpot off to the back room where the cribs were. The other girl continued to work on Curly until he asked her to bring him another beer.

"What's matter," she asked when he paid her. "You don' like girls." She squeezed his crotch and found nothing doing there.

He couldn't help it. All he could think of was Louise and her tight little body. "War wound," he said, his mind clouded with thoughts of her long red nails running across his back. "I can't."

She looked sympathetic. "I fin' a way," she said. "Fi' bucks. No bullshit."

"It's all right," he said, handing her an extra dollar for a tip. "I'm drivin'."

That seemed to satisfy her, although she left with a pout when she sauntered back to lean on the bar and resumed her bored, tired posture.

———

After two more beers, Curly felt the need to piss, so he rose and went to the john. It was padlocked, and a sign that said Out of Order in both English and Spanish was nailed across it. Judging from the rust on the nails, it had been there a while. Four or five "Gig 'Em's" had been scrawled across the lettering, and they had been, in turn, marked out and "Hook 'Em's" painted across them.

He left the cantina and went out onto the street. It had been deserted when they arrived, but now, it was full of people moving here and there. Kids bugged him to pay for a shoeshine or to buy chewing gum, a woman, or almost anything else he might want. He found a café with a working toilet three doors down, and after he came out, he wandered off toward another "Cantina" sign four blocks away. Women now were everywhere. They leaned out of windows of the old adobe buildings and spoke suggestively to him in Spanish.

This was one of the things he liked best about Mexico, he thought. The people came out into the streets and moved around without worrying about cars and work. He had never been deeper into the country than the border towns, but he suspected that the whole place was like this. Bright, warm, a lazy place, where there was no pressure. Sex was open and aboveboard, and if he couldn't find it for love, he could always find it for money. The prices, in fact, fell with every offer. Twenty dollars dropped to fifteen, then ten, and finally he found the two-dollar bargains Charlie had promised offered from the mouth of a scabby urchin of about twelve. She kept pointing toward an alley and saying, "Dos bucks, Estadas Unidas?" in between making jerking motions with her hand.

He wasn't interested in any of the offers, particularly that one, and kept shaking his head. Try as he might, he couldn't get Louise off his mind, and he now felt bad for being here when he might have sent Charlie and Jackpot down here on their own and stayed there with her. The thoughts bothered him, and he started actively looking for Charlie to try to put things back into perspective. This trip was threatening to put him right off Mexico.

He found him in the fourth place he tried. Charlie was drunk. He had two girls, one on each knee, and a half-dozen empty bottles on the table in front of him. The marks on his face from the beating the night before were bright red, and huge sweat rings descended from his armpits. His hands wandered from bobbing breast to naked hip to exposed crotch and back again as he fondled the women who were laughing and drinking right along with him. Unlike the other bars, this one seemed full of men, and most of them were scowling at the big loud American in the center of the room.

"They don't speak *no* English here, amigo," Charlie yelled when he saw Curly coming up. "An' they take credit cards for poontang. Glad you found me. I must have a forty-dollar tab. I already nailed Lolinda, here," he pinched one of the girls on the bottom and made her start up and playfully slap out at him. "Soon's I get the tank refilled, I'm goin' for Maria. You might give one of'em a try. She's a pistol." He pinched her, too, and she slapped him a little harder than her friend did.

The girls were prettier than the pair at the other place, Curly noticed. For a moment, he felt sorry for Jackpot. He started to sit down and waved at the bartender for another round of beers. "Dos, he said. "Quatro," he amended in answer to the man's frown and gesture toward the girls.

The pinching-slapping game did not stop with one round and was now escalating. Every time one of the girls slapped him, Charlie would pinch her again. Then when he picked up his beer, the one he pinched last would slap him again. The girls, Curly realized, weren't just prettier, they were older, too. This was more like the Mexico he liked, and his thoughts of Louise began to fade.

The bartender sent a different girl with the round of beers. There were five bottles on her tray. Like the others, she was just barely wearing anything at all. But she was prettier, better built, softer, somehow.

"Hee rohnin' a tahb," she smiled, then started to sit down on Curly's lap. "Me llamo Madonna. Como la cinema star, big time. Verdad?"

A barking slap like the shot of a pistol rang out, and Lolinda jumped up and started rubbing her buttock. Charlie had his hand to his cheek, which was growing redder than it already was. "Son of a bitch!" he yelled.

"Cabrón!" she said.

"Puta!" Charlie replied, and she slapped him again, hard. This time his head snapped to one side, and before he could look around, Maria, who was still on his lap, opened her hand and hit him on the other cheek, flashing his face around the opposite way. She giggled and looked at her friend for approval. "Shit," Charlie yelled. "That hurt!"

Curly stood up and pushed Madonna away from him. He heard other chairs squeaking back in the bar. "C'mon," he said, glancing at the door. The bartender vaulted over the bar, a baseball bat in his hand.

When he looked back, Charlie had picked up the full beer bottle and dumped it on top of Maria's head. She screamed and raced to Lolinda and the other girl. Charlie grabbed up two full bottles, one in each hand, gave them a quick shake, and sprayed all three of them. "Hose down these bitches," he laughed. "Cool'em off."

The girls backed off. Their doused negligees were clinging to their bodies, and they pulled at the wet, sheer fabric and looked around the room in embarrassment. It suddenly seemed very quiet. Curly scanned around the bar. Two dozen angry male faces stared at them. The bartender stood where he was, bat at the ready, a dark threat in his eyes. "Let's get the hell out of here," Curly said, and he turned and ran out the door. Charlie was right behind him.

———

It was Curly's intention to run back to the first bar, pick up Jackpot, and then hightail it back to the U.S. That might have worked, but when they swung by the pickup and looked inside, Elwood was gone.

"Think he went inside?" Charlie was breathing heavily, but he went over and watered the side of the building in the same place he had before. The dog was gone, but the same two kids stared wide-eyed at him.

"Maybe," Curly said. "But we weren't there. Jackpot's in the back with a girl."

They split up and started looking up and down the streets, but Elwood was nowhere to be seen. Curly noticed that the formerly friendly and solicitous faces had now turned angry toward him. No children swarmed around him trying to sell him anything. He kept asking for "gringo largo," which was the only way he could think of to describe Elwood, but his question and hand-signaled descriptions were met with hostile blank looks and indifferent shrugs. Charlie had also disappeared.

"Hey, gringo," a kid of about ten said when Curly passed him. "I know somethin' you don'."

Curly approached him. The kid looked at him evenly and stuck out his hand. "Ten bucks. American."

"Here's two." Curly pulled the bills from his pocket.

"I want five."

"People in hell want ice water."

The kid shrugged. "It's valuable shit, man."

The kid tried to take the folded bills, but Curly kept his fingers firmly on them. "What?"

"The federales is looking for you."

"Who?"

"The cops, man. They is looking for you an' your frien'. The fat one. They know where your trucks is, an' you better get the hell out of Dodge."

"Elwood?" Then Curly remembered. He and Curly had run out of that bar without paying, to say nothing of leaving behind three beer-soaked women. "Gracias," he said, and he let go of the bills.

"Hey, no sweat, man," the kid said and ran off. Probably gone to tell them where I am, Curly thought.

He looked up and down two side streets and finally gave up and went back to the first cantina. He was surprised to find Elwood sitting next to Jackpot, drinking a beer. His clothes were splotched with dried mud. "We're low on cash," Curly warned when he walked up.

"It's my first round," Elwood whined.

"You have any money?"

"Nope."

"Well, go easy." Curly sat down and waved at one of the girls to bring him a beer. "And we need to shake a leg. Soon as Charlie gets back, we need to split." He accepted the beer and paid their tab with the last of their cash. "What I want to know," he said as he wiped his face with a handkerchief, "is how it can be so goddamn cold up at home and so goddamn warm down here."

"I got a th-th-theory on that," Jackpot said. "It's them ch-ch-ch-chili peppers all these Mu-Mescans eat. They m-m-make the air hot when they br-br-br-breathe an' f-f-fart." Curly snorted and sneered at him. "I'm su-su-serious," Jackpot insisted. "I read that in a m-m-magazine. It's tu-tu-true in India, too, on account of all the ch-ch-cheyenne p-p-p-peppers."

"Cayenne," Curly said.

"Ch-ch-eyenne." Jackpot put his long legs out on a chair in front of him. There was a hole in the toe of one of his boots. He was a different man, now. Full of himself. "I r-r-rodeoed over there. I know somethin' 'b-b-b-bout it. That c-c-curry j-j-j-junk is f-full of ch-cheyenne p-p-p-pepper."

"You don't know shit," Curly said. He looked at the door. He wished Charlie would show up.

"What *I* want to know," Elwood said, moving his hand up to the obvious knot on his head, "is what the hell I'm doin' in Mexico. I got me a headache."

"We told you we was g-g-g-goin' to Mexico," Jackpot said. "Du-Du--Don't you remember?"

Curly looked at the round lump on the back of Elwood's head and braced himself for an outburst. He hit him harder than he should have, he thought. He about decided he should have hit Charlie instead.

"I don't remember much of nothin'," Elwood said. "All I know is that I wake up with a headache the size of Dallas, 'bout a hundred Mescan kids lookin' at me in the back of Curly's pickup, an' when I get out, I'm in Mexico."

"Du-Du-Don't you r-r-remember beatin' h-h-h-hell out of Ch-Ch-Charlie last night?" Jackpot asked. Curly looked away.

"Me? Why'd I do that? I like ol' Charlie. We're lodge brothers."

"On account of L-Louise."

"Louise." Elwood moved his hand down and rubbed his chin. His eyes went soft. "Oh, yeah."

The door to the cantina burst open, and Charlie barreled through the room, upsetting tables and knocking over several of the sleeping men. "Goddamn cops is right behind me," he yelled. "Run for it!" He disappeared through the back hallway.

"What?" Elwood stood. "What's he talkin' 'bout?" He took a step over toward the door to look out and was immediately confronted by a short, fat Mexican in khakis, a white shirt, and a small, straw hat. He had a badge the size of a Mexican dollar pinned to his shirt pocket, and he carried a steel automatic in his hand. He seemed as shocked to find Elwood's massive frame in front of him as Elwood was to see the pistol rising toward him.

"Now, hold on," Elwood said. "Just a second, amigo."

The Mexican didn't hear or understand him. He jammed the pistol into Elwood's generous belly and pulled the trigger.

No one could move. Curly saw the whole thing as if in slow motion. He saw the fabric of Elwood's mud-stained shirt pressed inward from the pressure of the pistol's barrel, he saw the Mexican's brown finger tighten on the trigger, and he saw the hammer falling a millimeter at a time toward the back of the slide. He wanted to yell, but he didn't have time. Aside from the heavy breathing of the Mexican policeman, the only sound audible in the room was the flat click of the hammer striking an empty chamber and the sudden outrush of air from Elwood's lungs.

Elwood's eyes rolled back into his head and he fell like he was cut off at the ankles. There was a loud thud when his head hit the floor.

"Landed right on the same place where you hit him at," Jackpot said.

———

It was after dawn, Sunday, when they got home. They had talked it nearly to death before they reached San Antonio, and Curly was so tired of thinking about it that he had let his fantasies about Louise take over and run wild just to keep him awake. Elwood was in the middle of the cab, asleep, and leaning alternately on him and Jackpot. Charlie was huddled under the comforter in the pickup's bed, his body swathed in Ace bandages. A new norther was blowing, and the temperature seemed to drop five degrees with every mile they covered. All Charlie had for help from the cold was the remains of a twelve-pack Curly bought for him at a convenience store in Laredo.

"I don't r-r-reckon I'll g-g-g-go down to Mu-Mu-Mexico no more," Jackpot said. His words startled Curly, who had just finished a drawn-out fantasy about taking a bath with Louise in a huge tub filled with bubbles. He wondered what her legs looked like. He'd never seen her in anything but tight jeans. He had forgotten all about Jackpot, about why they went to Mexico in the first place.

"Why not?"

"Too du-du-dangerous," Jackpot said. "'S-S-Sides, I think I already g-got somethin'. When we st-st-st-stopped back there to pu-pu-piss, it was already b-b-b-burnin'. Ch-Ch-Charlie said the same thing."

"You don't feel it that fast."

"Well, I p-p-probably got somethin' anyway. Cr-Cr-Crabs or some-thin'. You n-n-know my luck. I c-can't see su-su-su-spendin' any time in a Mu-Mescan jail, n-n-either," he said. "That's g-g-g-good enough reason."

Curly had to agree. It had cost him over five hundred dollars to keep them all from being locked up and to get them out of the country. He had to go to the mercado, where the jefe arranged with one of the merchants to ring up a phony charge for merchandise on his MasterCard, then hand over the cash, with a nice gratuity, of course.

They rode in silence for a while longer, and then Elwood woke up. The lights of town were apparent on the horizon. The sun would be up in a while. Elwood picked up the conversation where he had dropped it somewhere south of Waco when he fell asleep.

"Son of a bitch like to got me killed. A lodge brother. Don't that beat all?" It was about the four hundredth time he'd put the question to them since they left the Valley behind them.

Curly and Jackpot didn't say anything. There was nothing to say. Curly never was sure whether the Mexican cop's gun misfired or if the cop knew it wasn't loaded and was only planning to use it to scare Charlie. It didn't matter, though. It scared the piss out of Elwood. No sooner had he hit the floor than he was grabbed up by the two women and hauled to the back. When they brought him to the jail several hours later he had a huge swath of bandages wrapped around his head like a turban and a silly grin on his face that disappeared the second he saw Charlie.

Charlie was in bad shape. Five or six of the guys from the other bar were waiting at the cantina's back door with baseball bats when he ran on through and tried to get away. They cracked two of his ribs and knocked out a couple of teeth before the cop got around to breaking it up and arresting him, Curly, and Jackpot and hauling them in. They took him to a doctor who put Ace bandages around Charlie and charged Curly another fifty dollars. The MasterCard felt heavy in his wallet.

"I could of died, you know that?" Elwood asked them when the silence continued. "Died in Mexico. Did he ever think of that? What'd

Estelle-Lee say? She thinks I'm at a church retreat up at Lake Lugert this weekend. I'd of been in the doghouse forever if I'd got killed, an' it'd all been that son of a bitch's fault."

Curly and Jackpot stayed quiet, and Elwood became more awake and fumed. "Prob'ly got the clap, too," he muttered. "Them girls wouldn't let me 'lone." They let him off at J.D.'s parking lot where his pickup still waited for him.

"Next time you go to Mexico," he said, "wish you'd count me out. Man can get hurt down there."

"We'll l-l-leave you home n-n-next time," Jackpot promised. "It's no p-p-p-place for men lu-like us."

Curly saw the telephone cable lying in the parking lot where Elwood had dropped it on Friday night.

"I don't think there'll be a next time," he said.

Elwood nodded and glanced into the back of the pickup. "I'm not due home till tonight," he wondered aloud. "What'll I tell my Estelle-Lee?"

"Tell her it br-br-br-broke up early. There's wu-wu-weather comin'," Jackpot offered with a glance up at the sky.

There was, too, Curly thought. The air felt like snow.

Elwood nodded and looked back toward Charlie, who hadn't moved. "You goin' to take him to the hospital?"

"It's up to him," Curly said. He honestly hadn't thought about it.

"Well, you ought to. Twenty-four-hour observation," he said wisely. "The lodge'll pay for it. I'm treasurer. I'll see to it."

"He's got bu-bu-benefits out the ass," Jackpot said.

"I know that," Elwood said. "You ought to take him to the doctor, anyhow." His brow furrowed in sincerity. "That man belongs in a hospital. Promise me you'll do that. I mean it."

Curly nodded and touched his cap's brim in a salute of acknowledgment. Elwood straightened the bandage-turban, which was threatening to fall off, and staggered toward his truck. "Get him inside," Curly said. "Colder'n a witch's *tit* out there."

Jackpot helped Charlie into the cab, out of the cold, and they took off toward Jackpot's camper-trailer on the northwest side.

"Don't r-r-rreckon I'll be g-goin' back down to Mu-Mu-Mexico," Jackpot repeated when he climbed out of the pickup and shut its door.

Charlie rolled down the window to hear what he wanted to say. "R-R-Reckon I had enough of that for a s-s-spell."

"I'll remember that," Curly said. The countryside seemed gray, cold, dead. In his mind, even with all that happened, Mexico seemed golden, warm, and lively. The wind was whipping dust all around Jackpot, and he had to hold his cap on his head. Low gray clouds pushed toward the south in a panic of frosty air. "Though I'd have to say, I preferred the weather."

"Eat more ch-ch-cheyenne p-p-p-peppers," Jackpot advised. His teeth were chattering. "I'm gu-gu-glad I don't live d-d-down there. Place stinks."

"You can say that, again," Charlie muttered. It was the first thing he'd said since they left Laredo.

"See ya," Jackpot said, and he turned and started away toward his trailer.

They turned around on the highway and headed toward the east side of town. The pickup rocked in the wind. Freezing rain pecked at the glass.

"Reckon you can let me out here," Charlie said all of a sudden. They were approaching the blinking light that marked the junction where the by-pass skirted the town.

"What?"

"Said, let me out anywhere you want along here."

"This is the middle of the goddamn highway. It's freezin' out there."

"That's right."

"You'll get run over."

Charlie looked at him and grinned. "Naw. Just let me out."

"Don't you want to go to a hospital?"

"Hell, I been hurt worse'n this wrestlin' with my kids. Pull over."

"Ain't you goin' home?" Curly steered the pickup off to one side and started slowing down.

"Nope," Charlie said. "I been doin' some thinkin', an' I decided I ain't goin' home."

"What about Louise?" Curly asked. He felt something drop inside him, like an elevator falling from the top of a building. He saw her bottom sticking out of the refrigerator once more.

"She'll be all right," Charlie said. He lit a cigarette. "She never liked me much in the first place. Only married me 'cause she was knocked up an' I had a job. An' there's Elwood." He sighed heavily and winced with pain. "She's got lots of friends. More'n I ever had. An' then, there's you."

"Me?"

"Better'n Elwood," Charlie said, scooting over a bit and putting his hands out of the comforter and into the stream of hot air from the heater. "That dumbass son of a bitch. This was all his fault."

"You sayin' I ain't your friend?" Curly felt hurt, but not much. He just needed to ask the question.

"You are today," Charlie said. "But sooner or later, it'd be you an' me goin' at it just like me an' Elwood was. An' Louise'd probably just be standing there rootin' you on. She always liked you. Like as not, one of us'd kill the other. Just stop the truck. I'll get out here."

Curly stopped, and Charlie looked down between his legs. "Any beer left?"

Curly helped him look and came up with one can. "It's hot. It was wedged up against the cooler and the heater vent."

Charlie took it, opened the door, and stepped out. "It'll cool down out here," he said. He pulled the comforter out behind him and threw it over his shoulders. "Take that cooler back to Louise. It's her mama's. Make her pay you back for all the shit you run up on your card down there. Cash is in my billfold. An' tell her to get a tune-up on the goddamn Chevy." He grinned. "Tell her I'll write sometime. An' give her a kiss for me." He winked and stood back from the truck. "Kids, too," he yelled over the wind. "But be careful. They bite."

"Where you goin' to go?"

"Anywhere but Mexico," Charlie hollered. He was still grinning.

Curly pulled back onto the highway. The last time he saw Charlie, he was bundled under the ragged comforter and drinking down the beer.

———

It started to sleet by the time Curly pulled into the muddy gravel driveway that led up to Charlie and Louise's mobile home. He jumped out and cursed the wind while he dragged the cooler out of the cab and pulled it up onto the rotten wood of the porch. He could hear the TV blaring through the glass louvers of the door when he knocked. He banged twice more before the door swung open. He couldn't say exactly what he was feeling. But he wished his heart would quit pounding.

Heat from the inside washed over him when the door opened, and one of the kids stood before him, in a pair of ragged, dirty underwear. Cartoons jumped on the TV. The other child was torturing a hamster in the middle of the room, and several boxes of cereal were ripped open and scattered everywhere.

"Your mama home?" Curly asked. He wondered how Louise would act. The kid didn't answer but jammed a filthy thumb into his mouth. His underwear, Curly could see, was sopping wet. His face was covered with chocolate.

He started to go on in, holler for Louise, but then his eyes fell on the counter where he had sat and enjoyed watching her rear end display two nights before. A bundle of bandages, like a turban, was piled next to a coffee cup and two empty beer bottles. Charlie's wallet lay next to them. He stepped back. A chill deeper than that caused by any north wind shocked through him.

"She got company?" he asked the kid. No answer. The child's whole hand joined his thumb in his mouth. Urine ran down his leg.

Curly stepped inside and cast his eyes back toward the hall that led to the rear of the home. He heard the baby yowling over loud country music. "Well, you tell her her cooler's here," he said to the kid. He opened Charlie's wallet and counted out three hundred dollars in twenties. He didn't take all the cash that was there. "An' tell her . . . never mind."

He pushed the door to, got in his pickup, and backed out. When he used a bandana to wipe the fog off the windshield, he saw Elwood's green Ford Supercab parked by a hedgerow three lots down.

There was still over a thousand dollars credit left on his charge card, he remembered. "Mexico," he said to his reflection in the rearview mirror.

He guided the truck back onto the highway, out into the wind, shivered once, then he pointed it south.

THE BAPTISM

Wayne Henderson slowly moved his broom back and forth in front of his hardware store and enjoyed the cool air of the shady side of Agatite's Main Street. Cars, minivans, SUVs, and pickups moved slowly up and down the brick-paved thoroughfare, their windows rolled tightly up against the advancing warmth of the morning. Pulling in and out of parking places, the drivers—most of whom had cell phones jammed against their heads—jerked in stops and starts as pedestrians, many of whom were also on the phone—jaywalked in front of them. In spite of the sight of such peripatetic electronic mass communication, which Wayne disdained with an almost unconscious scowl as an inevitable sign of the times, it was an hour of the morning he normally enjoyed. It reminded him of a time when he was a boy coming "to town" with his grandmother on her weekly shopping trip.

Wayne's grandmother had lived on a family farm way out in the country, five miles from the paved farm-to-market road that ran southwest out of Agatite. Once a week, she would pile Wayne and his sister, Pearlie, into a battered old 1936 Ford sedan and drive them into town. She would stop first downtown and walk slowly up and down Main Street, speaking to people she met, and buying cloth, thread, or maybe a new pair of cotton stockings. Sometimes, she would stop at the hardware store for something more substantial, and she almost always found a "pretty" for Wayne and his sister at the Ben Franklin store.

In his memory, it always seemed to be summer when they came to town.

By the time she had finished her shopping, the heat of the summer sun had become intolerable, even to small children, and they would climb into the rusty old Ford and putter down to Rayson's IGA so she could pick up her weekly supply of "vittles," as she called them, and usually a popsicle for Wayne and Pearlie before heading back to the farm and a supper of fried chicken or baked ham.

When he was graduated from high school, Wayne left the farm and enrolled in Baker School of Business in Wichita Falls, and with his graduation certificate from there, he came back to Agatite and went to work as the assistant manager of the Main Street Hardware Store, owned and operated by M. Greely. Wayne often wondered if Greely had any real first name—even his tombstone read simply "M. Greely," and Wayne never heard anyone call him anything else.

When Mr. Greely died, Wayne used his savings to buy the store from Mr. Greely's daughter, who had come home from Chicago to sell everything as soon as possible and take her mother away with her. He got it for about half what it was worth and had been running it ever since. There was a while when he feared he might be drafted, but he was exempted when he claimed he walked in his sleep. He had to talk it over with three army doctors, none of whom believed him, Wayne knew, but he stuck to his story and finally was declared unfit for military service, except in cases of national emergency, which Wayne didn't anticipate.

Now, he was the sole proprietor of Henderson's Main Street Furniture & Hardware, and he hired no assistant manager. He kept his inventory records carefully up to date so in case anything happened to him, no one could buy it for the cut-rate he had paid, even though he wasn't married and there was no one but the First Security Bank to sell it for him—Pearlie had been killed in a car accident his senior year in high school, and his grandmother died a year later, just after his mother's body was shipped home for burial. Wayne never knew where she died or how. He didn't much care. He had no cousins or uncles or aunts he was aware of. He kept the farm, which was his only inheritance, and dutifully paid taxes on it, but he didn't work it or even visit it. The fields were allowed to go fallow, the pastures to be overtaken by mesquite, the ramshackle old farmhouse to fall into dereliction.

Instead, Wayne worked hard in the hardware business, expanding the stock and taking over a vacant storefront next door and enlarging his inventory, and it had paid him well. He spent little money on his lifestyle, preferring to live in a garage apartment in an old section of Agatite, and to walk to work rather than drive. He did own a car, but it was a "stripped-down" model, a 1963 Chevrolet Biscayne, which boasted no other luxury than a heater. Even though it was virtually an antique, it had fewer than twenty-five thousand miles on it. Wayne never went anywhere. He wore one of five sets of identical outfits to work each day—a white shirt, black trousers, and Sears Best work shoes—and he alternated his lunches between a tuna sandwich at the Town and Country Dinette and a chicken-salad sandwich at Central Drugs every other day. He skipped breakfast, except for three cups of stout instant coffee, and usually a can of Campbell's soup heated on an ancient hotplate was more than he could eat for dinner. He didn't like television, cared nothing for sports, but he checked out books on gardening and horticulture from the Sandhill County Library to fill his evenings, although he had never in his life planted a seed or cultivated any plant. He didn't drink or smoke, and while he often thought in profane terms, he never swore aloud. He never went out, socially or otherwise. He'd never attended a parade, civic festival, or other public ceremony, never been to a play or a concert. He hadn't seen a movie in more than thirty years.

In a small town, old bachelors were often regarded as "queer," but that mattered not to Wayne Henderson. He was content to allow his fellow citizens to form whatever opinions they might about him. He never thought about sexual congress with either women or men, and romance was a concept alien to his consciousness. A slight figure of a man, he had not been popular in high school, and his only attempt at a date had been a disastrous affair when he accepted an invitation from a somewhat forward girl, Sally McMichaels, to attend the Senior Picnic, where the bill of fare consisted mostly of garlicky hotdogs laden with chili and onions. She wound up going home with another boy when Wayne refused to kiss her on the moonlight hayride. Even though his rebuff had more to do with a fear that she might be offended by his breath than with any genuine shyness, it had fed rumors about him that continued to flit around the town from time to time, like bullbats swooping around streetlamps in the summer twilight.

Wayne's life was a quiet one. Except for an all-but-mandatory Chamber of Commerce membership, he joined no clubs, no lodges, had no friends—male or female—and conversed casually with no one, except his cat, a nameless stray that decided five years before that the stairs leading up to Wayne's apartment were going to be home, and who refused to be discouraged by Wayne's attempts to drive him off. He had no telephone in his house and never felt the need for one. There simply was no one to call. He was totally indifferent to the snickering gossip he occasioned at the women's clubs and card parties and around the domino parlor and country club bar because he was a "rich old bachelor" who preferred the company of an alley cat to that of the town's eligible females.

Wayne had no passions in his life, no desires, no wants. Even the money he religiously deposited and counted in the pages of his ledgers and checkbooks had no meaning, as money. It was merely a convenient set of figures by which he could measure his life's work, a chart of profits and losses that meant nothing in terms of buying power or access to luxury and comfort. Dollars were only numbers: exact, predictable, impersonal, and reliable. He knew precisely how many he had, and he knew precisely how many he would spend in any given endeavor. Although not particularly miserly or stingy in any mean way, he carefully guarded every dime he earned as if it was all that stood between him and starvation.

His single joy in life, though, was his recollections, and every summer, the sweeping of his sidewalk reminded him of Mama Henderson and his childhood, which, he decided, was the best time he would ever have. Recollecting it relaxed him. He also thought it was good for business for folks to see a store's proprietor out front and handling a menial task. It was not the sort of thing they would find at the big discount stores, he assured himself.

Three years before, he had reluctantly hired Warren, a junior college dropout who had come back to town after several stints in a detox clinic down in Lubbock. Warren, the son of Waylon Attaway, who owned the Ford dealership, appeared one morning, begging for a chance and assuring Wayne that he was "straight" and would be reliable and a hard worker. When asked why he didn't work for his father, Warren confessed that he was on his "last chance." If he didn't find work on his own, he said, his dad would banish him from the house and family. "I'll be here every day," Warren whined. He noticed that Wayne was looking at his exposed arms. "And no more trouble," he said. "I'm clean."

Wayne admitted that he needed someone to take care of minor chores and the heavy lifting around the store, but Warren was hardly the sort Wayne felt comfortable around, and in spite of his assurances, he didn't look "clean." The boy's pimple-ravaged face sparkled with various sharp bits of jewelry that pierced his lips, nostrils, and eyebrows. He had a colorful tattoo of nothing Wayne could identify on one forearm and ink-colored stars on the other, and he cut his black hair short on the sides, then swept the topknot up in a sharp, bright blond spike that seemed to be held in place by a pound of greasy gel. Wayne wasn't entirely sure, but he believed the youth also wore eye makeup. Why he gave in and hired him was a mystery Wayne could not explain even to himself.

At the same time, steady help was hard to find in the small town, and the kid accepted the job for minimum wage and no benefits apart from two afternoons a week off, a time when he could usually be seen riding up and down Main Street in a small convertible with a nearly emaciated blonde girl whose face and visible body parts boasted even more piercings and tattoos than Warren had. Although Wayne sometimes believed that Warren was probably an excellent candidate to become the village idiot or a prison convict, he was permitted to handle the snow and ice in the winter. But in the summertime, Wayne found the shady side of Main Street soothing and nostalgic. "It is pleasurable," he sometimes said to Warren to explain why he chose to do the sweeping himself.

In time, Warren proved to be as good as his word. He remained something of a painful annoyance to Wayne, all the same. The sight of such physical self-abuse and torture as Warren had inflicted on his flesh made Wayne's whole body tingle in sympathetic reaction, a phenomenon he could not seem to shake. A pair of miniature earphones were perpetually plugged into Warren's earring-laden lobes, their tiny cords joining in a Y beneath his perpetually unshaven chin, then snaking down to hook into some mysterious music-making apparatus inside his baggy clothing.

Wayne could hear the tinny vibrations of sound whenever he came near Warren, but he never had seen the device that made them, and he seldom came near enough to him to conduct a more detailed inspection.

The morning sweeping, then, also gave Wayne a reason to be outside the store during business hours, something he came to enjoy even more because it kept the painful vision of his young employee out of his sight and the indistinct rhythms of his music at bay.

That particular August morning, though, Wayne Henderson was not thinking about Warren's tortured body, or about Mama Henderson and popsicles, or about his bucolic youth. He was disturbed by two separate and unrelated problems. First of all, he was developing an ulcer. Secondly, he had to go to a funeral. Either of these was sufficient to depress him, but taken together, they formed a lump in his stomach that aggravated it even more than usual, and the rhythmic swinging of the broom was no relief. It actually seemed to accentuate his pain.

The ulcer had been brought about by overwork, Doc Pritchard had told him. "You need a vacation, Wayne," the medical man had said as he handed Wayne his shirt following his examination. "You're a textbook case of workaholism. You've got high blood pressure, a bad back, your 'indigestion' is a duodenal ulcer that needs immediate attention, maybe surgery. All the Pepto-Bismol in the world won't cure it, and it could kill you. Hell, man, you're only sixty-four. That's not that old, these days."

Wayne shook his head. It was true. He hadn't had a vacation since he bought the store except for one quick trip down to Nuevo Laredo to buy some Mexican lighting fixtures the previous summer. That had been a nightmare journey. The heat was oppressive, and the confusing bustle and filth of the border town seemed to envelop him while the clatter of jabbering Spanish surrounding him across the border disoriented him completely. All this combined with a spicy lunch the factory owner pressed on him to create a distress so severe that on the return trip he developed severe diarrhea and nausea. He was so bad off that he had to spend an extra night in a pricey Holiday Inn in San Antonio, alternately hugging the commode or perched on top of it, sure he was about to defecate away all of his internal organs and not caring very much, if doing so would relieve his misery.

To make matters worse, the venture was a total bust, since the market for the Spanish design proved to be more limited than Wayne had imagined, and the fixtures were wired so poorly that he had wound up spending more than he paid for them to restring the wires and make them safe. To boot, when he got back, the kid, Warren, had screwed up the books and lost a whole shipment of fishing tackle by refusing to accept it because he didn't know Wayne had planned to enlarge his line of sporting goods. That had cost him double shipping to get them back, and when they came in, half of the rods and reels were damaged or missing. The whole trip had been a complete disaster and had left his already ailing stomach in ruins.

To leave again, even for a day or two, meant leaving the idiotic kid in charge again. Kid. Hell, Wayne thought, Warren was well past twenty-one, but he looked like a freak of nature and didn't know enough to clean the shit off his shoes. Wayne couldn't leave town again without closing the store, and that meant losing business, possibly forever, to the Wal-Mart over in Vernon, or the Costco they'd put in in Childress. He had the only hardware store in thirty miles in either direction, and he made good money with it. But he couldn't let people get in the habit of driving over to the cut-rate discount stores. They might soon figure out that a quarter tank of gas was not that bad an offset if they compared too many prices. He had waged what he often saw as a one-man campaign to sustain local businesses in the face of the constant spread of big-box stores. He'd heard about the ruin they caused to mercantile concerns elsewhere, and he couldn't bear the thought of the same thing happening in Agatite. Once one opened there in town, he'd be ruined.

He was counting the potential loss such a thing would mean when he realized that Doc Pritchard was still talking.

"Now, all this prescription will do is relieve some of the stomachache," he said. "What you're going to need is surgery if you don't take some time off and relax. Go fishing, man. That's what I do. Hell, you don't even play golf." Wayne's eyes went blank again as he figured the cost of a country club membership, golf clubs, one line of sporting goods he didn't stock. He wondered how that game actually worked, anyway, and why so many people were addicted to it. Pritchard shook his head in disgust. "Wayne," he said. "Listen to me." Wayne raised his eyes, and Pritchard sighed and went on in a sincere tone. "You don't want to mess around with this thing. You could lose half your stomach, or more."

Wayne's mind drifted off again. He was looking right at Pritchard, but he was drifting back to the store where he remembered that he needed to inventory the hand tools and was wondering if he could trust Warren to do it.

"Hell," Pritchard said, disgusted. "You'll lose a month flat on your back in the hospital. Then, what'll happen to your goddamn store?"

That, at last, penetrated Wayne's mental fog. A month! What would happen then? Warren would run the whole thing into the ground, and if he closed down completely, his customers would find that thirty-mile drive to Wal-Mart or Costco not to be so much trouble after all, even if they didn't get local credit, interest free, and an unconditional guarantee on all tools and appliances. He'd lose a fortune either way. But a vacation! Golf! Shit. Where would he go, anyway? He could think of nowhere in the world he might want to see, no one he might want to visit.

Wayne told himself that instead of a vacation, he would just slow down, let Warren do even more of the heavy work and take care of more of the niggling little chores that always seemed to need attention during the average day. He'd cut the boy's afternoons off down to one, offer him a small raise, maybe give in and hint at a promotion to assistant manager, something he could postpone indefinitely, he thought.

Tattoos, piercings, and all, Warren was at least reliable. He'd never taken a day off sick or come in late, Wayne reminded himself. He might have potential. He might teach him how to keep the books properly. Then he remembered when Warren had tried to talk Wayne into putting his inventory and accounts on a computer. The kid had shown up one morning with a flat plastic box, which he unfolded and fiddled with until a screen lit up. Wayne had only a vague idea how computers worked from his visits to the bank and library. When he moved around behind Warren and peered over his shoulder at the screen, what he saw nearly struck him blind.

On the screen, so vivid he felt they might speak to him, two nearly identical young women, both completely naked except for high-heeled shoes, struck provocative poses that left utterly nothing to the imagination. Their arms were entwined, their legs laced together as they stood close to one another, their swollen breasts and bright red nipples nearly touching beneath dual cascades of long red curls, their pubic mounds barely covered with gossamer-thin hair, their eyes bright and mouths seductively open, white teeth and red lips inviting attention, even as their brightly painted manicures curled over one another's creamy shoulders.

Wayne reeled backward and knocked over a complete shelf of baseball equipment. "Good gravy!" he'd yelled at Warren. "Shut that thing off! That's—that's—" He stammered, felt his breath grow short and a sudden pain arise in his chest.

"That's Miss June," Warren said, shocked by Wayne's reaction. "Or Miss Junes. They're twins."

"That's filthy!" Wayne yelled. "Obscene!" He grabbed at the counter and tried to force his breathing to return to normal. He was as amazed by his reaction as was Warren. He'd seen naked women—or photos of naked women—before, naturally, had two or three times in his youth actually been exposed to raw pornography. But the grainy, poorly posed photos in cheap men's magazines he'd previously viewed did not compare to the brilliant, lifelike images on Warren's laptop screen. More, though, was the surprise of it, the graphic, almost tactile reality of it that caught him off guard. They looked so real on the small screen, it was as if they had been miniaturized and were somehow standing behind it, so three-dimensional in their aspect that he felt if he put out a finger, he would reach right through the screen and touch them. It appalled him.

"It's not disgusting," Warren said, his eyes narrowing in defense. "Shit, it's just *Playboy,* for Christ's sake. From their calendar." He looked proudly down at the screen. "It's my wallpaper," he said.

"Shut it," Wayne yelled, grabbing his broom and heading out the front door. "Unplug it, shut it, close it, unboot it. Whatever you do with it. Get that thing out of here and don't bring it back." He stalked off to the back of the store, pausing only to fling over his shoulder, "And watch your mouth."

That had been an end to any attempt to computerize Henderson's Furniture & Hardware's accounts and inventory with Warren's help. Wayne now eyed any computer in any business, even on the counter at the drugstore, with high suspicion of what vile pictures it might display, and he took an even dimmer view of Warren's character.

No, he decided, realizing that Pritchard had left the room, apparently deciding that Wayne's mental departures weren't going to subside while he stood there. Giving Warren more responsibility wouldn't do. But he could use him for more heavy work. Moving those sofas and tables, double refrigerators and washers and dryers around was backbreaking, and the newer model television sets were huge and heavier than ever. Maybe, he half-promised himself, he'd start taking a regular afternoon off a week. He could have a telephone installed in his apartment, and Warren could call him at home if he had any questions, if something came up he couldn't handle.

But on this Wednesday, the first planned afternoon off, he wouldn't be at home mowing his landlady's lawn with one of the new electric mowers or napping on the new Luxury Lounger—both items being tried out with the idea of possibly carrying them in the store. He would be down at the First Baptist Church attending Bill Castlereigh's funeral.

Along with his pleasant recollections of Mama Henderson, Wayne's dread of funerals went back to his childhood. Before he and Pearlie had gone to live with their grandmother, before his mother had run off with a wholesale liquor salesman from Altus, Oklahoma, before his father had gone after her, getting himself shot to death in some bar in Oklahoma City, his parents had been strict members of the Church of Christ. They dragged him and Pearlie to every service, two on Sundays and every Wednesday night, held in the yellow-brick church on Grove Street. He had sat squirming in prickly wool suits as the preacher screeched and screamed about the horrors of hell and the wages of sin, punctuated by toneless, unaccompanied singing and the occasional "Amen" shouted from some half-asleep soul in the congregation.

But the church funerals had been the worst part of it. His father drew the line at attending them, unless he knew the deceased, but for some reason, his mother was fascinated by them, and she would dress up both kids and march them down to the front pews to sit and listen while the preacher—now subdued and somewhat morose—droned on about the earthly virtues of whatever corpse lay encoffined in front of the pulpit. Wayne had curiously watched the weeping families mourn for whoever had died, wondering all the time what all the crying was about, since, from what he could understand, the "dearly departed" had gone on to a better and happier existence, although Wayne in his youthful innocence never could understand where the place was.

After a measure, the droning was deemed sufficient, and the congregation would sing another off-key hymn, and then they would all pile into steaming hot cars and caravan out to the Sandhill County Memorial Cemetery. There the coffin would be prayed and sung over again before being lowered into the red clay soil, and Wayne would have to spend an hour getting the mud or dust off his Sunday shoes.

It seemed like all funerals—like all trips into town with Mama Henderson—had been in the summertime. And the pleasant memories of trips into town were often balanced by the sticky, hot memories of burying the dead. That is, all the memories but one.

When Wayne was seven, a man, a drifter—a "bum" was how Wayne's father described him—was found starving and nearly frozen on Agatite's Main Street. He languished in the county hospital for nearly a week before a combination of pneumonia and exposure and starvation brought him to what Wayne's mother called the "death throes." In the course of his demise he was visited by every preacher and minister in Agatite, even the Catholic priest, but it was Brother Hays, from the Hendersons' own church, who made the greatest impression on the dying man. In the final moments of lucidity, the drifter agreed to "give his soul to Jesus" and be baptized in the church.

Over the objections of Doc Taylor, Brother Hays and a couple of elders bundled up the old man—his name was Roosevelt Grady—and trundled him out into what people were calling the worst norther in memory. The mercury hung at the zero mark, and the wind howled down the streets of Agatite as the preacher drove Grady over to the church, where a party of the faithful had been roused from their warm living rooms to witness this eleventh-hour conversion and saving of one of God's chief sinners.

Wayne, Pearlie, and their mother had also come, his father refusing to go out in such a storm for such "nonsense," and they were in the first chorus of a hymn when word was whispered around that Roosevelt Grady had arrived.

Inside the church, the temperature was below freezing, it being midweek and the heating system not having yet caught up to the expanses of the sanctuary. Wayne and his family had come wrapped in coats and scarves, and they huddled on the front pew beside other frozen brothers and sisters of the congregation. The hymn was faltering through the vaporized breaths of the icy building's occupants, and Wayne watched fascinated as the vapor that came from people's mouths played in the spotlights over the pulpit.

Just as I am, without one plea,
But that Christ's Blood was shed for me . . .

The curtains of the baptistery opened, and Wayne saw Brother Hays wade down waist-deep into the icy water behind the half-glass panel that fronted the tank. Hays was wearing rubber waders and had a scarf wound around his neck, but his hands were turning blue from the freezing water. He had to return to the concrete steps to help Clarence Underwood bring Roosevelt Grady down into the baptistery. He was still wearing his hospital gown and was only about half-conscious, and several of the women in the congregation averted their eyes as Hays and Clarence held him awkwardly up, trying to keep him from slipping and exposing more of his bare backside to the hymn singers than was already visible through the slits in his hospital garb.

And that Thou biddest me come to Thee . . .

The icy-cold water had an awakening effect on Roosevelt Grady. His eyes opened wide, and he began struggling to free himself from Clarence's hold on his hands and now from the grip Brother Hays had on his head and shoulders. But his illness had weakened him, and with a minimum of effort, they maneuvered him to the center of the tank.

Oh Lamb of God, I come, I come . . .

"Brother Roosevelt Grady, by your Profession of Faith and Acceptance of Jesus Christ as Your Personal Savior, I baptize you, my brother . . ." Hays began. But Grady had had enough religion for one occasion. He began to struggle violently, sloshing water out onto the carpet behind the pulpit and all over Brother Hays's shirt. "In the name of the Father, the Son, and the Holy Spirit . . ." Hays placed one hand in the small of Grady's back and the other on his forehead. Grady's arms flailed wildly, splashing water all over Hays and Clarence, who had begun to lose their grips in the numbing, icy bath, but somehow the minister managed to hold on and dunked Grady into the tank. Whatever strength the old man's body still possessed came suddenly to bear.

Feet and legs whipped out, thrashing the water and knocking Clarence back onto the baptistery stairs and pushing Brother Hays away, causing him to lose his footing and sink to the neck in the freezing water. Grady's arms beat the air above the tank, and he tried to stand, splashed down again, and finally gained his feet and stood up.

Wayne would never forget the horrible expression on Grady's unshaven face as he lunged up for air, gasping and working his toothless jaws in bewilderment. He hoisted himself up as high as he could, steadying himself on the glass panel along the front of the baptistery, then peered out through the spotlights into the darkened church at the small group gathered to witness the formal saving of his soul.

"God fucking damn!" he spluttered through a wracked and choked throat, spraying water and spittle as far as the feet of Wayne and the others in the front pew. "What are you people trying to do to me?"

Silence fell on the church as if a thunderbolt had sealed their doom. Several faces peered up to the ceiling as if they expected God to open the building like a tin can and vent His wrath on them directly. Brother Hays, now back on his feet and trying to compose himself, but shivering so hard he could barely speak, waded over to Grady and placed a dripping hand on the old man's shoulder, now naked, since he had kicked off the hospital gown in his struggles.

"Brother Grady—" Hays began, but Grady would have no part of it. He spun around on Brother Hays and punched him squarely in the middle of his face. Clarence, who had also waded down toward the candidate for baptism, caught the collapsing Hays full in his arms, and they both went completely under the waist-deep water, flailing and sputtering, trying to escape Grady, who was now swinging wildly in their direction.

All of a sudden, strength left Grady's body, and he turned and hung both arms over the partial glass partition, looking out into the congregation, gasping for air, completely naked. His gray eyes seemed to grow to twice their size and to take on a glow in the spotlights, and he slowly thrust out a long, bony arm and pointed a crooked finger at the stunned congregation, sweeping it back and forth, until it finally stopped, its cracked, yellow nail pointing directly into Wayne's face.

"You're all a bunch of fucking lunatics!" he said. Then his legs gave out and he collapsed, sliding back into the water of the baptistery. He was dead when they fished him out.

Everyone gathered in an arctic Sunday school classroom and tried to decide what to do about all this. Clearly, Grady had died as a result of the icy water and the exertion he had put forth resisting baptism. Some of the older women began debating whether he was baptized at all, since he had not let Brother Hays complete the rite. Hays, shivering and chattering in a blanket, nursed his broken nose and stated flatly that, of course, he was baptized, and it was a blessing that they had gotten to him in time.

No one mentioned what Grady had said, his language or his blasphemy uttered at the point of death, but Allen Underwood, Clarence's brother and one of the most respected members of the church, worried out loud about whether they had killed him. Most shouted that down, but their voices weren't that convincing, so they all swore a vow not to repeat what had happened there that night—something that was sorely disappointing to Brother Hays, who had proclaimed all afternoon how many souls would be moved to come to Jesus by his anticipated sermon on the event and how influential a monograph about the miraculous event would be if it was sent to missionaries. Instead, it was to remain a secret. Everyone was instructed to warn their children to keep their mouths shut also. Doc Taylor, who was on duty at the hospital, would be informed that Grady had expired immediately after the ceremony. God's Will be done.

Finally Brother Hays recovered himself sufficiently to decide on a plan of action. He called Doc Taylor and Everett Hardin, Agatite's only mortician, and the body was soon pronounced dead and picked up and taken to Hardin's Funeral Home to be hastily made ready for burial. The church paid for the service, although Hardin was instructed not to perform any extraordinary measures or to attempt any restoration—it was to be a closed-casket ceremony, using the plainest, cheapest box Hardin had—and those present scurried around, awakening more members and finding flowers. The church was warming up by four in the morning when about half the congregation filed in for the funeral of Roosevelt Grady, age unknown, who had been taken into the arms of the Lord at the very point of accepting Jesus as his Personal Savior.

In Wayne's experience, it was one of the longest funerals he'd ever witnessed. Later, he learned, it was the shortest service Brother Hays ever conducted.

At the graveside, Hardin's gravedigger, grumbling and complaining about the unnecessary overtime and frigid climate, managed to scrape a hole from the frozen ground in Pauper's Corner, and Roosevelt Grady was laid to rest with Brother Hays and Clarence Underwood and almost a hundred congregation members wheezing and sneezing a handful of hymns over his coffin as the winter sun rose.

Throughout the service, though, at the church then at the cemetery, Wayne had stared almost mesmerized at the stark blond wood of Roosevelt Grady's coffin. He fully expected that at any moment, the lid would pop open, and the old man, still full of baptistery water and blasphemy, would rise up and point an accusing finger directly at him. Even later, when the family visited the cemetery and his parents' grave sites, which were thankfully distant from Grady's, he refused to go anywhere near Pauper's Corner.

The memory of the ludicrous baptism and following funeral, of Grady's flailing arms, the splashing water, the accusing look and cursing haunted Wayne all his life. He steadfastly refused to commit himself to Jesus Christ or to anything that would lead to a baptism. After he and Pearlie moved in with Mama Henderson, he refused to join her at church services. He absented himself from his sister's funeral, then later from Mama Henderson's, claiming stomach pains for the former, and pleading the flu for the latter. He couldn't abide the idea of being inside a church at all for any reason.

Years later, to his horror, he discovered that the plot he blindly commissioned Everett Hardin to purchase for Pearlie and Mama Henderson's final resting place—there being no room in his parents' small lot—was only a few dozen yards from the weedy patch of indigent graves where Grady's unmarked remains had been interred. He could hardly bring himself to visit at all. The vacant spot reserved for him between the two principal women of his family seemed to point directly to the spot where

Roosevelt Grady lay waiting to spring up from the ground and accuse him once more of mortal lunacy. The thought that his own bones would occupy the same ground as Grady's stalked Wayne and caused nearly a week of nightmares.

After he purchased the hardware store and resigned himself to the fact that he would live out the rest of his life in Agatite, he went to Hardin's Funeral Home, now run by Everett, Jr., and made special arrangements for himself. He paid in advance for a guarantee that his remains would not be buried at all, but would be cremated—there was to be no funeral, not even a secular service. He objected even to the notion of embalming or buying a casket, until he was told it was required by law. His ashes would be taken out to the old Henderson farm and spread over some mesquite-choked pasture. That, he thought, might give him some peace.

But in the meantime, there was still the memory and the nightmare that always took for its subject that macabre baptism and funeral. In the dream, Grady's coffin would suddenly rise from the earth, clods and clumps of winter-dead weeds spilling off of it, and then it would open. Grady, his face dripping water, would be revealed from behind the swinging lid, his scrawny chest caved in with starvation and rot, and his horrible eyes would open and glow with preternatural light. His hand would slowly rise and point directly toward Wayne, and he would open his mouth to say something. But he never did. Instead, his hollow, toothless jaws would remain open and blue water from the baptistery would dribble out. Wayne always awoke bathed in icy sweat, remembering the cold stare of Roosevelt Grady from the nightmare throughout the next day. He hated the dream, and he always had it right after he so much as heard of a funeral in town or spotted the motor processional filing down Main Street toward the cemetery. He had it Monday when he had to serve as a pall-bearer for a girl found dead in an abandoned building. He knew he would have it tonight. Twice in one week. His stomach revolted at the thought.

Suddenly, Wayne realized that he had been sweeping the sidewalk longer than usual—far longer. The sun was heating up, and the pleasant and unpleasant memories of his childhood had vanished along with the shade on the storefront's side of Main Street. Normally, the sweeping gave him such pleasure, he thought, but not today. It was the damned funerals. Another one this afternoon. Just because he had foolishly agreed to join the Chamber of Commerce's Goodwill Committee, a move to rally more merchants and businesses to his plan to resist the arrival of a big discount store in town. That hadn't worked out nearly so well as he hoped, though. Most of his fellow Chamber members either refused to believe that it would ever happen, or they saw it as an inevitable fate, or in some cases, they believed it would benefit the entire community. Some simply said they hoped they'd be able to retire before it took place.

Even so, he'd had no idea that funerals would be part of the obligation he'd made. Pallbearers to half the goddamn county, it seemed. Ironically, it had been Bill Castlereigh who had talked him into joining and volunteering for the committee. Now, it was his body that Wayne would help carry that day.

Wayne walked slowly into the store, pausing only to adjust a display of camping equipment in the window. Then he stalked to the gloom of the back where Warren stood at the gun counter counting boxes of ammunition, his metallically decorated ears plugged by the ever-present earphones. Wayne could hear the distant, tinny sounds of a rhythmic beat emitting from them, and Warren's head bobbed and his feet shuffled slightly to the beat. He shot Wayne a look that said, "Look, see? I'm working," as Wayne replaced the broom back on the display rack with its companions. He used a different one each day. No sense wasting a good item. He'd just knock off a few cents if anyone noticed that one of them was soiled. Not much traffic in them, anyway. Rayson's IGA, now run by Rayson, Jr., undercut Wayne's price on household products like brooms. He idly wondered if Rayson could survive discounted competition from elsewhere. It would serve him goddamn right, Wayne thought. He was one of those who saw the coming of a Wal-Mart as progress.

Wayne watched Warren work for a moment. Counting the ammunition was a twice-a-month chore, although the government didn't require it nearly so often. Wayne didn't like guns, and he would have stopped carrying them and the ammo, except they were high-profit items and, for some reason, always in demand. Customers also stocked up on other items when they came in for a box of shells. He'd never fired a weapon, and he didn't like touching them. This was always Warren's work.

"Did Adam Moorely call while I was out front?" he asked as he straightened the rack of fishing lures on the wall behind the counter.

"Nope," Warren said absently.

"Would you have heard the phone if it rang?" Wayne asked softly.

"I hear you, don't I?" Warren replied, again astounding Wayne with his aural perception.

"If he comes in while I'm out this afternoon, you remember to get cash from him. No checks. His mother's account is in the register there, and you check it to make sure of the amount he owes on it. No checks. He's given me two checks already, drawn on some California bank. Both bounced. Don't take a check, you understand?"

"Sure, sure," Warren said. "No checks." Then he lost count and slammed his hand down on the counter. "Why tell me?" he asked as he irritably restacked the boxes of shells and cartridges to start over. You'll be here, right?" He then looked carefully at Wayne, suddenly remembered, and brightened. For once, he unplugged his ears. "Oh, hey! That's right. Today's your first day off on the new rest and relaxation program." Wayne turned away toward the weather stripping and made a mental note to restock—never too early to get ready for winter, he lectured himself. "R and R is good for the soul," Warren assured him. Wayne didn't reply but busied himself fussing with items around the cash register.

"Hey, you got a hot date or something?" Warren asked. Wayne stared at him, trying to decide if the kid was being a smart aleck. Then he remembered that he was wearing a dress suit instead of his usual outfit.

"No," he said. "Funeral."

"Another one?" Warren said, his pierced eyebrows shooting up. "Didn't you just go to one on Monday?"

Wayne swallowed hard and steeled himself against the stomach pang. "There's no quota on them," he said. "People die. People have funerals. It's inevitable."

"Whole town's fucking inevitable, you ask me," Warren said.

"Watch your mouth," Wayne said automatically. Warren shrugged, replugged his ears, and turned back to his counting. "When you get done there," Wayne said, "dust off the wood furniture, then go to lunch." Warren nodded, although it remained a mystery to Wayne that the boy heard anything he said over the music continually blasting into his head. Wayne went back to the counter and saw an alien piece of paper near the register. He thumbed it around and saw that it was a job application—for

Wal-Mart. Warren's name was filled in at the top, but he hadn't completed the rest, except to check off a box to indicate the position he was applying for. It was hardware manager trainee. Wayne's stomach turned over once more.

He glanced at the boy, whose back was to him, his body once more moving to the music, and then down again at the paper. The address on the top of the page wasn't in Vernon, as he expected, but was for a PO box right there in Agatite. Wayne looked up, surveyed the store, packed as it was with goods and merchandise, every item of which he knew, every inch of which he cleaned and organized regularly. The store was dark and musty, always smelled of linseed oil over a faint metallic odor of tools and implements. But at the same time, it was homey, inviting in a cozy and comfortable way. It offered what people needed with no apologies, no frills. He wondered what would become of it if he went out of business. What would become of him?

He sighed and his stomach panged hard. He went to the back to take stock of the snow shovels and tire chains. He wondered if he'd still be open when the first snow flew. That was a long time. He might be closed by then, driven out of business by forces he couldn't control. In the meantime, he had a long afternoon ahead, and a long night, and a long tomorrow. That was as far ahead as he dared think. The rest, he thought, was inevitable. Just goddamn inevitable.

THE PRODIGAL

She really screwed up this time, Melissa thought as she stared down at the bright glass blade and brilliant crimson stain that ran from the middle of her bed down to the floor. It was her fault, of course. It always was. The plan was far from perfect, but it was the best she could come up with, and God knew she had had plenty of time to think of alternatives. There just weren't any. And it should have worked. Even when it went wrong, she should have been able to salvage something, enough to save herself. It took courage to go through with it, and timing. She had never been very good at timing, and she'd always been something of a coward. It probably didn't matter anyway, since there was nothing she could do about it, now. She told herself that even had it worked, it might have caused her a bigger problem, might have sent her to jail. But that was a hard argument to swallow. Right now, jail sounded pretty damned good.

She lifted her pale blue eyes away from the bloody edge of glass and cast them hopelessly around the basement. Her bed sat iron-headboard-first against a paneled, finished wall. Behind her, bright posters of movie stars and flowers decorated her end of the underground room, and a window—bolted firmly shut, heavy carriage bolts going right through a thick board into the cinder blocks behind the paneling, just as all the windows were—was covered with a sampler that read "Jesus Loves You." Mama had gave it to her for Christmas, her second Christmas in the basement.

Next to her bed was an upholstered chair with a reading light and a small shelf full of books, video- and audiotapes and DVDs, and two remote controls for the stereo system, TV-VCR and DVD setup in a cabinet just out of reach of the foot of her bed. If she stretched, she could exchange the tapes or CDs in the decks, but the units themselves had been strapped to their shelves. A paperback book was the heaviest thing she was allowed to handle without supervision, and the weightier volumes had their covers removed and were cut into sections. A computer—even a PalmPilot—was out of the question, but there were some video games with a controller that stretched to her bed. The cord connecting it to the game console, though, was interwoven with heavy wire, wound so tight it cut into the plastic insulation and defied cutting or removal. The other remote controls for the electronics were mounted on brackets and screwed down. Papa was nothing if he wasn't careful, and he was smarter than he was careful, and he was stronger than he was smart.

On the opposite side of her bed was another shelf filled with crackers, cookies, nuts, and soft plastic tubes of cheese and peanut butter and fruit paste. There were PowerBars, candy, and soft drinks in plastic bottles amid an array of other snack foods kept in plentiful supply. She wanted for very little in the basement. There was a treadmill for walking or jogging, a rowing machine, and a dance bar for stretching. A sunlamp could even be wheeled over to her bed, and there was a special player that broadcast sounds of the woods, ocean, or meadow. She was only allowed to use the exercise appliances when Mama or Papa could watch her, of course—twice a week, on average—but they kept her fit so long as she moderated the snacks. The only thing she didn't have was real sunlight and wind and rain and other sensations of the outdoors, those and her freedom. Freedom she had forgotten.

Melissa folded a long naked leg beneath her and leaned back on the bed. Her thin lips made a familiar pout. Her bare breasts sagged down toward her stomach as if in imitation of her mood. The chain that led from her wrist where a handcuff encircled her left arm in a tight, padded cuff tinkled slightly. She was used to it. It didn't even awaken her when she turned in her sleep. Another cuff and chain dangled off the end of the bed's iron footboard. Like the hand restraint, its chain led down to a stout ringbolt driven into the concrete floor of the basement. Holes had been drilled deliberately through the pink wool rug underneath the bed for the purpose of anchoring her firmly to her immediate surroundings. She hadn't had to wear the leg cuff for a long time. Not since Christmas. It was for special punishments, special misbehavior. Right now, she felt a slight qualm of guilt for not having it on.

Across the basement, Mama's washer and dryer sat like squat white gods that stared disapprovingly at her. A dark blue cloth handbag rested on the dryer only twenty-five feet from the end of her bed. It might as well have been twenty-five miles.

In spite of the dehumidifier, the basement was always damp. Mama's work with cleansers gave everything a faint bleach and pine smell that made Melissa feel nauseated. There was no hint of that now, and the dehumidifier was off and out of reach. Melissa stretched out her legs and wiggled her long toes. A tiny tattoo on her ankle caught her eye. Papa hated that tattoo. His reaction had surprised her, because he had a tattoo of his own, high on his arm. She had the impression that it was of a hula girl, but she couldn't be sure. She'd never gotten a good look at it, because he always wore long sleeves and never removed his shirt in front of her.

His tattoo was large, but Melissa's was no bigger than a dime, and pretty: a blue heart with an arrow stenciled in red. She got it when she was thirteen and had gone with Matt on his motorcycle down to Dallas. She was out all night for the first time. She was so excited, the spring night air blowing her long blonde strands out behind her, holding onto Matt's taut stomach with both hands while he raced the big bike along the highway. Nothing—except getting the tattoo—had happened. Not then, not ever with Matt. But he had talked her into the tattoo, and when Papa saw it, he was furious, angrier with her than he had ever been before. He bellowed and raged at her and yelled that only tramps and harlots got tattoos, so she spat back at him, asking if he was a tramp, too. That just made him angrier.

That was the first time he locked her in the basement.

Then, the basement was more frightening. It wasn't scary like basements in horror movies. It was just junky and dirty, wet and cold, full of cobwebs and mildew. Although some homes in that part of Texas had cellars, not many had basements. They were either impractical or out of fashion, Melissa remembered Papa explaining. Apart from the parsonage—built sometime before World War I, and never remodeled or upgraded—as Papa often reminded everyone who came by—no other house she knew of in town had one. The skinny staircase that led down from the kitchen was concealed by a door that looked like part of the rear wall in the walk-in pantry. There was no doorknob even, just a piece of wood that looked like a short shelf and opened the door when it was lifted. They had lived there two months before she and Mama discovered it and went down like children investigating a pirate's secret cave.

The basement was jammed with broken furniture, boxes of clothing, drapes, and discarded junk from the church. When he saw it, Papa was annoyed and said that the elders were just saving themselves the cost of a rented storeroom. One Saturday, he hauled away all the clutter, then over the next several months he put in overhead lights, some shelving and plumbing, and installed the washer and dryer for Mama, who had been going out to the unheated garage to do the laundry. He also made a workshop for himself. But there was no outside entrance, so he couldn't build anything large down there, nothing that couldn't be hauled up the narrow staircase. After he set up a tool bench next to the washer, he never built anything else. Before he got in the habit of locking Melissa down there when she misbehaved, he almost never went down there. Neither did Melissa. She hated the basement the first time she saw it, thought that it seemed creepy and gross. Now it was her home, truly her whole world.

She had lived down there for nearly two years, since she was sixteen. That was when she came back from Fort Worth sick and hurt, after a painful and humiliating abortion. She was hoping to forget it as soon as she could, and to tell no one. Papa was wise, though. He quickly figured out what had happened to her. He went through her room and found the crack pipe, the rolling papers, and the half-full wine bottle, and the diary where she had written about her experiments with marijuana, cocaine, and some pills a truck driver named Harlan—the father of her child that never was—gave her after she slipped into the back of his cab where it was parked out by the truck stop. She wrote a lot about drugs, a lot about sex, and not just with Harlan. She had made most of it up, and she said so. That hadn't mattered to Papa. He told her she had "sinned in her heart." The only remedy for sin, Papa said, was punishment until the sinner repented. "You will repent," he told her. She tried, but she made most of that up, too.

———

The abortion was Harlan's idea. When she told him she was pregnant, he gave her the name of a clinic in Fort Worth that would "fix things" without her parents finding out. He told her if it came out that he was the father, they'd both go to jail. She was too scared not to believe him, even though Eve told her that was a lot of bullshit, that the only one who'd be in trouble would be Harlan. Melissa figured if Papa found out, she'd be in worse trouble than jail would offer. But he found out anyway. The procedure hurt, made her sick. She got an infection and a fever, and she bled for two solid weeks, but Papa wouldn't let her go see their regular doctor. He said she was trying to ruin him in the church, ruin him in town. He bought medicine from a drugstore in Wichita Falls, then made her stay in her room and told her if she misbehaved again, he would have to take "drastic measures." And Mama agreed with him. That hurt Melissa worse than anything. She had counted on Mama's understanding.

She supposed that was when she learned to hate Mama, truly hate her. If Mama had stood up for her, kept Papa off her back, then maybe things would have worked out differently. But Mama sided with him as she always did, made her stay in her room, and only spoke to her at all through lips tight with regret. No one could be strong in front of Papa, and Mama was never a woman to be strong in front of anyone. In a way, Melissa believed, that was why she and Papa were married in the first place. When he asked her, she couldn't find the courage to say no. A small, gray, mousey woman who seldom spoke in public above a whisper, she sometimes seemed startled by her own reflection in a mirror, and Melissa learned early in her life that if she yelled loud enough, she could usually get what she wanted from her. But Mama was too afraid of Papa not to go along with whatever he wanted, and that meant that she could be firm, even mean to Melissa. During that time, the only kind thing she would say to Melissa at all was that she was praying for her. Fat lot of good that did a girl who was worried about bleeding to death.

She escaped her room as soon as the fever broke and the bleeding stopped. As always, she jimmied up the window Papa kept locking and went down to the Conoco station on the corner and flirted with Ralph, the pimply attendant, until he let her use the phone. She called Eve. Then, when Eve picked her up, they went looking for Harlan.

She was just going to give him a piece of her mind. But when he didn't show up on time for his regular rest stop during his weekly run between Fort Worth and Denver, she wound up going with Eve to Oklahoma, where they sweet-talked the guy in the joint just over the river out of a bottle of tequila.

She had never drunk tequila before, but Eve practically swore by it, said it was just what Melissa needed. They stopped by an Allsup's and bought some salt and a couple of limes, and they drove around town and drank "solos" for about two hours, popping the pills Harlan had given her and Eve had kept, and trying to find some boys to hang out with. They got drunker and drunker, and Melissa felt wilder and wilder. She also became angrier and angrier with Harlan. It was past midnight when they took one more swing by the truck stop's parking lot and saw his rig. She barely remembered what happened next.

Harlan was high himself, and he was glad to see them. He opened up the cab's door and helped them in. He was grinning and had a big coffee can of pills and some crack he offered to share. In spite of having all the paraphernalia, Melissa had never done more than a hit or two before, but this time, she was too far gone to care. She giggled and winked at Eve while Harlan tried to make them comfortable in the cramped quarters of the tractor's cab, then passed around handfuls of pills. Then she saw his lockback knife in a leather case dangling from a knob on the truck's dashboard. She stared at it. It was as if God had put it there for her to use. Eve, all the while, was flirting with him, kissing him and licking his ears. At last, he let out a whoop and ordered them to "get naked" and wiggled out of his pants. Melissa just lost it. She started screaming at him, then grabbed the knife and tried her best to stab him to death.

If Eve hadn't been there to stop her, she probably would have. She wanted him to hurt the way the abortion had hurt her. She slashed at his exposed crotch, but he arched back, so the blade ran into his fat stomach. She then cut up his arms as he tried to escape her reach in the narrow cab. The knife was sharp, and blood spurted everywhere. Eve wrestled with her, grabbed her arm, tried to get the knife away, and Harlan kept trying to get his pants on and open the door. She wrenched free of Eve's grasp and stuck him in the face. She was going for his eyes, but she missed again, and just as the blade jabbed through his cheek, the door opened and he tumbled backward into the muddy parking lot. The last she saw of him, he was scuttling away through puddles and mud. She thought that he looked like a run-over rabbit.

It was nearly two when Eve took her home. They gobbled more of Harlan's pills and drank the rest of the tequila straight out of the bottle on the way. Mama was pacing in the living room, worried sick. Papa had been to Abilene to a meeting and was, Mama said, late getting back. "Thank the Lord," Mama said. Then she saw all the blood on Melissa's clothes and took a good sniff of the alcohol reek of her and went to pieces. For the first time in her life, she slapped Melissa.

The blow wasn't hard, but it was shocking, electrifying. Melissa could still taste Harlan's blood where it had splattered into her mouth. Cutting him had felt so good, so satisfying. But Mama's blow had stung. She couldn't believe that this tiny little woman had struck her, and her anger returned. Her head swam with a sudden rage, and she shoved Mama down, then hit her with a lamp, then threw the mantle clock at her, then anything else that came to hand—vases, books, pictures. She wrecked the living room before she lost all her energy and collapsed across Mama, who had crawled up behind the sofa to get away from her. Before she passed out, she wondered if Mama was dead, then decided that she didn't care. Mama shouldn't have hit her.

Mama wasn't dead. Papa came in after about an hour and dragged Melissa off of her, leaving her lying on the floor, then took Mama to the hospital. Melissa later learned that Mama had a concussion and a broken wrist, and she was in shock, but otherwise she was all right. Melissa was far from all right, though. After she awakened and sobered up, she went to her room, tried to self-impose the punishment she knew Papa would give her. Sober now, she felt guilty about hurting Mama. Mostly she felt ill. She couldn't stop throwing up, and she had fever and shakes and a terrible headache. She heard on the local radio news that the sheriff was looking for "party or parties unknown" who had assaulted a trucker sleeping in his cab behind the Highway 287 Truck Stop. Somebody coming in for breakfast the next morning found him lying unconscious in a culvert near the parking area. He had lost a lot of blood and was in "serious condition." Melissa was too sick to worry. She expected the sheriff to show up and take her away at any moment, but she didn't much care. Her only regret was that she hadn't killed Harlan, and she also blamed him for making her hurt Mama.

She couldn't keep any food down for two days, which was just as well, since there was no one at home to cook or buy groceries. Except for trips to the bathroom, she stayed on her bed and stared at the ceiling, lived on sodas and peanut butter spread on stale crackers. Papa didn't come home from the hospital at all, or if he did, she never saw or heard him. She had really sinned this time, and she knew she was bound for more serious punishment.

She finally decided to run away. She had no money, but she knew where Papa kept the Sunday offering receipts. He brought them in after church and stored them in a mahogany box until Monday when he took them to the bank. Even though theirs was a modest church, members were often generous. Sometimes, there would be as much as a thousand dollars there in cash, plus checks she might be able to cash. On Sunday noon, she heard him for the first time in nearly a week. He came in from church, and, as always, went to his office. Then he left. She thought he must have gone back to the hospital to see about Mama. Melissa was just in the act of replacing the small wooden box in his desk drawer when he walked in on her.

He didn't say anything. He didn't rage and he didn't hit her. Instead, he stared at her, his gray eyes studying her as if she was some stranger he'd never seen before. Then he took her by the wrist and dragged her down into the basement and made her get down on the cold, wet concrete floor. He tied her up and gagged her and left her there on her knees until the next morning. Then he let her up, but he didn't let her out. Except for her weekly bath, she hadn't been upstairs since.

Mama recovered nicely, and she even came down once and told Melissa she forgave her for hurting her, that she understood that it was the Devil inside her that made her behave so awfully. "You're our prodigal," she said in her familiar small voice. "Or we hope you will be when you come back home to us—in a spiritual way."

In the meantime, Papa said Melissa had to learn her lesson. He couldn't stand having her running around town drinking and taking drugs and sleeping with every boy who smiled at her, and he couldn't stand for her to be arrested for cutting up that truck driver. Melissa never learned how Papa found out that it was she who had done it, but he knew. He said it had "cost him a pretty penny" to keep it quiet. He said it would ruin him completely if any hint of her outlandish behavior got out. She should go to jail, he said, but he also admitted that he couldn't have that. He looked at her the way he might look at an abandoned dog. She was a sinner more than a criminal, he told her, a bad child and a disgrace to him and to the church, and she would have to stay down in the basement until God saw fit to "cast out her demons" and "heal her spirit." He would lock his hands together and bow his head. "You're a sinner," he said. "You will repent."

"And when the time comes," Mama concluded over her own hands, clasped together as if in prayer, a small smile appearing through the bruises, "we'll welcome you back upstairs, back to our family. As our prodigal."

"How long?" Melissa asked her, almost afraid to hear what she would say.

"Until God sees fit," Mama said. "Maybe for a long, long time."

———

Melissa didn't believe Papa was serious at first. He had never kept her confined in her room for more than a few days. He always gave in and forgave her, cried with her, made her pray, heard her say she was sorry, that she repented, and then he let her out with a stern warning to behave herself. But this time was different, hard as it was to believe. Even when he came down and paneled one side of the basement and brought down the bed and set the iron legs in cement, she thought he would relent and give her freedom. He was only trying to scare her, she told herself, to put "the fear of the Lord" into her. The chains and padded cuffs came from a store near Wichita Falls, he explained when he installed them.

"It was one of those places," he said with a sideways glance. Papa had lived a wild life before he got the call to preach, and he often renounced his past sins as coming from when he was "possessed of Satan." He claimed that he had been saved as much from himself as from Hell by his conversion. He never wanted to revisit that time, not even in his memories, although he wasn't afraid of making it the topic of a sermon at least once a month. "You have no idea how hard it was for me to go inside a place like that," he said. "Let alone buy something there. I took an oath I never would again. But I did it. For you. I did it for you and for your soul."

The chains were light-weight steel, shiny and pretty to look at and to hear when they tinkled against each other. The cuffs were covered with a dark blue padded fabric to keep them from chafing. She still believed he was bluffing, though, trying to frighten her into genuine repentance. Eve, she thought with a secret smile, would get a kick out of this when she heard about it.

But when he soundproofed the underground room, boarded up the windows, and put in the electric heater and dehumidifier, she began to grow frightened. After two weeks, her fright gave way to resignation. The basement became her home, her cell.

———

As weeks passed, Melissa's parents worked to create a decent environment for her prison. There was no regular commode, but a small camping toilet with a chemical tank was installed. Mama cleaned and emptied it regularly, and she brought down warm water and soap for daily sponge baths. Melissa received meals on a rolling tray Papa bought from a hospital supply store. They moved her stereo down and bought other expensive electronics items she would never have dreamed of receiving before. Papa ran a cable wire from the TV upstairs and subscribed to cable so she could receive more than a hundred channels. They supplied her with DVDs, CDs, tapes, books, magazines, and other materials to amuse her, and for Christmas her first year, they gave her the exercise equipment so she could keep fit.

At first, Melissa had not taken to her imprisonment quietly. After crying and begging failed to placate Papa, she took to sulking, refusing food, and allowing herself to grow unkempt and dirty. That hadn't worked, either. Mama patiently brought down soap and water, presented the meals, then wordlessly took everything away, whether Melissa had touched it or not. Once a week, she led her, still chained to a heavy leather belt Mama wore around her own waist, reluctantly upstairs for a proper bath. Papa sat on a chair outside the bathroom and guarded her with a threat she knew was genuine that she would be "more than sorry" if she tried anything foolish. They let her sulk and fret and refuse to wash until she couldn't stand the hunger and filth any longer and gave in and resumed better habits.

Her one try to run away turned out to be a painful lesson. One bath night, as soon as Mama unlocked her cuff with a small, silver key to let her go on into the bathroom, Melissa pushed the small woman against the wall and bolted down the hall toward the front door. Papa was on her like a bear. He grabbed her by her hair and dragged her backward to the bathroom door. Then he produced a miniature hardwood baseball bat he had won on the midway at the State Fair in Dallas when Melissa was a little girl and began hitting her all over. As she screamed, he struck her arms and legs, her breasts and stomach, and when she curled into a ball, he hit her head, shoulders, and back. Each blow was exquisitely painful, and Papa seemed to know just where to inflict the most hurt. Every time she tried to rise from the floor, he poked and slapped her with the small club. He was a whirlwind of jabs and thrusts, grunting and bellowing his rage over Mama's high wailing pleas for him to stop. When he finally did, she lay whimpering on the hallway rug while he stood over her, his face aglow with a fiery red blush. His breath heaved in huge, rattling gasps. Sweat dripped from his face and mixed with mucus running from his nose. But as she peeked up at him through her tears, what frightened her most was the glee she saw in his small, gray eyes. She knew then that he had enjoyed hitting her, that he had been waiting for the chance to hit her, that he was sorry he had stopped.

She was covered with ugly yellow-brown bruises. Her fear of him grew every day, for now she was convinced that he hated her. For the first time, she realized what a big man he was. She had always seen him as large, but now, she saw that he wasn't fat. He was strong. She knew he had worked as a merchant seaman when he was young—the photograph of him in his dress uniform was one of the few things she hadn't broken the night she attacked Mama—and he had also worked as a long-shoreman. That was when he met Mama, she recalled. He was tall—over six two she knew—and probably weighed more than twice what she did. But he surprised her when he moved so fast to catch her, and when she felt his huge, square hands on her hair and shoulders, dragging her down, she realized that he was still a powerful man and a dangerous one. The next time he hit her, she decided, he might not stop. He might really hurt her, might even kill her. She was careful not to provoke him again.

Terrified now, she started throwing things at them whenever they came down to the basement, especially when Mama came alone. She desperately hoped to coldcock her with a lucky toss, grab the keys to the cuffs, dangling from a leather thong and temptingly close as she came to care for her. But they soon stopped her tantrums. They removed anything heavy from her reach, and if she threw the CDs or tapes, they took them away, leaving them lying in sight but out of reach until she promised to behave.

Weeks flowed into months, and Melissa gradually came to accept her situation. She knew a quick run for freedom would never work, and pouting and sulking had no effect. So she changed tactics and acted as sweetly as she could. They changed in their attitude toward her, as well. Every night, Papa came downstairs and sat in the chair and read Bible verses to her, prayed with her, and sometimes even held her hand. It was almost more than she could do to allow him to take her slender fingers in his rough paw, but she somehow managed. If he ever came down when he thought she was sleeping, he would come over and gently kiss her forehead and whisper a prayer for her. She sometimes fantasized about grabbing him by the throat, holding him until she could capture the keys. She imagined what it would feel like to sink her sharp nails into his fleshy triple chin, to grab his larynx, crush it. But her memory of the fierceness with which he used the small bat that he always carried in his belt, like a blunt sword, convinced her that beneath his gentle manner, he was still capable of losing control, of hurting her badly if she crossed him. Mama also grew more careful and never came close enough for them to touch unless Papa was there, his gray eyes watching—eagerly, she thought—for any provocation.

After nearly six months of imprisonment, she tried to convince Papa that she was truly repentant. It was Christmas Eve, and he had just come home from the midnight service. He was glowing with the Spirit of Christmas, and he and Mama came down to sit with her beside the small, artificial tree Mama had put up in the dank basement. There were gifts for her, and she opened them with the professed innocent excitement of a six-year-old. They drank spiced tea and ate fudge and fruitcake. She hugged and kissed them and even offered an impromptu prayer of thanksgiving for such loving, caring parents.

"I've learned my lesson," she told Papa, who smiled warmly and puffed a twice-yearly cigar, his one indulgence that came at Christmas and on his and Mama's anniversary. "I've had time to think about things and I'm ready to show you how much I've changed." She lowered her eyes humbly. "I love you so much—both of you—and I'm so sorry I've hurt you. I want to become your daughter again. In every way. I want to show you how good I can be." Her voice shook with just the right amount of contrite sincerity. Tears welled in her eyes as she spoke, ran down her cheeks, and she looked up, letting them see how sincere she was. She had heard people in the church use the exact same tone when they came down front to make their public confessions, and she knew how such demonstrations moved Papa.

Papa looked at her over his cigar. His hair was as silver as the tobacco smoke, and Melissa noticed for the first time, it was thinning. His complexion looked sallow and unhealthy. His stomach had expanded during her confinement, she thought. He looked almost like a somber Santa Claus in a dark suit and bright red tie, smoking and studying her in the soft glow of the Christmas tree lights. Mama wrung her hands and looked anxious while he considered Melissa's profession. She looked no healthier than he did. She was almost ten years older than Papa, but she seemed to have aged even more. Her cheeks were sallow, sunken, and her chin fell away into wattles of soft flesh that wobbled when she spoke. Her hair, always teased and stiff with spray, had been disheveled by the wind. It now flew away from her head, and Melissa could see her pink scalp in places where her hands had tried to repair it.

Melissa knew that she had been an "accident," that they never thought they could have children. They actually had never planned to marry. Mama had been the cook in the boarding house where Papa lived in Galveston when he was a longshoreman. She was already an "old maid," she once told Melissa with a small, private laugh, when Papa started paying attention to her. She told Melissa that she hadn't liked him very much at all. "He was wild and wicked," she said, "and he scared me." But he pursued her, wouldn't be discouraged, and he wore her down. Still, the only place she would let him take her was to church. They attended a revival meeting in a tent, and that night, Papa was "caught in a rapture of the spirit," Mama said. He not only "gave his soul to God, but he heard the call to preach, too." When she spoke of it, her eyes went misty. "He said God wouldn't take no for an answer, and he wouldn't, either. So how could I stand against him, myself?" She sighed, sadly Melissa thought. "I guess I couldn't."

The rest of the story was vague, and Melissa half listened when Mama told it to her. Papa was eager to start his work, so in a few months they were married and then off to a seminary on money she'd saved for herself. Ten years later, Melissa was born, and they had moved to Agatite, where Papa got the small, clapboard church on the outskirts of town. It wasn't much of a church, then, but Papa poured himself into it, practically rebuilt it from the ground up, and recruited members from anywhere he could. The elders admired how he nearly doubled the membership in only a few years and how, even though he had come late to his ministry, his enthusiasm was boundless. He soon made himself an important figure in the greater assembly of the congregations in the region.

"He's a smart man," Mama assured Melissa. "He had a sinful past, but he knew enough to change. When you came along, he said his salvation was complete." Melissa wasn't so sure.

Papa was nearly forty when she was born, and Mama almost died on the delivery table. They had thought of her as a "blessing," a "gift from God." But in the course of his consultations with her over the past several months, Papa confessed often that he now wondered. He said she was a "test," a "cross I must bear," and a "task God has given me to complete." Apparently, the test was far from over, and it wouldn't be complete until she returned to his good graces and he believed her.

"I deal with sinners every day," Papa growled gently as he turned his cigar and studied his imprisoned daughter. "And I know the nature of sin, deep and black. I have seen it, have wallowed in it myself. I know how it smells, how it feels, how all-consuming it can become. And I have repented myself of it through trial and pain." He took a deep breath and stared at her. "Sin is never ugly, my dear. People often think it's nasty and revolting, but I know better. It's beautiful and tempting, lustful and eager to please. I know that. I have given in to it. But I have repented." He sighed deeply. "I believe you want to repent. I believe you can repent. But I'm not convinced that the time has yet come for you to go out into the world. Or that it's safe."

His voice rose and deepened into what Melissa recognized as his "preaching tone." He clasped the lapels of his coat and rocked on the balls of his feet. "The world is full of sin," he continued, "full of temptation." He lifted his eyes to the basement ceiling. His words seemed to fill the entire space as they became louder, rounder. "You're still a child. Still weak. You cannot distinguish between the false beauty of sin and the true beauty of salvation. You need a firm and guiding hand. You need to repent." He stopped, as if he realized where he was, and cast his eyes down and softened his tone. "I'll pray about it for a while. God will tell me when it's time."

Melissa wailed her disappointment, then threw her presents at the small tree until it was smashed and ruined. Papa nodded sagely to Mama as they left, pausing only for a moment by the washer and dryer to clasp hands and pray. Her birthday and the second Christmas went pretty much the same way.

———

Melissa often wondered what people thought of her disappearance. Her imprisonment had started in summer, but surely someone must have missed her at school, at church services. She asked Mama, but the little woman only smiled tightly and said that Papa had taken care of things, that she shouldn't worry. Melissa knew that it wasn't that uncommon for recalcitrant preachers' kids—especially daughters—to "disappear" for a while. They were sent away to live with cousins or aunts when they got into "trouble." But Melissa had no cousins or aunts. Papa was an orphan, and Mama was an only child whose parents were dead before Melissa was born, so there wasn't even a grandmother to inquire after her.

There was Eve, of course, and other friends, but Eve wasn't, Melissa realized, the sort to worry about anyone, and neither were most of her school friends. They would probably assume, especially when Eve told them about Harlan—and Melissa had no doubt that Eve would tell everything to everyone—that her parents merely sent her away.

During her weekly trips upstairs to bathe, she saw that her school picture was still on the mantle, but there was no other evidence that she ever existed. It was as if she had died. From time to time, she wondered if she had. Maybe this was Hell, she sometimes told herself. It sure wasn't life.

Sometimes, people came by to visit. Melissa could hear their movements overhead, and she thought of screaming until they heard her. But the thick insulation Papa installed muffled all sounds except the footfalls on the uneven floor above. She never could hear their voices or even Mama playing the piano, something she always did when they had guests. Melissa didn't have anything long enough to pound on the basement's ceiling to gain their attention. Most of them wouldn't know about the underground room, anyway, so she kept silent and listened to the world overhead as if in a dream.

Nearly two years of her life were slowly wasted. She decided sometime after the second Christmas that Papa would never release her from the basement. He wanted to keep her there until she died. Or until he died. The thought took root and grew inside her. He grew visibly older with each passing month, heavier and thicker, and she began to say prayers of her own. She wished as hard as she could for his expanding corpulence and worry to become too much for him, for him to drop dead. He had had "heart trouble" for several years, and she knew he took medicine to control it. With any luck and divine mercy at all, she told herself, he would collapse and fall on Mama and kill her, as well. At times, her daydreams of such an event were so deliciously real that she became excited. As she envisioned it, she began perspiring heavily, her breathing quickened, and she grew aroused by the prospect of their both collapsing right in front of her. Sometimes, she would lie naked on top of her covers and focus on the prospect, massaging herself, furiously crying out a feral roar as her climax coincided with a vision of the horrific, suffering deaths of the two people who loved her most in the world.

The truth, Melissa admitted to herself after such moments of fantasy had passed, was that she was far from repentant. She had learned to play the part of a guilty and unworthily pardoned sinner almost before she had learned her multiplication tables, and she wasn't sure she would know what genuine regret might feel like. She wasn't a pretty girl or smart. She was tall with long, thin legs and big feet, and she had gossamer thin blonde hair, pale blue eyes, and millions of freckles. She had developed unevenly, growing small buds of breasts when she was still in elementary school. In sixth grade, the buds suddenly blossomed and grew embarrassingly large. They looked freakish on such a skinny, gawky girl. Boys called her the "balloon smuggler" and "casaba queen," and even the teachers seemed to look at her oddly when she walked by. As the daughter of a minister, she found herself outside the social mainstream. Her presence among the majority of kids was a reminder of their own guilt whenever they engaged in harmless forms of juvenile mischief. The only girls who would be friends with her were those to whom being a preacher's kid was something of a joke. They were usually the "wild" girls, those whose experiments with sex and drugs and alcohol were a way of showing the "Ins and Ups"—as they derisively called the kids who participated in sports, clubs, who made higher grades—what was what. Outraging teachers, parents, and the "Ins and Ups" was their top priority.

Eve, Melissa's best friend, was the acknowledged leader in this group of "Outs and Downs," as they derisively named themselves—"ODs," for short. Eve had failed two grades and was older than average. She had a driver's license and access to her stepfather's car whenever she wanted. "All I've got to do is be 'nice' to him, if you catch my drift," she told Melissa with a wink, then made quick up-and-down motions with her fist over her crotch. "A hand job always works, a blow job'll get me a full tank of gas and booze money." Black-haired and brown-eyed, Eve was pretty and street-smart, but she was what Papa called "hard around the edges." He felt sorry for her because of her "broken-home situation." He said he had known girls like Eve all his life, and what they wanted most was discipline and a good example. In spite of his apparent suspicions, he encouraged Melissa to provide that example.

Eve was also a good actress. When she agreed to come to church with Melissa every Sunday and Wednesday night, Papa was delighted and encouraged their friendship in the hope that his daughter might bring the older girl to God's Grace. Of course, he had no idea that Eve used the meetings to meet more boys, whom she charged for light sexual play after the service. He could not have imagined such a thing. Melissa knew that up until the night she hurt Mama, he had never doubted Melissa's potential for salvation. "They're just girls," he would say gently to Mama whenever a doubt was raised.

It had been Eve's idea for Melissa and several other girls to buy matching jackets and to stitch "OD" on the back. She taught Melissa to smoke, cigarettes first and then marijuana, and it was she who gave her the crack pipe, although they couldn't get their hands on the yellow crystals with any regularity, since neither of them ever had much money. They only tried it twice, and every time, Melissa became ill. When Melissa realized she was pregnant, Eve revealed that she also had been in trouble—twice. She had an abortion the first time, which her stepfather paid for. She was only fourteen then, but the next year, she went away for the spring term to a home for unwed mothers and carried the second baby all the way, then gave it up for adoption. "It wasn't fun," she told Melissa. "Either way. It was a literal pain in the ass. But, trust me, a quick D & C is better than labor. I'll never do that shit again."

Eve delighted in showing Melissa the darker possibilities of adolescence. They would take off for Wichita Falls to go to porn movies. They would giggle at the silly films and imagine what it would be like to do the things the women in them did. They also went into bars out on the old Seymour highway. Usually, the bartender refused to serve two obviously underage girls, and they left behind a string of curses to the amusement of the airmen, roughnecks, and cowboys who called them "jailbait" and made fun of their attempts to flirt their way into a drink. They stayed out all night several times, but Melissa managed to fool Papa, lying about spending the night with a friend.

When they visited the mall in Wichita Falls, Eve instructed Melissa on the finer points of the "five-finger discount." Melissa was too afraid to take anything after the first time she palmed a lipstick and came out of the store, her hands shaking and so hot and sweaty that it nearly melted. Eve loved doing it, though, and Melissa was usually right with her. They never got caught, but a couple of times Melissa noticed that the sales clerks followed them around more closely when they made a return visit. Eve also showed her how to put a prophylactic on a man, how to douche herself to avoid pregnancy, and suggested various prices she might charge truckers such as Harlan who didn't mind risking arrest by taking a teenager into the sleeping compartment of his semi for a quick blow job, or maybe something more.

Melissa thought the whole possibility was disgusting. Harlan was hardly her idea of a lover, anyway. He was sort of nice looking in the face, but he was also stupid and nearly forty. He seldom shaved, had a beer gut, dirty fingernails, a long, greasy ponytail, and he smelled of diesel fuel. She never saw him when he wasn't high and didn't have a jawful of snuff. She knew he was married because he kept pictures of some ugly fat woman and three children taped to his sun visor. He was always glad to see them, though, and he always had plenty of pills and grass, and he was eager to share them. Still, the thought of him—or anybody like him—touching her in some intimate way revolted Melissa. Eve's lessons continued, though. She said that there was only one way of getting what she wanted in the world. "It's not so bad," she said glibly. "I just close my eyes and think of chocolate. It's over quick, most of the time, and it's not like it's forever. Nothing a hot shower and a bottle of Listerine won't cure."

Melissa's role as Eve's prodigy didn't last long. Soon enough, the younger girl had displaced Eve as the leader among their clique. She felt it was her responsibility. She was smarter than Eve, for one thing, and she proved quickly that she was more daring. Eve's motto was "Cover your ass."

"Never leave your butt hanging out," she would advise Melissa. "Somebody's liable to kick it."

Melissa didn't care. She soon developed a reputation as a girl who would do anything on a dare, never admitting that the risk of getting caught carried a double penalty for a preacher's kid, that the thrill of misbehavior was stimulated even more by the pain she could cause her parents. Even Eve was sometimes shocked by the chances Melissa took.

The irony, Melissa told herself often during her basement confinement, was that she rarely enjoyed the things she did to impress Eve, and she had really done very few of the things she was supposed to have done. She was an expert in deception; she knew how to pretend. A preacher's kid learns such tricks early, and after years of fooling her parents and the dour elders of the church, practicing them on a bunch of naïve teenagers was no challenge at all.

Melissa took up with Matt, who was three years older and had a motorcycle. She liked hanging out with him, liked being thought of as "his girl," but Matt was too immature, too sweet. He treated her more like a naughty schoolgirl than Papa did, and even scolded her when she behaved too outrageously. They were always off and on, because Melissa understood that she could never maintain her leadership role if she was anybody's "steady." It was, in a way, to prove that she and Matt weren't serious that she took up with Harlan. But that hadn't worked out very well, at all.

The beer and wine the ODs swilled while riding around searching for boys and trouble often made Melissa sick to her stomach. She smoked cigarettes, but rarely inhaled, and she easily faked the effects of marijuana well enough to convince everyone that she was higher than they could ever hope to be. Sex—mostly light petting—with anyone also was unpleasant for her. While the boys groaned while she touched them or let them touch her, she took Eve's advice and thought of more pleasant things. As she often did during the three sermons a week she was obliged to endure, she drifted away from the moment. For some reason she could never completely understand, she clung to her actual virginity.

With Harlan, though, her resolve ended. At first she just gave him hand jobs, but he quickly demanded more. In spite of Eve's assurance that gross as it might seem—even with a smelly jerk like Harlan—it could be fun, Melissa couldn't bring herself to perform oral sex. He grew more insistent, though, and began to make vague threats to tell Eve that she was "frigid"; so, fearful of losing her status with the ODs, she finally consented to climb into the small bed behind the cab of his truck and let him do whatever he wanted. He didn't have a rubber—said he wouldn't wear one anyway—but he promised, breathlessly, to quit "before anything happens." She put her mind on automatic, prepared to endure ten minutes of Harlan's groping touch. Still mostly clothed, they cramped into the tiny compartment of the big tractor, and she allowed him to sweat and grunt while he wiggled around on top of her and pawed at and slobbered on her breasts. She found it hard not to giggle when she imitated the porn queen actresses by pretending to be in ecstasy until he finally shuddered, hunched his shoulders, then relaxed and allowed his stinking weight to crush her for a few moments, his breathing hot and raspy in her ear, the smell of alcohol and tobacco filling her nostrils and making her nauseated. She never felt him inside her. Still, he got her pregnant. Timing.

Melissa decided that she had never felt much for her parents but fear and contempt. From the earliest age she could remember, they had always been sad, strict people, and she couldn't recall doing much of anything that they approved of. When she started menstruating at ten, Mama made her feel guilty, as if it were her fault that she was becoming a woman too soon, as if she was dirty somehow, as if she should be ashamed. When she was old enough to start choosing her own music, clothes, friends, and activities, they greeted everything she did with a sad shake of their heads. Then, they usually forbade whatever she wanted to do. They criticized the way she sat, walked, talked, ate, and behaved. They hated the way she wore her hair, polished her nails, and applied makeup. Having her ears pierced had caused a breach that was two weeks in healing.

Of course, they expected her to be in church every time the door was open, and if she refused, they grounded her for a week. She was reminded every day that she was a minister's daughter, that things were expected of her that normal kids didn't have to do. Being a child of a preacher removed anything that was fun and left nothing but boredom and depression. If Heaven was, as Papa assured the congregation, like "an eternal church service," she decided that any degree of Hell would be preferable. She was marked from birth, as if she wore a huge sign that said "Preacher's Kid. Beware!" around her neck. But murmuring along with the tuneless hymns and prayers was better than staring at the four blank walls in her room. Papa never tolerated movie posters and pictures of motorcycles and beer and wine ads up there the way he permitted them in the basement. In that way, her room was never half so nice as her subterranean cell. But there was a difference: She could leave her room whenever she wanted.

There were times, of course, when she felt warm toward them. Christmases, her birthdays, when Papa would beam his love and pride like a soft light and talk about her going to college or being married with children. Mama sometimes came into her room and brushed her hair or went with her to select a special dress or pair of shoes. She told her how pretty she was, although Melissa soon learned that mirrors don't lie the way mothers do. As she grew into her teens, and the rest of her body caught up with her chest, Mama's compliments became increasingly rare. She would never be truly pretty, Melissa realized, but she was becoming attractive, sexy and alluring, if she managed her assets right.

Her parents were never cold toward her, never reluctant to put an arm around her or offer a hug or a kiss. From her earliest memories, Papa had always been a big, gentle bear of a man, eager to sweep her up in his arms and hold her tight. Mama's touch was always sweet, almost feathery. Their home was old and out of fashion, but it was cozy, filled with the sense of family and solid, comfortable values. But the loving glow she felt there was usually tinged with more disapproval than admiration, more caution and suspicion than acceptance and understanding. Beneath every kiss or hug was a lecture or admonition, a correction or warning.

As she aged and developed, her rancor became more demonstrative. She still attended church regularly, sat primly on the front pew and sang all the hymns, and that seemed to be enough to bring her back into Papa's good graces when her transgressions were small. But for the large ones, those that hurt more than they angered him, the punishments became more severe and of longer duration. Her groundings and confinements seemed to come almost monthly. First to her room, and then to the basement, forever.

In the nearly twenty-two months she had been permanently confined to her underground room, she had wanted for very little. In a way, her parents seemed more loving, more solicitous than they ever had been. Aside from her freedom and the outdoors, every reasonable thing she asked for was provided with a warm, sad smile from Mama, and Papa never objected, even when the item violated some former prohibition. She was even allowed chewing gum, something he despised and had forbidden her all her life, but he would never bring her cigarettes, no matter how nicely she asked. She read more books than she ever thought she would, and she had seen great movies on videotape. She could probably qualify for a college degree of some kind, even though she had never been quite average in school.

She kept a diary for a while, but there was little to write about once she had catalogued her frustration and anger. Nothing different ever happened, and she was miserable when she considered how much of life was passing her by. She awoke late one night to find Papa leaning against the washer and reading her words in the dim light from the stairs. She thought of trying to use the diary to show him how sorry she was, but she knew he was smarter than that, so she abandoned it.

As time passed, serious depression set in. For once, she wasn't pretending. She became indifferent to everything, lethargic, wouldn't open a book or magazine or turn on the stereo or TV. She lay on her back and stared at the ceiling, rousing herself only when her body demanded, her hands folded over her stomach, as if she were a corpse in a coffin. That, she told herself, was precisely how she felt.

Whenever Mama or Papa came down to see her, she wouldn't talk to them, but that didn't seem to faze them. They smiled and chatted with her as if she were responding cheerfully, as if it was the most ordinary thing in the world for two people to keep their child chained to the basement floor.

Finally, she roused herself from the doldrums of self-pity and began renewing her interest in amusements at hand. She hated herself for giving in, for actually enjoying television programs or books or music, for putting her all into her exercise, but she couldn't stop herself from the indulgences. Still, she made a point of never smiling at her parents, of never giving them the satisfaction of seeing her with anything but a scowl or a pout. She avoided eye contact and seldom answered even the most direct question with more than a nod. If they noticed, they didn't seem to care. She decided they had lost their minds. She also believed that, once free, she would likely be arrested for what she had done to Harlan, but she had watched enough TV cop and lawyer shows to understand that, as a minor, her punishment would be light, at least in comparison to a life sentence in the parsonage basement. Even so, she clutched tightly to her belief that this couldn't last forever—something had to happen to gain her a reprieve. But as more time went by, that hope diminished and, ultimately, died.

———

Two weeks before her eighteenth birthday, Melissa resolved that no matter what it took, she had to escape. She had no idea, though, what it would take. She had gone over every possibility a thousand times and found no chance in evidence. The only time she wasn't chained to the basement floor or the leather belt around Mama's waist was when she was taken upstairs to bathe, and that usually happened late at night. With Papa standing guard with his vicious little bat, there was no opportunity there. She went over the routine minutely, seeking some oversight in her parents' vigilance, some chink in their armor.

Then, without warning, the schedule changed. Papa became involved in regular committee meeting work to revise the church hymnal, and the meetings were in Abilene. The business took him away from home every weeknight except Wednesday, when he had to preside over Prayer Meeting. As a result, they started escorting Melissa to the bathroom on Friday mornings. At first, she was delighted, contented to be upstairs in the daylight. The early summer sun streamed through the sash window over the toilet in the bathroom, and through it she could see green grass and blue sky. It was the first time she had been aboveground in the daytime for nearly two years, so she was careful to behave and act as well as she could in the hope of making the schedule change permanent. She even asked if she could take a while longer than usual to wash herself, so she could lounge in the tub and bathe in the sunlit room.

Papa was, at first, reluctant to grant her more time, but when she sang softly to herself as she stretched out her long legs in the bathwater, he joined in from the other side of the door, humming his deep bass. She overheard him tell Mama that it was the "first positive sign" he had seen. Mama beamed when Melissa emerged from the room, her long, blonde hair wrapped up high on her head in a towel, her freckled skin red and shiny from the hot water. She even suggested that, if Melissa continued to behave, they might start letting her come up two or three times a week. It pleased them so that she found something in her life to enjoy. Mama said they were "making progress" at last.

But happy as the newfound bathing schedule made her, Melissa discovered that her bouts of depression returned, and they were becoming harder to shake. She now understood that her parents would never let her out of the basement, that she would stay there until she died, that they might even bury her there, cover her grave with cement and forget about her once she was gone. No matter what she had done, she argued with them in her mind, she certainly deserved better than that. Surely, she should eventually reach a point when her debt to them, "to society"—to God—was repaid. Even a kidnapper, murderer, or rapist was eligible for parole at some point, she knew. TV taught her that. What she had done, she debated with herself, horrible as it might have been, wasn't as bad as any of that. She had tried to hurt Harlan, maybe even kill him, but she hadn't succeeded, and he deserved it, anyway. She wasn't like some serial killer. Even those maniacs had lawyers, someone to speak for them. She had no one. Lots of kids did worse than she had done, and they were outside, walking around, surrounded by friends and family who forgave them and accepted them. She had been punished enough, she assured herself. She didn't deserve to be imprisoned for life, to die in a dungeon alone and forgotten.

But there was no clemency in sight, and a pardon was out of the question. One night, she watched a TV show—a docudrama—about a child who filed charges against his parents for abusing him, beating and eventually crippling him by maiming his hand. The abuse only lasted for a few months, when he turned twelve and misbehaved in some way that made them angry. Although outwardly respectable and well liked, his parents truly were monsters. They kept him locked in a closet for days at a time, starved him, left him to lie in his own filth. When he told his teachers and friends about it, they thought he was exaggerating, making it all up. No one would do anything. But when he tried to escape and his father hit him with a hammer and crushed his hand, they had to take him to a doctor. Even then, the authorities did nothing, as the parents were too prominent in the community for anyone to believe them capable of such abuse. Finally, he found an attorney who believed him, took him as a client, and demanded an investigation. In the end, his parents were arrested and sent to prison.

"They violated the child's fundamental rights as a human being," the actor-prosecutor said somberly into the screen. "The major tragedy is that Frankie had to wait until he was permanently maimed before anyone would believe his claims and bring this heinous crime to light."

As the show's credits flickered on the screen, Melissa considered Frankie's dilemma and her own. She hadn't been beaten, and she wasn't kept in a dark closet. Truly, she was well fed and allowed to keep herself reasonably clean. She had all kinds of comforts. And while Papa had hit her, he hadn't crippled her. But in a way, what was happening to her was worse. She now knew why her punishment continued and seemed to have no foreseeable end, though. She would be eighteen in a few weeks, a legal adult. If she were free, she not only could embarrass Papa and Mama, ruin them with the scandal of what they had done to her, she also could take revenge on them: send them to prison, give them a taste of their own medicine. But she wasn't free, and she wasn't about to gain her freedom, not by their hand. She thought of how much kinder they had been toward her since her last outburst at Christmas, how they seemed to cater to her every wish. They had grown used to the fact that she was their prisoner. They would never let her go, not when she might go to the police, confess what she had done to Harlan when she was just a kid, take whatever punishment they might give her, and then tell them that her parents had locked her up, beaten her, mistreated her—no, she corrected with an affirming nod, "abused" her—for almost two years. The cops would be outraged, she convinced herself. So would a judge and a jury. What would they give Papa and Mama? Ten years? Twenty? It didn't matter. She would be free of them forever. That was all that counted.

But the fantasy of what she might do when she was free always was tempered by the obvious fact that unless she escaped, nothing was possible. Unlike Frankie, she didn't go to school, could never talk to anyone, least of all a sympathetic lawyer. She had no way of convincing anyone of how bad things were while she was locked up in the basement. Escape was her only option, and it became her obsession.

She reviewed every detail of her life's routine, counted every item around her to see if she had overlooked any potential weapon. There was nothing. She didn't even have a belt or cord that might be used as a garrote or a whip, certainly nothing to serve as a club or knife. Although she was in better physical condition than she had ever enjoyed in her life, Papa was still much bigger and stronger than she, and his advancing age and deteriorating health wouldn't progress far enough quickly enough to benefit her. He might live another twenty years or longer. Besides, she finally acknowledged sadly, they might have softened toward her in some ways, but they were still wary of her, and they weren't about to let their guard down even for a moment.

———

Escape, though, obsessed her. Every day, she was alive to every detail of her routine. When she was taken up to bathe one Friday morning, though, she gradually realized a possibility, something she had overlooked, forgotten about. Ironically, it came while she soaked in a bubble bath and enjoyed the summer sunlight streaming through the same bath-room window that gave her such pleasure.

When she entered puberty and her breasts were first budding, she dis-covered to a mixture of horror and amusement that Old Mr. Toynbee next door was watching whenever she passed in front of the small sash window above the toilet. There was a shade, of course, and it could be drawn, but that made the room seem dark and close. Melissa was a tall girl, and at her height, even as a preteen, when she stood by the toilet, she was fully visible from the waist up to anyone standing outside. The only possible onlooker, however, was Old Mr. Toynbee, since his house and fenced backyard abutted the parsonage's western side. All he had to do was look to see into the bathroom window.

Her parents had never had much to do with Mr. Toynbee and seldom spoke of him. It was as if he was someone with a contagious disease who might infect them. When they mentioned his name, they nearly whis-pered it, but that, Melissa knew, was because the Toynbees were Roman Catholic. It nettled the minister and his wife that the Toynbees made their home so near the parsonage, but they made it worse by putting up a grotto in their front garden that featured the Virgin Mary. That, Papa said, was "idolatry," and he and Mama mostly pretended that the Toynbees weren't there. Many times, Melissa had seen the old man wave at her par-ents when they were outdoors, but they always looked away, embarrassed to have been acknowledged by such a "pagan." All at once, though, Melissa came to realize that when he looked into the bathroom window, he was acknowledging her in a quite different way.

The bathroom was small and narrow, but it was long enough for her—or presumably Mama—to avoid the window while she was dis-robed, so once she realized he could see her, she simply stepped away from it whenever she was naked. After a while, though, she discovered a deliciously naughty game in exposing herself to Mr. Toynbee whenever she spied him working in his garden. If she found herself bathing in the morning, particularly in the spring and early summer when he was hoeing his tomatoes, she would stand, brazenly bare, allowing her over-sized breasts to jut out while she pretended to apply body lotion or to do some other toilet chore, all the while giving Old Mr. Toynbee an eyeful and pretending not to notice him.

An eyeful was probably more than enough for the old man, Melissa thought. Mr. Toynbee was aged, ancient, it seemed. His one apparent pleasure in life was tending the vegetables that grew along the fence line between the two houses. He had a large garden, and he was almost always out in the cool of the morning to cultivate his crop. He walked hunched over and wore a battered khaki hat that was ineffectually pulled down over stray wisps of white hair. He smoked a pipe, usually had not shaved and looked unkempt, and he wore glasses as thick as telescope lenses.

Melissa understood that he knew she was deliberately exposing herself to him when she stood naked in front of the window. She also knew that he would never say anything to Papa or anyone else, including and especially elderly Mrs. Toynbee, who often could be seen in a wheelchair taking the sun on the porch. But the effect of Melissa's homegrown peep show on the old man vastly amused her. Although she never made eye contact with him—or tried to speak to him or gesture toward him in any way—she watched from the corner of her eye as he stopped and stared, his pipe forgotten in his hand, his mouth hanging open in a pink gape as she stretched her body as tall as she could or soothingly rubbed lotion or oil onto her hard red nipples and ran her tongue around her lips in mock pleasure.

It was as if he imagined that she couldn't see him. Sometimes, it was all she could do to keep from laughing out loud, from throwing open the window and yelling, "Peeping Tom," or "You dirty old man!" But she enjoyed the moment too much to ruin it. In a way, it was flattering, and the naughtiness thrilled her. After a while, Melissa couldn't help herself and played the game every chance she had. Even at night, when she had no idea if he was peering from one of the darkened windows of the Toynbee house, she would perform, flaunting her youthful sexuality against the black windowpane and imagining that the old man was receiving an equal jolt of excitement while he watched her, fondling himself while he feasted his eyes on her youthful beauty.

As she grew older, though, and her affair with Harlan and sexual flirtations with other boys became more frequent, she became more sensitive about her little game. It started to disgust her, and she finally stopped it entirely and took care to don a garment or towel when she was out of the tub, finishing her bath routine. She knew that he was there, though, and if he caught a glimpse of her form in the window, he would shamelessly stop whatever he was doing and stare hard in her direction.

And after her confinement to the basement and her bath schedule was regularized to a once-a-week treat that took place usually well after anyone the age of Toynbee would have retired for the night, she forgot about him. Now, as she soaked and began singing softly to herself, listening to her father's humming on the other side of the door, she remembered him with a wan and nostalgic smile. She idly considered that perhaps the old man had died. After all, he was an *old* man, and it had been well over two years since she last saw him. On the other hand, she suddenly considered with a spark of hope, maybe he wasn't dead. Maybe he was out there right now.

A chill broke out all over her body, and gooseflesh rose as she contemplated the possibility with growing excitement. Fighting the impulse to move too fast and alert her father, she unfolded her lanky body and slipped slowly from the water, remembering to keep singing to cover her movements and hide any noise. Naked, she moved to the narrow window, straddled the toilet, and put out her hands to lean on the sill. Mr. Toynbee was nowhere in sight, but his vegetables were in full flower, and his old pitchfork and wheelbarrow were in place, just as they always were when he was gardening, right next to the fence.

She peered at the house, but no one emerged. The old man was surely somewhere nearby, she thought. She scanned the yard across from the parsonage, then stopped singing and breathed, "Come on out, you old fart. I got something for you to see you won't believe." She had no idea what he might do if he saw her after all this time, only that he would have to do something. She hoped he wasn't too senile or stupid to realize that something was terribly wrong, to call the cops. Even if he was, surely he would tell someone that the minister's daughter—whom no one had seen in two years—was alive and well but was living secretly somewhere in the house. How could he *not* tell someone?

Her entire body trembled with anxiety as she went up on tiptoes astraddle the toilet, leaned over the tank, and brought her breasts hard against the glass. Her nipples flattened against the cool pane, and her breath frosted the ripply old window. But Toynbee stayed out of view. Minutes slipped away.

Her father's voice startled her so much she lost her balance and almost fell. She suddenly realized that her abrupt quiet might have alarmed him, and she immediately began singing again, quickly let the water out of the tub, and called that she was fine, that she must have dozed off. From beyond the door, Papa immediately admonished her how that was dangerous, that she might drown. She silently answered that that might be just what he hoped for, but aloud, she merely continued to sing.

As she toweled off, her eyes raced around the bathroom. Papa and Mama had carefully removed anything that she might use to harm them. Even the beaded chain that used to hold the sink's stopper was gone, and the shampoos, soaps, oils, and lotions all were in soft squeeze bottles. There wasn't even a comb or a hand mirror in the room. The medicine cabinet was empty, and aside from thick, cotton towels, the bureau along the far wall away from the tub was void of anything that might be of use. Papa was as careful as he was thorough. Even the inner workings of the toilet tank were plastic.

She wrapped up her hair and put on her robe. Her eyes fled through the window once more, and she again raised herself up onto her toes so she could see directly over Toynbee's fence. She absently noted that Papa had screwed the window down with heavy carriage bolts, countersunk into the frame. The sash was painted shut. Papa called again to ask if she was ready, and she said that she almost was. Then, just as she was about to turn away, she saw him.

Toynbee stood up straight. He had been concealed, down on his knees doing something right next to the fence. His clothes were muddy and his hat was askew, but he had been there all along. He pulled out a red bandanna and mopped his forehead and glanced up toward the bathroom window briefly as he relit his pipe. She took a halting step forward, and then three quick knocks on the door behind her caused her to freeze. It was Papa's signal that he would be coming in after a brief, silent count of ten.

"Just a second, Papa," she cried in as steady a voice as she could manage. Toynbee turned and started walking back to his house; then she heard the rattle of the doorknob and gathered her towel and turned to face Papa as he gently opened the door, Mama right behind him. He automatically averted his eyes from his daughter in case she was not yet covered, but his tiny gray eyes scanned the room, sought evidence of treachery. The small wooden bat gripped tightly in his hand did not escape Melissa's notice, and she almost cowered before she caught herself and smiled as warmly as she could.

She was raging inside, frustrated nearly to madness that the opportunity of her life had slipped away. Her heart was pounding and she felt her breath shorten, but she fought for control and stood meekly while Mama rehooked the chain and cuffed it to her wrist, then led her down the stairs to her cell. Papa followed at a distance and leaned against the washer and read a small book while Mama used a blow-dryer and brush on her hair. Melissa's heartbeat slowed to normal, and she felt disappointment settling over her. Mama finished, then bundled up the wet towels for the laundry bin and went upstairs. Melissa waited, considered, then found her voice and called to her father, as he was turning to leave.

"Papa?" He stopped. "I have a question." He turned his broad face on her with a slight smile. For a moment, she saw the man who had once doted on her, loved her, but almost instantly he turned serious, and she saw her jailer's mask again. "Are you ever going to let me go?" she asked.

"We've been over that, Melissa," he grumbled behind a darkening frown as his shoulders sagged. "You'll be free when I decide the time is right. Not before."

For a beat, she chewed silently on his words, then lifted her eyes and studied him. "You're never going to let me go, are you?" He sighed. "That's the truth, isn't it?" He stepped toward her slightly, the bat under his arm, his hands opening to start explaining all over again, but she put up her hand, as if she were a cop stopping traffic. Then she sighed. "The truth is that you can't let me go."

She saw him stiffen, then stand utterly still, giving her a narrow stare. Finally he cleared his throat as she had heard him do a hundred times just before starting to preach. "No," he said, "that's not the truth." He paused and licked his thick lips, cast his eyes around the basement, as if looking for something to help him. At once, she could see, even in the dim light of the underground room, that he was afraid. She couldn't tell, though, whether the fear she heard in his voice and saw in his face was fear of lying or fear of her. It didn't matter, she thought. It was all of the same piece.

"The truth of it is . . ." He cleared his throat, then adopted the minister's sonorous tone, "God hasn't yet revealed to me what I should do about you. You must repent."

"You're never going to let me go," Melissa repeated softly, her eyes down, her finger tracing a circle on her exposed leg. "I know it. I think I've known it all along. You're not waiting on God or anybody else." His mouth opened to protest, but she looked him directly in the eye and went on, her voice rising, but only in volume, not in anger. She could hardly believe how calm she sounded, how in control she was. This wasn't like the Christmas tantrums. This was steady, solid. It came from something inside her that had appeared then settled like a stone in her stomach. "You don't know what to do with me," she said. "You're scared, aren't you? Because you know you're breaking the law!" Her voice now reached a quavering soprano, and cold sweat broke out all over her body as anxiety and anger broke open. "You can't let me go. Why won't you just tell me that? Why are you lying to me?" She wanted to cry, felt the tears forming, but she fought them back. Not this time, she told herself. She swallowed hard, pressed hysteria back. She wanted to wound him, hurt him, so she used his own words. "You've always told me that lying is a sin, Papa," she said. "It's your sin!"

His head snapped back, as if she'd struck him on the jaw. His face grew red and she could hear his breathing thicken. "I think you'd better take a nap," he said as he turned and stepped to the stairs. He held onto the banister. She could hear his rattling wheeze across the room. "I think you'd better pray a little and take a nap." He lumbered up the stairs, chugging as he climbed.

Melissa sat on her bed for nearly an hour without moving. Her entire body quaked with raging emotions. But she refused to cry. She would never cry again, she promised. But she made another promise, as well. The next time, she would make damned sure Old Mr. Toynbee saw her.

———

The week dragged by with painful slowness. Papa came down on Sunday and brought her quarterly ration of grape juice and a crumbled saltine cracker for quarterly communion. Mama wasn't with him, for once. He said she had a headache and gave Melissa an admonishing look, as if that was her fault. He seemed more reserved, somehow, colder and more formal. She didn't respond to his brief attempts at conversation, but she was civil to him, trying to show contrition and a pleasing face as he went through the rite in an automatic tone. She bowed her head and said nothing smart, fearful of any word or action that might jeopardize the next week's bath trip. She desperately feared that the hymnal committee would complete its work, and she would once more be on the late-night schedule.

Mama, apparently recovered, allayed her fears on Monday as she changed Melissa's bed linen and chirped stupidly about the importance of Papa's committee's work. "Music has always been his first love," she nattered. "Before he came to Jesus, he was quite a dancer, too." She lifted her face, and her washed-out eyes seemed to look into the past as a small smile creased her wrinkles. "Oh, how I used to love dancing." Then she blushed. "Long time ago," she said.

As the old woman smoothed the clean sheets, Melissa sat in the chair and stared at her in dumb silence, a smile pasted on her face. She no longer saw her as her mother or as anyone with whom she had any connection at all. Her contempt had grown from a benign to a malignant hostility, fed by scorn for Mama's idiotic behavior. She suddenly struck Melissa as a silly bird, fluttering about the room, bobbing her head up and down as if in agreement with her own words. She chattered about Melissa's welfare, her health, her appearance, as if she was reading from a script she'd memorized. All at once, Melissa's impassioned hatred for the small, wrenlike woman roiled into a flame. She wanted to hurt her, but not in the same way she hurt Papa. She wanted to hurt Mama badly. You're supposed to be my mother, for God's sake, Melissa mutely insisted from behind her plastic smile. How could a mother allow this to happen? Although she maintained her show of polite indifference to her mother's banter, she boiled inside. She felt murderous, her heart thudding in her ears. She wanted to wrap the confining chain around the woman's frail neck, but the chain was too short, and Papa was right upstairs. She could hear his footfalls in the kitchen.

Melissa fully understood that she could kill them with no remorse. She fantasized that she could fill the entire basement with their blood and feel nothing but triumph. She remembered that even through a drunken haze how immensely satisfying it had been to stick Harlan's knife into his belly, how shockingly gratifying it was to see gore pouring out of his surprised face when she laid open his cheek, how wide his eyes were with terror as she slashed at him with the sharp blade. Her mouth almost watered at the prospect of seeing the same terror in her parents' eyes, of creating in them such fear that they could do nothing but cower and beg. Oh, how she would enjoy killing them, in watching them suffer.

"You seem fidgety, dear," Mama said, noting that Melissa's hands were fisted, the ball of her foot bouncing on the floor in a rapid beat. When Melissa didn't reply, Mama patted her knee. "That time of month," she said in a sad whisper. "I know how it is. I'll make you some tea."

———

Friday morning, Papa and Mama arrived to take her upstairs for her bath. She swallowed a throatful of bile and smiled sweetly as she moved up the stairs behind Mama, and she suppressed a shudder of revulsion as she gave Papa a slight hug as he unlocked her cuff and ushered her into the bathroom.

As soon as the door shut, she latched it silently and went to the window. Her heart skipped into a quick rhythm and her mouth went dry. Old Mr. Toynbee was idly spraying water over his tomatoes, his thick glasses peering around in dreamy boredom over his pipe. She stared at him for a few moments, then nearly panicked when she remembered where she was and what she was supposedly doing.

She quickly began running the water in the tub and stripped off her robe. A light melody came from her lips as she stepped over to the toilet. It had to be today, and she had a plan. If her upper torso had caught Toynbee's eye before, she was certain that a full portrait would attract his total attention. She climbed up onto the stool and stood as provocatively as her ungainly position would allow. Fighting for balance, she cocked one hip and ran her hands up and down her stomach. Look, damn you, she mentally shouted while her voice sent a tune through the door to her father who, as usual, picked up the harmony.

At first, she was sure Toynbee would never cast his thick lenses in her direction. She stamped her foot on the stool in frustration. Then, all at once, he turned his head toward the side of the parsonage. He looked up and froze. His pipe fell from his mouth to the ground. After a few seconds, his hand rose to his thick spectacles and adjusted them on his bulbous nose. His eyes, magnified by the glasses, seemed to grow larger as he stared. She almost giggled to see the waterhose pointing downward, dousing his shoes.

For a full minute, they stood like two absurd statues. She didn't dare move except to stroke her finger from her blonde pubic pelt up to her breasts, pulling on her nipples, playing with a strand of hair, desperately hoping to hold his attention long enough for him to do something—anything—to acknowledge her. He stood, though, as if rooted in place. He shook his head slowly, as if the vision in front of him was a hallucination, but he continued to stare, the water continued to run forgotten down into his muddy shoes and away into the garden. His mouth hung open, and she could see his tongue running again and again over his lips, but other than that, he seemed to be dead, struck in place like the statue of the Virgin in his grotto.

The sound of the water in the tub behind her came to her ears, and she remembered what it meant just in time to scamper down and shut it off before it overflowed. She splashed around with her hand, sang another verse of her song, then went back to the window and resumed her former posture.

Her disappearance apparently animated the old man. He was stamping around in his sopping socks now, the hose lying dormant. He retrieved his pipe but kept glancing up toward the window, never looking for more than a few seconds. Finally, she saw him gathering his tools and putting them into the wheelbarrow. Panic spurted, then coursed through her. He was leaving! He glanced over his shoulder, apparently embarrassed. Frantically, she gestured for him to come toward the window, but he only stopped, turned, and stared once more. He rubbed his whiskery chin and shook his head. His face was bright red, and his eyes blinked behind his lenses. He turned abruptly and was once more retreating.

That wasn't what he was supposed to do! she silently insisted as sweat broke out all over her body. Perhaps he didn't know anything about her. Maybe he never had. Or maybe he did! Maybe Papa told him she was crazy, that she was being kept away from the public, that she had some dread disease. Frantic and horrible possibilities swirled around her like seeds on the wind, seeking someplace to root.

Toynbee was her last chance—her only chance. Old and crazy or not, he had to help her. She looked rapidly about the bathroom. There was nothing. Her fingers tested the pane in the window. She pushed against it hard enough to make her nails go white, and though the glass bowed slightly under pressure, it remained firm. It would shatter easily, she sensed, but she couldn't just push it out of the frame. She saw him going up onto his porch. She had to act now! Grabbing her bath towel and wrapping it around her fist as she had seen people on TV do, she smashed it through the window and screamed.

The sound of breaking glass filled the bathroom and covered her cries. Her right arm thrust out the broken window, and blood jetted from dozens of cuts. Behind her, she heard two loud thumps, then the bathroom door crashing open, and she felt Papa's huge hands grab her shoulders and jerk her backward. He spun her around, and she saw in his boiling face a deeper fury than she had ever imagined. His eyes glowed with madness, his nostrils flared, and he was snorting like a raging bull. She recalled a phrase, "Wrath of God," as his fist slammed into her mouth. She heard a bright bell ring just before she fell back and away from him into the full tub of water. She sensed no pain, only fear, and blood filled her mouth. Papa had never before struck her with his hand, let alone his fist. Now, he was reaching for her again with his thick knuckles doubled, his arm cocked, but his fingers slid off of the slick skin of her shoulder, and she fell back once more, striking her head hard on the faucet. Bursts of light filled her eyes, and a sharp and piercing pain screwed through her head and smashed up behind her eyes.

Mama's shrieking screams suddenly lit the small room, and Melissa saw her scramble to the broken window and drape a towel over the bloody, broken glass that toothed angrily away from the frame. Papa still groped for purchase on her body, but Melissa, panicked, wiggled and scooched back into the tub of warm water, her legs dangling over the edge, touching the floor, trying to lift her. She twisted to avoid his grasping square fingers. Her head throbbed, and her lips and jaw stung. Her mouth was full of blood. Finally, Papa grabbed a fistful of her wet hair and yanked her up from the tub. Mama still screamed, and Melissa steeled herself for a punch, but he paused, blinked, then opened his hand and slapped her twice and roughly dumped her down on her face beside the toilet.

"Get up!" Papa bellowed. "Face me, you slut! You harlot! You whore!"

Purple and red spots danced before Melissa's eyes and she felt herself slipping into darkness, but then she felt a large piece of sharp glass beneath her palm. She closed her fingers around it and sobbed while her father bent down and yelled in her ear, his breath rasping, choking, "You will repent, you whore! You will, so help me!" He slapped her again, but he couldn't get leverage, and his blow glanced off. "I will not have a whore in my house!" he screamed at her. "You are wanton! You will repent!"

At last, Mama pushed between them and pulled her up. She whimpered at Papa to leave Melissa alone while she wrapped a towel around Melissa's bleeding arm and hand that still clutched the glass shard. Melissa couldn't tell how large it was or even the shape, but she knew it was sharp. The sting of it slicing her palm kept her conscious.

Papa had the bat, now, and she could hear him huffing like a locomotive as he stomped around the bathroom and whacked at the tub, countertop, and sink. The basin shattered, and tile cracked under the blows. "Wanton whore," he wheezed over and over. "Filthy. Vile. Whore." He was out of control, and she knew he wanted to hit her again, but Mama wouldn't have it. She dodged and feinted, keeping her small body between them. He started making loud guttural noises, roars and grunts and exclamations of pure rage, all the while puffing and blowing snot and slobber around the room as he slung the bat at the thin air. She could think only of a bull gone mad as he stormed, and she half expected to see horns sprout from his forehead and smoke blow from his spewing nostrils.

Finally, Mama pushed by him and led Melissa into the hall. He continued to roar and groan in deep tones. She hustled Melissa through the pantry and down the steps to the basement where she quickly hooked the cuff to her left arm and left to fetch bandages. Through the open door Melissa could hear Papa still stomping around, still raging, still unable to speak in words, gulping in heaving sobs of air that rattled like autumn leaves in a high wind when he let them go. Melissa's head throbbed and her jaw ached, but she sucked her smashed lips and watched the stairs carefully for Mama's return. She unwrapped the bloodstained towel and opened her slashed palm that still held the piece of glass.

The shard was jagged, curved like a miniature cutlass blade. It was almost three inches long, sharp on one side but beveled on the other, as if it had popped out of the window frame when she smashed her hand through. She admonished herself that she should have used it on Papa in the bathroom when she had the chance, but his size and anger cowed her. Her cowardice dismayed her. Now, she vowed, she was ready. She ran her index finger across the edge, and a bright red line of blood rose immediately across the pad. With a grim smile on her narrow lips, she sucked her finger for a moment, then shoved the glass into the pages of a thick paperback book and put it on the shelf next to her bed, only rewrapping her hand and rearranging herself moments before Mama returned to dress her arm.

Papa had gone quiet, and he didn't come down while Mama worked. Melissa locked her jaw against the pain and remained silent while her mother doctored her. Many of the cuts were deep, Mama said, and a few had tiny pieces of glass imbedded in them. The old woman worked in silence with tweezers, plucking out the splinters, then poured peroxide over all the wounds, making them foam up in pink bubbles and causing Melissa to feel faint. She fought to stay conscious.

Mama washed the bump on her head and wiped the blood from Melissa's split lip, then wrapped her arm in gauze and tape. "You're a naughty girl," she mumbled. It was as if she were speaking to someone else. She never looked Melissa in the eye. "A wicked and naughty girl," she went on. "Papa is upset. You've made him sick, and he's had to lie down. You're a wicked, naughty girl."

Melissa said nothing. Mama finished and stomped up the steps, still scolding her for her "nastiness," her "naughtiness." When she was finally alone, she lay back on her bed, a grim smile of satisfaction on her face. Her head and face, arm and hand ached, pulsed with pain, but her plan had worked. It had been worth it. Old Mr. Toynbee had to have heard. If he didn't call the cops, surely he would tell someone. Word would get out. It was just a matter of time.

She wasn't surprised when Mama didn't return with lunch or supper. She wasn't hungry. Her head now throbbed with an angry, dull beat, and her mouth was swollen and sore. Her arm itched and burned, as well. At eight o'clock, her anxiety almost unbearable, she turned on the TV and forced herself to watch an old movie until she fell asleep. The set was still on when she awoke early the next morning. There were no footfalls in the kitchen upstairs, no sounds from above at all. Something had happened, she sensed. For a time, she fantasized that her parents, fearful of Toynbee's sounding an alarm, had turned themselves in. They were probably being interrogated at the police station. They would soon confess, she was sure. She convinced herself that at any moment the basement door would burst open and the cops would come trooping down the stairs and save her. In a rush of anticipation, she threw all her clothes away from the bed across the room and lay naked except for the bloody bandages on her arm. She wanted to look as pitiful as possible when they arrived, hoped that reporters would come and take pictures to put on television.

Hours passed. No one came. She finally concluded the obvious: Old Mr. Toynbee had told no one about her. In a sudden attack of despair, she gave in to tears and cried for nearly an hour, sobbing hard into the pillow and kicking her legs in frustrated disgust. That soon gave way to anger with herself. It had been a stupid plan. He was old, likely crazy, and probably hadn't believed his eyes when he saw her, probably thought she was some sort of apparition of his memory or imagination. More likely, she decided with a thin compression of her lips, he looked upon her as his one private little sin, something he didn't want to risk losing if he told someone about it. He had never told anyone about her exposing herself before. Why should he now? Furiously, she chastised herself. She had put too much faith in him, blown it all out of proportion, let her fantasies carry her away to false hopes. Then, she made a new resolve. None of it mattered, she told herself. For the moment, she was still imprisoned, but she had, at least, done something. It was a start. She'd find a way to escape, no matter what it took. It wasn't a total loss, she suddenly remembered. She opened the book, removed the piece of glass and turned it over carefully in her hand, then sat for a long time and just stared at it. This, she assured herself, was the key.

———

It was three in the afternoon on Sunday when Mama reappeared in the basement. Melissa had gorged herself on snacks and soft drinks, and she lay, still naked, still bandaged, her arm aching, itchy, and hot, on top of her counterpane where Mama had left her the day before. She imagined she might have a slight fever. She ignored all the discomfort, shoved it away from her mind as soon as she heard the door open. She closed her eyes, but slitted them just enough to see her mother's shadow descend the stairs.

She waited and watched as Mama stopped at the foot of the steps and stared at her. Her mother's small, dark figure was barely lit as she waited by the laundry area to catch her breath. She seemed to waver a bit. Melissa saw her set a bag of some kind on top of the dryer, then slowly move over to the bed. Melissa felt her skin go clammy. She fought the temptation to tense her body. Her left hand, cuffed and chained, was under the pillow where her head lay. In it was the sharp piece of glass. If Papa came down in a moment and drew close to her, she would sit up. Her nudity would distract him, she believed, long enough for her to move up onto the pillow and keep them from finding her weapon. She must be careful. There would not be another chance.

Mama came into the glare of Melissa's reading light and stood looking down at her. She was saying something in her inane, whispery, chirping voice, but Melissa's heart was pounding in her ears, and her mind was racing too fast to hear her. Papa hadn't come down! she mentally cheered. She and Mama were totally alone. If Mama stepped another two feet closer, she would be in reach.

The old woman continued to mutter in breathy tones, but Melissa concentrated on the glass. Her fingers were tingling, so she flexed them to prevent them from falling asleep. Her right arm and hand throbbed angrily, and she reminded herself that she would have to change the bandage before she got away from the house. She hadn't many clothes to worry about, and aside from the money she hoped Papa still kept upstairs in his office, there would be little to pack. She had planned it all out: Find the key in Mama's pocket, free herself, race upstairs, grab the money, and run to the Conoco station and call Eve. If Eve was still in town. She would call somebody. Matt, maybe. Somebody. Then she would go away. She would get a safe distance from her parents, and then she would go to the cops, turn them in. If that didn't work—or they didn't believe her—she'd get a lawyer, just like Frankie in the program. Either way, the authorities would have to become involved. That would settle Papa and Mama for good.

Mama was still standing there, talking softly. She might have been praying, Melissa thought as she peeked through the slits in her eyelids.

She looked older and smaller than ever. Her face was drawn and gray, her complexion ashen, and dried streaks of mascara ran down her shrunken cheeks. That was odd, Melissa thought idly. Mama was always fussy about her makeup, since she was older than Papa and hated for anyone to notice. She also was still dressed for church, which was strange for that hour of the afternoon, with a little old-fashioned pillbox hat and veil dripping down over her faded eyes. She had on a dark suit and a white blouse with a navy blue ribbon tied around the collar. She had black gloves on, and there was something white—a paper of some kind—folded in her hand. Melissa suddenly noticed how gaunt and weak her mother looked. She had never been a strong woman, but somehow she had always found energy. Now she looked worn, abused, tired beyond endurance. Melissa had the impulse to feel sorry for her, but hate quickly welled and drowned pity. She couldn't permit herself any sympathy, any weakness. Mama, after all, had been her warden as much as Papa had.

Melissa was about to resign her ruse of sleep. She refused to act impulsively, to blow the chance. But her mother hadn't moved any closer and might go away and get Papa if she thought Melissa was truly ill. She would have to lure the old woman near enough to put the glass to her throat, force her to unlock the cuff. Then she would chain her up and leave. That was the plan. It called for timing. She waited while she listened to her heart drumming in her ears, trying to decide on her best move.

Then the old woman did the unbelievable. She stepped forward, not one pace but two. She was right beside Melissa's bed. Melissa sternly fought the temptation to move. She couldn't afford to lose another opportunity. She had to wait for just the right moment to spring or the chain would catch her and she would be caught short. Mama would call Papa down. There was no telling what he might do if she attacked her mother again. His rage, his violence, his mad brutality terrified her. She breathed deeply, faking a sleeping sigh, tried to calm herself.

She saw from her narrowed eyelids her mother leaning forward and realized that Mama was going to kiss her on the cheek. She shut her eyes for real and waited for the buss of her mother's lips on her face. That would be the moment. That would be perfect. But the kiss never came. She could hear her mother's voice close, very close, but she wasn't kissing her. Still, Mama's breathing was almost right over her. With a thrill rushing through her, she decided. She rolled over in one quick movement, and with an animal cry, she whirled her left hand and its glass blade out in a wide circle.

"Oh my!" Mama said as she stood up and arched back, startled. The only sound Melissa heard was the metallic jingle of her chain when it caught its limit and stopped her arm's arch.

Dark disappointment instantly flooded Melissa's mind and coursed through her like pitch. She had missed Mama entirely. She had never been good at much of anything with her left hand, and her whole arm tingled with a million numbing prickles. It had been partly asleep, after all, weak and useless. She scrambled to sit up, frantically tried to think of something to say, anything to protect herself, to keep Mama from fetching Papa, when the old woman took a step backward and flung her hand to her throat, her narrow mouth wide open. Her other hand reached down and groped for the iron footboard of the bedstead. Her light eyes were wide under the veil, and her whole body visibly shook. She had scared her, Melissa said to herself in disgust, merely scared her. That was all.

Then, between the black-gloved fingers, a bright red fountain began to seep, then flow, and Mama's eyes glazed as her mouth spread wider to make a scream that never came. Blood gushed in a scarlet flood down the front of Mama's white blouse and, as her hand fell away and revealed a gaping tear across the white wattles of her throat, it spurted out and all over the old woman's suit and painted scarlet ripples on her legs. Melissa stared. She was looking at a dead person. She had killed Mama.

Mama slid down to her knees onto the pink rug, and as she lay, almost gently, down on her back, her legs folded beneath her in an absurd lady-like movement, more blood jetted, pumping out in brilliant red spasms as if someone was pumping it. By the time her head rested on the floor, the red pulses spurted into the air, and a thick smell of gore struck Melissa's nose, made her gag. She scrambled to pull her legs back out of the way of the splashing bursts and stared at the twitches and spasms that wracked her mother's body before she finally lay still, her eyes open, life steadily flowing in a crimson river from her lacerated throat out across the uneven floor of the basement.

It was a long time before Melissa could bring herself to move. Her legs were numb and her chest felt hollow. A knot formed in her stomach, then rose to her throat and refused to go away. Her lungs refused to hold her breath, and she could feel her heart pounding in her ears. At once, she leaned over and vomited onto the floor beside the bed. After the wracking heaves ended, she sat up again and tried to calm herself, to follow the plans she had made. With one eye on the stairs, wary of Papa's roaring charge, she kept the glass blade in her hand as she rolled Mama over and went through her clothing. The fabric was slimy with blood, and Melissa fought back gags and stomach heaves while her fingers raced around, searching for the key. She was breathing heavily, fighting the impulse to start screaming and never stop. This was no fantasy, she kept telling herself, no dream, no TV program or movie. But it didn't seem real, either. It was nearly too much to accept.

Her jaws clenched against more nausea, she ransacked her mother's dress. The key was not there. It was *always* there, Melissa insisted frantically to herself, dangling from a leather thong outside Mama's or Papa's pocket. They wore it that way on purpose, she believed, to taunt her, to tempt her to reach for it just to prove that she was still in need of punishment. She scooped up Mama's small, black clutch that had fallen on the bed. But it wasn't in the purse, either. Lipstick, mascara, a big wad of soiled tissues, and a small brush fell out onto the bloody counterpane. The key wasn't there.

Melissa took a deep breath, then leaned back and chewed a blood-stained fingernail and pondered where Mama might have secreted the key. She was about to undress her to search for secret pockets inside her clothes, when she spotted the paper lying on the floor. That had been in Mama's hand when she approached the bed. Suddenly, Melissa realized that when Mama had bent over her, it wasn't to kiss her but to place it on the bed next to her, where she could find it when she woke up.

One corner was soggy with blood, but she unfolded it and read it quickly. It wasn't long.

Dearest Melissa,

> *At last, you shall have your freedom. Your little stunt in the bathroom on Friday upset your father so much he couldn't get over it. He*

wouldn't talk to me or do anything but fume. I guess his poor heart just gave out. I think you broke it for good and all. I took him right to the hospital, and they did everything they could, but it was too late. So he's gone now. And I guess that means any reason to keep punishing you is gone, too.

You hurt him very bad. You did it on purpose, and it was not fair. He was a good and decent man, and he helped so many people find the Lord. He loved you so much, but you kept on hurting him. I guess you finally hurt him too much, and God called him Home.

I have left the key to your chain in a blue bag. I will put it where you can reach it. There's some money there (not much, we never had much), and some new clothes, your birth certificate, and other things you might need. You're old enough, now. You can go anywhere you want. I don't know where you'll go, but you probably do.

Don't try to find me. I am going to stay with an old friend. You don't know her. She lives far, far away. You can't stay here. Ray Hobbs told me at your father's funeral today that they are going to close the parsonage. They plan to tear it down and build a new one. That would break your father's heart, I guess, since he wanted a new home so bad all his life. Now it will go to someone else.

You may not believe this, but I love you. You hurt me, but you never hurt me as much as you did Papa. But I forgive you and I love you anyway. I know Papa did, too. You'll always be our little girl, our blessing, in spite of the Devil that's inside you. We called you our Prodigal, and we wanted so bad for you to come home, to the bosom of your family. But you just wouldn't. I hope this has taught you some-thing and I pray that someday God will forgive you as well. Good luck and God bless you. I love you.

Mama

Melissa read the letter a dozen times, then she sat still, staring at the distance across the basement to the dryer where the blue bag that held the key and her freedom sat squat and silent. It might have been a million miles away. She knew better than to try to pull her chain free from the floor. She had tried that for years. Mama hadn't so much as a nail file in her bag. There was nothing that would help her in any way, and the glass, sharp as it was, was useless against concrete and steel. She went over such thoughts again and again. She was surprised when she discovered that more than an hour had passed.

Unpleasant odors suddenly caught her attention. The blood stink had faded, but now, she could smell her body, and she wrinkled her nose in disgust. She wished she had gone ahead and taken that bath first. Timing, she thought. She looked at the portable toilet. It was full, and it also stank. So did the pool of vomit on the other side. She had certainly soiled the counterpane and rug, she thought, as she lowered her eyes and examined her immediate area once more. Mama would have been angry with her, if Mama wasn't the cause of the soiling herself. Bloodstains were hard to get out, Melissa considered, especially after they set. From the looks of things, she thought as she looked at her mother's torn body sprawled across the bright pink rug, they were going to have plenty of time to set.

It could be weeks, Melissa realized, months even, before anyone came into the house. Mama probably told everyone she was going away, and no one would come looking for Melissa, because no one would have imagined that she was there. Even when they tore down the parsonage, there was no guarantee that they would find the basement door, hidden as it was in the pantry. They might not find it until they tore the house completely down. Eve was the only one Melissa knew who was aware of it, and Eve was the last person she could hope would come looking around in a parsonage. She looked around and gradually understood that she was inspecting her own grave.

Melissa still had plenty of food, snacks and drinks, peanut butter and candy. She wouldn't starve for a long time. But there was no doubt about it, she reminded herself. She had really screwed up, this time. Once more, her timing was completely off. She was hungry, suddenly, and she almost reached for a package of cookies before she bethought herself and determined that rationing should start now. But then, as she drew back her bandaged arm and felt the sick, throbbing reminder of the festering cuts beneath the bloody gauze and tape, she changed her mind and drew the package over and began stuffing her mouth with chocolate chips. No point in postponing the inevitable, she thought. "Procrastination is a sin," Papa always said.

While she chewed, she used her remote control to turn on the TV. A *Leave It to Beaver* rerun was on, and Ward was giving sage advice on good manners to Wally and his buck-toothed brother. Wally had a black eye and looked dour. Beaver's hair was unusually mussed and there was a dark smear on one cheek. Melissa thumbed up the volume. Ward was telling the brothers about the importance of working out differences without fighting, of understanding, forgiveness, of trying to bring out the best in people.

Melissa looked down at Mama's body. She said she had forgiven Melissa. But for what? Could she ever forgive Mama? And for what? For being afraid of Papa and doing everything he said? No, Melissa thought, it wasn't all Papa. It was Mama, too. It was both of them. Her letter made it clear. She was as much her jailer as Papa had been, as cruel as Papa had been, and she never tried to understand, to work it out. Mama's fear wasn't of Papa. She was afraid of Melissa, afraid enough to keep her chained and locked away forever. How could she forgive her for that?

Melissa then thought of Papa, unable to hurt her anymore. He had never forgiven her, never tried, and he would never want her forgiveness. He kept her locked away because he, too, was afraid of her, not of what she might do to him, to his reputation, but of something else. She was far from a blessing. She was his curse, his demon, a living image of his own sin, of his failure to truly repent. She was a constant reminder of who he really was, of what he might become.

She glanced at a shampoo commercial on the screen, shook her dirty hair. In a way, she thought, she might have brought out the best in both of them. In a way, she might have saved them from knowing themselves.

In the concluding scene, Beaver quipped a malapropism, drawing her attention back to the set. She shut off the tinny, canned laughter and familiar theme song, grabbed a Dr Pepper and opened it, drank to wash down the cookies. Maybe, she thought, she was ready to forgive them, now. Maybe. But truly, it didn't matter. It's all a matter of timing, she thought, and in the long run, probably that didn't matter, either.

DOGSTAR

Four rats were caught suddenly in the brilliant jab of a flashlight's beam and quickly scurried away into the steaming heaps of trash and junk behind them. Their noise was small, scratches of their nails swallowed by the grating crunch of leather soles on the rocky soil of the trail that led from the dirt pathway between the mounds to the gravel road at the edge of the city dump. There was the sudden sound of a steel-toed shoe striking something metallic and unyielding in the darkness.

"Jesus," a voice came across the frigid stillness that followed the noise. "Why do they always have to die in the middle of the goddamn night."

"Because that's what makes overtime," another voice said. A second flashlight beam sliced through the darkness and joined the first. "Okay, Will, we're here. Where the hell is he?"

"Over there." Will's voice was timid, weak and strained from too much smoke, too many nights coughing into the cold, too much cheap wine. "I found him like I told you."

The shadowy forms now came to the area at the edge of the dump. Weeds and thick stumps of what once had been trees but were now nothing more than blasted shapes in the starlight held a natural defensive line against the encroachment of the stinking trash.

"Colder'n a witch's tit out here," the first voice complained. "Why do they always have to die in the goddamn cold?"

"It ain't that cold. Not freezin' yet," the second voice responded. "Will be by morning." A dry chuckle followed. "Wait till February. They freeze up like popsicles in February. Bums on a stick," the voice finished with a louder, grimmer chortle.

The forms followed the sharp points of their flashlight beams to a patch of grass, then to a spot where it had been parted. Against the naked dead trunk of a limbless tree, a small lean-to shack was visible. It was short, too short for a grown man to stand up in. Three sides were constructed from various anonymous bits of this and that. The fourth side was the dead tree. There was no window, but an opening too small for anyone who wasn't on his hands and knees to enter gaped into the face of the dump. The doorway seemed darker than the night around it.

"Flip you to see who goes in," the second voice said.

"Hell, no. You're City. It's your jurisdiction. I'm just along for the ride."

"This is County," the second voice argued. "Where's the goddamn sheriff."

"Home in bed, likely. Ain't an election year."

"You called him?"

"Sure, I did. He's apt to send a deputy. Probably Eddy."

"Piece of shit."

There was a space of silence. The second voice sighed. "All right. I'm going in. But you cover me."

"Cover you? He's dead." The first voice followed the flashlight's beam that revealed Will, a shriveled little man dressed in a thin raincoat three sizes too big for him. The belt was a piece of electrical wire. He had a woman's floppy hat tied down around his ears with a scarf. "You said he's dead. Right?"

Will nodded. "Dead as a doornail." His eyes were pale, watery in the flashlight's beam. "I checked. But why—"

"Dead men don't shoot," the first voice said again. His light's beam shifted toward the other man, who had on a city policeman's uniform. It was neat, sharply creased, well fitted to a muscular body. He wore a down-filled coat over it. A short-brimmed felt cap covered his head.

The cop put his light on the speaker, a state highway patrolman. "It ain't dead men I'm worried about," he said. The state trooper's dove-gray uniform was also neat and nicely tailored. His boots were shined, glossy in the occasional wash of the flashlight's beam. He, too, had on a heavy western-cut coat, leather, with a fur collar. He wore a ten-beaver Stetson.

"It's live rats," the cop continued. "Rats out here'll climb your leg and bite your nuts off."

"What'd'you care?" the trooper laughed. "You're married." The cop didn't say anything. The trooper went on: "You know the only difference between being married for twenty years and being on the job for twenty years?" The cop stood still, silent, his breath vaporizing into the flashlight's beam. "The job still sucks," the trooper finished the joke.

"The job's always sucked," the cop said.

"That's the point," the trooper said, then shook his head. "You too chickenshit to go in there?" The cop gave him a slanted look. "Oh, okay," the trooper said. He pulled a black automatic from his holster, held it into the light, then pulled back the slide, cocking it. "You're covered against rats and other vermin." With his other hand, he moved his light over to the lean-to's door. The beam did not penetrate the interior. A piece of dark fabric was hanging over it.

The cop drew his nightstick, pushed it aside. "I hate rats," he said.

"There ain't no rats in there," Will said. "Danny didn't like rats."

"Right," the cop said. "That makes me feel all better." He bent down and peered past the small opening. "God, I hate this," he said.

"He ain't in there. Why're you going in there?" Will asked, and the cop stood up quickly and once more trained his light on the small man. The highway patrolman did the same.

"Don't screw around with us, Will. It's too damn cold to be screwing around."

"You said he was here," the trooper said. "In the dump, you said." He put his beam into Will's narrow face. "If you're jerkin' us off, you little shit, I'm goin' to whip your ass."

"He's over yonder," the small man said, and he pointed just beyond the shack into a patch of tall grass and wild growth. Some tall weedy stalks had been bent back, leaning away from the dump as if the odor and steam offended them. Their yellow coloring looked white in the flashlights' glare.

"Why didn't you say so, for Christ's sake?" The trooper stepped off. He kept his pistol out and ready. "There's skunks around here, likely. Maybe coyotes, God knows what. Watch where you step."

"Now, who's chickenshit?" the cop teased.

"A rat is one thing. Skunks are something else. They don't have to bite you to fuck you up. You want to spend all night in a tub of tomato juice?"

"All I need," the cop growled. But he, too, drew his weapon, a regular revolver, from its holster and followed the trooper.

"If I tear my pants out here, Will, I'm going to kick your butt," the trooper said.

"Watch where you step," the cop warned as he flashed his light around on the ground. "There's broken glass, rusty tin, all kinds of shit. Put a nail through your shoe, we'll spend half the night in emergency talking them out of tetanus shots. Those sons of bitches hurt."

"Here," the trooper said. "I see him."

Their flashlights' beams twinned, then fell on the body of a man. He lay on his back, his face to the ice-clear sky overhead. His hands were folded across his chest. He had on gloves, but the fingers were cut out and they laced themselves precisely over his heart. His legs were outstretched, feet akimbo. The shoes were worn completely through and tied on with rags and bits of string. He wasn't moving. His eyes were open to the blinking stars.

"Dumpster Danny," the cop said. The two officers stood on either side of the corpse and looked down at him. "Dead as Aunt Roadie's old gray goose."

"Sure it's him?"

"Sure, I'm sure. Seen him every day since I was a kid. Look at that hat." It was a bowler. Moth-eaten and full of holes and stains, it lay off to one side as if it had been placed carefully by the owner. "I'd know that anywhere. Used to do tricks with it."

"Tricks?"

"You know, juggle it, pull stuff out of it. Like W. C. Fields."

"Thought he used a top hat."

"Danny didn't."

For a moment the two officers stood quietly and studied the body. "Dumpster Danny," the cop said, again. His breath vaporized in the cold, windless atmosphere.

Will offered a correction: "Dogstar Danny."

"What?"

"We always called him 'Dogstar Danny.'"

"I never heard that."

"You never come out here."

The cop raised his head and looked around him. He sniffed the stench of the dump. "Wonder why." It was a statement, not a question.

"Go call it in. We'll need the coroner or a JP out here," the trooper said. "I'll check his body for effects."

"Why should I call it in?"

"Your jurisdiction."

The cop shook his head. "Outside the limit. It's yours, 'less Eddy or somebody from County shows up."

"Call it in," the trooper said. "Please. We need a coroner, and it's cold."

"We ain't got a coroner. JP's Earl Blankenship. He's gone to see his kids down on the coast."

"You got a county ME."

"That'd be Doctor Blake. He does it for the extra money."

"Go call him."

Neither moved.

"Wonder what killed him?" The cop's voice broke their vigil.

"Cold, likely. Cold and stink." The trooper picked up a board that was alive with rusty nails, dropped it. "Lockjaw, maybe. He live there?" His beam fell on the shack.

"Hell of a place to live," the cop said by way of answer. Again, they stood silently.

"All right," the trooper said. "I'll go call if you won't." He started off. "C'mon Will." He stopped. "Will?"

"I'm here," the voice was smaller now, farther away.

"C'mon. You can wait in the car."

"You promised me a sawbuck if I showed you to him."

"You'll get it. C'mon."

"I'll wait here, all the same to you."

"What's the deal?" The trooper searched for Will with his light. He was over by the shack, squatting down.

"He wants to see if there's something he missed stealing before," the cop explained. "That right, Will?"

"No!" Will cried out, his voice sudden, shrill, soprano. It echoed across the dump. "You got no right to say that. Danny was my friend."

"Danny was worth ten bucks," the cop said. "Leave him alone. We'll pay him and let him take what he wants later."

"What time you got?"

The cop pointed his light at his wrist. "Twelve thirty-two."

The trooper started off. "Check the body for effects."

The cop remained where he was. "What about protecting the crime scene?"

"What crime?" The trooper moved off quickly, following his light.

The cop waited until the highway patrolman was out of earshot, then he said in a soft, frosty breath, "When a man lays down and dies in a city dump, it's a crime." He put the flashlight under his arm and bent down over the body.

―――

Two halogen floodlights mounted on telescoping tripods filled the area with silvery white artificial sun and drove the rats and skunks back from their center of focus, the paper and broken particleboard shack at the edge of the dump. A rusty piece of tin served the triangular residence as a roof, and the barkless dead tree reached up above the surface of the light and fingered black into the darkness overhead. The highway patrolman stood off to one side with a deputy sheriff, who kept watch on the small path that led back to a half-dozen official cars and a hearse that doubled as an ambulance. There, three other men in uniform paced up and down the path nervously. Their breath was cloudy and thick. It had grown colder.

The city policeman remained on the opposite side of the light. His hands were full of worthless sundries. He turned them over and studied each carefully before dropping it into an oversized ziplock plastic bag he held between his ankles on the ground. His nightstick was back on his belt opposite his holstered pistol. His flashlight hung by a lanyard around his neck and blasted a strong beam on his hands.

A man in a thick wool overcoat was bent over the body. He had on a stocking cap, wore a stethoscope around his neck and blue rubber gloves. Everyone spoke in low tones, and expelled breath froze and hung suspended in the atmosphere. All around them, beyond the false perimeter created by the light, the dump steamed and stank, and they all now heard the rattle and scraping of animals sifting through the garbage in the distance beyond the globe of light. The trooper lit a cigarette and pretended to listen to the deputy while he studied the cop's work.

The cop looked young, though he was well past forty. His stomach was flat and taut, and his shoulders were straight. Ballplayer, the trooper reminded himself, ex-Marine, Southern Baptist, wife and four kids, huge mortgage, lousy job, no future. The police cruiser was the nicest car he'd ever drive. Nice guy, though. Good man to drink coffee with at midnight. Followed baseball. Nobody follows baseball, anymore.

The deputy sheriff was still talking, hadn't stopped since he arrived, though he hadn't said one thing worth hearing. The trooper turned back to him. The county officer was older, maybe fifty-five at the inside, pushing sixty, maybe. Hard to tell. But he looked every bit of it: dumb, fat, ugly. Backslid Methodist, the trooper thought, maybe Church of Christer. Hadn't heard a sermon in years. Divorced at least once, always broke, probably drank when he was off duty, maybe when he was on. Definitely a soup-over-the-sink eater. Football fan, probably. Not likable at all. His belly hung over the oversized cowboy belt buckle that held in his too-tight jeans' waist. He had on roach-killer boots with roping heels and a plaid shirt with a badge clipped to the flap of the breast pocket. A large-caliber pistol—.44 magnum, the trooper noted—swung at a jaunty angle from a western-style rig. He wore a straw hat tilted back on his head and a short, sheepskin jacket open over his stomach. He spoke with an easy, familiar drawl that hid mischief, meanness. His eyebrows were bushy, danced when he talked. From time to time, he would spit as if his cigar was bothering his tongue.

The city cop looked at the items he found in the body's pockets: a braided brass finger ring, worn almost in two, green with corrosion; four bottle caps with redeemable liners inside, all expired; two books of matches, mostly burned; a box of wooden matches, half full; a miniature Swiss Army knife with a broken blade; and a crumpled cigarette pack with three half-smoked butts. These, along with a cracked telephone pager and a piece of electrical cord, were inside the plastic bag already. In his right hand he held a broken bottle opener, three C-cell batteries, some miscellaneous metal and plastic pieces of things the officer didn't recognize, and what appeared to be two pork ribs, old, well chewed, and dry. He sifted these items into the bag and looked to his left hand's contents. A broken spoon and a whole fork, two toothpicks, and a small wallet greeted him.

He put the utensils into the bag with the rest and opened the wallet. It was so old it almost crumbled as it unfolded. In a brittle plastic card holder was the photo of a woman and a little girl. It was originally a color shot, but it was faded. Only the outlines of their faces met him in an odd sepia tone in the silver light of the floodlamps. She had an antique hairdo—Betty Grable's name came to the cop's mind—and her long, lacquered nails were draped over the shoulder of the little girl. The girl looked to be eight or nine. She had long curls and bright eyes, wore an old-fashioned pinafore.

There was half of a two-dollar bill in the wallet. The date was missing, but it looked like one from the thirties or earlier, not one of the reissues. The cop thought of movies he had seen. The note wasn't casually ripped. It had been torn neatly in half. There was nothing else there.

The cop moved over to where the man in the overcoat was making some notes on a clipboard. He didn't want to look at the body again, not in the bright lights, but he did, anyway. The clothes were open, now, a fishbelly white stomach exposed to the cold. Large red sores raced here and there across curly gray hair that matted across a thin chest. There was a bruise on the ribs, but the palomino tone around the edges told him that it was an old injury. He'd seen that sort of thing before—on prisoners. Men who didn't eat well and often were slow to heal. Above the beard line, more sores were open and unhealed. Part of the forehead seemed chewed. Rats, the cop thought, and he shivered.

Still, he thought, the corpse looked peaceful, as if he had fallen asleep and just died. The fingers were black with grime. So were the four toes that stuck out of his shoe tips. The beard came down almost to where his hands had been folded before the doctor had begun working on him. The nose was hawk-beaked. It hooked so low it almost touched the chin. There were sores on it, too. The mouth was slightly open, and black teeth were exposed in a sort of smile.

"Not much to show for a life's work," the highway patrolman said as he walked up.

The city cop turned to him with a puzzled look. Then he glanced down and realized he was still holding the wallet. The trooper squinted down at it. "This was all there was," the cop said. "The rest is just junk."

"So's that."

"What about the picture?"

"Probably came with the wallet. Look at it. God, it's fifty years old." He held it up into the light. "Wonder where the other half of this is?" He exchanged the photo for the bill.

The trooper took it, held it up to the light and peered through it. "God knows." He squinted. "It's old, too." He looked down at the body.

"Kind of a dirty old fart," he said as he handed the torn banknote to the cop who replaced it in the wallet and dropped it in the bag and zipped it closed, then pulled his leather gloves back on.

"What'd'you expect, when you live in a dump?" the cop asked. "Who the hell would want to live in a dump?"

"Oh, I don't know," the deputy said as he walked up. "Lots of neat shit in a dump. I used to come out here all the time and shoot rats."

"Eagle-eye Eddy," the cop said. Eddy didn't laugh. "No wonder it stinks out here so much."

"I thought you farted was all it was," Eddy said with a smirk. "Got your ass out of a café booth after dark, and it didn't know what else to do."

The doctor looked up at them with an irritable expression on his face, and they stepped away.

The trooper pulled out a little pad and started writing. "You say his name was Danny?"

"Yeah," the cop was momentarily distracted, looked off toward the sky. "We called him 'Dumpster Danny.' I never heard that 'Dogstar' stuff before. Nobody knew his real name. He went through all the Dumpsters and trash barrels downtown. Looked for anything he could find. Aluminum cans, mostly, I guess. The rest of it wound up out here, anyway." In the distance, he saw how the ambient light cast from the town's street lamps reflected on the icy horizon.

"Ever arrest him?"

"Naw. Picked him up on a D and D or a PI, now and then. Tossed him in a cell and let him sleep it off. Harmless old guy. I think he just got a snootful when the weather got bad so he'd have a dry place to sleep."

"Sounds good to me." The trooper made another note.

"You writing a book?" The deputy looked over the highway patrolman's shoulder and squinted. The cop snapped to at the question, stared at the notebook.

"Report. Commander wants me to write it up."

"I thought you said it wasn't your jurisdiction. 'Just along for the ride,'" the cop recalled.

He shrugged. "Not my decision. He wears the rank. Guess he wants me to earn my time."

"Bet you're hell on the coffee and doughnut beat," Eddy said, smirked. "Never pass Connie's but you and Dick Tracy here ain't in there sopping it up." The trooper didn't reply. "It ain't really the slurp and burp that draws you in, though, is it?" he said, tilting his head. "That Connie's got a rack worth a long, low look. Great legs, nice ass. She gets the home fires burning, right?"

"You got a mouth on you, Eddy," the trooper said. "You know that?"

The cop nodded in agreement. "Wonder if I'll have to write it up, too?"

"That'd be a switch." Eddy tossed his cigar butt onto a nearby trash heap, stepped off a few paces, opened his pants, and began pissing into the garbage. "Last time you guys wrote something up, I must have been on vacation." Small wisps of steam rose from the flow. "This one's your problem."

"It's not City. It's County," the cop said. "We're outside the limit."

"You see the sign by the highway?" Eddy asked, hunching his shoulders. "Says, 'City Landfill.' Not 'County Landfill.' This is City. You write it up."

"Least he can write," the trooper said. Eddy just chuckled as he buttoned up, then wandered away.

"Where'd he come from?" The trooper clicked his pen in and out quickly. "Danny. Not that dick with ears."

"Who knows? I've heard all kinds of stories." The cop looked into the plastic bag. Trash. Nothing but trash, he thought.

"Some say he came here during the oil boom and stayed," Eddy said, strolling back. He pulled out another cigar and lit it. A stream of tobacco smoke trailed up into the light and on into the night sky overhead. "But I always heard he was a railroad bum who came through town on a freight. Bulls caught him, threw him off, and he just decided to stay. Regular hobo."

"My dad talked about seeing him when he was a kid. He's been here for goddamn ever," the cop confirmed. "Kind of part of the town. Like a statue or something." He took a breath. "My mom used to give him food out the back door."

"You sure it was only food she was passing out?" Eddy said.

"He came around begging?" The trooper scribbled a note.

"Naw," the cop said with a sideways look at Eddy. "He'd offer to do something for it. Weed the garden. Trim around the curb and sidewalk. Shit like that. Nothing heavy. Just something to do for something to eat." He paused, made fists, gave Eddy his chance, but the deputy was silent, just rocked on his heels and smoked. The cop glanced over at the body. The doctor was pulling the clothes to. "He used to scare me," the cop said quietly. "Always wondered where he came from. What he thought about. Who he really was."

"He was a fucking bum," Eddy said. "Now, he's a dead bum. Case closed."

The trooper turned away from the deputy, who shrugged and took up a casual stance, continued to smoke. "You check the shack?"

"Not yet," the cop said. He didn't move.

"I'll do it." Eddy said with a sigh. "Hate for you to wrinkle your creases. Gimme your light."

"Get your own," the cop said. "This one's City."

Eddy shrugged, then went to get a flashlight from another County man down by the cars.

———

"Who closed his eyes?" Doctor Blake came walking up to them. He had a wet cloth in his hands and was cleaning them. The clipboard was under his arm.

"I did," the cop admitted. "How'd you know?"

"Dehydrated. They'd been open a spell."

"Any obvious cause of death?" the trooper asked.

"Offhand, I'd say NCs," the doctor said. "Heart, most likely. Could be a stroke. Strange, though. Lying out here like that. I'd say he's been dead four, maybe five hours."

"Like he just went out there and went to sleep," the cop muttered.

"If it smells any worse inside than it does outside, I can't blame him," Blake said. "What makes it smell this bad?"

"I've been to a hundred dumps, I guess," the cop said. "They all smell the same."

"It's just shit people don't want," the trooper said. "Cast-off consumerism. Crap like that."

"They all smell the same," the cop repeated. "Wherever you go in the world, they all smell the same."

The trooper was checking his notes. "It was eleven forty-five when Will found us. He had to walk in to town. That took an hour, maybe two. Took us thirty minutes to find him, call it in. You took an hour getting here."

"I was already in bed. I have a surgery in the morning," the doctor said. He opened his coat and revealed pajama tops underneath. "Must have died around eight, eight thirty. Maybe nine."

"Sounds right," the highway patrolman said. "Close enough for government work." Blake nodded. They stepped out of the light. The cop lit a cigarette and offered one to the trooper who accepted, to Blake, who shook his head. The trooper produced a lighter and lit both of them. Blake looked away, scanned the sky for a beat, then sighed. "Oh, shit. Give me one, too."

"Thought you medical guys all had a lecture for this," the trooper smiled as he lit the smoke the cop provided the doctor.

"I'd rather have a cigarette," Blake smiled. "Nicotine, caffeine, whiskey, and sex. That's medical school. Keeps you going. You never quite get over it. Well, maybe the sex."

"Know the difference between twenty years on the job and marriage?" the cop asked suddenly. Blake shook his head. "The marriage still sucks," the cop said.

Blake looked blankly at the trooper, who chuckled. "I think you got that backwards," he said.

"No, I didn't," the cop replied. "Believe me, I didn't." They laughed briefly, uncomfortably, and then stood silently and smoked for a moment.

Blake nodded toward the body. "Guy had a whang on him a yard long."

"What?" the cop was confused.

"No kidding. Never seen one that long. Not on a white guy."

"No shit," the trooper whistled through his teeth.

"Hung to his knee. Must've been a real pussy-getter once."

Maybe that's what killed him," the trooper suggested. "Advanced hernia or something. Carrying all that weight."

"You should be so lucky," Blake said.

"Nothing lucky about dying in a dump," the cop said. He sounded angry, and the men fell silent.

"Boo!" The deputy came up behind them and stuck out his hands. Two skulls grinned into the silvery light, and all the men jumped. The trooper put his hand on his pistol butt. The cop cringed and reached for his nightstick. The doctor dropped his clipboard and scurried into the floodlights' circle.

"What the shit, Eddy? What the shit?" the trooper demanded. He was flustered, annoyed. When he stepped back, his boot went ankle-deep into a pile of unidentifiable garbage.

"Got you, didn't I?" the deputy asked. "Shit your pants?" The skulls in his hands were small. Dog skulls. "He must have fifty of the goddamned things in there. All lined up on busted crates and stuff. Some scary shit."

The cop looked at the bones in the plastic bag. Dog bones. Ribs, he thought.

"You're an asshole, Eddy." The highway patrolman was shaking his boot and leg to throw off whatever he had stepped in. "But you'll never be worth a shit."

"Funny guy, you are, Eddy." Blake looked warily at the skulls and retrieved his clipboard. He was angry, too.

Eddy grinned to match the skulls. He held one up and placed his face next to it, and poked two fingers out the eye sockets. "What'd'ya think? Doberman?"

"I'd say canis assholus," the doctor growled. "You, not them."

"Why don't you go watch the road, Eddy?" The trooper had relaxed again. He was in charge, his jurisdiction or not. They all felt it.

The deputy didn't move. "Nothing else in there. For your report," he said, contrite. He was now trying to be helpful. "Just some empty wine bottles, other trash. Nothing worth nothing."

"What name?" Blake finally asked, biting the cigarette in his teeth and positioning the clipboard to write on.

"Danny," the cop said. "Guess that's all."

"Danny Doe," Blake said as he wrote.

The trooper brightened. "Hey, Will? You still here?" The small man shuffled into the light. It hurt his eyes and he pulled the woman's hat down over his forehead. "You know his real name?" The trooper also had his pen ready.

"Danny's all I know," Will muttered. "Dogstar Danny. Can I get my ten-spot now?"

"What do you know about these bones?" Eddy asked. "What was ol' Danny? Some kind of nut?"

Will looked up from under the brim, wary of Eddy. "Oh, he just liked'em."

"Where'd he get them?" the cop asked. He thought about hunger. They ate dogs in Korea. His stomach clenched. "Did he steal people's dogs?"

"Naw." Will frowned. "Folks was always bringing their dead dogs out here and throwin'em out. Didn't wrap them up or nothing. Just drove up yonder," he pointed toward a high point on the gravel road, "tossed them off in the trash. Danny'd get them and bury them. After a while, he'd dig them up. Take the heads, you know. They was all clean from the worms and stuff. Just skulls and bones. He liked to look at them. Called them his only real friends."

"There's a county ordinance against that," Eddy suggested. "S'posed to take them to the incinerator out south of town."

"That's why they come at night," Will said. "Didn't want nobody to see, I guess. Danny'd see'em coming, be waiting on them. He'd know what they was doing."

"Nutcase," Eddy said.

"Depends on how you see it." Will grinned at him. He had no front teeth at all. "Folks'd love them dogs. Love them up. Take them for walks and car rides and stuff. They'd feed them dogs like they was part of their families, Danny always said. Feed them, take them to fancy dog barbers. Even dress them up in sweaters and hats and shit. Then they'd die, and they'd bring them out here at night when nobody was around, and they'd just dump them. Danny felt sorry for them. Said they deserved better. I guess that's why he done it. Couldn't bear to see the rats get them."

"Danny the Dog Man," the trooper chuckled.

"Dogstar Danny." Will laughed, too, but nervously, weakly. He was shifting his weight back and forth, brushing his arms across his chest. Everyone else had a warm coat, but his oversized garment was threadbare, out at the elbows. He was shivering. "He liked the Dog Star. Said it was his star."

They all looked up automatically.

"Right there." Will pointed up into the lighted night, but no one could see beyond the canopy of the floodlamps' glare. "He liked to come out and lie down and look up at it." They stared silently at the firmament. "Can I have my sawbuck, now? It's cold. I can get a room with a ten-spot down at Ethyl's."

"That fleabag?" Eddy said. "Shit. I wouldn't bury a dog there. Place should be condemned."

Will shrugged. "It's warm and it's indoors," he said.

"Would be condemned," Eddy went on, "if she wasn't banging half the city council."

"You promised me a ten-spot," Will whined.

"Well, it's too late to buy a bottle," the trooper said, then reached into his pocket and pulled out two bills and handed them over. Will took the money and shuffled off.

"I'll give you a ride back to town," the cop called, but the little man kept going, across the garbage heap, into the darkness.

The cop drifted back over to look at the body. A blanket was folded across the abdomen. Pieces of twine and wire were neatly coiled on the chest. They had served in the place of buttons, the cop realized. The naked black toes stuck out like individual obscenities. How many miles had they walked? the cop wondered. A filthy necktie lay off to one side. The cop remembered Danny always wore a necktie, even in the hottest weather. He looked again at the fingers. They were long and straight where they protruded from the ragged gloves. The nails were silver in the light, almost pure against the grime of the skin beneath them. The cop suddenly saw them gripping the steering wheel of a big car—a Cadillac, one of the old ones, with huge fins, holding it tight but confidently. He saw a red tie—why red? he wondered—but it had to be red. Red silk, with an old-fashioned print—knotted tightly up against a starched white collar, custom made. Sharkskin suit. Alligator shoes. Snap-brim hat with a wide ribbon-band. Fancy shit. High roller. Sinatra on the radio. A half-dressed blonde bimbo in the seat next to him. Tits and ass, a roll in his pocket that would choke a horse. The world was his oyster. He was a star. The vision evaporated when the cloud of his breath hit it. Now, he saw the greasy collar of a woolen shirt bunching the wattles of Danny's neck beneath the matted beard. The eyes were half open again. He turned away.

What kind of man lived in a dump but took the time and care to put on a necktie? he wondered. Tears came up in his eyes and he quickly wiped them away. He had no idea why that happened. He was embarrassed, didn't want the others to see.

"You know, there was a story for a while that he was a really rich dude," Eddy said.

"I heard that," Blake put in. "Banker or something from Atlanta."

"New Orleans," the cop corrected. "Oil man."

"I heard stockbroker." Eddy was irritated. It was his story. He rolled his cigar around in his mouth, rocked on his heels. The dog skulls lay at his feet. "And it was Mobile, not New Orleans. Went bust in the depression."

"Got fed up one morning while he was riding the elevator up to his office in one of those big buildings down there." The cop spoke up as if he hadn't heard the deputy but was just picking up the thread of their thoughts. "Came right back down again. Just walked away and left everything. Wife, kids, family. Just drifted till he got here, and he stayed."

"I heard he went bust," the doctor said. "But it wasn't the depression. He lost it all in a big scandal. Women and drugs. Gambling."

"I remember, now," the deputy's voice rose. "I heard he was held up, robbed, and beaten—no, that's not right. He was kidnapped—"

"His wife was kidnapped," the doctor interrupted. "Wife and kid or something like that." Blake shook his hand as if to clear the icy air of doubt and poor memory. "He sold everything he had to pay the ransom, but they killed them, anyway. So he just walked away. Left everything. It was Memphis, not Dallas, now that I think about it. Maybe Nashville or Little Rock, maybe St. Louis, one of those places—no, it was Memphis. I'm sure." He suddenly rubbed his eyes. "Give me another smoke."

The highway patrolman was writing it all down. "Nutcase," he said to himself.

"I've heard that story," the cop said, shaking his head as he handed Blake a cigarette, then passed one to the trooper and took one himself. "You guys'll owe me a pack." The trooper lit them, again. For a moment, they stood, silently adding lung-cooled gray smoke to the vapor of their breaths. The cop shook his head. "I've heard all of it. Who the hell knows? There were lots of stories. He never said that I heard of. He's just always been here." He looked at the ember glowing in his fingers, studied it as if it were a miniature sun. "Doesn't matter much now. Just another dead bum." He sighed deeply, and a gush of frosty breath filled the circle the men had formed.

"Naw," the deputy said. "It don't matter, and that's the point." He puffed hard on the cigar. "I'm gonna sort of miss him, though. Always rooting around in the garbage. Hell, he was better than a watchdog around some places on the edge of town. Nobody'd fool around if Danny was back there digging around, likely to see them, turn them in for two bucks."

"He's been a part of this town long as I can remember," the cop said again.

"Yeah," the highway patrolman nodded. He put his notebook away, and for a moment they stood, finished their cigarettes, listened to the other officers and deputies out by the cars talking. The squawk of a radio occasionally broke through.

"Well, I'm done here," the doctor said.

"You got a for-sure cause of death?" The trooper pulled his notebook out, again.

"You want an autopsy, I can do it tomorrow," Blake said. "My money's on the heart, though. Maybe stroke, maybe something else. Probably had the DTs. I took some blood. I'd guess it's eighty proof. He wasn't stabbed or shot or anything, but you can smell the booze. Cheap wine, anyway. No foul play or blunt instrument, as they say on TV. He was just an old guy. Bum. Had to go sometime. Looks like he went better than most of us will. Just went to sleep. Save the county some money just to put him under and forget it."

The cop looked at him once more. "Bum." He let the word issue as quietly as the vapor of his breath. "Kind of old-fashioned. We're not supposed to use it. Call them 'homeless' or some shit."

"Used to call them hobos," Eddy put in. "If you stop riding the rails—you know, moving around a lot—are you still a hobo?"

"Bum," the cop said. "Says it all in a word."

The doctor turned and yelled for someone to bring the stretcher from the ambulance, then went over and spread the blanket over the body. In a few minutes, the corpse was loaded, covered, and wheeled through the miniature mountains of stinking garbage back to the vehicles on the road. The officers unplugged the lights, helped telescope the tripods, wrap the floodlamps, pack up the generator, then store it all away in their cars' trunks. Eddy led the way back to town for everyone but the highway patrolman and the cop, who continued to stand together in front of the shack, watching their flashlight beams rake the weeds and grass at the dump's edge.

"Hell of a way to go," the cop thought aloud again. "In a dump. Middle of the night. Cold. Alone. Wonder if anyone cared?"

"Give me the bag," the trooper said. The cop handed it over. "I'll inventory it and file a report, and your office can have a copy. No need to do much more."

"Didn't think it was your jurisdiction."

His beam found one of Eddy's cigar butts. "It's not yours," he said as he received the bag. "Don't care what that asshole said. Outside the limit. That makes it as much mine as anybody's." His flashlight danced quickly on the cop's face. "Somebody always cares," he added. The trooper thought again of how young the cop looked. They were the same age, about; but he felt older, knew he looked older. And he hadn't been married for twenty years. He'd never been married, never would be. That sucked, he thought.

"There's the Dog Star." The cop pointed with his flashlight, and the trooper's beam joined it. The white streaks quickly evaporated in the stars overhead, and they studied the blanket of twinkling lights without recognizing any single one as something more significant than the others. "Man, you can really see the Milky Way tonight."

The trooper lowered the light. "Coffee?"

"What the hell," the cop said. They started to leave. "Will?" he called, but there was no answer.

"He's hiding out there someplace," the trooper said. "Or he's drunk. Or both."

"Guess he'll be next," the cop said.

"Yeah. Used to be ten or twelve of these guys around here. I guess Will's about the last. He's been around almost as long as Danny. When he goes, that'll be the end of them."

"There's plenty down in Dallas," the trooper said. "More every day." They kept walking. "Danny's the first I know of to die out here, though," the cop went on. "Mostly they die in town. Alleys, doorways, even the hospital."

"Or the jail," the trooper suggested.

The cop nodded, then he stopped walking. "You know, we should have asked him his name. His last name. Will's last name." He turned and bellowed, "Hey, Will! You out there?" Only a scratch and scramble of tiny rodent feet answered him.

"He'll show up," the trooper said. "He's a regular. What's his story, anyhow?"

"Don't know," the cop said. "Some say he owned a mess of car dealerships in Houston or maybe it was Shreveport. Went broke, caught his wife fooling around and shot her and the boyfriend. Did time. When he got out he just started drifting, got here and stayed."

"When was all this?"

"Oh, back in the fifties or sixties. Maybe seventies. If it's right. I also heard he was tied up with a bad land deal out near Odessa. That Billy Sol Estes thing. Or maybe it was the Sharpstown scandal. Can't remember. I also heard he worked for LBJ in the Senate, but he hated niggers, and he got fired when Johnson became president and overheard him making a racist joke. Went to work for Wallace, I heard, till he got shot. But it all could be bullshit. God, it's getting colder. Bet it's way below freezing now."

"Bet this place is a picnic in the summertime. Stinks like hell, now."

"I don't want to die in a dump," the cop said. They stopped and looked at one another, their breaths mingling in the space between them. "Connie's?" the cop asked.

The trooper nodded. "Eddy's right about her rack, you know," he said.

"Being right doesn't stop him from being an asshole."

"Walking penis."

Their voices followed the jabs of their flashlights' beams and the crunching of the soles of their shoes as they made their way out of the dump. In a few minutes, their individual vehicle doors opened and closed, and they drove off into the night.

———

In half an hour, a waning moon rose, drowning the stars in its brilliant slivery shine. In the orb's cold gleam, a thin man's form emerged from behind the tall grasses and swept its way into the lean-to. The moonlight caught and reflected quickly from a wine bottle in his hand as he disappeared behind the dark fabric. There were bumping and scraping sounds from within for a moment or two, then all was quiet except for the scuttling of animals in the garbage. After a while, headlamps could be seen over the mounds of trash that now belched and rumbled and steamed higher into the subfreezing, early morning air. The sounds of the rats and other night creatures of the dump abruptly ceased as the auto stopped and the noise of a trunk being opened was followed by the dull, muffled thud of a small canine body being tossed atop the nearest pile to the road. In a moment, the car's door slammed, and the vehicle's lights stabbed away into the darkness.

BUSH LEAGUE

Katie Becknell smoothed the lines in her skirt and playfully swung her hips back and forth in front of the full-length mirror. "You might have spent a lot of years in the minors," she told herself, "but girl, there's nothing small-time about you now." At forty-four, she was still a good-looking woman, her image confirmed. The odd thing, though, what made her frown suddenly, was the notion that until she hit her forties, she never thought of herself as particularly attractive at all.

"Well, sweetie," she mumbled, "it took a lot of work." She ran her pinky across her lips to smooth out her lip-gloss one more time. "But the results are definitely worth it," she concluded, then leaned in close to check her eyeliner. "The trick to wearing makeup," she lectured her reflection, "is to look like you're not wearing any at all." She smiled brightly, then scowled in disapproval, then crinkled her eyes quizzically, raised her brows in surprise, and stepped back to admire the effect of a smug, disinterested expression. It was a flexible mask, one with a repertoire she had created, practiced, then mastered in all its variety.

No, she thought. Nothing needed. Too many women just pile on a pound or two of base, trowel in some mascara, hit each cheek with a red racing stripe, and then out the door. Not her. She had spent enough time in the right shops and salons in Dallas to figure out how to do it right. The results looked damned good, and this afternoon, she planned to make sure nothing was out of order.

She had changed four times in the past hour. This dress was pink, but not too pink, just right for early spring when flowers were blooming but there was still an edge to the temperature. The skirt flowed perfectly along the outline of her thighs—she worked out, ran three miles four times a week—then stopped at just the right length to accentuate her calves. Good knees, she thought as she took one more turn before the mirror, slender ankles, no varicose veins. Opaque stockings, four-inch heels, dangling earrings—half-carat diamonds set in gold—probably too much for an afternoon . . . an afternoon what? Business meeting? Nope, it was more than that.

The thought made her frown again, but she shook her hair to make sure of the correct lie across her neck, then she smiled. "Reunion," she chirped. That's what it was, a reunion. But not in every sense of the word. It really was a business meeting, although she couldn't allow herself to think of it that way.

She passed down the hall and into the living room, checking for any stray sneakers or random articles of teenage dross left in the wake of either of her children. There was none. Her orders that morning had been strict to both of them to clean the entire front of the house spic and span, and for once they did so. They thought they should have a housekeeper, and they were quick to point out that they were the only kids on the block who had to dust and vacuum. But Katie countered with the fact that their living on that block made the luxury of a housekeeper impossible. It was one of several hundred corners they cut every day just to drive the car they drove, to dress the way they dressed, to live the way they lived.

"So who is this guy?" Phil demanded while he stacked newspapers and magazines. He was tall and lanky, but muscular and quick: born to play ball. He was nothing like Ed, his father, she noticed with a satisfied study of his firm, seventeen-year-old body. A few small pimples dotted his forehead, and bright steel crisscrossed his smile, but quality and high-dollar orthodontics and dermatology ensured both those detractions would be gone before he was graduated in a few weeks' time. He always looked like he was wound up, ready to spring. He had grit, the coaches told her. They nicknamed him "Cobra."

"Just an old friend," Katie sang falsely while she rearranged unique knickknacks over the mantle. No old family photographs, no plaques or trophies or other tacky bric-a-brac, just expensive gimcracks and carefully posed shots of Phil and of Susan, sort of a pretty child, a slightly pudgy young teen, ready to blossom. A cousin, perhaps? That was the question she anticipated. But there were no shots of Phil in uniform, and none of her and the kids together. The perfect blend of studied domesticity and quiet good taste. "We used to be very close."

"Yeah?" Susan gave her a sideways look, almost a sneer. "How close?"

"Just close." Katie tried to keep discomfort from marring her composure, then turned to face her twelve-year-old. Her father was clearly stamped on her features. It was something Katie pretended not to see on a daily basis, but it was always there, like a ghost, mocking her. "We were close friends."

"I'll bet," Susan shot. She resented having to do housework before she left for school, but beneath her scowl, she was enjoying the teasing. She was still too much the baby to be the completely rebellious adolescent, and she was naturally curious about any of her mother's male friends. In her young life, there hadn't been any man in their lives. Ed left before she was born, so she had never had a father. But she listened to too much gossip, and she also watched too much TV. So long as she stayed on the honor roll, though, Katie didn't complain. There would be time for questions and answers later.

"Probably he's the reason Dad left," Phil concluded while he made half-hearted swipes with a dust cloth. He looked at her to see if she would rise to the bait. But that's what it was, bait. He had no memory of Ed at all. To him the word *father* was simply associated with the name on a child-support check.

"Your father didn't leave," Katie corrected in a flat tone. "I threw him out. If you're not going to do that right the first time, then you'll have to do it again. Anyway, it had nothing to do with Mr. Leder." She put her hands on her hips and glared at them. "Or with any man."

That much was true, or at least it was true if she didn't count her ex-husband as a man. And she didn't. He was like old furniture, worn-out carpeting, a clanking refrigerator, something that had outlived its usefulness and then been discarded, no sentimental value wasted on it.

"Now, finish and get out of here. Remember, you're not to come back before dinner. This is a business meeting, and I don't want it interrupted."

They bent to their work, arguing and snickering as Katie once more arranged the room's furnishings for the right effect. They would sit across from each other: he on the sofa, she on the slightly higher chair. She had taken a lot of psychology in college. She knew how these things worked.

The children departed in the stormy middle of an argument over who would have to wash dishes that night. After a final inspection, Katie moved into the kitchen to set up the snack tray. It was mean of her, she knew, but it was too perfect to resist. Finger sandwiches, which Byron would hate, along with tea, which he never drank, a few sweets, which he would probably like, but not enough of them for him to really enjoy himself. Bone china, Waterford crystal, Spanish silver: classy stuff, all costly, all proper. It looked precisely like what she wanted it to be: a tea party, a fine tea party. Byron was strictly a bourbon and beer nuts guy. Scotch was his idea of a class act. No booze today, she promised herself. It was part of her plan.

This was to be the most miserable afternoon of his life, and she was going to enjoy it.

A car door shut somewhere outdoors, and her eyes nailed the wall clock: two thirty. He was early, by a half hour. She remembered that trait of his, to show up before anyone was ready. "Keeps assholes off guard," he always said. "Makes people like you because they think you're anxious to spend more time with them." She was glad she remembered so well. It made things easier. He would be counting on her to be someone who would want to spend more time with him.

She moved back through the living room and peeked through the window. He stood on the sidewalk, his back to her. He was paying Buster, the cab driver. A navy blue raincoat was slung over his arm. He seemed heavier than before, closer to the ground, somehow, but his back and shoulders were familiar. She felt a twinge deep within her, but she suppressed it. A small suitcase and a carry-on bag sat on the sidewalk next to a briefcase.

"Son of a bitch came to stay, didn't he?" she whispered to herself. Her breath fogged slightly on the pane, and she stepped back, studying his form in the afternoon sun while he replaced his wallet, picked up his bags, and started up the walk. The familiarity of him momentarily rocked her, but she quickly recovered and applied a critique. He was balding severely, she noticed, but he was wearing a casual but expensive suit—sporty and nicely tailored, but not sufficiently well cut to hide an expanding middle—white shirt, tasteful tie—green, for the Eagles' colors, no doubt—light-weight Italian loafers. It was the sort of outfit that could be easily converted with a sweater or blazer to a more casual attitude. Take off the tie, roll up the sleeves, and he was ready for a beer at the bar or maybe a tailgate party. "Ever the good ol' boy," she snorted. Ready for anything.

Otherwise, though, he looked the same, and the prospect of his being there, right in her home, in the flesh as it were, frightened her suddenly. She again felt old stirrings, steamy, ghostly feelings that were long dead, a long-forgotten tingling sensation in her abdomen. These, too, she had anticipated, though, and she brought her will to bear, suppressing them, quenching them before they moved from spark to flame.

He stopped for a moment and studied the house's exterior, then swiveled his head to inspect the neighborhood at large. This was not what he expected, she knew. The last time she saw him, she lived in a two-bedroom dump on the wrong side of town. He was in for a few more sur-prises, though. She counted on it, and she was almost exultant to see him behaving precisely as she had planned. The lawn's late spring growth was lush but well trimmed, the shrubs carefully, if irritably, manicured by Phil and two of his friends—no gardener either, she reminded her son—the Mercedes in the driveway too prominently visible to ignore. The damned car cost more than she made in the last two years, but it was a necessary expense. Prosperity wants more of itself. You can't park a five-year-old Chevy in front of a house like this. Her only regret was that he missed seeing Phil's new RAM pickup, a graduation gift presented two weeks in advance. That had nearly busted her.

He stepped forward, then stopped again and contemplated the car. She read what was going through his mind. He had come for something, and he had to find out what they needed, wanted, in order to get it in trade. He couldn't appeal to their needs, she interpreted his thoughts with satisfaction, that much should be clear to him. She hoped that he had counted on doing just that.

———

It had taken years, twelve years to be exact, but she had made it, on her own, without him, without Ed or any other man, either. Working all day, driving damned near two hundred miles three times a week to finish the degree, then scrimping and saving, borrowing carefully and repaying early, cutting every dollar into a hundred pieces every month, trying to make sure each place that needed a penny or two got one. And she had done it. Gradually, she climbed out of the red and into the black. She was successful, now, and she intended to stay that way. Anyone who looked could see that she didn't want or need one damned thing, at least not anything she could get from a man, a married man, in particular. She had focused on her goal so hard that she almost lost sight of her children, of Phil, anyway.

Then, somewhere along the way when she wasn't looking, Phil moved from Little League to the high school varsity team. The boosters called her and astonished her by telling her how good he was. They offered to provide a scholarship for him to attend summer baseball camps in Austin, and as a sophomore, he made the All-State team. Now, in his senior year, he had nine college scholarship offers. And they still had two weeks to go before they played again for the state trophy. Tomorrow, they scrimmaged a team from the next higher division in an exhibition game. That had drawn the pro scouts. And it drew Byron. Somehow, she thought, she had known it would. Somehow, she believed, she had planned all of this for the past ten years.

———

He glanced around again, this time allowing his eyes to linger on the car, then he rolled his shoulders back as if to work out a kink and approached the front porch. It was a familiar gesture, one she'd seen him make a thousand—a hundred thousand—times before. Her throat closed, and she had to look away and swallow hard before returning her gaze to him. His mouth was sealed in the pensive grimace he always wore in her memories. She knew that at the slightest provocation, his lips would part, show those big front teeth formed into what had always been his trademark of victory, a wide smile. But there was another trademark as well, she also knew. Just as easily as they signaled a sure win, they could turn down in a frown of disapproval that could drop her heart into her stomach. That, too, had happened thousands of times before.

But it wasn't just her heart that had so often dropped. He had done the same to hundreds of youngsters who looked to him for approval, for a chance to be more than they were. God, she thought as she studied his portly walk and almost completely bald head, how could everyone have been so foolish? How, indeed, could she have been?

The doorbell chimed, and she stood still for a moment. She felt herself all over with mental fingers. Her tongue sliced out and wet her lips, and a bright smile formed on her face. She moved to the door and pulled it open.

For a moment, they stood like idiot statues, staring at each other through the ornate glass outer door from behind large, false grins.

"Good to see you," he said, at last. "Came straight from the airport, if you call it an airport: two strips of concrete in a cow pasture. Some things never change. Hope you don't mind that I'm early."

"I expected you early," she said, still not opening the door. "You always came early." She curled her mouth up and sighed, wondering if he would catch the pun.

"Yeah." He dropped his smile and his eyes and studied his shoe tops for a moment. "Silly habit, isn't it?"

She was so thankful for the glass between them that she almost reached out and stroked it. She hadn't thought that he might want to touch her, to hug her, to hold her, maybe to kiss her. Old friends did that sort of thing, but they were much more than old friends, and it would have been awkward.

"Come in," she said, taking a breath and at last swinging the door open. "I've been looking forward to this for a month."

It was only a partial truth. She had been looking forward to it for years, for almost twelve years.

He levered his bags past her into the entryway, then stood and inspected the house's interior while she hung his raincoat in the closet. It was small, as houses in that neighborhood went, but it was elegant. She had wanted elegance, and she achieved it. At that moment, she thought, she had less than a hundred dollars in the bank. But what of it? She had what else she needed, and she didn't owe a single thing to anyone.

Just for a moment, while she held the coat and caught the mixture of familiar odors—Old Spice dominated—she wondered if it was only for this moment that she did it. Was any of it for her, for Susan or Phil? She tossed her head—a practiced gesture of nonchalance that showed her jewelry to advantage—and turned to face him.

She was acutely aware of how she looked standing in the opening to the living room, one hand lightly floating in the air, the other graciously down by her side. Every hair was in place, her makeup was perfect, and she was attractive, pretty. She could see it in the way he refused to look directly at her while she watched him. Then she felt his eyes leave the furnishings and rest at last on her.

It was one thing she knew that would be hard: his eyes on her. There had been a time when they followed her every move when they were in a room together. They made her so self-conscious that she would drop things or scurry into the bathroom to check and see if anything was wrong with her clothes or makeup. It wasn't until later that his looking at her made her so hot and wet that she didn't dare wear light-colored pants whenever they were together. It disgusted her now. But then, it had excited her. She thought it was love. So, she believed, did he.

"You got a really nice place here," he said, moving past her and stepping down into the living room. "Can't believe it."

"Why not?" she allowed an edge to sharpen her voice. "Didn't you think I could do it?"

"Course, I did," he amended, but not before a slight blush touched his cheek. "Just meant . . . well, I mean, it's not . . . it's just so different from . . . from—"

"From what I had before," she finished, moving rapidly past him and into the center of the room. She gestured toward the sofa. "I know. It's been a while, and it's taken some doing, but I finally 'made it,' I guess." She enlarged her smile. "Sit," she ordered, and to change the subject, "Let me get us something to drink."

"God, yes," he said, taking his place on the sofa. He immediately reached inside his coat and simultaneously cast his eyes around the room. There wasn't an ashtray in sight. "Thought I'd never get off that plane, and they don't serve anything on these puddle jumpers. Hell, they're doing good to get them off the ground." His eyes fixed on her, then moved up and down, taking her in, drinking up the image of her she had so wanted to present to him. "God, you look great, Katie. Mean it. You really look great."

"What did you expect me to look like?" she sang lightly, but before he could answer or even react, she spun around and walked into the kitchen.

A dancer's move. A graceful exit. There was a grim smile on her face. She felt his eyes on her every step of the way.

———

So, what the hell was she up to? Byron Leder wondered as his eyes roamed around the room. He couldn't let himself look at her again, for every time he did, she glared at him, tried to fix his eyes with hers, hold them, force their minds to lock together the way they used to. That was dangerous. He remembered how they could be at a big party, lots of people, them sitting across the room from each other, not even speaking, yet through their eyes they said it all. It was hot, he thought, and it was great. It was also dangerous as hell. In a way, he remembered, he enjoyed the danger more than the sex. But the sex was all right, too. Or so he thought at the time.

Now, all he was sure of was that things had changed and that she was up to something. Whatever it was was serious, and it probably spelled trouble for him. It wasn't enjoyable, but it was still dangerous.

It had been a long time: eleven, nearly twelve years. The last time he saw her, she was standing in the rain in front of that dumpy little house on the south side, like Lauren Bacall or somebody, crying her eyes out while he drove away. He hadn't completely understood that. She knew the score. What did she want him to do? Take her with him? Say to his wife, "Hey, Paula, you don't mind if I bring my girlfriend along, do you? I mean, she won't eat much, and you two will have so much to talk about." Shit.

So what was this all about now? Tea and finger sandwiches, for Christ's sake! No ashtrays, no booze, just silly small talk about this hick town, probably leading to a series of "remember whozzits?" people he had forgotten so completely he couldn't even picture them in his mind when she mentioned them, and her talking and sitting there with this stupid look on her face, like she was discussing gardening or flower arrangement or something. Jesus.

She had some memory, he'd give her that. The "Remember when we . . ." sentences all ran together in a steady lane of bad memories each of which reminded him of how desperate he had been to leave this town. He noticed, though, that she never hit on one that had to do with them and them alone. That topic she avoided completely.

"So," she said in one of the steady parade of subject-changing transitions she had made since they sat down, "tell me about what you're up to. What brings you back here after all this time?"

"Told you on the phone," he said, genuinely surprised. He had called from Chicago two weeks ago, as soon as he read that the kid made All State for the third season in a row. It was a stupid thing to do, but he decided that facing her all at once, alone and up front, would be better than waiting until the deal went down for them to meet. After he hung up, he had that sick feeling of having made a major mistake. Maybe he should leave the kid to somebody else, he kept thinking. But Phil's stock was high, and Byron was determined to make the best of it.

Should have checked into the motel first, he thought. But then, all the scouts would be there, and he wasn't ready to meet them, not yet, not without a couple of drinks under his belt. And theirs.

"Came to see Phil," he said.

"Phillip," she corrected. "He likes 'Phillip.'" She remembered his annoying penchant for nicknames and diminutives. She had always been "Kathryn" before he started calling her "Katie." Now, she was Katie to everyone.

"Thought he liked 'Cobra,'" he said. She didn't react. He shrugged. "There's the scrimmage tomorrow. Talked to Coach Grissom and he's starting him. Want to see him play, and want to talk to him about representation." He flashed an innocent grin. "You know what I do."

"That's right," she said. "You did say all that on the phone. And you want to see him play." She paused, licked her lips with one quick strike of her tongue. He nearly flinched. "But you also said you wanted to see me first."

He nodded and took another finger sandwich. It fell apart in his beefy fingers. "Kid's got more potential than anybody I've seen since Stan Musial."

"Did you know Stan Musial?" she asked.

"No," he frowned. "Course not. Hell, I wasn't even born when Musial retired. You know that. You know how old I am."

He put the kneaded and shapeless sandwich in his mouth and chewed. It evaporated instantly, and he sipped the lukewarm tea. It was bitter as citrus peel. "Good tea," he smiled thinly.

She grinned. "So, what about Phillip?" she frowned in mock serious-ness. "I guess he's pretty good, huh?"

God, he thought, it was like being in a play. Get the right line, offer the right expression, complement the whole with the right gesture. He was playing a part, all right, but he hadn't seen the script. He had less trouble signing an illiterate PR or a ghetto black, who'd never seen an acre of grass. "I mean," she went on, "I know he's good—for high school—but is he really *that* good?"

"There's six scouts here right now—or there will be—just to see him pitch tomorrow," he said. "The A's, the O's, and the Sox and the Rangers are all here. Expect the Boston guy will be, too, and the Cleveland Indians' 'Hotdog,' Shorty Robarts. But he travels incognito. Doesn't like to adver-tise." He winked. Robarts didn't like to show any interest in a prospect, not till he's champing at the bit, he added to himself, and if the kid's stupid, he'll sign his life away for twenty cents on the dollar just to play in a farm club for a team that has a century lease on the division cellar.

She poured more tea for both of them. "Who else?"

"Well, no National League clubs have shown much interest, or at least they're pretending not to. But they will. The kid can hit and throw. A ninety-mile-an-hour fastball gets everybody's attention, even out here in the bush league."

"Bush league?"

"Yeah. You know. Small towns, Nowheresville, USA. Lots of guys think that because the competition isn't what it might be in the city schools, that the kids are overrated. I think different."

"I know." She gave him a demur smile. "I read that about you."

He frowned. That damned article in *Sporting News,* he remembered. The reporter cozied up to him in a bar, bought him about a dozen drinks, and under the pretense of asking his advice for a story he was writing on emerging players, he grabbed some juicy quotes for a feature on sports agents and their trade secrets.

"The bush league is where the talent is," he was quoted in the article under a quarter-page photograph of him slapping his most recently acquired client on the back. "Too many guys spend all their time hustling big-city kids, because they get all the press. But look at the record. The best players—the phenoms—come out of nowhere. Big old country boys, raised on heavy, hard work, who don't have anything better to do than throw hard, hit hard, and run like hell. Don't tell me. The bush league is where future Hall of Famers grow, and that's where the smart money can be made."

The article pissed him off. It took away the one thing every agent craves: his anonymity. Now, every time he showed up at a game anywhere, he was hounded by would-be players or their parents or even their coaches.

"Who you scoutin' tonight, Byron?" they'd ask him. "Listen, I got this kid who can hit a frozen rope five hundred feet into a hurricane with one eye tied behind him." The scouts were worse. If a scout thought he was even mildly interested in a kid, they'd stumble all over themselves trying to get him to sign before he even thought of the word *agent*. Shit like that had stalked him for two years since the goddamned piece was published. Even she had read it.

"Seems everybody read that damn article," he sighed. "Gotten to the point where I have to make plans in secret. Half the time, the competition gets there before I even know I'm going. Half surprised that I didn't have to stand in line to get past your front door."

"You never had to before." She looked deliberately at her nails. The manicure was perfect.

He pretended to ignore the comment and the discomfort it stirred deep inside of him. "What'll sell them eventually, especially the NL," he went on, "is his .475 average—lifetime, well, three years on varsity, anyway. This year, he's only .425 so far, but that's a slump. Can you believe that?" He sat back and laced his fingers behind his head, forgot he wasn't alone, almost talking to himself. "A .425 slump! Christ!" His mind swam with figures, and he began listing them in the proper order, speaking to her as if she were a skeptical general manager. "He's got the lowest ERA and the most strikeouts in the high school region—number four in the whole goddamn state in both categories, and that's against 5-A pitchers. Also, he's got one of the best pickoff moves I've ever seen. Slick! You add all that to a yearly average of fifteen home runs, twelve stolen bases, and twenty-two—count'em—RBIs, not counting sacs—and you've got yourself one hell of a versatile player. Shit, a pitcher who can hit and run and sacrifice and plays right field when he's out of the rotation! And he's a righty! Jesus, it's like having a half-dozen Hall of Famers rolled into one!

And he's white, speaks English! You just don't find guys like that hanging around a city park."

God, he thought with a shake of his head, I love baseball.

"I guess there's a lot of money involved," she said. He snapped back to where he was, to whom he was speaking, and he lowered his voice and called forth his most earnest tone. He had to sell her before he sold anybody, he knew. If the mother falls, the kid's a can of corn. And of all mothers, he figured he knew this one well enough to know how to make her fall.

"Say we're talking half a mil a year anyway, maybe more, with a signing bonus, and a five-year contract, minimum. If he has the right representation."

"And what do you get?" she asked.

His eyes searched her face once more, then, because he could find nothing there, relaxed. "Fifteen percent. Nothing, if he wants to work without a net."

"Or with a different 'net,'" she smiled slightly, but there was no irony in her voice. "I thought ten percent was the standard."

"Fifteen's my commission." He frowned and stared at her, but her face continued to say nothing. "Who've you been talking to?"

"It's really up to him, you know."

He sat forward. A slight panic pressed behind his eyes, and he felt sweat break out on his forehead. If he'd wasted all this time and money coming out here, he'd kick himself. "What has he said? Is there somebody else sniffing around here?" Maybe he had misjudged her, he thought. Maybe she was playing him. What the hell was going on? Maybe he ought to get the hell out of here and call the kid tonight. Fuck the scrimmage. Somebody else could be clicking his Bic right now. Right now, the kid could be tooling around in a new convertible with a chesty redhead some club had imported. Robarts wasn't above that sort of thing. He'd done it before. Had a whole stable of eighteen-year-old cunts ready to hop a plane at a moment's notice. Called them his "Motor Pool." "Helps to know the type. Know what I mean?" he always said with a wink.

Byron squirmed and fingered his tie. Sitting here and sipping tea was just wasting time. That Mercedes out there ran seventy grand if it ran a penny—so maybe money wasn't an issue—but that's chickenfeed for a down payment on a kid like that. He gave Katie a long look. Hell, he thought, some asshole like Robarts could have paid her off to stall me, wait for the kid to cut his own deal.

He studied her face, but there was a barrier there, something impenetrable. It wasn't familiar to him at all. He didn't expect her to fall into his arms or invite him into the sack or anything—hell, that was over long ago—but he did expect her to be more open, less cagey. For sure, he had expected her to be warm if not willing. Was she running a game on him, or what? What the hell ever happened to "old times' sake"?

She sipped her tea and pretended to wince because it was too hot. He knew better and just as suddenly as it came, anxiety left him. She was acting out a role, just as he was. She didn't know anything, and even if she did, it wouldn't matter. The kid couldn't even talk to a scout before the state finals, not legally, couldn't accept anything, not even a Coke. He could queer himself and his whole team. An agent was different. All they were doing was discussing possibilities. There were no other agents in town. He was almost sure of that.

He thought about the Mercedes again and let his eyes drift around the room. It fit with the house, with her classy clothes and makeup. There was no payoff, at least not recently. On the other hand, there must be something. How much money could somebody like her make in a year in Sticksville? Not much, he guessed. Probably in debt up to her tits.

The thought drew his eyes to her body. She had held up well, he thought. Or she was a master of the foundation garment. He admired the narrow waist and well-rounded breasts beneath the light pink fabric, then he shook off the pitch. He was no rookie, and he wasn't going to swing wild at junk. She delicately fingered a sandwich into her mouth. She was still the key to the whole thing, and she knew it. He was giving too much, losing his edge with her, letting her get too far ahead in the count. It was what he feared he would do the minute he called her. But whatever she was trying to pull off wasn't anything to worry about. She wasn't bright enough to work a dodge, not on him. He was in the bigs now. He could tell when things were hinky, and this setup was too hot, fast, and down the middle to have anything fancy on it.

"So," he said, trying her own conversational technique on her for a change. "What's he like?"

"Who?" Her eyebrows shot up, then relaxed into a crinkle. "Oh, Phillip? Oh, I don't know. He's just a typical teenager. I really don't know much about baseball."

"But what's he like personally? Is he a good kid or what?" Does he have a heart? he wanted to ask. Does he have an attitude? The last thing he needed was a "dude with a 'tude," a kid who knew exactly how good he was, how good he could be. Confidence was great. It could be developed, bartered. But an attitude was like a bad hamstring. It always acted up at the wrong time.

"He's a good boy," she said. "Like his dad in some ways. You do remember Ed, don't you?" She folded her hands in front of her and smiled, but for the first time, he saw a chink in her armor. Her fists were clenched around a napkin, the muscles in her forearm tensed.

"Uh-huh." He drained the china teacup and set it down. Time for a new topic. "So, how've *you* been, Katie? You really do look good. Been one hell of a long time, you know." He offered her his patented scowl, then turned it up into a promising grin. "Say, you got any scotch?"

———

She stood in the kitchen and gripped the edge of the sink. Her fingers turned white with the pressure, but she welcomed the pain. She had given in, and she hated herself for it. Every time she looked at him, she tried to conjure the image of what he used to be. She had counted on keeping that image in front of her, for she wanted to hate it as much as she hated his memory. But hatred wouldn't come. All she could feel was a kind of breathless anxiety, a sense of something happening that was outside her control.

All the little traits of his came back. His eyes—those damned eyes—feasting on her, lingering on her body, and just when she noticed, moving back to her face. That smile. That goddamned smile. That tendency he had never to say "I," in any sentence, seeming to avoid referring to himself, but somehow, always keeping attention on him and only him. God, how that infuriated her.

She wanted to wound him, but he wouldn't take the blow. He seemed to be dancing just outside her reach, taunting her, daring her to feel something for him, to react to him.

There was a long, narrow mirror on the internal wall over the sink, her attempt to make the area seem brighter, more spacious, create the illusion of a window. "Damn," she said to her reflection, "he probably figures the next step's to the bedroom." Well, he's wrong, she silently added. He couldn't be more wrong.

When they started, Byron was the assistant high school coach, not so young and kind of paunchy even then, with a receding hairline and a bulldog's personality. She was fresh out of high school, a teacher's aide, mother of one child and, it usually seemed, wife to another. She and Ed hadn't made love since Phil was conceived, and from all she could tell, Ed hadn't missed it any more than she had. But none of that lasted long. Byron moved rapidly up the ladder in the high school's athletic office. When Coach Gray had a heart attack and resigned at midyear, Byron stepped in. He took teams to state four years in a row. At the same time, she was promoted to a clerical position in the principal's office and was in charge of keeping records on the athletes' grades. They worked together often. First it was just long, lingering, almost painful looks across his office's desk. They attended the same Methodist church, had several friends in common, and were together a lot, particularly during the summer, at barbeques and at the lake for youth fellowship outings in the summer. Then she dieted severely—made herself ill—just to look good in a swimsuit. She told herself it was for Ed, then told herself it was for her. But finally, one night when she stayed behind with Byron to lock up the field house and he drove her home, she realized that it was for him. It was raining hard, and they parked in front of her dumpy little house and waited for it to let up. There, alone in the dark, and suddenly talking openly about how they felt about each other, she admitted to herself that it had always been for him. Words soon gave way to kisses, and before the rain quit, they had steamed up the windows and each other. Embarrassed, suddenly, they pulled apart and wiped the fog away, half expecting Ed to be peering in with a shotgun in his hand.

They agreed it was too adolescent, too stupid to do anything about it. And it was dangerous. They agreed to laugh it off. But she loved him. There was no way around that.

It was months later, another rainy afternoon after school—it always seemed to be raining when things happened to them—when she took some athletes' grade records by for him to sign. She hung around his office, talking, then naughtily smoking cigarettes and sipping cheap whiskey he kept hidden in a locked drawer of his desk. Finally, they were touching and ultimately half-falling into a major petting session right on the floor. They wound up in a giggling, sweating tangle on a blue workout pad in the girl's weight room. Every time afterward she always thought she could smell the sweet-and-sour odor of a gym about him when they made love.

They didn't risk meeting on the school grounds after that, but they didn't laugh it off again. For the next several years they met in motels in nearby towns, abandoned barns in forgotten pastures, and vacationing friends' houses and apartments whenever they could find one. They couldn't stay away from each other, couldn't get close to each other at school or anywhere without finding some reason to touch. They made love in the backseat of each other's car, other people's cars, once at church, on the sofa of the pastor's office during an Easter Sunrise Service while they were supposed to be counting offertory receipts. When they came together, they devoured each other. They didn't just kiss and embrace, they tried to absorb each other's bodies. They traced every inch of skin with their tongues, knew one another's likes and dislikes, one another's weaknesses and strengths. They doted on themselves, and they behaved like shameless teenagers in love.

And all the time they were married, to other people. But it was all right, because she loved him, and she thought he loved her.

But that was twelve years ago, she insisted to her fingers that were now unbearably painful in their grip on the porcelain sink. Twelve years ago. She was married to Ed and had a kid, and he was married to Paula, who was childless but who "needed him for her sanity," he told her. And that was the way things were. There was no way it would ever be anything more than what it was: a dirty, tacky little affair.

Then it became less. He got a job offer as hitting coach for the Tulsa Drillers, and he was gone. He wrote to her, sent her meaningless, noncommittal letters in plain envelopes to the school. They looked like bills or junk mail, and that's precisely what they were, she thought: worthless pieces of unsigned writing scrawled on a legal pad, full of chitchat and his personal hopes for himself. Nothing about her, nothing to remember, nothing to hold onto. After Tulsa, he moved to Oklahoma City—assistant manager, but AAA, now. That lasted two seasons when he decided the air above him was behind glass—he didn't have the connections for the bigs, he wrote her—so he hired on as a scout for the Padres and went to California. Then he moved to the Dodgers, and then to New York to work for the Yankees. Then he was on his own, an agent.

The letters became notes, then postcards, then they stopped entirely.

She had seen the article about him. And she had memorized the quote, cut it out and kept it. He knew the bush league, all right. He was strictly bush league, himself.

She stood back from the sink and fought for a grip. All of this had been planned so carefully, and it was now threatening to fall apart. He had been here less than an hour, and she had already found him an ashtray—even suggested that he might want to smoke—and now she was out here looking for a bottle of "whiskey or something." What did he want? she wondered. Was he really only here to make Phillip his client? Or did he want something more? It was hard to tell, harder to push to find out.

"Scotch? I really don't know," she had answered his question curtly. But he didn't blink. "I don't keep it regularly. Not anymore."

"Hey, Katie," he had said with that same little smirk that used to make her heart turn over and her stomach feel hot and hollow. "Not particular. Something else'll do. Beer? Wine? Just can't drink any more of this tea."

And he sat there with a cigarette in his hand and that stupid little smile on his face and expected her to jump up and say something like "Oh, I'm sorry, I didn't even think. I mean—I'm just so stupid," or something and then to go out to the kitchen and pretend to search for something. And that's exactly what she said, and that's exactly what she did. A bottle of Dewar's and a bottle of Wild Turkey sat on the counter. They were both new, both full, both bought last week. Why? Because she knew he liked whiskey? That wasn't in the plan, that was never part of the plan. She put them on a tray, added a small bucket of ice, a pitcher of water, two highball glasses, and swung through the doors back out into the living room.

His face brightened immediately, and her heart jumped, just as it always had. She loathed herself. Then she realized what she had just told him. If she didn't keep liquor on hand, then where did this come from? Her mind raced, trying to find a convenient lie. Nothing seemed plausible. She'd just tipped her hand, she thought. This was a mistake. She needed to stick with the plan, take charge again, stop merely reacting.

If he noticed the quality of the liquor selection in front of her, he didn't show it. He immediately took charge and opened the ice bucket and began pouring two highballs.

"What if," she said as she accepted her drink, "Phillip wants to go to college or something? What if he doesn't want to play professional baseball?"

A cloud formed over his face as he sipped the scotch rocks. The liquor was the exact color of his eyes, she noted. "Everybody wants to play professional baseball," he said. The coach he once was emerged. He suddenly looked ten years younger. "You can't tell me there's a kid who ever picked up a bat and ball who hasn't wanted to be Mickey Mantle or Joe DiMaggio. Your kid could be another Sandy Koufax, Vida Blue, Nolan Ryan."

"Well, he might want to play ball in college. His father said—"

"Ed?" he cut her off and grinned. "What does Ed know about baseball *or* college for that matter?"

She felt herself redden with anger. Byron was right, of course: Ed didn't know anything about either. Hell, she thought, Ed wouldn't recognize Phillip if he met him on the street, wouldn't care enough to say anything to him if he did recognize him. The one time he'd come home to see him, he never did. All he did was shuffle around out in the hospital parking lot, smoking cheap cigars and sneaking drinks out of a glass flask. She was bluffing, and Byron caught her. Bad move, she lectured herself. Get it right or quit trying.

"Anyway," Byron went on, "college'd screw him up. Played enough with metal bats and small-timers who can't hit or throw. Time he moved up. Can take classes, work on a degree in the off-season, if he wants. Lots of guys do that."

"Do they?" She arched an eyebrow, found some strength inside her and tried to use it.

"Yeah, sure. Some even make doctor or lawyer."

"Or coaches or agents?" she purred, but he didn't react.

"Listen." He narrowed his eyes and almost whispered. "It's a hell of a lot easier to get through life with a couple of million in the bank than with some knocked-up coed on your arm and no way to pay her off."

The shock of his remark hit her like a wave of cold water. "That's disgusting," she shot at him and stood up. She found indignation to be a comfortable ally, a welcome defense against the other emotions assaulting her. "And you're talking about my son." She paced a bit, now enjoying herself once more. "You've never even met him. He's not some stupid jock."

"Talking about athletes," Byron said, leaning back and opening his hands. "Face it: College is fine for the football and basketball boys. Toughens them up, gets them ready for the pros. Separates the men from the boys, and the scholarships are worth the money. Perks, too. Also get a lot of press, TV coverage. All helps in the draft. But baseball players get shit for scholarships, no perks, and never make any TV outside of cable. Can wind up injured or worn out by the time they're ready for the minors. Baseball's a young man's game. Hell, half the players in the league peak before they're twenty-one."

"Is that right?" She faced him. Her voice was still indignant. Studiously, she cocked one heel back and rested her weight on one hip. The entryway mirror opposite her revealed the pose to be perfect for her mood.

"No," he grinned and sat back. "But it's a damned good sales pitch. Look, he wants to go to college, fine. Can be worked out. He wants to get laid regular and safe, that's okay, too." He put up a hand, palm out, stopping her protest in her mouth. "Boy gets to be a man quick in college or baseball. Know how to protect him from everything from athlete's foot to AIDS. Just let me handle it."

"Fuck you," she said, still standing, still holding the position.

He said nothing but just smiled even wider. "So, anyway, how's old Ed doing these days?"

———

She doesn't know one thing about the kid, Byron told himself as he watched her calm herself, return to the sofa, and fix a second round of drinks. Her own son, and she doesn't even know what's going on in his head. Probably thinks he's still a virgin, something he hadn't seen in a high school senior athlete in twenty years. At least, not in a good one. Not a trophy or photograph of him in uniform around anywhere in sight. He bet she hadn't seen him play more than a dozen times. She was sitting on gold and didn't even know enough to have it assayed. Instead, she was fouling off the junk, playing for time, and she knew that he knew it. This was turning out to be easy, a pop-up.

He sat back and looked around the room once more. What had she done to herself? When he left, she was poorer than Job's goat. Trailer trash in a clapboard house. Glorified file clerk at the school. Ed worked a double shift at the mill just to keep them out of hock. It was a good thing, he thought with an inward smile. Otherwise, they'd never have had all that time together.

He accepted the drink from her, noticed her perfect pink nails, the tennis bracelet dangling on her arm. Her hair looked soft and natural— no dye. No matter where she came from, she was a good-looking woman, he thought, better looking than she had ever been before, that was sure. And there was something else, something hard about her, not unattractively hard, but taut, firm, appealingly solid. When he first came into the house, he thought it was confidence, self-assuredness, the kind of thing he recognized easily in a pitcher who was down four runs in the seventh, but who knew he could go the distance if only he could get the hitting to back him up. But who was the coach here? Who was writing the checks? It was a safe bet somebody was. You don't tell a major league agent to fuck off unless there's somebody in the dugout giving the signs.

"I'm sorry," she said at last. She sipped her drink. "That wasn't called for. It's been a long time, Byron. Things have changed."

"Haven't told me what you do," he said and lit another smoke.

"What I do?" she looked surprised. "Why, I thought I'd mentioned that. I'm in business. I do interior design."

"Interior design." He looked for the fortieth or fiftieth time around the room. The walls were dark blue and trimmed in off-white. It was a fine effect, neat. It made the room seem smaller, more intimate. The furniture, the wall hangings, even the junk on the mantle made the entire place look like a fancy, high-dollar gift shop. It wasn't warm or personal, just perfect, tasteful and carefully planned. There was no hint that anyone actually lived there. It made him uncomfortable. He was glad she finally broke out the booze and let him smoke. He wasn't sure he could have stood it much longer. He wondered if the whole house was just as well appointed. He wondered briefly about the bedroom, then forced the thought away. "You do good work," he muttered.

"I'm good at it," she said, then added, "I think. After . . . after Ed and I split up. That's what happened, you know. We split up."

"Caught him tomcatting around?" He hoped it was true, but he wasn't sure why he wanted it to be.

She lifted her chin. "No," she said. "I just came home one night and decided the sight of him sitting there in his underwear, drinking beer, smoking cigars, and watching TV was too much. I told him to leave, and he left. That simple."

He could believe it. Ed was never the brightest of men. It was a trait he counted on finding in Phil. "He just left? Just like that?"

"He left. I've only seen him twice since. Once in court, once when Phillip had his appendix out. He lives in Colorado now. I'm not sure . . . oh, what difference does it make?" She sipped her drink.

"None. What'd you do, then?"

"I went back to school. Midwestern University." He raised his glass in acknowledgment. Small-time school. Middling-fair team from time to time. Nothing recently worth a second look, though.

"Then I went to work for Naomi Havermeyer. You remember her?"

"Havermeyer's Furniture and Appliances," he recalled. Nice lady, took over the business for her husband's family after he was killed in Vietnam. Pilot of some kind, spent some time in the minors right out of college, then got drafted, or he enlisted. Didn't matter. Dead was dead. And a ready-made upscale business wasn't something you turned down. She moved into town from somewhere in Florida. Had a kid, he remembered, her youngest of five. Played fair second base: decent glove, no bat at all. He suddenly remembered she had good legs, looked great in shorts, especially for an older woman.

"Right. Well, she wanted someone to go out to people's homes and do them up. I was working on the degree, and, as you say—or I said—I guess I was good at it."

"Must pay pretty good," he said, glancing out the window. "Isn't a cheap neighborhood."

She blushed, looked away, and then faced him. "Anyway, her children all grew up, moved away. She wanted to leave, too, go back home to her family. New Orleans. So I made an offer, and I own the store now. I do design, sell furniture, carpeting, all of it. I coordinate rooms, sometimes whole houses. Turnkey jobs. For a price."

"Didn't know there was still that kind of money out here in the sticks," he smiled. Shit, he wondered seriously. Was there? Maybe he shouldn't have left, after all. Maybe he should have hung around, opened up a sporting goods store, sold rifles to jerks who wanted to shoot Bambi, bats and balls to kids who wanted to be the next A-Rod or Derek Jeeter, retired early. It had to be better than following the league around like a hound on a bad scent, chasing around some snot-nosed kid with a good arm who couldn't care less about all the work that went into contract negotiations. Half the time, the ungrateful punks fired him if he didn't get some indecent figure more than twice what they were worth. Half the time, he didn't know what city he was in. More than half the time, he didn't care.

"Oh, there's money," she said, now pouring herself another highball, sitting back and holding it, not yet drinking. "Not spread around as much as it used to be, but it's still here. Still around."

"Got it," he said. He didn't, but it didn't matter. Now the image of the small town around them came fully to his mind. He remembered why he had wanted to leave so badly, how ambitious he was then. He remembered the games played under lights so dim that half the time no one could find the ball if it was hit to the deep outfield. A field that filled up like a toilet bowl every time it sprinkled. Weedy outfield, rusting backstop, broken benches in the dugouts. Bush league, he thought again. Couldn't even have a beer after a game, not legally, anyway. Another year in this place and he'd have gone nuts locked up in the sticks with no way out.

But now, ironically, that's the way he made his living, combing through the mesquite and prairie grass for some kid who was too dumb to throw a meaningful glance but who could hit a human palm from sixty feet, six inches, or connect a bat with a ball the size of an apple whizzing past him at one-eighth the speed of sound. But visiting places like this was different from being there all the time, under the watchful eye of everyone.

More than anything else, she reminded him of all that, of everything he had been, of everything he never wanted to be again, and of everything they had done in spite of those watchful eyes. He felt too warm, now. Must be the whiskey, he thought. All of a sudden and not for the first time that afternoon, he wanted her. The thought surprised him. But he knew it was true: he wanted her badly. His eyes drifted down to her slender ankles, lingered on the arch of her foot, then climbed up to her knees, finally resting in the narrow dark space where her thighs crossed beneath the hem of her dress. Expensive clothes, he assessed, and he again noted that she was in shape, had lost weight, looked really younger than she had been then. Oh yes, he thought, he did want her. But not the way she was now: hard, sure of herself, cunning. He wanted her the way she was before: soft, pliable, eager. But that woman was gone. He wasn't sure exactly who it was who sat across from him now.

She had moved up, he thought. She wasn't the same easy risk he had known before. Now, he realized, she was infinitely more dangerous, but this time, the danger didn't have the old appeal. He drank down his drink and sobered his thoughts, collected himself, focused his attention on the game at hand.

"So," he said, once again shifting the subject. "Guess you know, Paula's dead."

———

His words hit her hard. She was blindsided, frozen, and for the briefest of moments she felt herself fluster, go limp inside, search for the response she had planned to give when he mentioned Paula, only to realize that it wasn't there.

"Dead?" she asked simply, forgetting to work her quizzical mask. "When?"

"Three years ago. Car wreck," he replied, and he leaned forward and replenished his own drink. "Drunk driver, wrong side of the road. Raining like hell. Killed instantly."

"Oh, Byron," she gushed out. "I'm sorry. So sorry." She felt like crying all of a sudden, but she wasn't sure why. She fought it, forced it back. This was not going right, she thought. It just wasn't.

"It's okay," he said. "For me, anyway. Were getting a divorce. Hadn't seen her in six months, hadn't lived with her for more than a year. Things weren't good, hadn't been for a long time. Was on the road a lot. And there were other men. Ballplayers, mostly. Kids." He chuckled, then added sadly, "Turned out, she had a thing for the hot corner."

"I'm sorry," she repeated. She didn't know what else to say. She had barely known Paula.

"Hey, really. It's okay. Tell you the truth, things weren't good long before I left here. Not between Paula and me. In a way, you were what kept us together."

"Me?" That was outrageous, she thought, eyeing him carefully. "I kept you together?" She felt a prickle of perspiration breaking out on her neck.

"Yeah, in a way. Hey, I had you, you had me. Paula and I were content in sort of not having each other. You and Ed . . . well, never was sure about Ed."

"I think I know what you mean," she muttered. Her thoughts were racing, and she was now discernibly moist under her arms. A sudden drop of sweat drained down her side. Above everything, she had counted on him and Paula still being together, on things being like they were before, of his wanting her and her resisting him, putting him down, showing him she didn't need him. She planned to take the moral high road. And now, there was nothing to stop them. Nothing at all. It was as if a huge abyss had opened in front of her, and she felt herself tottering on the edge, threatening to fall in. Or did she want to leap? She had to concentrate to keep her breath from shortening. Once more, she felt his eyes on her, in the old way, the way that made her so uncomfortable and at the same time the way that made her so proud to be his lover, so content to be in his mind and heart. The tingling in her abdomen returned, and her mouth felt unbearably dry.

"So, anyway, thought you might have known. Mean, it was in the papers. Happened in Dallas, well, Arlington, really."

"I didn't know," she said, struggling to keep her voice steady. "And I am sorry, Byron."

"No big deal," he said. "Three years is a long time. Got over it. Things were going downhill for a long time before that. You know how that is."

"Was there . . ." she trailed off. Then she stood and walked slowly to the window, grappling with thoughts that now swirled through her mind. There was no pose this time. "Was there, uh, was there another . . . anyone else? After me, I mean?" She took a breath, hating herself for asking this. "Another woman?" She wasn't sure what answer she wanted. She glanced at the face of the mantle clock. Three forty-five, she thought. A half hour ago, she would have been more certain of the answer she wanted than she would have been about asking the question. Now, she didn't know. But when he looked up, his eyes caught and held hers. She felt her mask slipping away, revealing the hurt she had felt for years, the yearning she ached through every time she remembered his driving away in the rain, leaving her pregnant, longing for him, and knowing she would never see him again. It was all there now, she knew, openly revealed, but this time she didn't look away.

"No," he laughed lightly and without feeling. "No, Katie. There never could have been any other 'other woman' but you."

"Oh, Byron," she said, returning to the chair too fast and bumping the table. Her drink turned over onto the carpet. "I don't know what to think, what to say." She glanced automatically down at the spill, decided she didn't care, and she tossed her hand, wiggling her fingers in nervous dismissal, then rose again and stalked to the window. Was he going to ask her back? Was there another man? There wasn't, hadn't been. Should she lie about that? Make up something, invent somebody? What was her next move? Her mind was a whirlwind of confusion, her emotions more torn than if they were paper rent by a storm. Outside, she noticed, thick clouds had darkened the afternoon, and the room was gloomy, now cold and hostile. But she felt steamy, too warm by half. The air between them seemed dense, almost foggy. She was sticky. When she looked back at him, he was only a shadow on the sofa. He still hadn't moved. He wasn't going to ask.

"Don't need to say anything," he said as if he read her thoughts. "Mean, getting too old for that shit. Come to think of it, were too old for it when we were doing it." He drew in smoke, making his cigarette glow brightly in the gloom. Now was the moment, she thought. "I was, anyway," he sighed out a gray cloud. Ice clinked against his empty glass. "Anyhow, came here to talk to you about Phil. Phillip. About his future."

You didn't come here to see me, she mentally translated. She now knew: He wasn't going to ask.

"And we've done that." He glanced at his watch. "Probably ought to be going. Need to check in, take a shower, grab a bite. Ask you to join me, but it wouldn't look good. The scouts. Anyway, want to see him play before we talk about anything." He ground out his smoke, set the glass back on the tray, and stood.

"You think you'll change your mind. About Phillip, I mean?"

"Reading about a player isn't the same as watching him, if that's what you mean," he said. "Want to see if college would be the best thing for him. Is for some, no matter what they say. Was kidding, you know, about the girls. Might need to season for a while. Might not be ready for the big leagues or even the minors. Not yet."

"So, you're going, and you might not even talk to him at all?"

"Yeah," he said. "Hey, don't take it so serious. He's young. Got a lot of chances left if this one doesn't take. Thought maybe, I get to know him, help him if it comes down to having to make a choice. No charge," he added with a grin. "For old times' sake."

"I appreciate it," she said in a monotone.

"Mean, college might be right. Won't stand against what you want, anyway. You're the mother, right?"

"Right."

"And, hey, college might be the ticket. The CWS tourney always helps. And hell, he might need to learn a trade. Place to fall. Truth is, they all do, sooner or later." He stepped toward her so the purple light of the window fell fully on his face, on his smile. "Mean, hell, there's worse things than coaching. Or being an agent." He winked, then turned away.

"I wanted you to meet Susan," she said.

"Susan?"

"My daughter." *Our* daughter, she mentally amended, but she had recomposed her face, showed nothing. "She's twelve, or soon will be. Next month, in fact." She gestured gracefully toward a framed photograph.

"Didn't know you had a daughter." He glanced quickly at the picture, then away. "Congrats! Good-looking kid." He stepped toward the entryway, then gave her a narrow look. "You said you didn't want another baby."

"Did I?" Did he suspect? she wondered. Did he know? Care? Her underarms were awash.

"Twelve, huh?" he asked, his eyes shooting to the door.

"Next month."

"That's great. Maybe meet her at the scrimmage." He gave her a direct look, and his teeth formed once more into his memorable smile. "Pleased you've done so well. Really! But got to scoot. Scouts'll be crawling all over the motel." He glanced out the window, then pulled a cell phone from his pocket, flicked it open. It was one of the fancy ones, like a minicomputer. "Need to call a taxi," he explained.

"*The* taxi," she said. "There's only one. Never was more than one. You know, Buster's Cab Service. He still runs it by himself. Doesn't advertise. I'll call him for you." Now she felt numb inside. Dead. A silence grew up in the room, and neither of them moved. She wanted him to come to her, to reach out and take her in his arms. She realized it was what she wanted all along, more than anything. She had told herself her wanting it was so she could reject him, stiff-arm him away from her, laugh at his embarrassment. But that was a lie. She had only made it up to make all of this easier. She had never needed him more than she did right then, but she couldn't make herself move toward him. She only stood there.

He coughed, cleared his throat, and then walked to the closet. "Right," he said. "Thanks." There was one more beat of silence. "Wait out by the curb."

He found his coat and pulled it on against the gathering rain clouds, collected his bags, and stood for a moment in the open door.

"Damn good to see you again, Katie," he said. "Sure we'll be seeing a lot of each other, if Phillip's agreeable."

"I think he's got his heart set on college," she said. She meant it. He hadn't made any commitments yet, but she had *her* heart set on college, and that was going to have to do, whether he liked it or not. And he was not going to be a coach, either. She would see to that.

"Money has a way of changing a kid's mind."

"Not that boy."

"Well, see you—and Phillip and, uh . . ." He nodded toward the picture, although he couldn't see it from where he stood.

"Susan," she said.

"Right! Susan. See you at the park. Tomorrow." He looked out once more.

"Yeah," she said, distracted. "Tomorrow."

"If it doesn't rain. Remember that rain'll fill that place up like a, uh, punch bowl."

"I guess it's still not much of a park."

"Well, what do you expect out here?" he asked with a glance toward the sky. "Bush league, remember?"

"Yeah," she said.

He gave her a small, almost boyish grin, then turned and strolled down the sidewalk.

"Nice ride," he called, but she was shutting the door and pretended not to hear him.

She phoned Buster, told him to hurry, made herself another drink, a stronger one, then went to the window, stood back a bit to watch him stand on the curb. He removed a small umbrella from his briefcase and held it up when it began to sprinkle. He looked older than he had before, she now thought, a lot older—and wearier. His feet seemed too big, and his paunch now hung loosely over his belt. He wasn't really attractive, probably never had been. He was ugly. Bald. How could she ever have found him desirable?

He looked through the drizzle up and down the street with a firm expression of patronizing evaluation. She could read his thoughts. Small-town attempts at finery, small fish in an even smaller pond. God, how contemptuous and self-righteous he was! Thank God, she hadn't let on how she felt, hadn't weakened and shown him a thing. She had made it without him, and regardless of what he had done, of who he had become, he had to see that she didn't need him—that Phillip didn't need him—that she had put him behind her once and for all. Thank God, she had stuck to her game plan, that she stayed strong.

Byron stood uncomfortably on the sidewalk, his flight bag over his shoulder. He put the suitcase down on the rapidly wetting concrete, rested his briefcase on top of it, and tried to shield both with the small umbrella. He glanced quickly back at the house, saw her at the window, watching him, and he self-consciously looked out from under the umbrella, inspected the thickening clouds. Keeps up, it'll cancel the scrimmage, he thought, which meant this whole trip was wasted. More than two grand, by the time he figured airfare and the charter here from DFW. No return until day after tomorrow, either. Three days shot.

It was a waste, he thought; had been from the start. Good as the kid might be, he wasn't worth it. Dealing with her would be impossible. She'd gotten shrewd, clever. She'd be maneuvering all the time, trying to flank him, tease him, work the kid like a decoy, try to draw a wild throw. Never would work.

He shook his head, lit a cigarette under the cover. She hadn't heard about Paula, he mused. Not that it mattered. Maybe she figured he knew about Ed, about her success. He glanced once more up and down the street. Success? Hell, it was thirty miles to a Wal-Mart. Who wanted to be successful in this hellhole? Bunch of people with a little money in the bank, driving fancy cars and hiring maids, pretending to be high class in a place where there was no middle. Just them that had it, them that didn't. Didn't take much to have it, not here.

He glanced again at the window. She was still there, standing back, but he could see her shadow. Just for a moment there . . . he let the thought die. She was still a good-looking woman, better looking now than before, he considered. And she knew class, even if she wasn't sure how to use it. It might have worked. Might work yet, he thought, with hollow warmth growing inside him. Might.

He tossed the smoke away into the wet grass. "Nope," he whispered out the last of it, "never in a million years."

The rain picked up suddenly, began to wet his bags, so he picked them up, searched the street for the stupid old fart who drove the only taxi service in town. He thought back to when he first hit on the kid as an item. Who would have imagined it—the coincidence? Should have been an easy out, but somehow, he lost it in the sun. It wasn't going to work and it never could. Never, he silently lectured himself as Buster's cab hove into view through the sheets of rain. There's no replay, no do-over. It's over when it's over. New game, new plan. Batter up.

The rain pelted him. No scrimmage, he confirmed. Probably canceling it as he stood there. He wondered if he could hook a ride with one of the scouts back to Dallas. He didn't think he could stand one more minute here than he had to. "Bush league," he said. "All the way."

———

It was raining hard when the cab arrived, and Byron opened the door. Then he lowered the umbrella, turned and smiled that wide, famous smile of victory toward the house. The gesture struck her with the force of a line drive, knocking her backward. She stumbled away from the window, over an end table, and down onto the sofa. She looked at the drying stain on the carpet, the impersonal, indifferent décor around her. She tried to see herself there, in any object, any color, any texture of the whole room. She wasn't there. All she could sense was the lingering odor of cigarette smoke and the sound of rain pelting on the roof.

"Oh yeah," she said to the dark room, "bush league." And then she started to cry.

NICKLEBY

for Marion

O n the first really cold day of the year, Connie Kentworth clutched her tote bag full of student papers to her chest and sped up the walk toward her house. The neighborhood seemed even more dismal than usual under the gray sky of the Arctic front scything across the prairie.

"Nothing between here and the north pole but a bob-wire fence," the clerk in the bookstore tritely assured her that afternoon. "And it's down." He laughed, but she didn't. Cold weather had never appealed to her.

She lunged against a sudden gust of wind, then stopped, huddling into herself until it passed. She feared it would rip the tote from her and scatter the eighty-five essays she had to mark that weekend across the neighborhood's yellowing yards. The cold sliced right through her thickly layered garments. Her teeth chattered. If it's this bad in October, she wondered, what will winter be like?

Before she could resume her movement, a sharp, quick yapping caught her ear. She looked reluctantly northward into the yard next door, where a small, black puppy played happily with Dickey, the neighbor's son. Dickey was "seven goin' on eight," as he proudly put it. In Connie's opinion, he was well on the road to federal prison. She had already caught him throwing rocks at her windows, and she suspected that it was he who punched holes in her garden hose.

Today, though, he seemed charming. In spite of the shrieking wind, he was running and playing with his new pet. A bright flash of teeth opened in a smile when he spotted her watching them. He waved her over.

Pulling the tote tighter to her, Connie stepped across the crinkling dead grass and looked over the hogwire fence that separated the two yards.

"Puppy!" Dickey yelled over the gale. "My new puppy!"

The pup was part Lab, part everything else, Connie decided. "What's his name?"

"Ain't got one," Dickey said proudly. "Daddy says you don't give a name to a working dog."

"And what work is he going to do?" Connie asked. She thought of an illustration of a dogcart she had seen in a facsimile edition of a Dickens novel. It made her sad to think of this puppy hauling around even so light a weight as Dickey.

"He's our pertection," Dickey said seriously. "Daddy says the neighborhood's going to hell, and we need us a guard dog."

"I see," she said. "Well, he's a fine-looking dog."

"He's my dog!" Dickey announced. He reached down and picked up the pup by the scruff of the neck.

"Don't do that," Connie warned. "You'll hurt him."

"Naw," Dickey assured her. He held the pup up high. "Don't hurt'em none." The dog's legs dangled helplessly, and his teeth bared from the stretched skin. His eyes rolled back. "That's the way you pick up dogs. Daddy said so."

She didn't wish to argue, and she didn't want to contradict the boy's father, Tom Davidson, a night watchman at the grain elevator. She couldn't stand watching the torture, either. Without another word she turned and went into her house.

———

The house was Victorian, something she had always wanted, and only through a series of lucky breaks and serious compromises and not a few sacrifices had she finally been able to buy it. The luck came when she was hired to teach at Hardeman Christian College. It was a tiny school, relatively new and closely supported by an unusual alliance of regional and otherwise unaffiliated Bible churches, all strictly fundamentalist. The pronounced mission was to establish the "right kind" of institution of higher learning in a geographically central location that would keep youngsters close to home and watchful parents, and well out of the way of corrupting influences known to prowl urban campuses. The school boasted an enrollment of fewer than three thousand—there were no dorms, no fraternities or sororities. Students outside handy commuting distances were housed by local church members. But it was accredited, and it was also struggling for prestige by hiring experienced faculty and touting the value of a rigorous and highly traditional curriculum. Like most small parochial schools, though, the cheerful facade put on for trustees and benefactors hid more than it revealed. No one mentioned how tight the budget was, how strictly the faculty were supervised, or how far the administration was willing to go to retain students for four full years. They also kept those truths hidden from prospective employees until they had signed contracts, Connie learned.

She was ostensibly hired to teach Victorian literature, her single love, her one specialty. Instead, however, she discovered that she was assigned four courses in lower division writing—two in composition, two in technical writing—something she knew nothing about. At first, she thought it was because she was new, that they were breaking her in. She rationalized that there were too few English majors to justify frequent courses in a special area. But she learned in her third week of employment that in the spring term, a Victorian novel course was to be taught by Dr.—as he insisted on being addressed—Howard Wesson, EdD, the department head. He was an acerbic and myopic little man who served Earl Grey and boxed cookies to anyone who came by his office. He told her he was so pleased to have, as he put it, "another lover of Dickens and Thackeray on staff," that he couldn't find the words to express himself. He also couldn't find a course for Connie to teach. She soon realized that her assignment for the spring was four more overcrowded writing courses.

To complain was to risk contract renewal and eventual tenure. It would also risk the house, so she was forced to accept her schedule with a stoical stiffness in her upper lip.

A second compromise had to do with the neighborhood itself. Once prosperous and home to physicians and bankers, it had fallen into serious decline when the upwardly mobile of the small city began building modern and tasteless ranch-style houses in the suburbs, or in what passed for suburbs: a series of treeless developments erected on what had very recently been cotton fields along the highway by-pass near the edge of town. A new strip center was being built there, and a driving range and miniature golf course were being laid out. There were two new chain eateries, a Pizza Hut and a Sonic Drive-In, and she'd heard that the YMCA was talking about building a facility nearby.

Her salary was sufficient to allow her to buy one of the new condos also being built in conjunction with the developments, but she had chosen instead to sink what savings she had into the Victorian. She had a small hope that her moving in might reverse the neighborhood's decline.

The house suffered from long neglect. She paid for replumbing and rewiring before she moved in, and that had been expensive enough. But now she discovered that the beautiful hardwood floors were rotten underneath, and she hired a contractor, who agreed to replace the ruined boards, one room at a time, one room a month. It was all she could afford.

But the house was structurally sound. She would need a new roof before spring, and paint would be required then as well. Several windows had been broken while it was for sale and vacant, but she was competent enough to replace them herself, and she was pleased and surprised to discover a well of talent for wallpapering and minor carpentry. The house was shaping up, she constantly told herself, and it gave her more satisfaction than anything else she had ever done.

She came through the front door and used her back to shut it behind her. It was chilly inside. Heating was a constant—and expensive—problem. Built in a time when the only warmth available for homes on the rolling prairie was burning coal or wood, every room was equipped with a fireplace. When natural gas became available, the owners had bricked up all but the front room's chimney and installed outlets for space heaters throughout the house. More recently—thirty or forty years ago, she guessed—they were replaced by a forced-air gas-burning furnace that was built into what had once been a butler's pantry. The unit was ancient, and it wheezed and groaned anytime it was called on to produce any warmth above sixty degrees. The blower rattled horribly, as well. As a result, she relied primarily on wool and flannel to stave off the record-breaking autumn chill.

She was a realist, though. As soon as she could afford it, she planned to open all the fireplaces eventually, or at least those downstairs, and to replace the old furnace with a modern central system.

She dumped her tote next to her chair in the living room and removed her coat. The house was dark, gloomy, although it was still early afternoon. She switched on some lamps and then went to the kitchen to put some water on to boil for cocoa. It was Friday, so she didn't have to attack the stack of papers yet, but she felt the need to put on wool socks, snuggle up in a flannel housecoat, and sip a hot drink and read. One major advantage of an old house like this was that almost every room had built-in bookshelves. All of her books—more than two thousand volumes—were on display and available from the multiple floor-to-ceiling bookshelves the previous owners had installed in every room. She was feeling like George Elliot this afternoon, maybe *Middlemarch*.

———

It was nearly dark when she went into the kitchen to open a can of tomato soup for supper. The previous owners had kept a woodburning stove in service in the kitchen, although they also had installed a modern oven and gas range. She preferred the antique cooker. She kept a bank of coals in it whenever she was in the house, and one of the boys in her class, the son of a home builder, brought by a regular supply of scrap lumber, cut in blocks small enough to use in the stove.

While she waited for the soup to heat, she looked out the window over the sink into the neighbor's yard. Dickey had retreated inside, apparently, and the puppy sat forlornly on the front porch and yowled. She could barely hear it above the wind that rattled her house's windows and made the old shingles on the roof sing.

"Poor thing," she thought aloud, "they ought to let it in."

She poured her soup into a mug and returned to the living room and her book. She owned a TV, but only a cheap, black-and-white model. She used it only to watch the news or, rarely, something special on PBS. The small town was too far away from most stations to receive much on the set's built-in antenna, and she refused to pay for cable or to have an out-side aerial or satellite dish erected on the house. Her idea was that the structure be restored to as accurate a representation of its original form as possible. Besides, it was an expense she didn't need.

The house moaned with the wind. Around ten o'clock, she rose, stretched, and took her soup mug back to the kitchen, washed it out in the sink. She heard the pitiful cries of the puppy once more.

"Are they going to keep it out there all night?" she asked herself. She peered through the kitchen windowpanes, but only her reflection looked back at her. "I wonder if you even fed it?" she questioned them aloud.

She went to the stove and placed two small blocks of wood inside, stoked it briefly, and then opened a can of beef and barley soup and dumped it into the pot. It heated rapidly. She didn't want it to boil. As soon as it was just too warm for her finger to touch, she poured it into an old metal pan, then grabbed a flashlight and went out the back door.

The wind blasted against her so hard it almost knocked her down. Her teeth clenched, then chattered, and she thought of returning to warm the soup some more. The windchill must be below zero, she thought. She pulled her housecoat more closely around her and paced up the side of the house. The grass had a frosty covering and snapped and popped beneath her slippers, and her breath was ripped away in vapory gusts.

Connie made a couple of kissing noises and tried to whistle, but her lips were dry. Finally, she called, "Pup, come here, pup!" The black dog bounded up to the fence and the glow of the light, all feet and tongue.

She had to lean over to put the pan full of soup down, and it almost tipped over. The puppy was ravenous. He lapped it up greedily, putting both front paws inside and tilting the pan as he licked the inside clean. When he finished, he looked expectantly up at her and bounced, trying to reach her, finally settling for standing with his front paws on the hogwire.

She leaned over and stroked his head, thinking of how Dickey had picked him up. "Poor puppy," she said in a soothing tone. "Now, you go up there on the porch in the corner out of the wind." He turned around and around, suddenly fascinated by the sight of his tail. She watched him spin in insane circles for as long as she could continue to stand the windy chill, and finally retrieved the pan, petted him once more, and then returned to her kitchen to wash up.

———

Semester break was hard on her. Christmas was always lonely, but this year seemed especially difficult. With no family alive, no close friends anywhere in the region, no local colleagues who weren't otherwise occupied, nowhere really to go herself, Connie was isolated. She had long ago formed the habit of spending the holidays alone, reading, catching up on personal chores, ignoring the fact that, at nearly thirty-eight, she had no man in her life and never really had. She had just never met anyone who interested her or who was that interested in her. She didn't worry about it, but during the holidays, the absence of someone special sometimes haunted her with an unaccountable guilt and forced her to concentrate more on her personal needs.

She worried about becoming a spinster, an "old maid," a lonely, antique woman living in a lonely, antique house in a small town where eligible males who could read above an eighth-grade level were rare. But the thought didn't frighten her so much as sadden her. A plain woman with fine dark hair and too many freckles, she had never dated much. Mostly, she sometimes thought, she spent more energy fending off advances from men who thought she was too desperate not to fall for some silly line than in trying to develop relationships. There were available men at the school, married and single, and some had been more than a little friendly. But she wasn't interested, particularly in the married men. Not now, and not here. She had had her flings when she was younger. This was a time in her life when she had to think seriously about a relationship, about commitments. And besides, she reasoned with a grim smile, even the hint of a rumor of such a thing would probably result in them making her wear a scarlet "A." Sex was not an open topic at Hardeman Christian College.

Christmas was a tough season to be alone, though. This time promised to be a bit worse than usual, largely because of her new town. Winter arrived early and refused to give anyone a break to prepare for it. The cold weather that began in mid-October had not abated. Snow had fallen at Thanksgiving, and in spite of a quick thaw that left the ground muddy, shady areas around houses and along fence lines were perpetually spotted with remnants of ice. Recurring northers brought more sporadic falls, freezing rain and sleet, and one night a thundering hailstorm brought her from her bed in a panic.

She could have lived with the cold wet weather, even though her old furnace was threatening to quit every time she turned up the thermostat. But what finally brought her down was the plumbing. During the second week of December, while she was at the school administering final exams, an arctic front arrived. The morning temperature dropped from a pleasant midsixties to a chilly midthirties during the afternoon to ten degrees by midnight, and the wind was clocked at a steady twenty-five miles an hour with gusts to forty. Her water pipes froze and burst before she had time to consider the possibility that they might be in jeopardy.

The plumber charged her over two thousand dollars to repair the damage to what he had installed only a few months before. He refused to carry her on credit, and she had to take out a loan at the bank. It ruined her holiday plans, such as they were.

For Christmas, dismayed by the fact that the commercially cut trees never were more than about six feet in height, she purchased a large, locally grown cedar tree. It stood twelve feet tall and was perfectly shaped. Her idea was to put it in the bay window of the front room, to decorate it with the antique Victorian ornaments she had collected during collegiate trips to the British Isles, and to throw a big party for the entire department, students as well. She wanted to serve plum pudding and punch, show them what a true Victorian Christmas felt like. She even hoped to talk the head of the music department into drafting members of the student chorus to come and sing carols around a piano she impulsively bought through a lease-purchase.

Now all that was ruined. Aside from the plumbing bill, the cost of gas for the old furnace was much higher than she had anticipated. Matters weren't helped when, on the first of December, faculty salaries were unceremoniously cut by fifteen percent as part of a collegewide austerity program. She was amazed by the move, since no one on faculty was making anywhere near decent money. Everyone complained bitterly about it in private conversations in the faculty lounge, and there were rumors that the administrators gave themselves handsome Christmas bonuses. But no one did anything or suggested any action.

To make matters worse, the attic was awash with leaks, caused, a roofing contractor said, by the weight of snow and ice on the old shingles. Now, a new roof couldn't wait until spring. She renewed the fledgling loan and trebled her debt.

She put the tree up anyway, and she decorated it, but as she spent every night alone, uninvited to parties or other events going on in town, she became depressed. This year she seemed especially blue. Her only pleasure, in fact, was Nickleby, or so she had named the puppy next door.

He was hardly a puppy any longer. The student who kept her supplied with firewood for the kitchen stove estimated him to be about six to eight months old, and he was mostly Labrador.

"He'd be a good hunting dog," the student appraised, "if they'd train him. He's got big feet. That's the sign of a good dog."

She didn't care about Nickleby's feet or his potential for flushing birds from mesquite thickets. What she enjoyed was his companionship.

Every afternoon when she came home from school, he raced to the gate to greet her, then he shadowed her route up the sidewalk from his side of the hogwire fence and yelped and barked until she came over to stroke his ears. He was typically playful for a dog his age. He still chased his tail whenever its black tip entered his line of sight, and he slobbered all over her hand when she tried to pet him through the wire. He leaped up on the fence, and if his paw missed one of the wires and she was standing too close, her clothes were often splotched with the dark mud the Davidson's yard yielded under Nickleby's playful, romping gallop.

Dickey had apparently grown bored with him, Connie noticed. The dog had little attention. Davidson erected a crude lean-to next to the porch, and a pair of rusty bowls for food and water were next to it. But almost every night, the temperature dropped well below freezing and didn't recover until midafternoon, so the water stayed solid. Nickleby either didn't care for the food or it was inedible, since the bowls were perpetually full. Connie gave him fresh water and table scraps as well as whole cans of soup almost every day.

It was, in fact, her kindness to the dog, her feeding it, that brought her face to face with her neighbor for the first time since the day she moved in.

That original meeting had been as brief as it was awkward. Davidson drifted over while she lugged furniture and lamps up the rotting steps of the porch on the blistering hot Sunday afternoon she arrived. The U-Haul had to be back by six o'clock or she would be charged for another day, so she almost resented his unhelpful intrusion. No other neighbors had done anything but stare at her from the shade of their porches, though, so she tried to be cordial.

"You buy this place?" he asked when he walked up. He was more than six feet tall and must have weighed well over two fifty. His belly protruded roundly out, as if he were bloated. He had on a stained undershirt and a pair of what looked to Connie like boxer-short underwear. At first she was startled at his audacious attire. Surely, they were some sort of swimming trunks, she told herself, but a quick glance at the gaping fly revealed otherwise. She averted her eyes and turned back to her work.

"Yeah," she huffed at him. She was trying to wrestle a battered mattress up the steps one at a time. It had been her only bed for years. Now she would have a real house with a real bedroom, and one of her first planned purchases was going to be a big bed. She had already bought the four-poster frame for it. It waited in the trailer to be hauled in last.

She felt him staring at her and stopped and wiped perspiration from her brow. "I'm Connie Kentworth," she said and stuck out her hand.

He looked at her hand with flat gray eyes and sipped a beer he kept in his fist. "It's been for sale for goddamn near ever," he said. He eyed the trailer, the mattress, and then let his gaze drift back to her. "You got a lot of junk. Good thing it's a big house."

She was suddenly self-conscious. She wore a white tank top and shorts. Never a modest woman, she thought herself unattractive. She was now embarrassed by the freckle-dotted paleness of her exposed legs under his empty stare.

"It's exactly what I wanted," she said. "Now, if I can just get everything inside, I'll feel like I'm home."

"Cost you a arm and a leg to fix it up."

She felt his eyes on her breasts, and she turned away slightly. "That's something I'm looking forward to." She smiled.

"Name's Tom Davidson," he said absently. He pulled a package of cigarettes from the waistband of the boxers. "I'm watchman over to the Co-op. Work the night shift."

"I work—will be working—teaching—at the college," she said.

"Yeah?" He seemed curious. "What'll you teach?"

"English."

"Oh," his face darkened. "I never was much good in English."

She had heard the comment so often that she let the silence grow. There was never anything to say in reply.

"Bunch of damn Jesus freaks, you ask me," he said, now meeting her eyes with a challenging look. "Queers, too, you ask me."

There was nothing to say in reply to that, either.

"Don't be bothering me with no pamphlets and such," he said. "We're Baptists. Ain't likely to convert."

"I'm Episcopalian," she said. "We don't hand out tracts and pamphlets."

For a moment, he seemed dumbfounded, then flicked his cigarette butt into her hedge. "It'll shut down, soon," he said. "Shit like that's been tried here before. Never takes."

She wasn't sure what he was referring to, exactly.

"Well," he said with one more inspection of her bare legs. "Just wanted to see who you was." He turned to go. "You ought to get some help," he said as he walked off. "You got a lot of heavy junk. This heat'll kill you."

With that he was gone, and she continued to lug her belongings inside without him. No other neighbors came over, not that day, not since.

She met Dickey two days later. She found him in her backyard with a Crisco can full of oily tar. He was collecting grasshoppers and dropping them into the black sludge, then fishing them out and watching them as they tried to clean their legs. They exchanged names before she took his torturous toys away from him, and they didn't meet again until she caught him throwing rocks at the bay window. Fortunately his small size and poor aim prevented any damage, and she didn't tell on him, hoping to make of him a friend. She called him inside, gave him a candy from an antique jar in her living room, and explained why he had to stop doing that. It sort of worked. At least, his mischief was less blatant after that.

Dickey told her that his mother's name was Belle, but Connie hadn't seen her but twice in all the time she lived there, and even then, she wasn't sure that the woman she saw was Mrs. Davidson. Both times she had appeared on the front porch in a faded, gingham housedress, her hair wisping out of a poorly fashioned ponytail, and she had done little more than look up when Connie called a hello out to her. She raised her hand briefly and fled inside. She looked severe and old enough to be the boy's grandmother, Connie thought. No other person had been evident to Connie's eye in or around the Davidson house.

Aside from Dickey, she had rarely seen anyone next door at all. At night, lights were on, and she had heard a television playing too loud once in a while, but the windows were covered with yellowing shades, and the yard was completely enclosed, front and back, with hogwire. During the day the house looked deserted except for the dog. And she never saw anyone attending to Nickleby.

She took up the chore with an automatic pleasure. The dog needed someone to look after him, not just to feed and water him, but also to pet him, to talk to him. She toyed with the idea of bringing him over to her yard, maybe even inside on the colder nights. But she didn't go that far, and after Tom Davidson's second visit, she knew she never could.

On Christmas Eve, a knock startled her from her book. She had built a roaring fire of the remains of the stove wood and was cuddled up with a Daphne du Maurier mystery—one that had surprisingly eluded her notice—listening to music on the radio, and she was embarrassed to have cried out in fear when the banging of the old brass knocker rang through the house.

"I come to ask you something," Tom Davidson announced from the porch when she opened the door. He had on khakis and a tee-shirt. His stomach, if anything, seemed larger than before, and his face was unshaven. A sandwich that looked to be made of nothing more than a hamburger patty squashed between two pieces of white bread was in his paw. His fat fingers grasped it tightly beneath nails chewed down to the quick. The thermometer on the porch read twenty degrees, and the wind was up.

"Well, come in," she said. "You must be freezing."

He didn't move, only glared at her. "You been feeding that dog?"

"The dog? Why, yes, I have," she admitted. His frown deepened. "I mean, I give him some scraps from time to time. You don't mind, do you?"

"Yeah, I mind," he said. "You damn right I mind. I'm buying special food for that dog. I don't want you feeding it a bunch of crap."

She stepped back, shivering. "Won't you come in?" she asked. He didn't move but gripped his sandwich more tightly. Grease ran out from between his fingers. She gave in with a sigh. "I'm sorry," she said. "I didn't mean any harm. He just seemed hungry, and I did have the scraps."

"Well, don't be feeding him no more," Davidson growled. "I got him to be a watchdog, and it don't work if you go feeding him all the time."

"Oh," she said with a slight smile that she hoped was ironic enough. "I didn't know you were training him. I haven't seen you working with him at all."

Davidson narrowed his gray eyes and looked at her. "I'm training him just fine," he said. "I think you ought to just keep your nose out of my business. I ain't one of them prissy little Jesus students, you know." With that he did an about-face and stalked off into the Christmas night. He resumed eating his sandwich before he hit the bottom step of her porch.

━━━

In light of the warning, it was foolish of her, but she couldn't restrain herself. Something made the box of dog biscuits jump into her cart at the IGA store, and she didn't think twice about loading her pockets with them every time she left the house. To Nickleby, they were manna. He jumped and barked eagerly every time she approached the hogwire barrier with one in her hand. Soon, she had him rolling over, speaking on command, sitting, and even shaking hands through the wire in exchange for a treat. Her student was right: He was a good dog. She kept her eye out, but she never saw Davidson work with the animal. In fact, she didn't seen him at all after Christmas Eve.

That the Davidsons celebrated Christmas was evidenced by the tinder-dry tree she saw put out by their curb, and a new BB gun that was perpetually in Dickey's malicious hands. But the weather remained so cold and wet that she seldom saw Dickey playing outdoors. Except for Nickleby, the house seemed deserted. Only the daily disappearance and return of a beat-up old Chevrolet sedan in the driveway indicated that anyone lived in the residence.

The holiday continued. School wouldn't start until mid-January, and without money to continue her restoration plans, Connie soon tired of reading all day. Her Christmas cards brought her up to date on her correspondence, and she had reorganized her bookshelves twice. She took long walks down the small town's slushy streets, and she fed and played with Nickleby. She found that every morning she looked more forward to seeing the dog than to anything else. In spite of the cold, she discovered that she was content to stand for more than an hour at a time and talk to the growing black animal, pet him, and feed him treats in exchange for his expanding repertoire of tricks.

She was doing just that one bright frigid January morning, when Tom Davidson stormed out of his house and marched across the muddy yard.

"I thought I told you to leave that dog alone!" he bellowed.

"You told me to stop feeding him," she said, startled by his anger. She fell back a couple of steps in spite of the waist-high fence dividing them. Again, he had nothing heavier on against the temperature but a stained white tee-shirt. But strapped on his belt was a holster and an ugly revolver. He apparently had just gotten off work. Nickleby paid him no attention at all.

"Well, just what the hell do you think you're doin'?" He looked down at her hand that still held a bone-shaped dog biscuit.

"It's a treat," she said. "Not food. Just a biscuit. It keeps their teeth clean. Besides, he loves them." Nickleby groaned and sat up, expecting to be rewarded.

Davidson glared at her for a moment, then bent his knee back and kicked Nickleby squarely in the stomach. The dog rose two feet off the ground and then plopped down in a bank of muddy ice before springing to its feet and racing back to the lean-to.

"You!" Connie cried. "You . . . why'd you do that?"

"I told you to leave the goddamn dog alone," Davidson shouted. "He's *my* fucking dog. If you want a dog, why don't you go and buy you one?"

"I don't—"

"Well, then, leave my dog alone," he said. "I'm not fixing to warn you 'bout this no more. I'll have the sheriff on you. There's a law about messing round with a man's dog."

"I am not 'messing around' with anything," she said. Shock fled in the advance of outrage. She stepped forward, flushed with anger. "I was merely being kind to an animal who is receiving no attention, no love from its owner."

"Love!" Davidson sniffed and shook his head. "Lady, this is a *guard* dog! He don't need no love. Now, you mind what I say. Just leave him alone."

"You don't even let him in at night," she went on. Her ire was up. "And it's wet and cold. Too cold. There're laws about cruelty to animals, too."

"He's got him a house," Davidson said. "He's got a good deal, here. Or at least he did till you come along and started messing with him."

"That house—" she started. The shabby lean-to was so pathetically inadequate to shelter the animal, she found herself unable to describe it to its builder.

"I'm not fixing to tell you no more," he said. "You leave the dog alone, or I'll have the sheriff on you, and I mean it." He turned and stalked away toward his porch. Nickleby stayed inside his doghouse.

———

The main thing to come out of the confrontation with Davidson, Connie observed, was that he actually began working with Nickleby. Several mornings a week she watched from her kitchen window while he tried to train the animal to do what he wanted. What Davidson wanted, however, was never clear to her, nor to Nickleby.

Davidson usually came out for about twenty minutes. He called the dog up to him, put a chain on his collar, and then dragged him around the muddy yard, screaming at him to do various things such as "heel" or "sit," to no other end than the animal's complete bewilderment. If Nickleby refused to obey or tried to fight the chain, Davidson kicked him or slapped him on the head, screaming curses at him the whole time. Once, she saw the frustrated Davidson whirling around in a circle with the poor animal stretched out at the end of his collar until he was thrown like an obscene hammer into a crusty snowbank beside the house. The sight made her so nauseated she had to go lie down. But painful as the ordeal was to watch, she couldn't keep herself from bearing witness to the ongoing cruelty on a regular basis. At times, she was astonished to find herself nearly weeping with pity for the poor creature next door.

Most mornings, Dickey sat impassively on the porch and watched his father torture Nickleby, occasionally shouting "bad dog" when his father whipped or otherwise punished the beast for refusing to understand and obey. Although he never struck the animal while she was watching, he also extended no hand of compassion or friendship. It was too sad to believe.

Finally, she decided she could bear it no longer. She looked in the phone book for the ASPCA, but there was no chapter in the town. She called two or three nearby cities before she found someone who said that there wasn't much they could do outside their own counties, and suggested she call a local law enforcement official. He also gave her the statute numbers of laws against cruelty to animals. Connie phoned the sheriff.

She got the deputy. "Well, what's he doing, exactly?" he asked her.

"He's kicking him. Hitting him, choking him," she said. "Torturing him to death."

"He using a board or a whip or anything?"

"No, just his fists. But he's a big man."

"Well, most men are bigger than their dogs." The deputy sounded bored.

"He's going to kill that animal," she cried. "And that's against the law. You are the law around here, aren't you?" She cited the violations she had observed to him, and finally he agreed to come out and see for himself.

The deputy arrived about twenty minutes later. Nickleby slunk off as soon as the officer came through the gate and confronted Davidson. They talked for a while, then Davidson whistled, and Nickleby reluctantly approached his master. The deputy reached down and scratched his ears, and Davidson did the same, although the second his hand touched Nickleby's head, she saw his tail tuck and his body tense. After a few minutes, the officer left. Davidson waited until he was out of sight before he came over and knocked on Connie's back door. She didn't answer it.

"I know you're in there," he yelled. "And I know you can hear me. I ain't fixing to hurt you. But I'm gonna to say my piece."

She retreated to the hallway between the kitchen and the shadow of the stairs, out of sight of the windows. She was shaking uncontrollably, and she hated herself for being so frightened.

"You set the law on me," he said, "and it wasn't none of your goddamn business. How I treat my dog is *my* business. He's my dog. Now, you can see that he didn't arrest me or nothing. He can't. I ain't done nothing wrong. Now, I want you to take a lesson from this, schoolteacher. That's my dog, and he's gonna to *stay* my dog. I'll work him the way I want to. You want a dog, you go and get you one." He waited for a beat, and Connie could hear him pacing back and forth on the porch. "That's all I'm gonna say, but I'm telling you, you stick your pointy little nose into my business again, you're likely to get it bit off. You hear?"

After a while, she decided he had gone, and she went upstairs and lay down. Her head was throbbing, her heart wouldn't stop pounding.

She thought of filing charges on him herself, but she wasn't sure what the procedures were. Clearly, the deputy had seen nothing to substantiate her claims, and she might have to have a lawyer herself. That was something she was certain she couldn't afford. Besides, she told herself grimly, Davidson was right: Nickleby was his dog.

Two days later, she was not surprised to find that Davidson had erected a partial barrier along his fence line. Made of preformed cheap plastic lattice, it restricted her view of his yard from her window. To watch him "work" the dog, she would have to go outside, well into the front boundary between their properties, and confront him. That she wouldn't—couldn't—do. But in the evenings, after he had gotten in the battered car and driven off to work, she continued to sneak out and feed Nickleby scraps and treats. She found, though, that instead of energetically bounding over to her, he now seemed to cower and slink to the hog-wire and to flinch from her outstretched hand.

———

She welcomed the start of the spring semester as a diversion from her observation of Nickleby's continuing agonies and her growing worries, but she was quickly disappointed in her hopes of throwing herself into her work with enthusiasm.

There had been a meeting of the board over the holidays. Slipping grades and sliding GRE scores by the college's graduates during the past two years had prompted the trustees to take notice of the school's perilous academic standing and to lay down some strict new rules at a general convocation the first week. The failure to learn, they were told, was clearly a failure to teach, and the faculty was to be held accountable. Instead of raising standards, insisting on more difficult assignments and stricter grading policies, though, the administration increased teaching loads so every departmental member could "have more opportunity to apply him- and herself to the profession." Connie's four-course load went to five, and she still wasn't teaching a word of literature.

What was worse, she learned, was that she had been targeted by several students for special complaint. Apparently her suggestions of secular topics for essay assignments had aroused the notice of her more fervently religious students who wanted to write every paper on the subject of their faith in Jesus Christ. Since Connie was an Episcopalian—albeit a nonpracticing one—she was already suspected of spreading some sort of humanistic heresy. Now, she was called before both Dr. Wesson and Harvell Turner, the dean, who also insisted on being called "doctor"—although he held no such degree—and ordered to be more flexible in her acceptance of the "moralistic responsibilities of higher education."

"This is a Christian college," Turner said, astonishingly pointing his finger right in her face. "We will have no attempts to divert our young people from their mission and their faith."

"But you can't argue faith," Connie pointed out. "It's not logical."

"Logic has nothing to do with God," Dr. Turner intoned, tenting his fingers. "But essays may be expressions of personal belief. You do believe in freedom of religion, don't you?"

"Well, of course—"

"Then you take my point," he said, shooting his cuffs and waiving a dismissal in one grand gesture. "You are to permit—nay, encourage them to write about their faith, if they so choose." Then he smiled. "You might find it instructive," he said. "The Lord works in mysterious ways."

She felt helpless. To refuse was to resign, and she couldn't afford to resign.

She became more depressed than ever. How could it be, she asked herself, that she could find a house she loved in a place she really sort of liked, and have such a lousy neighbor and such a lousy job? She knew she had only taken it out of desperation. She had wandered from temporary position to temporary position for over a decade, ever since she completed her degree, searching for the right opportunity to prove her teaching ability and just get along. She thought she had finally found it. It wasn't exactly the kind of school she had hoped for, of course, not the sort of place that would engender her longing to conduct research, write criticism. The library, she sadly noted, wasn't adequate for the average junior high. The truth, she admitted, was that in the darkest most pessimistic moments of her graduate studies, she never thought she would wind up in such a hellhole of a college. But given the job market, it was what there was, and, in truth, she had been grateful to find it. And now, she was in too deep to just walk away. Besides, she reasoned, the thought of quitting and starting on the long job hunt trail again made her almost ill. She had been determined to make a good life here, to enjoy the serenity of her old Victorian house, to wallow in the wonderful solitude and peace of it. It was all she'd ever wanted, and she'd been willing to sacrifice everything else to get it. Now, it was all at risk.

But when she turned up her walk and stepped carefully around slick, icy spots on the sidewalk, her thoughts were mollified by the sight of a muddy black dog, pricking up his ears and waiting on her call. He didn't run to greet her anymore—almost as if he sensed that there might be a punishment for such an act—but he still trusted her judgment enough to come if she called.

Without a thought, she pulled a biscuit from her coat pocket and spoke his name. He met her at the fence, his tail sweeping the frigid air behind him, his head lowering almost beyond her reach as her gloved fingers stroked his ears.

"You poor thing," she cooed. "You're just like me. All you want is to be left alone, and all you get is kicked around."

Maybe this wasn't such a perfect life after all, she thought. Then she glanced up to the house. The cloud cover was imperfect that day, and stark blue sky cracked through it in places. The house's gingerbread trim, peeling and faded as it was, seemed to brighten under the distant promise of spring. She smiled. The house was worth all of it, she assured herself. She tossed Nickleby another biscuit, for which he obediently rolled over.

"It's a rough patch, boy," she said. "But we'll get through it."

The rough patch continued. Spring came in a stampede of windy, dusty days that were alternately cold and hot. She never seemed to dress to fit the weather. If the morning started below freezing, it turned off warm and balmy in the afternoon, and she returned home sweaty and exhausted from the weight of sweaters and coats. If it was warm in the morning and she dressed lightly, by afternoon the sky would darken, and she would race home in sleet or freezing rain and sit by the stove in the kitchen desperately trying to coax circulation back into her fingers and toes.

The situation at the school settled into a routine of puritanical intolerance. Insecure colleagues spied on one another and reported the least infraction of school rules. Threats of dismissal and rumors of a "hit list" with names of those not to be renewed for another year circulated through the faculty lounge. The students were in passive rebellion. They sensed that the administration had undermined the faculty's authority, and they took advantage by cutting classes with impunity, offering weak excuses or sometimes none at all beyond an indifferent shrug. Any grade below B was protested and often changed by the department heads over instructors' objections. If an exam or essay was failed, students received two, sometimes three makeups or do-overs until a satisfactory mark was achieved. Another ten percent cut in gross pay was effected in March with no explanation or apology whatsoever.

Many in her department were frantically scanning job lists and mailing out résumés, but Connie knew her own options were limited, particularly since she doubted she would receive a positive recommendation. Besides, there was no way she could afford to travel to the conventions or distant campuses for interviews, even if she could obtain any. One icy night in February, the old furnace coughed twice and died, requiring that she make an enlargement and extension of her loan to pay for its replacement. Since she walked the two miles to school, she put her car up for sale, but she still owed so much on it, that she barely cleared five hundred dollars by the time the kid who bought it finished bargaining. She felt the end of her rope passing through her fingers. All she had left now was a few threads.

She almost stopped reading entirely except for her student papers. Because of her increased load, she had as much as a hundred and fifty thousand words to read and evaluate a week, most of them copied by students one from another or just out-and-out plagiarized. To accuse a student, though, was dangerous. A math professor who had the temerity to fail two kids who were caught red-handed with cheat sheets during an algebra exam was immediately suspended. Dean Dr. Turner told him that the papers he found were not mathematical formulae at all, but were connected passages of scripture—chapters and verses—that they were sharing. He suggested that the professor clear out his office by the end of the week.

Connie rarely did anything to the house anymore, rarely went outside at all, but spent the blustery early spring inside, hunched in her chair over sheaves of sloppily prepared, error-filled student writing.

She didn't even see Nickleby for weeks at a time.

———

When spring break came, she sagged under the weight of the most recent writing assignment as she trudged back to her house. She had research papers this round, none of which was less than ten pages long, and in addition to marking the grammar and usage, she also had to check sources, form, and content for accuracy and logic. She also tried to ignore the obvious plagiarism, which had become epidemic. As she couldn't afford a personal computer, she was forced to use the single machine available in the department to search for suspect passages. Even if she could find them, she wasn't sure what she would do about it. Her depression was heavier than the ream of paper in her tote. She had earlier toyed with the idea of taking a trip, maybe going to visit an old college friend in Cleveland, but the new expenses and cuts to her salary prohibited that, so she resigned herself to a week's work, interspersed with as much rest as she could manage.

When she turned up her walk, she spotted Nickleby near his doghouse. Even though she had given up carrying the dog biscuits in her pocket, she whistled lightly and called his name.

At first, he didn't respond, but finally, when she came to the wire and called him again, he lifted his head and trudged toward her. He reached the end of a length of chain and stopped, instinctively knowing what his limits were.

"Fixed your wagon, didn't I?" Davidson's voice startled her. He had been at the side of the house, apparently heard her whistle, and now emerged into the windy afternoon. He wore a khaki uniform and his pistol. A small pointed hat such as she had seen policemen in old movies wearing was perched on his head, accentuating his receding hairline.

Dickey also came out of the shadows. He had on a toy army helmet and carried his BB gun.

"Hello," she said, determined to be pleasant.

"I know what you was thinking about," Davidson said. "I was fixing to put me up a high board fence along here to keep you out. But I said to myself, 'Why spend that kind of money? All you need to do is get that dog a short chain, and that'll be that.'" He strolled to a spot near Nickleby. "Worked, too, didn't it?"

"I wasn't going to bother him," she said. "I was just going to say 'hello.'"

"Well, you better say it from a distance, now on," he grinned and spat. She saw his jaw was full of tobacco. In imitation of his father, Dickey had a huge wad of gum in his mouth. "Let me show you something."

He went to the porch and picked up a mop handle. Advancing toward Nickleby, he announced, "Dog. Attack! Dog!"

She was astonished. Nickleby instantly laid back his ears, dropped his front legs, and went into a deep crouch. His mouth opened slightly and a low growl rumbled deep inside him. He opened his jaws, and saliva webbed his teeth. Davidson took two more deliberate steps and waved the mop handle absurdly out in front of his huge belly.

"Attack!" he commanded.

Nickleby leaped. He reached the end of the chain and was jerked off his feet onto his back just as Davidson reached him with the handle. At first Connie was horrified, sure that he was going to beat the dog, but instead of swatting Nickleby with the handle, he began poking and prodding at him, gouging his flanks and sides while he scrambled around in the dirt and tried to find his feet. When he scrambled erect, he looked like a monster, feet planted, fangs bared, his eyes red-rimmed, and a throaty threat rolling out of his mouth.

Davidson didn't back off but kept fencing at the dog with his handle, landing harder blows. Nickleby feinted and lunged again and again at his master, sending up a fierce and frantically snarling protest, but Davidson showed a surprising adroitness and parried each of the dog's toothy thrusts with a smart riposte, occasionally knocking Nickleby off his feet and onto his side. Connie felt bile rise in her throat.

Wheezing and laughing, Davidson stepped away, out of Nickleby's range. The dog continued to snap and growl, and finally he set up a gale of barking at the fat man who teased him with half-hearted swipes with the pole.

"What you think of that?" Davidson came over by the fence. Nickleby continued to bark and dig in against the chain's length.

"I think if he wasn't on that chain, he'd rip your throat out," she said evenly.

"Me? Naw," Davidson laughed. "Dog. Rest!" he ordered. Nickleby's barking instantly ceased, but she saw that the tension in his forelegs and eyes remained. His chest heaved, and his focus was totally on Davidson's back.

"I told you I was fixing to work with him. And that's just step one: Prowler with a stick or a knife. I'd had him already where he ought to be if it wasn't for your messing with him. You got to admit, I'm a pretty fair trainer." He looked proud of himself.

"All I can see is that you're a bully," she said.

His eyes narrowed behind his fat cheeks. "Well, I'll tell you this. Ain't nobody fixing to come into this yard with no stick or knife that that dog won't tear apart. Nossir."

"What's your next 'step'?" she asked. "Are you going to teach him how to call the police?"

Davidson gave her a sideways glance. "Nope. Step two is prowler with a gun. Watch this here. Go on, Dickey."

Dickey stood up to attention and gave his father a salute. "Yes, sir!" he snapped off. Then he lifted the BB carbine and took careful aim at Nickleby. "Dog!" he yelled in his high voice. Nickleby's ears pricked up expectantly.

"No!" Connie shouted. "You'll—"

Before she could say more, the metallic whang of the rifle sounded and Nickleby leaped high in the air with a loud yelp. He spun around before he came back to earth and raced into his doghouse.

"Time we're done," Davidson chuckled, "that dog'll take the head off anybody who comes in a country mile of him with a gun."

"By the time you're done," Connie said, "you'll have taken a sweet puppy and turned him into a monstrous brute."

"Good," Davidson nodded. "That's the idea."

"You're a bully," she said, turning away. She felt sick to her stomach. "You're just a cruel bully."

"Case you ain't noticed it, lady," he shouted after her, "this neighborhood's going to shit. I need protection for my family. You'd do to take a lesson here, schoolteacher. You'd do to get yourself a watchdog like mine. One of these nights, you'll be sorry if you don't. Skinny as you are, some ol' boy's liable to take a shine to you. Follow you home. Teach you a thing or two about your snooty ways."

Her stomach churned as she kept moving toward her house. When she climbed the porch steps, she had to fight to keep herself steady. Her head was swimming, her heart pounding.

"Step three's next," he yelled at her. She could hear the anger in his voice. "Know what that is? That's to teach him to attack anybody who tries to feed him. You better take a lesson in that, too. He'll bite the hand that feeds him. He'll bite your hand. I swear! You better—" His words were shut off when she slammed the door behind her and raced for the bathroom to vomit.

———

April brought a marvelous change to the rolling prairie. Buds sprang out on every branch, and grass shed its muddy yellow shroud and burst forth in verdant wonder. The mud-brown fields were now awash in green wheat that began to turn golden around the edges as harvest approached. Connie was delighted to find that the house's former owners had planted a variety of bulbs around the porch—cannas and tulips, mostly—and shoots soon emerged and blossomed a burst of color. She was inspired enough by the change in the weather to renew work on her floor repairs, although it meant that her diet would have to be restricted to canned soups and vegetables in order to make room in her budget.

All the good feelings that came with spring, however, seemed distant to her. A cold she developed at the end of spring break lingered, and she started every morning with sniffles and chills that sometimes worsened during the day. The school's health plan was inadequate for anyone without a ready supply of cash for the deductible and co-payments, so she treated herself with lemon tea and mentholated chest rubs, postponing a visit to a doctor for as long as she could. Her sinuses also seemed to be reacting unfavorably to the heavily pollinated air. Her ears and head were full and buzzed with infection.

Somehow, she dragged herself through her classes, read the never-decreasing mountain of essays, and struggled to keep apace of her other departmental duties, most of which involved long, dull meetings that were always opened and closed with longer and duller prayers. Her attention to Davidson and Nickleby waned, as the dog no longer responded when she called it. As she did what little gardening she felt like and had time for, though, she observed that Nickleby didn't come to Davidson when he called, either. The dog's refusal to obey a command to "C'mere" enraged her giant neighbor, and the result was usually a stiff beating with the mop handle. She noticed, though, that when he punished the dog, he made sure Nickleby was at the end of his chain. The dog's growls and snarls grew deeper and more vicious with each beating, and her heart ached for the beast.

Surreptitiously, she began feeding him again.

She waited until it was well past dark when Davidson had gone to work to make sure that Dickey and his mother—wherever she kept herself—would not venture out onto the porch. Then she would take whatever food she had left over from her meager suppers and toss it over the fence, well within reach of his chain length. Often it was nothing more than a piece of bread or a chunk of turkey or chicken, but he would approach it, sniff it, look up at her in the darkness, then gobble it down. When he finished, he would stare at her across the darkness, and his tail would sail briefly back and forth before he turned and plodded back to the lean-to. She longed to touch him, to pet him, to let him know that someone loved him, but she didn't dare enter the yard. She contented herself with some kind words whispered across the night's distance and a hope that he heard and understood the tone of them.

As her life trudged toward summer, things took a change for the better at school. Dean Turner suffered a heart attack during the first week of April. He was expected to live, but the associate dean, Calvin Munson, a youngster fresh out of seminary who had been hired really to do little more than attend meetings Turner found too minor for his attention, took over the office. Young Calvin immediately discovered a number of irregularities in expenditures and academic records-keeping, which he dutifully reported to the trustees.

The scandal was quiet but widespread. It was revealed that Dr.

Wesson and Dean Turner were implicated in what could only be called embezzlement and possibly extortion. Parents who wanted their children degreed and were not too picky about how it came about had been writing fat checks to the school. The money never made it further than the department heads' pockets. "Not to put too fine a point on it," Munson chuckled as he explained the situation to the faculty, "they were all trading grades for money, and God only knows what they were doing with the money." Wesson and seven other heads resigned immediately, and Turner's wife announced that he was taking medical retirement. The new English department head, Malverna Stone—who did have a real PhD, and from Northwestern, no less—worked with Munson to restructure everything and to try to settle the festering resentment among the faculty.

The salary cuts were restored with compensation for the past four months, and announcements of a return to normal teaching loads for the fall term were posted. Students were put on their guard that the luxury of indiscriminate grade inflation would be suspended forthwith. Everyone celebrated. Connie thought that even the students seemed relieved with the return to academic normalcy.

The best news for her, however, came when Professor Stone called her in and told her that in the fall, Connie would begin teaching Victorian literature. Her load would be cut to three classes per term to give her a chance to do some research as well. "You're an asset here," Malverna said, "the sort of person we had in mind when the college was founded. You need to be working in your area more than you need to be herding freshmen around commas and semicolons. Besides that, you need to work toward tenure."

Connie walked home after her meeting with Professor Stone feeling slightly bewildered. She knew she should be elated, but the combination of the cold and sinus infection in her head made her ears ring, and she felt weary. She was mentally arguing whether to use her restored cash to her income to have the house painted or to pay off one of her hefty notes or possibly to buy herself a computer, when she turned up her walk and spotted Dickey and Nickleby.

All year, the boy had continued his road toward the reformatory with a steady progress. He stayed home from school three days out of five, it seemed, but he never appeared to be ill beyond his perpetually runny nose and malignant mean streak. Although she continued to reprimand him gently whenever she caught him doing something he shouldn't, he persevered in his trek toward a life of crime without so much as a stutter-step. She continued to find a collection of slaughtered birds on her porch every few days, and the week before, she discovered a dead cat, its eyes shot out, stuffed under the hibiscus in her flowerbed. Every window in her house had a telltale BB hole in it, and she didn't own a garden hose that hadn't been sliced, punched, and otherwise defaced by Dickey, the mid-day marauder. He was always pleasant to her in person, overly respectful, obsequious to the point of obnoxiousness, but when her back was turned, he struck at her maliciously.

Dickey sat on his porch playing with something in his lap. The dog rested half in and half out of the doghouse. But the chain was loose on the ground. A sudden swell of good feeling unaccountably burst open in Connie's heart, and she pushed into her house, went to the kitchen. She had made sugar cookies two nights before—a rare treat for herself—and she grabbed a bunch of those as well and went out into the yard. If she was going to live by the reincarnation of Gradgrind and Son, she thought, she needed to make friends with at least one of them.

She nearly skipped out of the house and went directly to the fence.

"Dickey," she called. He had disappeared. Nickleby ignored her.

"Dickey, I have something for you." He must have gone inside, she thought. She started moving down the fence, wondering if she should just forget it. Then she made a quick decision.

"Nickleby," she called softly. "Want a cookie, boy?"

The dog's ears pricked up, but he didn't move.

"Nickleby, come!" she ordered gently. "Treat? Want a cookie?"

He rose slowly to his feet and ventured toward her. She saw the hesitation when he reached the point where the chain usually stopped him, but he only paused for a moment, then moved slowly toward her.

Although now huge, he was still very much a puppy, she thought. His legs were gangly and too long for his body, and his head seemed too large. A lack of care had caused his coat to mat, and there were splotches of dirt where he had been in the mud.

"Come, Nickleby," she cooed at him. "Good dog. Come!"

"Just what the hell you think you're doin'?" Davidson's voice shouted.

"I, uh . . ." Her breath caught.

"That's a dangerous animal you're fooling with there." He stormed down the porch steps. As usual he had on khakis and a tee-shirt, but he was barefoot. He had probably been napping, she thought, and heard her. He marched toward her, and she stepped back. His small eyes were red-rimmed, his fists clenched around the mop handle. His thin hair spewed up from his balding crown. "What I want to know is just who the hell took him off his chain?"

"Well, I didn't—" she started.

"Well, somebody did, and I don't see nobody else round here." He glared at her, then at the dog. "C'mere," he ordered Nickleby.

The dog turned his head slightly but otherwise didn't move. His eyes were on the cookies in her hand.

"Look, Mr. Davidson," she tried to sound calm, although her heart was thudding in her chest, "I just brought out some cookies for Dickey, and—"

"So, now it's my goddamn kid you're after," Davidson yelled. "I thought so! I told Belle that'd be your next move." He reached the fence and grabbed the top wire in his thick fingers. "What's wrong with you? Can't you leave people alone? Are you nuts, or what?"

She stood up straight. The ringing in her ears seemed worse. She felt feverish. "I didn't mean any harm," she said. "I was just trying to be nice."

"Nice, hell." His face turned almost bright red, and he put a bare foot in a bottom rectangle of the hogwire. I'll show you fucking nice."

She suddenly understood that he was going to climb over the fence and grab her, maybe hit her with the mop handle. She stepped back, stumbled, then caught her balance.

"I'm sorry—" she started.

"I'm fixing to show you sorry, you meddling bitch," he bellowed, trying to throw a heavy leg over the top of the sagging wire. Connie was frozen in place, unable to move or take her eyes off the hulking man struggling to climb a four-foot-high wire fence so he could reach her. The wire moved wildly, threatened to buckle beneath his bulk. "I was trying to get me some sleep," he yelled, "but every time I doze off, I hear you over here messing in my yard. I swear, it's time you learned something." His entire weight was now balanced on the flimsy wire, and it swayed alarmingly beneath him. Connie put out her hands, as if pushing the air between them would force him away. "I'm goin' to fix your wagon," he huffed. "I'm goin'—"

Nickleby hit him hard. Davidson, his eyes bulging, the dog locked onto his neck, rocked on the hogwire, both hands gripping the fence, fighting to keep his balance. His feet were both involved in the wire rectangles, then he fell backward, twisting his legs across each other. She heard a sickening snap of bone when he hit the ground.

"Oh, no!" she screamed, her trance broken. She raced for the fence.

"Get him off me!" Davidson cried. He swatted helplessly at the dog, but Nickleby was now all over him, his fangs slashing and biting. Davidson rolled over, and the dog's mouth once more gripped the back of Davidson's neck. He shook his head, sinking his bite even deeper. His forepaws were dug in around Davidson's head, and his hind ones burrowed themselves into his master's upper back as he snarled and growled. All at once, blood squirted all over the big man's back, instantly staining the tee-shirt with a crimson dye. "Goddamnit!" he screamed, batting his hands uselessly in the air. "Get him off me!"

Connie stood helplessly frantic, her fingers gripping the top wire. She glanced around and measured the distance around the end of the fence and to the gate. It seemed like miles. Too far to run around.

Davidson tried to roll over to push himself up, but his feet were still entangled in the hogwire, one now pushed all the way through and twisted. He couldn't move even if his leg hadn't been broken and Nickleby's fangs weren't sinking deeper and deeper into his neck. A fierce, bubbling growl poured from Nickleby's throat as he instantly loosened his grip, then clamped his jaws down even deeper, bringing forth more blood.

"Nickleby!" she shouted. "Down, boy!" but her voice was lost in the dog's snarling and Davidson's yelling. "Stop!" she screamed. "Nickleby! Stop!" She put her foot on the lower wire, tentatively trying to imitate Davidson's actions a few moments before, but the wire was moving wildly as Davidson kicked, trying to free his twisted leg while he futilely battled the beast chewing on the back of his neck.

"God, he's fixing to kill me!" Davidson shrieked. His arms flailed helplessly in the air. "Help me, goddamn it! Get the goddamn stick!"

Before she could even look for the mop handle, the solid bark of a pistol smacked hard against Connie's ear and almost threw her down on the grass. Davidson jumped and let out a wet grunting sound. She saw a fresh gash of red tearing across his tee-shirt just under his right arm. Her eyes flew to the porch where Dickey stood, his father's large black pistol in both his small hands. He was using his thumbs to cock the revolver once more.

"I'll get him," Dickey yelled. He lowered the barrel slightly to gain leverage. His tongue jutted out between his teeth and his eyes narrowed. Incongruously, she noticed a glistening trail of snot running down his upper lip. "I'll get him!" he repeated.

Connie took a breath to yell at the boy, but her throat filled with phlegm and her voice failed her. Only a choking gurgle came out. She leaped for the fence once more and this time scrambled over the top. Nickleby paid her no mind but shook his master's head and upper torso violently. Gore washed out of Davidson's side and neck. But she had no thought for Davidson, nor did she consider that after all these months, this was her first entry into the yard. Her only thought was to get to Dickey before he fired again.

When her feet hit the ground, her ankle turned violently under her with an audible crack and she went down on her knees. A brilliant ray of pain raced up her left leg and knifed into her mind. "Oh, God," she hissed, closing her eyes against the exquisite, excruciating agony that followed the first blast, a wave of white hurt that turned her stomach over and forced vomit into her mouth. Purple and white spots danced behind her eyelids, and she felt the earth tilt beneath her. With all the will she could command, she struggled to stay conscious, forced herself to look and saw with a horrifying clarity the hexagonal black barrel of the pistol only a few feet from her face. She was directly in the boy's line of fire. She swallowed hard and filled her lungs, steeling herself against the angry pain throbbing up her leg.

"Dickey!" she commanded. "Dickey! Put down the gun!" She gritted her teeth against the injury and gathered her right leg under her to spring for the porch before he could shoot again.

A heavy blow from behind struck her and knocked her flat, again summoning spots and making her ears ring. He shot her, she thought wildly, John Dillinger, Jr., shot her! She was going to die in the muddy swamp of a dog's yard, shot by a kid with a runny nose. She dug deep, mining strength she didn't think she had. With a grunt, she rolled over and scrambled to her knees and was at once confronted by the vicious maw of a ferocious dog, his bloody teeth bared only inches from her eyes, his hot breath washing over her. Panicked, she scrambled away, ignoring the blinding pain from her ankle, her feet kicking at the dirt between Nickleby's front legs, her hands thrust out in front of her.

Nickleby's paws dug into the dusty ground in front of him, his head lowered and muscles bunched. His red-rimmed eyes bulged, and scarlet saliva roped down from his jowls. There was no recognition in his eyes, no softness or hint of affection, only hot fury. Behind him, Davidson lay facedown and motionless. It appeared the entire back of his neck had been torn out. She saw white bone and a mixture of gray and red tissue spilling out onto his shoulders and down into the bloody mud. Nickleby, snarling, pawed the ground, then dug in again, his eyes glassy, his growl deep and throaty. His chest heaved as he gathered strength for a surge.

She clenched her jaws, pulled herself to her feet, wobbled on her injured ankle, found her voice.

"Nickleby!" she ordered in as strong a voice as she could, "Nickleby, down! Down, boy!" More pain jolting from her ankle defeated her resolve and stole her voice as the words emerged and trailed off into a whining cry.

He lunged. She coiled her forearms over her face and fell onto her back. His hind paws sank painfully into her stomach as he vaulted over her, racing, she realized in horror, toward Dickey, who remained on the porch, now with the gun cocked and waving uncertainly in the dog's direction. Nickleby took one more bound and launched himself into the air toward the boy.

The revolver's noise smashed the air, rocked her back again, and the animal fell like a dark heavy lump, striking the ground and rolling over in his own blood. His eyes were open. His tongue lolled out onto the ground.

"I done it," Dickey shouted and danced on the porch. "I really done it!"

———

There was a painful wait of three days while a laboratory determined whether or not Nickleby was rabid. He wasn't. Connie's ankle was seriously fractured, but even after it was set and plastered, she was admitted for observation. She had too many open wounds and scratches for anyone to be willing to take a chance that the dog had not also bitten her. Tom Davidson remained in intensive care for another two weeks, but he was expected to recover. He would be in a wheelchair forever, Connie learned, not only as a result of damage done to his spinal cord by the dog, but also because of the .357 magnum slug that his son fired into his side. He was, as one nurse confided to her, "damn lucky to be alive."

Dickey was proclaimed a hero by the local paper, and no less a personage than the mayor came out to the crumbling bungalow to present him with a plaque.

Connie returned to her Victorian house, but, at Professor Stone's urging, she took a medical leave for the rest of the term. She learned to manage her crutches well enough to negotiate the stairs. She would have to wear the cast, she was told, well into the summer.

Since the "accident," or so she came to think of it, she had felt numb. She hardly noticed that her cold and sinus condition cleared up entirely. She was listless and lethargic and barely thanked the few students and colleagues who came by to help her with shopping and household chores. After a week or so, they stopped coming entirely.

Somewhere in the course of those weeks, she gradually decided to resign. There was no moment of truth. She just accepted the notion that she was leaving as part of the natural evolution of her life. Once she realized that she had made up her mind, she discovered that the decision was firm. She wouldn't even take summer teaching, if it was offered. She didn't want to be there another minute longer than she had to. The very sight of the house that she had been so proud of now made her physically ill. She called old friends all over the country and asked if they knew of any position she might fill in the fall, even a temporary, part-time teaching job, and they all promised to ask around and see. She knew they wouldn't call back. She didn't care. She was leaving anyway, even if she had no place to go. It might seem pathetic, she thought, but it was what it was.

She telephoned a real estate agent and listed the property for sale. In spite of his warnings that she would never get out of the house what she had put into it, she insisted, so he came by and put up a sign on her gate. There were no immediate inquiries.

She was upstairs dressing after her bath on the first of May when she heard the knocker slamming against her front door, and her heart skipped into alarm for a moment. The noise reminded her of when Tom Davidson paid her the Christmas visit. She hobbled downstairs while the caller banged again. The echo seemed to penetrate every corner of the house, mocking her.

When she opened the door she was surprised to see the frowsy, almost emaciated form of her neighbor standing erect in the shadows across the threshold.

"My name's Belle Davidson," the woman said after a moment of awkward silence. "Thought I might have a word with you, if you don't mind." She paused and looked around the yard behind her as if she suspected she was being watched. "Live right next door," she said with a nod of her head toward her house and yard. Then her chin came up sharply. "We ain't never spoke, and I'm ashamed of that. I ain't been a good neighbor."

Connie moved back to allow her to come in. Belle was wearing the same gingham housedress Connie had seen before, and her hair was also the same. Its mousey wisps flew in a thousand directions away from a loose bun behind her head. She wore no makeup, and Connie wondered idly if she ever had. She timidly stepped into the hallway, swiveled her head to the dining room on the right and then to the living room on the left, and went in.

"Law, you got a lot of books," she said, it seemed, to herself. "Never seen so many books. Like a regular library in here." She swiveled her head around, then up and down the shelves. "You read all these books?" She glanced at Connie and lowered her eyes. "Sorry," she said. "Didn't come over here to gawk and ask stupid questions. Won't take up much of your time," she apologized. "I know how busy you schoolteachers are this time of year."

"Won't you sit down?" Connie asked, lurching after her. "I could put on some tea."

"Law, no," Belle Davidson said, her hand rushing to her throat in an automatic display of shock. "Didn't come over here to cause you no trouble. I just come to have a word or two. If you got the time."

Connie crabbed over to the sofa and almost collapsed onto it. Although she was mobile enough on the props, she had not yet mastered how to get into and out of furniture gracefully. She noticed that Belle was wearing old-fashioned cotton stockings rolled down to just above her knees. She had on worn oxfords, and her fingernails were dried and cracked. Connie tried to guess her age. Maybe twenty-five, maybe thirty, maybe fifty. It was impossible to tell. Her skin was coarse and wrinkled, and her blue eyes were so washed out, they looked almost white.

"Well, what can I do for you, Mrs. Davidson?"

"Law, don't you go calling me 'Mrs. Davidson,'" she said seriously. "You call me Belle. Everybody does."

"Very well, Belle." Connie winced at the unintentional rhyme. "What can I do for you?"

"Well, I just kind of come to talk. Have a word, don't you know."

"About what?"

"Well." Her pale eyes dropped to her hands that folded themselves in her lap. "'Bout that sign out there, for one thing."

"Are you . . . I mean, are you and your husband interested in buying?"

"Law, no!" she exclaimed and laughed. It was such an unself-conscious display of genuine mirth that Connie almost felt embarrassed. Then Belle caught herself and smoothed down the worn cotton fabric across her skinny thighs and smiled. "That ain't it. I come to talk you out of selling it. Out of leaving." She brought her pencil-thin eyebrows together in a curious frown. "You *was* thinking 'bout leaving, wasn't you?"

"Well, yes," Connie said, quietly. "I think that would be best."

"Well, I don't," Belle said quickly. "I mean, we don't."

"We? You and . . ." She couldn't bring herself to say "Tom."

"Me and everybody. Everybody who lives round here wants you to stay."

"I really don't see why," Connie said and forced an ironic smile. "I mean, no one has spoken to me except . . . except your husband. And he—"

"Oh, Tom," she said sadly. "I know how that is." She sighed deeply. "He can't help the way he is. Always was too mean to live. But he won't bother you none. Not no more." She glanced at the wall as if she could see their home right through it. "We're getting a good settlement out of the insurance. We're all right. But he won't bother you no more." Her faded eyes roamed quickly around the room. "He won't bother nobody no more."

"I see," Connie said. "But I don't understand."

"Look." Belle folded her hands in her lap and spoke clearly but softly. "When we seen you moving in here with all them books and all that fancy furniture, we didn't know what to think. Then when Tom seen you fixing this old place up . . . well, it sort of made us feel . . . I don't know. Sort of low-down. See?"

Connie was startled. "I never meant—I mean, I only wanted to make it decent."

"Law! Course you did. Course you did." She nodded hard and looked around the room again. It was the only one Connie had come close to finishing, and it was still raw, but Belle's study didn't seem to be so much admiring as amazed. "And from the look of things, you got a good start on it," she said. "But folks around here don't have much. Never did. And the neighborhood's going downhill. Has been for years. But there you are fixing and working. Well, Tom got to resenting it."

"I don't see why."

"Well, he's just a night watchman over to the Co-op."

"I know."

"And he don't make but 'bout eight or nine hundred a month. After they take out and all."

"I see." Connie nodded. She felt guilty. Her salary, small as it was, was considerably more than that.

"Well, he couldn't 'ford to fix up our place, don't you see? Made him feel bad."

"That wasn't my intention."

"Course it wasn't. Course it wasn't. Wasn't none of your fault. But, you see, that's why all this happened."

"I don't understand."

"With the dog. With Dickey." Connie shook her head, confused. "The dog was my idea," Belle went on. "Thought it would keep the boy out of mischief. He's too much like Tom sometimes. Got a lot of the devil in him. Thought the dog would make him a playmate. He ain't got no brothers and sisters, and he don't get along too good with other kids." She lowered her face as if she were studying her abdomen. "Probably just as well. I can't handle him by hisself."

"So you got him the dog."

"Uh-huh." She nodded. "Kind of reward for being good."

"But Mr. Davidson said . . ." Connie trailed off.

Belle frowned deeply and studied her hands again. "Tom wouldn't have none of it. He didn't want no pet, he said. He said he wanted him a watchdog." She looked up, meeting Connie's eyes. "I seen what he was doing. I seen him making him a mean dog. Then I seen you feeding him. I hoped that maybe you doing that would keep him from turning mean."

Connie sat back. "He wasn't mean. He was just protecting himself."

"No, ma'am," Belle said pertly. "That's not what he was doing. He was protecting you."

The idea startled her. She made a small sound in her throat, but Belle didn't seem to notice.

"You was kind to him. Good to him. And he was protecting you from Tom. I know it. And if you think on it, you'll know it, too." Connie studied the woman's face, tried to decide if she was as sincere as she seemed. "And I'll tell you something else," Belle sighed. "That boy didn't shoot his daddy accidental. He shot him full on purpose."

"I don't believe that."

"Believe it." Belle's faded eyes sharpened, again. "He told me he done it on purpose. And I believe it. He come in and got that pistol when he seen Tom going over the fence to get you. He told me what his daddy was fixing to do." She took a deep breath. "And I told him . . . I told him to go ahead on." Her right hand went to her left arm, then drifted up to touch her cheek, an automatic, absentminded, and familiar gesture. "I ain't sorry," she said.

Connie didn't know what to say. She could see it now. It was clear.

Belle sighed again and now looked out the window. The day was a collage of spring colors. "You see, I knew Dickey could do it. And I knew I couldn't."

For a moment the two women remained silent. Both focused on their folded hands.

After a bit, Belle's eyes once more found Connie's, but now they were soft, damp. "But that's fixing to change. You can count on that. Now, the man can't even go to the bathroom by hisself." She nodded her head once and with vigor. "Law, things're fixing to change." She pulled a ragged tissue from a pocket and wiped her eyes quickly.

"Well, that's what I come to tell you." Belle rose. "Now, don't get up. I've took up enough of your time. Tom's coming home tomorrow, and I got a world of things to do."

"Well, I thank you for coming," Connie said, feeling awkward in her seated position. "But I really am leaving."

"I wish you'd change your mind," Belle said. "I do. You've brought something here. Something good. We ain't seen it, yet. But we would." She fixed her once more with her light blue eyes. "I wish you'd think it over."

"I have," Connie said, but she was startled by the lack of conviction in her voice. "I think I have to leave. There's just too many—too much sadness here, now. It's a lonely place."

"Well," Belle sighed deeper than she had before. "What's done's done." She started out, turned, then stopped. "You called him a name. Tom wouldn't give him no name. What'd you call him?"

"Nickleby," Connie said. "It's from a novel by Charles Dickens. It's about an unhappy boy. A lonely boy."

"Sort of like Dickey, think?"

Connie felt herself flush. "Well, not really. Maybe a little. He endures a lot of hardship, but he triumphs in the end."

"You think you'd loan me that book sometime?"

"Well, yes," Connie said, ignoring an alarm that went off whenever anyone asked to borrow one of her books. "I guess I could do that." She reached for her crutches and stood. "Do you want it now?"

Belle put up her hand, stopping her. "Let's wait and see if you change your mind about staying." She smiled thinly. "Hope you do." Then she was gone.

Connie stood on her crutches in the soft light of the room. Outdoors, the brilliant sun of early summer vied with the flowers and green grass to capture her attention. She heard a child's voice somewhere in the distance. He was yelling, his shouts full of laughter.

She turned and looked around the gloomy house. Her bookshelves needed dusting, and she needed to reread all of Browning and Arnold if she was going to teach them in the fall. The hallway needed new paper, she thought. And a coat of varnish on the staircase banister wouldn't hurt a bit. It wouldn't cost too much. If she took her time, she could even do it on the crutches.

She wondered if hanging baskets of wandering Jew or moss roses would do well on the back porch, and if it would be possible to trim the wisteria off of the house's southern side without killing it. There was so much to do, but thankfully the summer would be long and warm, and she'd be back on two feet before she knew it.

Before she fully realized it, she had already decided to stay.

A TRAIN TO CATCH

Mattie Cummings swung her legs over the side of her bed and sat up. She stretched away the mustiness of sleep, ran mental fingers all over her body, searched for anything wrong. She was a bit stiff, but that was natural, given the weather. She had an aching in her fingers. Her fingers always annoyed her when it was about to snow. She rose, turning automatically to make the bed. Tight corners, nice tuck of the heavy comforter under her pillow. The mattress was too hard. She knew that hard mattresses were supposed to be better, but she liked to sink deep into a bed, feel it all around her.

In the bathroom, she completed her morning toilet, brushed her thick gray hair in the small mirror over the sink. Like everything in her life, the bathroom was cold, sterile. It defied her attempts to personalize it with a small basket of perfumed soap. There was no tub, only a hospital-type shower with an overlarge stall for a handicapped user. She thought of them as "cripples." She was a long way from being crippled. Her hair was unruly this morning, wiry and full of static electricity. She tried damp-ening the brush, but that only seemed to make it worse. She'd have to clip it to hold it down.

Back in her small room, she slipped off her nightgown and stood naked before the bureau mirror. Her body was sturdy. Age and hard work hadn't bothered it much. There was a little fat around her hips, a slight bulge across her belly, but her shoulders were level, her breasts still firm, still had some bounce left in them. Once, she went for a week without wearing a bra just to see if anyone noticed. No one said a word, but she detected envious disapproval in House Manager Yvonne Garrett's glances. Though she was thirty years younger than Mattie, Yvonne's breasts sagged to her paunch with gravity no brassiere could arrest.

Outside, the wind was up. A chill seeped into the room, and she shivered. She pulled out a housedress and put it on. She found a pair of cotton socks in the bureau, then her lace-up rubber-soled shoes. She refused to wear house shoes, never had. She saw them as a sign of laziness.

Rising, she walked over to the window. Brittle cold swirled on a bitter north wind. The trees were bare, stark fingers grasping uselessly at the sky, grass yellow and dead, clouds the color of gunmetal, darker around the edges of the morning horizon. "Snow before dark," she said aloud, rubbing her sore knuckles. Her breath formed a pear-shaped cloud on the window. She ran a crooked finger through the liquid fog.

She broke the finger when she was a girl trying to catch a chicken for Christmas Eve dinner. When the fat hen dodged away from her, she slipped on the ice, fell against the porch, and the digit snapped backward. She tried to remember the pain, but she could only remember her daddy setting it with string and a clothespin while she sat at the kitchen table and smelled her mother's cooking. It mended with a bending twist. "Christmas," she said softly. The childhood anticipation of the holiday took root deep in her and grew.

She smiled and allowed her crooked finger to continue its wet design, turning the pear into a tree-shaped triangle, then adding small circles for balls, ornaments. She'd always loved Christmas.

Across the norther-swept street a movement caught her eye. It was a young Spanish boy helping a girl into a battered old open-bed bobtail truck. "Mestizos." Mattie frowned and whispered the old term. Migrant workers, she mentally corrected, and not Spanish, but Mexican. Too late in the season for them to be here, whatever they were. Work was long gone. They looked dirt poor. The girl was fat—for a Mexican, Mattie thought. She absolutely waddled. People that poor shouldn't be well fed enough to be so heavy at so young an age, or at any age. The girl had trouble getting up into the cab. She had long, dark hair spilling out of a stocking cap over a threadbare denim jumper. Even from a distance, her hands and bare legs looked raw with the cold. Fat or not, she was pretty when she turned and flashed a bright smile at the boy, who was short, chunky. He jogged around to the other side and banged into the vehicle. Frost from their breaths covered the windows as the old truck lurched away.

She estimated they were heading out to the old boxcars by the Short Road where the migrants generally lived. No running water or electricity. Just shelter, and not much of that. They were poor and ignorant, Mattie thought. But they looked happy. She envied them and was angry at herself for admitting it.

It was time to go to breakfast. She hated breakfast. For more than six decades, she had arisen every morning and made biscuits, hard-fried eggs, bacon, and gravy, and set the whole ensemble out with a half gallon of strong coffee on an oilcloth-covered table for Dutch. He liked a good breakfast. She loved making it. Now, though, she knew that the dining room table of Willow Oaks would be laden with nothing more substantial than lukewarm oatmeal. There would be some yogurt, low-cal jellies to go on bagels or some other rubbery excuse for bread, some decaffeinated coffee and weak tea, a couple of pitchers of juice, and skim milk for those who wanted cold cereal with overripe bananas.

That wasn't breakfast, Mattie thought. That was just stupid.

She glanced around her room. The bed was against one wall, her bureau—the only piece of furniture she was able to bring with her other than a rocker—against the other. A rubber-backed, washable cotton throw rug occupied the middle of the area, covering green and white tile, gone black in the corners from years of wax and dirt buildup. She had put a few small mementos on the wall, but they seemed out of place, temporary, as, truly, they were intended to be. She had photos of her mother and father, and one of her and Dutch. It was a picture they took the day they paid off the farm. Ten years ago, she remembered. It seemed a lifetime ago. In a way, it was.

With a sigh, she left the room. There was little choice. It was nearly eight, and Yvonne would be coming down to check on her if she didn't appear. It made her feel helpless, at Yvonne's mercy.

The hallway smelled of camphor and antiseptic, human waste and the sickly sweet odor of age. Indefinable, it permeated the house, even the residents' clothing. No matter how hard people cleaned their surroundings, themselves, it remained, overcame everything. It had no source, it was just part of the stink of Willow Oaks. What kind of stupid name was "Willow Oaks," anyway? Mattie wondered as she padded down the sterile hall. A willow was a willow. An oak was an oak. There was no such thing as a "willow oak." In North Central Texas, there wasn't much of either one, anyway.

The dining room opened before her gaze. Maria Chivington, the girl Yvonne worked like her personal slave, scurried around helping the half-dozen residents seated at the table. Yvonne herself breezed through, gave Mattie an acidic smile, inspected the table, departed. Yvonne had been an ugly girl, Mattie thought as she sat down and reached for a piece of cold whole wheat toast. Now, she was an ugly woman. Too lazy to get a husband when she was young, she gave up on herself and decided if she couldn't be happy, she'd make it her mission in life to see to the perpetual unhappiness of others. So far, she'd been successful. As house manager of an old folks home, she'd found the perfect calling.

Yvonne forbade anyone to call Willow Oaks an "old folks home," Mattie reminded herself with a wry smile. This was a "benevolent care center." She thought it more closely resembled the death house of a prison. Yvonne was the perfect warden.

Mattie's fellow tenants didn't talk much at breakfast. At first, this distressed her. But after a few weeks, she realized that it wasn't that they were unfriendly. They just had little to say. Beyond complaining about their most recent surgeries or comparing medications, their lives had been reduced to dim memories. There were plenty of those. Enough to fill each eight-by-twelve room with a combination of misery and regret, laced only occasionally with the joyful recollection of something wonderful. No one needed to share another's. It hurt too much to drag the past out and dust it off for the indifferent inspection of someone whose life was just as disappointing as everyone else's.

The average age in the house was seventy-five. Mattie knew this because Yvonne kept a large chart on a wall in the kitchen, a running count. If someone died or moved in, she made the adjustment. At eighty-two, Mattie was the oldest ambulatory resident on the premises. This vexed Yvonne, who thought anyone as old as Mattie should have to rely on a walker or at least a cane.

Mattie reached for coffee, sniffed it, and asked Maria if there was any fresh made. Maria gave the kitchen door a brief glance, then winked and slipped through. Mattie's conspiracy with Maria was another satisfying element in her life. She slipped the girl five dollars a week to keep a thermos of regular coffee handy. She made it at home and brought it in. If Yvonne knew, she'd probably fire her. Mattie worried about that. But she needed and wanted her coffee, regular, strong, and black as Yvonne's heart.

———

Breakfast over, and two cups of Maria's stout brew consumed on the sly, Mattie retired to the "rec room." It really was just a living room, doubled in size from the original house's design when it was converted from a private residence to Willow Oaks. Four hard sofas were placed here and there, with some lumpy easy chairs—no recliners, as Yvonne explained she was afraid of lawsuits in case someone hurt something getting into or out of one. A few end tables held ugly lamps with low-wattage bulbs and stacks of outdated magazines that offered advice on cooking, home decorating, child-rearing, and, for some reason, sexual gratification. There were some old *Texas Monthlys*, advertising restaurants, boutiques, and luxury vacations no resident of Willow Oaks could even imagine. A handful of business magazines were for the investment-minded reader who might want to plan a prosperous future. Willow Oaks residents were in the middle of their future, Mattie thought, and it was far from prosperous.

The room was cheerless and as impersonal as a tire shop's waiting area. A nineteen-inch color TV on a wobbly stand was parked against one wall. There was no cable or satellite dish, only a rickety antenna that struggled to pull in three—sometimes four—grainy stations from distant towers. Four wheelchairs were aligned in front of the snowy screen that morning, their occupants waiting for the news programs to end and game or talk shows to begin. The volume was perpetually too loud to talk or concentrate on reading. Christmas music spilled out from commercials and network greetings. Mattie picked up a stack of *Southern Living* and *Better Homes and Gardens,* took a seat. She'd never developed an interest in television, as they never could get any reception on the farm. She had a radio in her room, but farm market reports and implement ads depressed her, political talk shows and screaming radio preachers bored her. She never learned to like modern music.

She glanced out the window. The weather was deteriorating. No walk today. She had nothing to do until dinner, which Yvonne called "lunch," and which like everything else at Willow Oaks was served on a strict timetable. Today, it would be a real thrill, Mattie thought. Maria told her that cream of broccoli soup and pasta salad were on the menu. "Just as soon have peanut butter on a stale soda cracker," Mattie told her. Yvonne assured her that that could be arranged. She liked to get in the last word, Mattie knew.

Mattie came to Willow Oaks three months before. It wasn't a choice she enjoyed making. Dutch's death caught her by surprise. It probably caught him a little by surprise, too. He had always been a strong man, brought eagerly to hard work. At eighty-four, he often bragged that he never saw a doctor, "took no patented pills," and "had every tooth he was born with." But against a brain tumor, none of that mitigated. He could have handled the pain, the discomfort. What he couldn't handle was the wasting away. She saw the change in him when he returned from the first chemo treatment: He was frail, required help just to get into bed. He might have gotten past that, too, she thought. Might have survived the indignity of peeing all over himself, of vomiting down his shirtfront every fifteen minutes. But what he couldn't get past was the fact that the tumor was inoperable. He'd never get better. All he could do was suffer the humiliation of watching the farm fall apart around him because he was too sick and weak to do the work. But his death wasn't exactly a well-planned departure from sixty-two years of marriage and a lifetime of building something. Just a quick jerk of the trigger and a mess to clean up in the barn. That was a year ago. It was a horror, at first. Now, it was just a galling memory.

She and Dutch never had children, had no siblings left alive, and never were close to any of their nieces or nephews. She'd survived all their friends who were her age. For a suicide widow, there is no insurance, only heartache and embarrassment. The farm was hers, but so were the expenses, and the taxes. A farm has to pay for itself to keep going. That meant work, more work than a woman her age could do or could afford to hire done. Each month since Dutch got sick, their reserves went down.

Finally, after burying Dutch, there was little left, so she had no choice. She put the place up for sale and followed her banker's advice, moved to Willow Oaks, hoped her funds would hold out until the place sold. Given the market these days, that wasn't likely.

Willow Oaks was the only old folks home in the county. Yvonne's daddy, who operated the town's funeral home, owned it, let her run it as she saw fit. She had a degree in something or other from Texas A&M, and she made the place her own private hell on earth with herself as chief devil. Mattie figured there was some kind of kickback for anyone Yvonne hurried along to her daddy's main business. There was a lot of profit in death, she knew, more than there was in dying.

Mattie had enough cash left to pay for a year in advance. If and when the farm sold, she could move to another town, maybe a better place. But for the time being, she was stuck. Willow Oaks was worse than jail, she thought as she flipped the pages of the old magazines. At least prisoners had some hope of parole. The only hope Mattie had was for transfer to a nicer prison. That, or the cemetery. Lately, she'd been thinking more and more about Dutch's final choice. She had thought it was the wrong thing to do, but maybe he'd known something she didn't.

She flung the magazines aside and looked around the room. Five or six more of the tenants had drifted in, found seats where they would wait out the morning. Most seemed to be waiting merely to die. There were twenty-four tenants at Willow Oaks, but ten were bedridden and virtually comatose, eight more confined to wheelchairs, and a solid majority were virtually deaf, or blind. The medicine tray Yvonne carted around twice a day looked like a portable pharmacy.

Mattie stood and went out onto the porch, patting her pocket to make sure she had her cigarettes. Yvonne forbade smoking, but Mattie didn't care. She never smoked more than four or five cigarettes a day, but the habit was a hard one to break. She took it up the night she met David "Dutch" Cummings at a Christmas USO canteen next to the Fort Worth and Denver Depot. Handsome in his sailor's uniform and on his way to "somewhere in the South Pacific," as the newsreels said, he shouldered aside a brawny GI corporal to get to the spot in front of the doughnut table where she sat, then offered her a wide grin.

"Want to step outside for a smoke?" he asked.

Her heart fluttered as she examined his curly red hair and bright blue eyes. "It's cold out there," she replied through a smile so big it hurt.

"I've got something to keep us warm." He winked, patted his bag, then extended his hand. "C'mon. It's Christmas, and I've got a train to catch." She stood, held out her hand. He spun gallantly and took her arm, and together, they stepped outside into the breathless cold.

They sat on wooden benches out in the frozen night of a depot platform and sipped Cokes laced with bootleg rum and smoked Lucky Strike Greens until his train left at daybreak. She wanted to go with him so bad, she ached. He wrote to her every week, and when he came home, they married, bought the farm, made a life.

It was blistering cold outside, and Mattie wished she'd brought a coat. As she pushed the door to against mild protests from those caught in the icy gust, her visible breath disappeared on wisps of wind rushing by her face. She cupped her hands and lit her smoke, drawing the heat deep and holding it before letting it escape into the frigid atmosphere. These days, having a smoke was about all she could do to connect her to Dutch, to his memory.

———

When she returned to the parlor, hugging herself against the cold, her attention was arrested by a large white box in the center of the room. Lettering on the side announced that it contained a "Full-sized, Life-Like Christmas Tree." Mattie walked over and nudged the box with her toe. Closer inspection announced that a six-foot Douglas fir was inside the box. All that was required was assembly.

"A plastic tree?" she muttered. "They're going to put up a plastic tree?"

"*We're* going to put up a plastic tree!" Yvonne announced from the doorway. Her arms were full of tinsel, ornaments. All were in boxes boasting Wal-Mart sale price stickers, each accompanied by a bright, round, yellow smiley face wearing a Santa hat. Mattie had always found that particular symbol to be insipid, reminding her of an idiot child's countenance. "We'll start right after dinner while the Perry Como special is on," Yvonne continued.

"I don't want a plastic tree," Mattie said. "I—we want a real tree."

Yvonne was already on her way out. She spoke over her shoulder. "People are allergic to real trees."

Mattie continued to stand in the middle of the room. A plastic tree. Not in all her life had she even considered such a thing. She remembered Dutch coming in with a fresh-cut cedar in tow. The smell of it, so fresh, crisp and green, filled the house, excited her out of common sense. Plastic had no odor. None. She looked around the room. A full majority of the ambulatory residents were now present.

"Who's allergic to real trees?" she asked. No one paid her any attention, so she stepped to the center of the room, spoke louder. "I asked who here is allergic to real trees?"

A few heads shook in denial, and several sets of rheumy eyes turned toward her. Finally, Leanda McGillicutty spoke up. "Yvonne doesn't like real trees. They make a mess, she says. And cause fires. You be quiet, now. Oprah's coming on."

Mattie stared at the dying forms surrounding her. Their total attention was fixed on the screen. Their entire lives had been reduced to sitting here, day after day, watching some silly box. They couldn't even have a real tree for Christmas.

"I think we should take a vote," she said. "We're paying tenants here. I think if we want a real tree, we should have one." Again, only a few gave her attention, so she stepped over in front of the set. "I said I want to vote on this. We have a quorum here. Let's have a vote!"

Herbert Bugerman, a onetime robust rancher and former All-American fullback, now a humpbacked, bald man with clawlike fingers and perpetual urine stains on his pants, raised his hand, palm out. "This ain't a lodge meeting, Mattie," he said. "Yvonne runs this outfit. She says no real tree, that's what she means. Ain't no telling what she might do, we take a vote against her."

Several heads bobbed in agreement. "He's right," Clara Florentine, once the town's librarian, said in a quaking voice. "We buck Yvonne, she's liable to take away the television."

That caused a stir. Everyone in the room began muttering, and one or two stood and started wagging fingers, lecturing Mattie. "You're new here," Bernie Cartwright, onetime high school principal, shouted. "You don't know Yvonne. She's too mean to live."

"That's right," Faye Newsome, who once ran for Congress on a populist platform, added, putting on her oversized glasses for a better view of Mattie. Her sparse hair was dyed pink and curled close to her head, giving her the appearance of a giant, mangy poodle with owl eyes. "She's took away the television before. Missed a whole week of my soap!"

"Fine!" Mattie yelled. "Watch your damn television!" She threw up her hands and left the room. Yvonne was there to meet her, her chubby cheeks red with annoyance.

"Do you see what happens when you get them all worked up? We have a way of doing things here, and everything's done for a reason."

"A plastic tree is not Christmas," Mattie said, feeling suddenly childish, hating herself for it. "Christmas is smells and sounds and tastes—"

"Christmas is just what we make it," Yvonne cut her off. "And it will be the same here as it is every year. A very nice time. They're rebroadcasting the Perry Como special tonight, and I plan to have the tree all up and ready for the ornaments. We'll have punch."

"With rum, or maybe some brandy in it, I expect," Mattie said with a sneer.

Yvonne ignored Mattie, brushed past her, and went into the dining room. Mattie stood for a moment, the odor of camphor and sickness swirling around her. She suddenly felt ill.

———

She skipped the noon meal, stayed in her room. The afternoon began to darken as clouds thickened overhead. She could hear the wind against the building, felt the cold through her window. This room, she thought, was like a tomb, a coffin in a grave. Christmas was here, and everything was dead, dying. She didn't expect gifts, not even a card. But she had expected that for a few moments there might be something, some recollection of years gone by. That's what Christmas was for, she thought. That's what it was supposed to be: memories.

From the window, she observed the gray street beneath the winter day. She and Dutch were Baptists, but they mostly went to church for weddings and funerals—especially funerals, it seemed. Farmers didn't take Sunday off when there was work to be done, so they weren't regular. Besides, Dutch told her, he lost his religion on Guadalcanal.

"You spend about a week burying several thousand rotten pieces of what used to be healthy kids, and you come to the notion that there ain't no God," he told her in one of the rare moments when he talked about it, "and if there is, He's not worth much of a damn." He said he was glad they never had children. "Kills you to bury a child," he said. "Kills your soul." He stopped, then got a faraway look in his eyes. "I never want to bury a child again."

Mattie kept her faith, but she didn't much care for the new brand of ministers. Most of them she saw as glad-handing fools with expensive haircuts and capped teeth, eager to squeeze money out of the faithful, but unable to deliver the kind of spiritual strength that preachers should offer. She knew what the meaning of Christmas was, and she acknowledged it in her prayers. But she also knew that it was so much more. It meant thinking of her brothers and sisters, her parents—all gone now—and of Dutch. And he was gone as well. Burying a husband isn't particularly good for a person's soul either, Mattie thought.

Disappointment welled in her heart, and tears filled her eyes. It seemed that without thinking about it she'd been looking forward to nothing more than Christmas, to putting up the tree, singing carols, eating rich foods tasty with bad-for-you ingredients and enticing with holiday aroma. She could almost smell the chicken cooking on Christmas Eve. More than any other, that scent was always Christmas to her. If Yvonne had her way, she thought with a sudden surge of bitterness, Christmas dinner would be a turkey sandwich and a fruit cup. "It's healthy," she could hear the home manager saying in her whiny, fat-girl voice. "We have to do things a certain way around here. There's a reason for everything we do."

Mattie wiped her eyes and looked out again. Parked off to one side of Willow Oaks was her old Dodge pickup. She remembered the day Dutch bought it. John Kennedy was shot that very afternoon right down in Dallas. She had no idea how many miles it had traveled—or how many rebuilt engines and transmissions and clutches Dutch had put in it—since that dark day. Held together as much by faith as by bailing wire and spot welds, the old vehicle had bounced its way over the crusted ruts of field roads for more than four decades. Its seats were worn out, windshield cracked, tires nearly bald. Its only virtue was that it was hers. She refused to include it in the inventory of things to sell.

She now remembered that she had excluded other things from the sale of the place and all its furnishings. A whole roomful of personal possessions. They were all boxed up back at the house, in the spare bedroom, awaiting some solution as to storage: her mother's china and silver, some quilts, old clothing, her wedding veil. There were most of Dutch's personal things: his hunting knives, his wallet and watch, his Navy Cross and Purple Heart, and that old flask from the night they met.

And among those boxes and bags, she now recalled with growing excitement, was something else: a large, green box tied with ribbon—her collection of Christmas tree ornaments. Gathered for decades, no two were alike. They came from all over, sent by friends and distant relatives, handed down from their families. She could see them dangling from the evergreen branches, glistening, sparkling in the excitement that, for her, always was Christmas. Her breath went short with the memory.

Those people—she pictured the somnambulant group in the parlor—had given up. Something like Christmas was what they needed to keep them moving, keep them hoping, make them remember something good in their lives. If they couldn't have a real tree, why couldn't they at least have real ornaments? Why not have something that would in some small way at least remind them of a real Christmas? There was no reason. No reason in the world, she thought. They would love it!

She turned suddenly and looked at the door. She half expected Yvonne to be standing there, shaking her fat face, insisting on putting up her cheap discount decorations on the plastic tree, telling her why her ornaments wouldn't fit in with the way things were done at Willow Oaks. But the doorway was empty. Mattie's eyes trailed to the bureau, to the jewelry box that held the keys to the truck, the house. She hadn't driven it in months, wasn't even sure it would start. But if it would, what could it hurt?

It was already after three. Supper, which Yvonne called "dinner," was at five. The farm was five miles out, but if she took the Short Road, she could get there, find the box, and return in an hour. Almost breathless with daring, she raced to the closet, pulled on a heavy coat, grabbed some gloves from the bureau, tied a wool scarf around her head, and slipped down the hall, out the fire exit, and bent her body against the icy pellets now peppering the town in front of a strong north wind. She trudged toward the ancient pickup.

When the old Dodge cranked on the first try, she began singing "Jingle Bells" as loud as she could. She slammed it into gear, and sped around the corner trailing a cloud of blue exhaust. For the first time since Dutch died, she was truly happy. For the first time in a long time, she thought, she was acting, not merely reacting to something she couldn't control. "In a one-horse open sleigh," she shouted at the web of cracks in the frosty windshield.

———

When she reached the farmhouse, the storm was worsening. Wind tore at the Dodge when it lumbered past the "For Sale 640 Acres and House" sign, crossed the cattle guard, and ground up the rutted drive to the dooryard. For a moment, Mattie peered at her old home through the cracked windshield. Stark, empty against the wintry blast, the house looked colder than even the weather could make it. The chimney was void of smoke, something that would never have been the case in weather like this. She saw the henhouse door was open, and she was sure she could see some birds inside. Percy Walker was supposed to have taken them, but some of the flock probably wandered off before he came, then returned later. She wondered why varmints hadn't gotten them. The garden was overgrown with onions and wild asparagus, and a piece of tin roof was peeled back on the toolshed, slapping in the icy gale. To her faded eyes, the whole farm seemed to be sulking because it had been abandoned at such a time.

She shook off somber thoughts and stepped out into the icy wind that now scythed unimpeded across the rolling prairie. The sleet had lessened, but snow now mixed in with it. The ground was soft, warm, not yet frozen hard, so that meant mud soon. She needed to hurry or the Short Road would be an impassable loblolly. It wasn't really a road, just a trail for irrigation workers cut along the edges of fields near shelter breaks and deep drainage ditches.

The wind nearly blinded her, forced her to duck her head as she mounted the old steps, holding the door key in her hand like a lance. Slippery ice covered the porch. All she needed was to fall, she thought, to break a hip or a wrist. Wouldn't that give Yvonne a thrill? She reached the door, ripped open the screen, jabbed in the key, remembering to give it a slight push on the right side to swing it wide.

Inside, she was halted by a gloom that haunted the raw emptiness of the front parlor. Motes and cobwebs swirled in drafts lit by the blue-gray light from the sash windows. The house sagged, moaned in the wind. Cold covered everything. The furniture, draped with bedsheets, squatted in a dusty room that had never been less than perfectly clean, with hardwood floors polished to a mirrored sheen. Sadness welled inside her, but she pushed it back, took a deep breath. She had a purpose here, she reminded herself.

She moved quickly down the hall, wishing she'd remembered to bring a flashlight, and wondering if the oil lamps in the pantry were filled. But her memory provided a sufficient beacon. In the bedroom, the bright green box was on top of a stack of other containers. It wasn't heavy, and she shook it lightly to hear the tinkle of a small, glass bell she remembered was packed in cotton down toward the bottom, cushioned by thick coils of wide red-satin ribbon.

Holding the box made her feel whole. Warmth built inside her like a newly stoked fire. She moved slowly out of the room, then back down the hall and to the door. She had trouble pulling it to, relocking it, but she finally made her way back to the pickup and nestled the box securely in the seat. This was a victory, she knew. A small one, but a victory nonetheless. And that's what Christmas was about, she thought to herself: victory.

———

Eager to return before she was missed, she took the Short Road. That was a mistake. The storm was now fully arrived and coated the land with white powder that rapidly deepened. No mere snowfall, this was a blizzard that blotted out natural light, and Mattie's visibility was soon reduced to a few feet in front of the old Dodge's hood. The ineffective defroster wheezed uselessly against the thick vapor in the windows while the wipers clanked against the thickening snow.

The one-lane trace was sandy and uncertain in the best of weather. It took two miles off the same trip by the highway, but it was liable to washouts in heavy rains. The steering wheel seemed to have a life of its own as the truck's tires fought to find reliable ruts to guide it. More than once when rounding a curve beside a plum thicket or copse of overgrown mesquite, she felt the rear wheels lose purchase, skid onto the edge of one of the deep ditches alongside, as if some monster was trying to pull her into its icy maw below.

She fought fear and cold away, concentrated on steering the truck around the winding curves, longed to see the highway emerge after each. How long was this road? It only seemed to take minutes when she used to drive it. Today, it was more like hours. The clouds were lower, darker than ever. Her headlights shot an anemic yellow beam into a white curtain that billowed almost parallel to the ground. It felt like midnight, though it couldn't be later than four. She slid around one more curve, certain that this time she would see the highway ahead, then spotted the old bobtail truck blocking the road immediately in front of her.

She jammed both her feet onto the brake, stood up on it, and was sure she was screaming when her head struck the windshield and, after a brilliant flash of light, everything went from stormy white to utterly black.

———

She was having a dream about the time she had the flu. That, too, had been at Christmas. Her body was racked with fever, but she shivered with chills. Her head ached, and Dutch was wiping her forehead with a cool cloth, talking to her in soothing, low tones. Through a haze, she could see the lights of the tree reflecting off her ornaments.

Then, her eyes fluttered open, and all she saw was a circle of darkness floating in a sea of white specks, like alabaster moths encircling an ebony flame. Dutch's face slowly transformed into the swarthy features of a Hispanic youth only inches away, his chocolate eyes wide with fear. He was applying a dirty rag to her forehead. As she came more to herself, she realized he was speaking to her, but his words made no sense. At last, she understood he was speaking in Spanish.

"I don't—." She choked, swallowed, continued: "I don't habla the lingo," she finished gruffly. She pushed his hand away, tried to sit up. Dizziness spun her head, forced her to lie back. He held the rag over her like a charm, but no longer touching her, merely staring at her, wide-eyed. She was now aware that she was out of the pickup, down on the ground. Snow swirled overhead, but he had pulled her around behind the vehicle, out of the wind. "I'll be all right," she said. "Just let me get my breath."

It took a few moments, but she sat up. There was an instant swimming behind her eyes, but the pain settled into a dull throb in the center of her forehead. She touched the spot. Bright blood stained her gloves. The youngster was jabbering at her in rapid Spanish.

"I don't speak it," she said. "You might as well talk Greek to me."

He nodded as if he understood, then sat back on his hams and stared at her. He looked familiar, but she discarded the thought, started again to rise. He tried to stop her—or maybe help her—but she pushed his hands away. "I'm all right. Hell, I've been hurt worse than this slopping hogs." She made it to her feet, but her head gyrated and the ground beneath her wanted to shift. It seemed very dark, and the blizzard blasted by her like a train. She took a deep breath, steadied herself.

Her mind flew to the box of ornaments. She stumbled around to the side of the pickup and jerked open the passenger door. The box was shoved against the dash, and there was a large tear in one corner, exposing the red-satin ribbon, but the container was otherwise intact. She wondered if any of her precious treasures were ruined. Angry now, she spun on the boy, "What're you doing out here? Blocking the road like that? Are you crazy?"

He stepped back and spoke in Spanish.

"Loco? Are you loco?" she demanded.

He gave her a bewildered look, then grinned nervously, spoke again in Spanish.

"Fine," Mattie said, pointing at the box. "If even one of those are broken, I'll have the sheriff on you!" He stared incomprehensively at the box, but she ignored him, braced herself against the truck, and walked down to inspect the damage. When she got around front, she saw what had happened. The larger vehicle had slid sideways, clipped a utility pole. The truck was hopelessly stuck across the narrow passage, blocking it entirely.

She limped around to the front of the Dodge. It was wedged into the bobtail, and the windshield over the steering wheel was webbed where her forehead shattered it. "Damn it," she said. "Yvonne'll sling a litter of green cats!"

Over the howl of the wind, she became aware that the boy was still talking to her, more rapidly now, mixing heavily accented English words with Spanish. He pulled frantically at the sleeve of her coat and gestured for her to follow. She resisted, but he kept waving toward the bobtail. She now remembered where she knew him from. The Spanish couple, the mestizos. She had seen him earlier that morning. Where was the girl? Maybe he took her home—back to the boxcars that passed for homes among these people. He kept tugging, blabbering, and finally she shrugged, followed him. If he was bent on doing her harm, she thought, he already would have.

They skirted the narrow margin of sandy ledge around the bobtail. Mattie looked up into the cab's window where he was pointing, jabbering constantly and with increasing anxiety. Finally, she grabbed the handle and stepped onto the running board. Her head spun once more, but she found her footing and looked inside the cab.

Now, she understood what he was saying, what he was trying so hard to make her understand. Now, she knew why he had taken chances and was speeding along this road in such weather. She looked down at him. He was no more than twenty. The beginnings of a mustache formed on his upper lip, but his cheeks were smooth under dark eyes that showed more fear than concern as he babbled. He was practically dancing under her gaze, but she couldn't tell if it was from the cold or from panic. Should be both, she thought. And she peered again into the cab.

There lying across the spring-scarred front seat was the girl, wrapped in the old denim jumper and shivering in pain as well as cold. She was alive, and she was well, and, Mattie saw, she wasn't fat at all. She was, however, in imminent danger of having a baby.

It took more than a half hour to loosen the pickup from the smashed side of the bobtail, get it started, and turn it around on the narrow trail. Eventually, they had the old Dodge on its way. Mattie let Julio—a name she learned through gestures and mimes—drive, and she sat in the bed, her coat and two ratty blankets wrapped around the girl—Mariana, she determined—who was now having regular and more frequent contractions and kept Mattie in a panic that warmed her more than any covering could have. There was no question that the baby was coming, and soon.

Mattie had delivered calves, colts, piglets, puppies, and kittens when their mothers were unable or unwilling to do it alone. She once had gone along with Dutch when he was called to assist Bob Dalhart with the birth of a llama calf—or whatever they were—during his misguided experience in trying to raise the beasts for wool. But she had no experience with a human baby or with a terrified teenaged mother. Mattie's teeth clenched against the fear that jumped in her heart with every bump. She frequently pounded on the back glass, flattening her hand to try to make Julio slow the vehicle over the rougher spots. She didn't know if he saw her. Because the windshield was smashed, he was driving with the window cranked down, leaning outside, trying to penetrate the blinding white storm that raged around them. Next to him, the box of ornaments bounced high with every bump. Mattie yelled about that, too.

The pickup was not as "okay" as Julio assured her when they backed it up and got it going, either. She could hear the engine coughing, the gears grinding roughly when he downshifted. It would take a miracle to get them back to town, to the hospital, even to a telephone. Almost every house in this part of the county was either for sale or abandoned, she knew, recalling what the banker told her when he convinced her to sell out. Those that weren't, were probably empty, their residents in town at church or off visiting relatives for the biggest family holiday of the year. The only two homes they passed along the way exhibited nothing but cold, dark windows and snarling, barking dogs against the approach of the old truck out of the blowing snow. Each time, Julio slowed, but Mattie shook her head, pointed down the road. They drove on.

Mariana cried out with every bump, every turn that caused her to move. Her knees kept hunching, and Mattie pressed down on her bulging stomach, unsure of what to do for her.

It was full dark when they finally made the highway turnoff—five miles back to town or at least a telephone—but Julio stopped, jumped out, yelling in a panic. Mattie stared over the top of the cab. A bright geyser of steam whiter than the swirling snow around it was spewing from the hood. Mattie's resolve sank. If the Dodge died, they were done for. Even if someone came along, who would stop on a night like this to help two Mexicans and an old woman in a beat-up pickup? She peered into the snow dancing across the blacktop highway. Who but a bunch of fools would be out on a night like this?

She peered across the highway to the pasture gate. The house was just over a mile away. She pointed toward the gate. "Go," she yelled at Julio who was staring at her finger. He stood looking dumbly at her. Panic swelled her voice. "Vamoose! We got to move, now, or this child's going to drop her calf right here beside the road! Go!"

With no more assurance than his faith in her voice, he leaped back inside, gunned the ailing pickup across the highway, bounced through a barbed-wire gate and onto the pasture road. He was moving too fast, the truck swerved and veered, careened dangerously near fence posts and mesquite stumps. Over the wind, she could hear the engine whining high and loud. She held Mariana to her own body, tried to soften the bounces, heard the girl cry out with every bump. Mattie gritted her teeth and turned her eyes up where the snow blotted out the night sky, the flakes iridescent in the reflected headlights of the old pickup as it made its familiar way back home.

———

When they skated up on icy mud to the dooryard gate, the truck whined, coughed, then died with a hissing expulsion of steam. Mattie leaped down, pulled the bewildered boy out, and grabbed the key ring. "Inside!" she screamed over the howling wind. "Get the girl." She stumbled across the yard and up onto the slick porch. She stopped, saw him still standing by the pickup, gaping at her.

"Inside! You stupid—" She stopped herself, took a breath, searched her memory for the right words. "In el casa!" she yelled, pointing to the house. "Mi casa. Mi casa!" She spun, slipped on the slick porch, and went down on one knee. Pain, sudden and sharp, shot up her thigh, into her hip. She tried to rise, couldn't. Her eyes shut against the agony. "Oh, Dutch," she hissed through gritted teeth, her eyes wet with tears of panic and pain. "Give me strength." She saw Julio's form lumbering through the snow toward the porch, Mariana in his arms. "Don't you dare let me bury a child tonight."

She took a cleansing breath, pulled her feet under her, then staggered toward the door, keyed the lock, and shoved the door open. Once inside, she limped around, jerking sheets off furniture and carrying them to the front bedroom—their bedroom. Julio, Mariana in his arms, stumbled through the door. He was, the fleeting thought passed through Mattie's mind, the first Mexican ever to cross their threshold. As if he read her thought, he stopped in the entryway, staring at the dark, empty room.

"Don't just stand there, you idiot," Mattie snapped. "We've got work to do."

There was no power. No heat. Julio, though, proved adept at building a fire in the old woodstove in the kitchen, pumped water from the cistern and set it to boil while Mattie found an oil lamp and brought it to the bedroom. She spread the sheets on the mattress, then stripped the girl's threadbare dress off her while she screamed in the agony of almost constant contractions. Mattie went to the bathroom and located enough pieces of soap to cleanse her hands in a bowl of hot water that Julio, jabbering constantly, finally brought in. Unable to abide him any longer, she shoved him from the room, shouting "go make yourself useful" into his frightened face.

"Go on!" she insisted, pointing out the front door. "Get the blankets, at least."

"¿Qué?" he asked.

"Blankets, you idiot!" she shouted, pointing again. "In the truck!" And she slammed the door. She was panicked enough for both of them, she thought, and she wanted him out of the way.

She turned to Mariana, writhing on the soft mattress, her knees spread, her face twisted in pain. "Damn it, Dutch," she whispered. "What do I do now?" Then she went to the girl. "It'll be all right, honey," she said. "You're not the first one to go through this, and I'm sure you won't be the last."

————

It was over quickly, almost before she knew it. Mattie barely had time to reach the bedside before the screaming girl's pretty face scrunched once more, then she delivered into Mattie's waiting hands a suddenly squalling baby boy.

For a moment she stood there in the dark room, the tiny, bloody infant writhing in her arms, his eyes squinting against the faint light of an old oil lamp, his fists opening and closing in reflexive samplings of the frozen air around him. Mattie traced his perfect chin with her crooked finger and something warm touched her heart. "Merry Christmas," she whispered. "You're right on time."

She handed the baby to Mariana, whose eyes in the yellow lamp's reflection were as large and black and beautiful as anything Mattie had ever seen, then talked softly to the girl as she finished the business of the birthing. She took her time and washed the baby and mother, found the box of quilts in a closet and made a decent bed on the bare mattress, then stood back for a moment, admiring the scene. It was frigid in the room, but the mother and babe lay snug and peaceful in the bed Mattie and Dutch had shared for so many years. She felt her eyes moisten, but then shook away the sentiment. "Time to meet your daddy, I guess," she said and went out to fetch Julio.

He sprang to his feet when she came through the door and stared his question. But she could offer him no attention. Her shock when she came into the old living room stunned her speechless, motionless. Julio had found candles. Dozens of them. The entire room was ablaze with golden light. He asked something, but she could only nod, too amazed to say anything. He leaped past her into the bedroom, but she never saw him. Instead, she stepped forward into the candlelight, overcome. The old wallpaper, faded and torn over the years, outlined with the bleached shadows of frames and hangings now packed away, seemed brilliant, almost new. The floor was freshly swept, the reflected candles dancing in its shine. But what captured her eye, what amazed her was something else, entirely, something utterly astonishing. "Oh, my," was all she could say. "Oh, my."

Draped across the walls, strung from windowsill to windowsill, door jam to door jam, was a rope of wide red-satin ribbon, and hanging from it, spaced carefully against the wall, were all her ornaments, each sparkling and twinkling in the candlelight. The tiny glass bell was over the front door.

Her hand went to her throat, and she turned round and round. Her eyes were wide and glistening in the reflected beauty of the room. "Oh my," she repeated and turned to see Julio standing in the doorway. He put his hands together and lay them to the side of his inclined face. Mariana and the baby were asleep.

She swallowed, then stepped toward him. "How?" she started, but had no words to finish.

He shrugged, then smiled timidly. "¿Le gusta?" he asked. "¿Bonita, verdad?" She continued to stare, and he shrugged again. "Es navidad," he said, bowing his head slightly.

All at once, to her nostrils came a wonderful, familiar aroma. She looked down the hall toward the kitchen, then back at the stocky boy, who grinned self-consciously.

"Pollo," he said. He made a gesture of wringing a chicken's neck, shrugged again. "Para las tamales navidad. Is okay?"

Her smile began slowly, then widened. "It's okay," she whispered. "It's very okay." Then she said aloud, "Very, very okay."

Weariness suddenly swam up from her feet like a wave. Pain from her forehead returned with a spinning throb. She also felt a lurching jab from her knee. Standing was too much. Julio rushed to her as her legs buckled, and she slumped into Dutch's old chair and sighed deeply. Julio fluttered around, speaking quickly, concern wrinkling his brow.

"Just leave me be for a minute," she said, waving him away. "I need to rest." He looked at her, a wide smile on his face. "You're grinning now," she said. "That won't last."

She looked once more at the stunning decorations of the room, savored the scent of chicken boiling, basked in the warm gold light of the candles, and sighed. This, she thought, was Christmas. Then her eyes fell to her hands, folded on her lap. A large scarlet drop had fallen onto her crooked finger. Another soon joined it. She thought to reach up, touch her injured brow, but somehow, her hand lacked the strength. She looked at Julio. His dark face and black eyes shone in the soft lights of the candles, the sparkle of her ornaments. What would become of him? Of them? They had nothing but each other. But, then, she thought, that was more than most had, more by a long shot. It was more than she had, but not more than she remembered having.

She smiled and settled into the soft warmth of Dutch's chair, utterly satisfied with the comfortable inner peace she felt. Willow Oaks and Yvonne were far from her mind, from her life. For the moment, it seemed enough to sit quietly in her house, to look at her ornaments, to smell Christmas, and to remember.

She looked up once more at Julio, but he wasn't there. Instead, there was Dutch. He wore his sailor's uniform and looked as tall and handsome as the night they met, his grin stretching wide, his red curly hair piled high on his head, and his blue eyes sparkling.

"Want to step outside for a smoke?" he asked.

Pain and weariness fled before a fluttering heartbeat. "It's cold out there," she replied through a smile so big it hurt.

"I've got something to keep us warm." He winked, patted his bag, then extended his hand. "C'mon. It's Christmas, and I've got a train to catch."

She stood, held out her hand. He spun gallantly and took her arm, and together they stepped outside into the breathless cold.

ETTA'S POND

Walker P. Sloan and Mickey stopped chewing at the same time. It was the first really warm night in a while, and the windows were open. They were having supper when the terror of screaming rubber came through the rusty, thin screens on the house's south side. They immediately looked at each other. Walker P.'s fork, laden with mashed potatoes and redeye gravy, stopped halfway to his open mouth. Mickey's cornbread froze in his fingers. Their eyes locked. They both knew what was the matter without saying it, and a hollow feeling replaced the half-eaten meal in Walker P.'s stomach.

"Maybe it was a skunk, or a armadillo," Mickey said.

"Them folks don't stop for that." Walker P. put his fork down, picked up his napkin, and wiped his chin. "Rabbit or possum neither. It's Butch."

Out on the porch twilight was passing. The silver sky in the west outlined the bare trees. It was early spring. Buds hadn't yet appeared on the burr oaks and cottonwoods, and the Johnson grass was still yellow and crackly. Walker P. walked to the edge of the warped, gray boards and peered out toward the highway. A pair of taillights blinked away into the night.

"One of them Surburbans," he said. "From over to Punkin Center. Goddamn town people got no sense. Drive too goddamn fast. Don't they know folks live here?" The man and boy stared off into the darkness. "Get my rifle," he said, "and a lantern." Mickey turned and went back into the house.

"You ain't gonna shoot him, are you?" he asked when he returned and handed the 30.06 to the old man.

"May have to. If he's hurt bad an' ain't dead, I got no choice. Animals can't live with pain. Couldn't keep that damn fool dog out of that road. Should of shot him when they put it in."

"You couldn't of done that, Walker P. He was my dog."

"He was Etta's dog."

Walker P. hefted the rifle in arthritic fingers and limped down off the porch. Mickey lit the kerosene lantern and followed. It was a scant fifty yards out to the barbed wire alongside the paved state highway. Mickey put a worn sneaker on a lower strand to push it down, and pulled the top wire up. Walker P. leaned the rifle against a cedar post and stooped through the opening, then he held the fence and the lantern for Mickey.

"Butch!" Walker P. whistled. "Butch? Yo, Butch boy?"

"C'mon Butch," Mickey pleaded. "Yo, Butch!" His voice was high and plaintive. It rang off the mesquite scrub along the fence line. The two waded through the dead Johnson grass in the ditch.

The rifle wasn't necessary. Butch was dead: back broken, teeth bared back in a fierce grimace against the lantern's glare. Whether it was pain or fear, Walker P. couldn't say. There wasn't much blood. He had died clean.

"Stupid sons of bitches," Walker P. said. "Damn fool dog."

"This is where the pond was, an' this is where he liked to be," Mickey said.

"Pond's gone. Damn fool dog should of seen that."

As the last of daylight slipped behind the horizon, Mickey picked up the dog and carried him back through the wire. They buried him on a knoll a hundred yards behind the house, next to Etta's grave.

"There was a time," Walker P. said while he tamped down the newly turned earth over his—Etta's—dog's grave, "when she'd of done anything she could for that animal. Worthless as he was. Who'd of thought he'd outlive her? Hadn't of been for that road, he'd of outlived me, bet you."

"Don't say that, Walker P.," Mickey's voice cracked. He was crying, or fighting it, Walker P. realized. "Somethin' happens to you, what'll become of me?"

"You'll get on, boy," Walker P. said. He gave the grave a final pat. The lantern's yellow light spilled across it and illuminated them only from the knees down. The night was moonless, dark. "You got on before. You'll get on after." The wind picked up slightly, and Walker P. thought he heard a hymn being hummed from far off. He cocked his head suddenly, but it was gone.

"He was a good dog," Mickey said. Walker P. knew the boy felt the need to say something, wanted Walker P. to say something. He had wanted him to say something when Etta was buried, too. But he hadn't. He'd be damned if he was going to now.

"Yeah, well, what the hell," he said. He picked up the lantern. "Get the pick. We got a early day tomorrow."

"We got a early day every day."

"Yeah, well, what the hell." They went back to the house to wash up the supper dishes.

————

Walker P. had been getting up at five o'clock for so long that he had no need of an alarm clock. Occasionally a thunderstorm would awaken him earlier, or maybe Etta would turn in her sleep and bring him to consciousness. But usually, he just opened his eyes, cleared his throat, and shifted his legs over the side of the bed. By the time he did the milking, gathered the eggs, fussed with whatever piece of equipment he would need that day, the sun was up. Etta would have ham frying along with eggs, biscuits, gravy, potatoes, hot coffee, and cool, sweet milk.

Since her death five years before, he sometimes forgot she was gone. When he returned to the kitchen, stopping to remove his dirty shirt and boots before entering the house, he was shocked to discover the stove cold, coffee unmade, the room still dark and still. It was then her death hit him the hardest, then and one other time: when he looked out over the highway and remembered where the pond had been.

The pond was a unique phenomenon in the county. Lots of farmers had tanks, most filled by windmills pulling gyp water deep from the earth and pouring it into man-made sandy ditches for stock to drink. But Etta's Pond was fed by a natural spring. Maybe it was the only one in the whole county, or at least the only one left since irrigation dropped the water table. Walker P.'s father, Sean, found it one Sunday when he took off from the backbreaking toil of laying down the Fort Worth and Denver City

Railroad route and went on an aimless walk through the fields nearby the line camp. He had been the son of a farmer in Ireland, and he knew enough of the trade to know that rich soil and sweet surface water meant success was possible. He marked the spring, hiked to town, and sat on the sidewalk outside the county court house until they opened on Monday. He filed his papers, went back and built a dugout, and two years later had made enough farming cotton to marry Elizabeth Walker, a sixteen-year-old beauty who gave him Walker Patrick and three other children before she died of pneumonia thirty years later. Sean had a stroke ten years after that. He spent his last year sitting in a rocker on the porch, looking out over the encroaching mesquite around his spring and the small creek that ran out of it, watching Walker P. take over the farm. The other children—girls all—married and moved away. Walker P. got a Christmas card from each of them and their children, whom he'd never met, every year. Two were dead now. The third was senile.

The spring wasn't a pond then, only a creek, a run really. When Walker P. arose the morning after he and Mickey buried Butch, he peered out into the predawn gloom and imagined that he could still see cotton bolls waving just outside his window. Cotton was his life when he was young. It was hard to grow, hard to keep healthy, hard to pick, cheap to sell. Every square foot of the farm was planted, even the dooryard to the house that Sean had completed after Walker P.'s second sister was born. There were no strippers then, no combines, not even tractors. Black laborers and white trash from town hoed the weeds, pulled the bolls, sacked and loaded the cotton onto mule-drawn wagons that Walker P. and his father drove to town. Walker P. was only ten when he drove his first team to the gin. He was past forty when he gave up cotton for wheat.

He started the coffee boiling and went out to the barn and milked his single cow. She was heavy with a calf, and that pleased him. He'd fatten it all summer, butcher it next year: keep half, sell half, eat well for a year. He heard Mickey fussing around in the henhouse, talking to the chickens, gathering eggs. Walker P. poured out a quart of warm white foam into a plastic container, then took the milk pail and set it next to the barn door for Mickey to find. There was no market for fresh milk anymore. Or for eggs. Mickey would slop the hogs with most of both before he came in for breakfast.

The sun was up when Walker P. finished hard-frying six eggs and crisping ten strips of bacon so brittle that they broke from a mere glance. He used store-bought biscuits—never had the knack for bread-making—commercial jelly, too, no gravy. They ate the last of Etta's preserves two years ago. The coffee was bitter and hot, but yesterday's milk was sweet and cold. The two men ate in silence and listened to traffic swishing past on the highway. As was their custom, they didn't speak during a meal.

———

There was a series of mornings—several months' worth—when Walker P. was aroused for his morning chores by something other than his internal clock. The noise of earth-moving equipment started the din. It was followed by bulldozers, heavy trucks, then rollers and asphalt machines. The slamming of doors and curses of working men brought the sun up, put the cow off her milking schedule, stopped the hens from laying. The sows ate their litters that spring. Everything was wrong, but there wasn't a thing Walker P. could do about it.

"We're putting the highway right through here," a khaki-clad engineer told him.

Walker didn't like the man the minute he saw him. He drove up in a new Chevrolet pickup with TX DOT markings on it, sent Mickey looking for Walker P., and sat there smoking a cigarette while the farmer shut down his ancient International Harvester tractor and trudged up to the house. The man wore a shiny straw hat, short-sleeved white shirt, and a clip-on tie. He introduced himself as Clyde Dayton and told Walker P. what was about to happen: he was going to lose his farm.

———

"Eminent domain," the young lawyer in town told Walker P. "There's nothing you can do about it, I'm afraid." The young man's name was James David Leftwich.

Walker P. scowled at the youth across the mahogany desk in front of him. He never had trusted any man who went by two whole first names. He had been Walker P. since grade school where there was also a Walker K. and a Walker T.

"Never knew that name was so popular," the teacher said. It was the way she had of telling them apart when she called on them, and it stuck.

"Where's Buddy Henson?" Walker P. asked the attorney. "I always do my law business with Buddy. He won't let'em take my farm."

"You know Buddy's retired," James David smiled sadly. "I'm his nephew, and I'm handling his practice. Have been for two years." He adjusted his cuffs underneath his suit coat. "And they're not taking your farm. They're just building a highway through it."

Buddy never wore a suit coat inside of doors in his life, Walker P. thought. His only fault was that he sometimes drank too much. It was a vice Walker P. respected. James David Leftwich didn't look like he had ever had a sip of decent whiskey in his life. No backbone, Walker P. scowled to himself. Half-decent shit pain would cripple him.

"Now," Leftwich went on as he scanned the papers Dayton had given to Walker P. "They're offering you a fair price. Twenty dollars an acre more than you could get on the open market, the way things are for farmers these days."

"Don't want to sell."

"You don't have a choice. The state has the legal right to come right through there with that highway. It's only a spur, really. I think you might squeeze them for a few dollars more. We could demand another five, maybe ten an acre. They would beat us in court, initially, but it would hold them up, and they don't want that. I can prepare a letter and see what happens. It would help if you would list it with a real estate broker at the price we want."

"Don't want no goddamn broker. Don't want their goddamn money. I want my farm. It's *my* farm. Born there. Lived there all my goddamn life. My folks is buried there. Wife, too."

"Well, you can still live there." Leftwich glanced at a fancy, black-faced clock on his desk. "They won't touch the house."

"They're cutting it right in two. I don't see the need for it. That road's done just fine goin' up by the bridge. Just who the hell wants a paved road through my farm anyway?"

Leftwich leaned back and tented his fingers. "You know as well as I do about the new development out at Pumpkin Center."

"Punkin Center," Walker P. corrected. "Never was no pumpkins there.

Named for folks named Punkin. My daddy knew them." Goddamn city people, he thought. Come out here, mess up everything. Ran half the town now, maybe all of it. Sure as hell ran the county.

"It's a five-mile drive up to the highway bridge and then into town. This spur'll make it a straight three-mile shot." He pursed his lips and then reached out and adjusted the clock. "You know also that every farmer in Texas thinks it's his God-given right to have a paved road running right up to his front door. You probably voted for the men who passed this law."

"Ain't no farmers livin' in Punkin Center. Just a bunch of yahoo town people, bankers an' the like. Come out here 'cause they've already messed up things where they was. Buildin' a country club an' a lake an' sittin' round on their asses listenin' to the TV. I'm a farmer. That's my farm they're cuttin' up."

"You have a whole section. This isn't going to take up that much of it."

"They're going to fence off the whole damned place. Can't run no stock, got to take the tractor the long way round. Can't get combines into my fields. Half what I got is overrun with goddamn mesquite an' fire ants anyhow. They're goin' to ruin what I got left."

"Well, maybe it's time you thought about retiring. They're going to pay you a considerable amount. Why not sell out, lock, stock, and barrel? You could relax, take it easy. How old are you, anyway, Mr. Sloan?"

"None of your goddamn business."

"You're over seventy. You're a widower. You have no children to care for you."

"I got Mickey."

Leftwich frowned. "You ought to look at one of the rooming houses in town. There are several that cater to men your age. Your friends, farmers like yourself who've retired. They get together and have a great time. Uncle Buddy's living in one," he added hopefully.

"Sit round on their goddamn butts an' drool on each other. I been there. I seen them."

"They're your friends."

"My friends is all dead." He clenched his fists. "Look, I'm a healthy workin' man. I got all my own teeth, don't take no tonic or pills. My heart's good, an' I think clear. See things clear, too. I can see they're stealin' my farm from me, an' I come to see ol' Buddy for help. Now, you tell me Buddy's over yonder pissin' on his boots, so I guess it's up to you."

"There's nothing I can do. I'm sorry. I have another appointment. I'll write the letter asking for more money, and I'll let you know—"

"Ol' Buddy'd never let them sons of bitches take my farm. That's a good farm. It makes its way. I never had to borrow extra on it, always paid my bills. I got money in the goddamn bank to carry it. They got no right to take it."

Leftwich rose. "They have the right. It's the law. And, I say again, they're not taking your farm, just running a highway through it." He looked hard at Walker P., but the old man saw only pity in Leftwich's eyes. It infuriated him. It saddened him.

The lawyer stuck out his hand. "I urge you to remember that. They're not taking your farm, just cutting through it. There's nothing you can do to stop that highway."

"No." Walker P. came to his feet and stuck his gnarled hands into his overalls' pockets. "I guess they ain't."

"That's the way. Look at it positively. I mean, in the final analysis, you'll be better off. What have you really lost?"

"Etta's Pond," he said. "Sons of bitches'll ruin Etta's Pond."

———

It was really Walker P. who made the decision to ruin Etta's Pond. He had little choice. Clyde Dayton came into the house, sat down, and ignored the mug of reheated ebony bile that Walker P. put in front of him. Walker P. was no happier about the man's presence than the engineer was about how bitter the coffee was, but Etta had never turned away any person from her kitchen without some kind of refreshment, and the leftover breakfast coffee was handy.

Dayton didn't even take off his hat. He spread a map out on the oil-cloth of the kitchen table and used a silver pen as a pointer.

Walker P. tried to listen, to understand, but the map looked like nothing he had ever seen before. It had swirls and lines going in circles. No landmarks were identified, only elevations, geographical problems, geological faults. Dayton lit a cigarette and continued to talk, sweeping his pen out toward the walls of the room in different directions, oblivious to the old farmer's confusion.

"So, we'll leave it up to you after this point," he said. Walker P. peered down to see the pen's point resting between a maelstrom of wavy lines. The name "Sloan" had been penciled inside a tiny circle a few inches away. Walker P. decided that was his farm. "We have three choices: We can go straightaway, which would run right through the house, here. We can cut to the north or south of it. We try not to take a man's house if we can avoid it. Costs too much." He winked. "So in this case, either route is fine. We'll just curve away in whichever direction you think is best for you."

Dayton went on about how they would erect fences along the right-of-way to protect the house and fields they were interrupting, suggested ways of moving the road coming up to the house to improve Walker P.'s access, and discussed the number of gates they would be required to place in the fence. Walker P. wasn't listening anymore.

"So, which is it to be? North or south? It really doesn't matter to us." He walked out onto the porch. Walker P. followed. "I can come back next week, if you want to think about it. But we'll need an answer, soon. The road crews are already to the cutoff on Grangerford's place where the old road ties in. Surveyors will need to go to work here, soon."

What Dayton was saying finally registered in Walker P.'s mind. "Which away you want to go?"

Dayton patiently outlined the alternative routes once more. The rolled map substituted for the pen as he pointed north of the house, toward the knoll where Etta's grave was. Walker P. felt a chill in the summer air. She hadn't been in the ground but a few months. It was where she wanted to be, said so to him a million times. Now, this Yankee feather merchant was sent from Austin to build a road right over it.

"No goddamn way," he said. "There's a grave up there, cemetery. My daddy's up there. My mama, too." He paused. "My wife's up there."

Dayton studied Walker P. "Well, we can go south. It'll cut closer to the house, right across that tank. But if that's what you want."

"Ain't a tank, it's a pond," Walker P. corrected automatically. It was a common mistake. "Natural spring."

"Well, it's that or the cemetery. Which?"

"Can't you cut south of the pond. Maybe way over yonder someplace?"

"Nope." Dayton lit another smoke and shook his head. "Soil's unstable down in there. We did a preliminary shoot last month. Core samples and seismograph readings say it's almost a swamp. And if we go over to the north, we have to blast through solid rock. This is the only route."

Walker P. went in to see Buddy at that point. But Buddy wasn't there. Leftwich was, and was no help. When he saw Dayton again, he told him it would have to be the pond. Etta's Pond.

———

While Mickey finished the breakfast dishes, Walker P. went out on the porch with his coffee. He set it carefully on a rusty metal table and rolled a cigarette. For more than forty years, he had smoked four hand-rolled cigarettes a day: one after each meal, one right before bedtime. With the last one of an evening, it was also his habit to take a sip or two of whiskey from a pint bottle he kept under the kitchen sink.

Etta hated strong drink, but she never complained about that. In their forty years together, she complained about very little.

Looking out over the gray surface of the roadway, he observed morning traffic passing. There were plenty of pickups, some heavier vehicles, Suburbans, Expeditions, Tahoes, a variety of foreign-made SUVs, some big cars and some small, sporty models. Mostly they were spanking new and driven by men and women dressed for office jobs. He doubted any of the vehicles would ever be worked the way he worked his old Ford truck or IH tractor. He doubted that any of the drivers had ever really worked at all. "Goddamn speed merchants," he said aloud when three in a row raced by.

For a while after the highway was completed, motorists waved to him when they saw him sitting and sipping his coffee. The road was close to the house, too close, and they could see him clearly. He never waved back, and soon they stopped. He never drove or walked on the asphalt surface, except to cross it, either. When he went to town, he took the old county road by the bridge, which he could see they were letting go.

He hadn't planted any crops the spring they built the highway. He intended to, and the wheat was already up by the time they started, but instead of putting in alfalfa and soybeans, he spent the mornings watching them ruin the pond. He stayed on the porch every day until mid-May. Then, he left only to supervise the wheaties who took the grain from his fields. It was a good year, first in a long time that hail or excess rain hadn't ruined at least part of the golden crop before he got it out. Prices were high, too. It was a chance to replace worn-out equipment, fix up the house and outbuildings. But he hadn't. His heart wasn't in it.

The year before Etta had still been alive. Ten inches of rain in two weeks washed the wheat down and rotted it in the fields. What he got out didn't get to the elevator for weighing until the price fell.

"Maybe next year," she said. She said that almost every year. When next year came, she was gone.

He banked the money and watched the workers destroy the pond. Butch and Mickey sat with him. The only work they did was essential chores: the cow, the chickens, the hogs. When they had the pond all filled in but a few thousand square feet out in the middle, they tossed in some dynamite and killed all the fish. Perch, channel cat, smallmouth bass floated to the surface, stunned, dead. The construction workers gathered them up and put them in plastic coolers. They brought a mess up to the porch where Walker P. sat and offered them to him: his own fish. He told them to go to hell, and they stayed away from him after that.

Butch didn't even like them. He ran up and down the new fence they put up and barked at them constantly when they were working near the house. It was a wonder he didn't have a heart attack, Walker P. told Mickey. He ran and yelped for hours: Etta's dog, protecting Etta's pond.

———

Walker P. met Etta just after his youngest sister married and left home. It was at the State Fair. He had a prize mule that year, and friends urged him to enter it. She was the last working mule he would ever own, he realized, and it seemed a good thing to do. It was his only trip to the Dallas event in his life, and he met Etta in the neighboring swine exhibit. He strolled over to admire the hogs, and she smiled at him and introduced herself.

"Name's Etta," she said. "For Etta Place. Know who she was?" Walker P. acknowledged his ignorance. "She was the Sundance Kid's sweetheart. He was an outlaw. My granddaddy was conductor on a railroad they held up. Always said she was the prettiest girl he'd ever seen, made my folks name me for her. Said he didn't want me to be an outlaw, but he was sure I'd turn out pretty. What do you think? Am I pretty?"

Walker P. admitted she was.

She was a farm girl from down along the coast, lived right on the ocean, she said, place called High Island where her daddy ran cattle, and she continued her 4-H work with hog-breeding long after she was too old for the club. They talked for hours, and when he got back to West Texas, he wrote to her. Four letters later, he proposed, and she accepted by telegram. He was impressed, and she *was* pretty. They were married at her aunt's house in Waco, about halfway between. She told him on their honeymoon night that she knew they would get married the minute she saw him. He was glad. He had felt the same way.

She took well to farm life in the arid climate, kept breeding hogs, the only husbandry he continued to practice after she died aside from keeping chickens and one good heifer for milk. Cheerful always, happy to be Walker P.'s wife, she asked him for very little he didn't provide and paid him back by becoming more beautiful every year. Her main oral expression of regret was that she missed seeing water.

"You live on the ocean all your life, you come to miss it. I never look out the kitchen window, I don't miss seeing a body of water," she told him once. Once was enough.

The next day he hired a dozer to come and dredge out the spring's creek and build a small earthen dam: The pond was born. That was when he stopped farming cotton. Irrigation was now possible from the runoff, and he sank three wells elsewhere on his property and began growing wheat, alfalfa, soybeans, even watermelon and cantaloupe. They planted a peach orchard alongside the graves where his parents were buried, had pecans along the old dry bed where it meandered off toward Blind Man's Creek and into the copper breaks, and they planted grass and flowerbeds in the house's yard where Sean Sloan grew cotton years before. Etta revived his mother's vegetable garden as well.

The pond was popular. FFA and 4-H boys who lived in town and needed a place to raise their livestock projects came out to swim and fish in the summer while they tended and pampered their animals that occupied pastures and pens Walker P. provided without charge. It was they who named it "Etta's Pond." They also provided a bit of labor around the house—mending things, chopping weeds, mowing grass—sometimes even taking a turn on the tractor when the wheat stubble needed plowing or hay needed baling in return for the farm's hospitality. Often, Etta would ask them to crank up a freezer of ice cream she made to go with some fried chicken for an impromptu picnic along the banks. Eventually, they even built some rickety tables and benches to set out there. Some of them spent more time on the Sloan farm than they did at home. Some said they would rather be no place else in the world.

"It gives me such a warm feeling to see those kids out there," Etta always said. They were five years married then, and two doctors had confirmed that the Sloans would never have children of their own.

The best part of the pond, though, was the way he and Etta used it. In the heat of summer, when he would come in at dusk, filthy with soil and grease from the implements he had wrestled around all day, he wouldn't even go to the house. In the twilight, out among the crickets and bullfrogs, he would strip off his grimy overalls and swim out to the middle. Etta pretended to be outraged to see her naked husband cavorting in her pond, but after a few pretended scoldings, she, too, would respond to his calls, undress, and enter the cool, healing water, swim out to him, and they would splash and play until full dark.

"Don't need no bath when you got the pond," Walker P. would tell her when they came shivering into the house for supper. "Can't fill a tub with nothing as good as what we got right out there."

———

Walker P.'s coffee had gone cold, though he had barely sipped it. Mickey seemed to sense the problem, and before the old man splashed the black liquid into the dead flowerbeds alongside the porch, he emerged with the pot.

"We gonna work today?" he asked.

"No more'n usual," Walker P. said.

"Thought I might go find some flowers to plant on ol' Butch's grave."

"It's too early for flowers."

"They's some daisies out yonder," Mickey said. He pointed off toward a north pasture. "I could dig up the roots while they're dead. See if they'd seed out. It'd be real pretty come summer."

Walker P. doubted it would work. They were more likely sunflowers than daisies. He sipped the scalding coffee and nodded. "Go ahead on," he nodded. "Get back 'fore dark. Tend them hogs." Etta's hogs, he amended. He hadn't been able to bring himself to sell or kill one since she died, and they had grown fat, lazy, and plentiful in their pen. It was all he could do to cut the boars in time to keep a new litter from appearing.

The boy scampered off.

Boy, Walker P. thought. He was nearing thirty, maybe. "Put some on Etta's grave, too," he shouted. Mickey stopped and turned.

"Miss Etta always did like flowers," Mickey grinned. He waved his gimme cap and took off at a dead run. Didn't even take a shovel, Walker P. thought. He'll be back in a spell.

———

Walker P. watched the roadbed grow to a completed highway. In a way, he told himself day after day as the trucks and machines worked in the increasingly hot afternoons, it was worse than if they had gone over the cemetery. It was almost as if they were burying all those kids who came out here. But then, it was worse than that, too. The kids were long grown and gone, and Walker P. and Etta were only old people, dim memories to them. By July, the workers had moved on, out of sight. Only a distant noise told the farmer that they had passed beyond the boundaries of his property and were now cutting up someone else's: Dutch Cummings's, he reminded himself, but then he remembered that Dutch Cummings died. No one had lived on the Cummings place in years.

A group of people named the Sandhill Grain Syndicate farmed it now. They'd sent him letters from Dallas asking if he was interested in selling out to them. They offered him "top dollar," they said. He wondered if it was as much as the state paid. But he didn't wonder long. He burned their letters with the rest of the trash.

When the bright yellow truck came down painting stripes in the middle of the gray asphalt, it was over. The fence was up and sang in the summer wind, and vehicles were soon speeding past, hauling people from town to Punkin Center and the swimming pool and golf course they had put in alongside a small, man-made lake built for the exclusive use of the wealthy residents who lived there. Of an evening, when the wind lay,

Walker P. could hear the high whine of their speedboats. Sometimes they reminded him of Etta's humming when it came across the fields.

He continued to go out to the porch and sit the rest of the summer. Only the greatest of effort forced him away from the rocker to gather his crops. The melons mostly rotted in the fields. He didn't have the energy to harvest them regularly.

The next year he did better. He put in his winter wheat, also planted in the spring, and did fairly well with all his crops, made money for the second year in a row. Mickey worked with him, but Mickey was little help at all. He never could master the intricate gears of the old tractor, and he didn't move a plow or handle anything more complicated than a hoe without hurting himself or destroying the implements. He couldn't even milk properly. It was only through the greatest effort he taught the boy to swim. In the pond. But Etta had loved him. Just as she had loved Butch. So Walker P. never complained or scolded him. He gave him chores to do that he knew he could do, saw to his needs, and let him alone.

One September noon almost fifteen years before, Walker came up from the fields for dinner and found Mickey sitting on the porch eating leftover stew. He gave the farmer a wide, dirty-faced grin when Walker P. stripped off his shirt and boots and stomped barefoot past him into the kitchen. It wasn't that unusual for Etta to feed a drifter, although in those days drifters weren't as common as they had once been. It aggravated Walker P. nonetheless.

"They're like cats when they're that young," he said. His skin was milky where the sun hadn't touched it. His neck and hands were dark brown, almost mahogany from heat and dry wind. Bare-chested, he looked twenty years younger than he did in his sunbaked overalls and workshirts. "Feed them, an' they'll never leave."

"He was hungry," she said before he could go on. "He's going to clean out the henhouse after dinner. Says his name is Mickey. Don't say anything else."

"He'll be here a week if he's here a hour."

He was there all day, Walker P. discovered when he came in at dark. He had a plate of chicken and dumplings balanced on his ragged trousers and a huge tumbler of iced tea next to him on the porch. Walker P. noted that his shoes were bound together with strips of tape. He had no suit-case, no bindle, nothing in the way of belongings besides what he was wearing.

"He's just like that goddamn dog," Walker P. growled over supper.

"Hush," Etta warned him. "And watch your language. He's just a boy."

Normally, Walker P. knew, drifters liked nothing better than eating but talking. Starved for company, they would sit and talk about their lives for hours: where they had been, where they were heading, what big things they planned to do. This boy was different. When Walker P. came out after supper for his smoke, the boy sat quietly and stared out over the pond.

"There any fish in there?" he asked.

"There's fish."

That was it. They sat silently in the darkness until Etta came out with a lantern, apologizing good-naturedly about Walker P.'s continued failure to wire the porch for electricity, and then sat next to her husband and pre-tended to crochet a baby blanket for a newborn grandniece they would never see.

When he was still there two days later, they questioned Mickey closely. He didn't know his last name—or wouldn't give it, Walker P. sus-pected—or exactly how old he was. He claimed to have finished eighth grade, but he couldn't remember—or wouldn't say—where. In fact, he said he didn't know where he was from, where he had been, exactly, or where in the world he was going. He slept in the barn. The next morning, they put him in the back of the pickup and took him to town.

Doc Wilson examined the boy, gave him some simple tests, then told them he was mentally retarded: not "crazy," as Walker P. suggested, just "slow." He said it would take a specialist to know for sure, but to him it seemed like a syndrome—"Asperger's," he thought, a form of autism. "Won't get worse, won't get better. He's pretty much the way he'll always be. He's not stupid. Just slower than us."

"How'd he get it?" Walker P. asked, then glanced protectively at Etta. "Can we catch it?"

"He didn't get it," Wilson said and fired his pipe. "He was born with it. And no, you can't catch it. He's harmless, but he's helpless, too. In a way."

He sent them to Sheriff Schroeder for advice. Schroeder told them he would make some calls, see if anyone had reported him missing. In the meantime, they could take him home. Two days later he drove out and told them that there was no record of Mickey that he could find anywhere. He would keep looking. He suggested that they let him take Mickey back into town, call a social worker from Wichita Falls.

"What happens then?" Etta asked.

"Well, if they can't find his folks, I reckon he'll have to go down to Austin or maybe somewhere else. There's places for boys with his problems."

"You mean an asylum, don't you?" Etta asked. Her hands were bunched in her apron.

"Well," Schroeder shifted his weight. "They don't call them that. But yes."

"Where you reckon he come from? Where's his folks?"

The sheriff looked down the old county road as it trailed dusty into the distance. "Sometimes, people just can't handle boys like that. They just dump them. Let somebody else worry about it," he said. "It's not pretty, but it happens."

"I know," Etta said thoughtfully. "That's how we come by Butch."

Walker P. walked away and went down to the barn. He knew that Mickey wasn't going with the sheriff. He wasn't going anyplace.

They bought him new clothes and enrolled him in school for one term, but he was too far behind to catch up, too slow-witted to follow much of anything. He obsessed on things, ideas or items, collected junk, or became fascinated with some casual event. Other boys picked on him; even those half his size and years younger than he was sent him home with a bloody nose or black eye. He didn't even have the sense to be ashamed of it, and it never occurred to him to fight back. Doc Wilson filled out a form saying that he was seventeen, old enough to quit school if he wanted, and he stayed on the farm, played with Butch, and helped Etta out with chores. He was worth less than Butch as a hand, but he could do a few things, and he made Etta happy. She called him an "angel unawares," and that would have to be enough for Walker P.

When he had been there five years, they talked of putting him into a special school that was starting in Wichita Falls, maybe help him learn a trade. "Something to do with himself when we're gone," she said. She never considered his leaving before then, though Walker P. often wished he would. She wrote off for information twice. The principal at the high school in town said he would help arrange things. Walker P. never saw the need for it. "Good money after bad," he told her. "We feed him, give him a bed. If he wants more, let him go after it."

"He don't know his name, not even what day it is," she said. "He's God's gift to us. Just like that pond out there. Just like you and me are to each other."

"We'll see when the time comes," Walker P. promised. He then pointed out that Mickey's going away might mean his staying away. That put an end to the argument. To Etta he was like the pond, like Butch, like Walker P. and the farm: her life.

———

To his surprise, it was afternoon when Walker P. finally rose from the porch and moved into the kitchen. He ought to make some dinner, but he knew that Mickey, wherever he was, wouldn't come back until he spotted his shadow long on the ground and saw that it was getting dark. Etta gave him a watch one Christmas, but he never mastered telling time. He didn't even cry at her funeral, Walker P. recalled. But then, neither had Walker P.

The old farmer didn't grieve for Etta, never had. She was a woman with a good heart, and one day, the heart just quit: like a piece of land that would grow fat crops year after year, then just quit. She wore out. Walker P. didn't begrudge God for taking her. In a way, he thought she was relieved to go. Farming was hard on a woman. Hard on a man, too. He missed her, but he never resented her leaving him behind.

He went into the kitchen, got some ham from the refrigerator, and made himself a sandwich, boiling up a new pot of coffee to go with it. There was a bucket of scraps by the sink, and he whistled and called Butch to come eat the bacon rind. He was out on the porch before he remembered. A car sped past to remind him.

Sometimes, he had trouble remembering exactly where the pond was. Now, as his eyes roamed over the highway and fence line, he couldn't recall it ever being there. There had been a stand of hackberry trees next to the spring, but they were gone. There was nothing left to mark where it had been.

Butch never forgot. Like Walker P. and Etta, he loved to swim in the pond, would go down on his own and cool off when the weather was hot and prowl the banks, barking at migrating ducks when they stopped over. After the highway went in, he'd roam the blacktop like it was a blanket covering a buried bone, sniffing at the ground and looking lost and quizzical when he couldn't figure out where the water was. Walker P. stood on the porch and realized that he had marked the pond's boundaries by Butch's antics, much as they aggravated him and made him fear for the dog's safety. Now Butch was gone. So was the pond.

For years, of an evening when the season didn't demand constant, daylight-to-dark labor, neighbors would come by and sit on the porch, sip iced tea or coffee, and look out over the pond, watch Butch or the boys from town swimming out there. Once in a while, they would take one of the cane poles Walker P. kept stacked by the barn and put a few grasshoppers out on the water. It didn't matter if they caught anything; it was the company that counted. On hot summer evenings, they would sometimes sit and watch the water rippling in the heat. From time to time a fish would jump, and through the cicadas' buzzing the sound of that cool splash was the next best thing to an early norther.

More than once, when Etta was in town buying groceries or on some other errand, the pond was full of naked farmers, playing like schoolboys in the blue water. She wouldn't have minded, Walker P. thought. The pond was for friends, neighbors. It was for her and her life there.

Now, there were no more friends, no more neighbors. The county agent told Walker P. just before the highway was put in that he was only one of four resident farmers left in that end of the county. The rest had moved into town long ago. Or died. The farm had died, too. He wouldn't fool with the gates Dayton's people put up, and he leased out the fields and pastures across the highway. Last year, he had leased out all but the twenty-five acres immediately surrounding the house. It was still good land, mesquite and ant infested as it was. People were glad to have the use of it.

Walker P. looked around the yard. Rusty equipment, a falling-down hogwire fence, some broken pens greeted his eyes. Everything needed paint. Wind had almost pushed the barn over. The tractor hadn't been started in a year, probably wouldn't. Weeds choked the flowerbeds, and a failure to water had killed the grass last summer. Large bare patches of dusty ground spotted the yard. Etta's—his mother's—vegetable garden was overgrown with Johnson grass and tumbleweeds. There was a trash heap next to some sixty-gallon oil drums. He needed to do some burning, another chore he didn't trust Mickey with, and probably there were snakes under the henhouse. The weather was warming: they'd be out and after the chicks and eggs soon.

He went back inside and discovered the coffeepot boiling over. When he reached out his hand to grab it, the black liquid spilled out and scalded him.

"Goddamn!" he cried, turning and flinging the coffeepot across the room. Grounds splattered across the cracked linoleum. "Goddamn, god-damn!" He stepped to the sink and ran cold water over the burned area. That made it hurt even worse, and he jerked his hand away. "Son of a bitch!" he hissed.

"Etta," he called. "Etta! I burned myself, goddamnit." She would be mad about his swearing, he thought. Can't be helped: A man has to swear out the pain. "Etta!"

His voice came back to him in a slight echo, and he remembered. The kitchen seemed to close in on him. Outside he heard the fence keening in the wind. Corner shadows raced toward him and made his head swim. He shook it, cleared his mind.

"Damned old fool," he said. "Not worth a good goddamn to nobody."

He stalked through the house back to the bathroom. It was an add-on, something his father had not seen the need for when he constructed the house. And it was modern. Etta insisted on the best plumbing they could afford, and they had it. A well provided the water, and they had a Culligan softening system. He entered and opened the medicine cabinet.

An array of ointments and creams were stacked on the top shelf. Some had been left open and dried up. Others were hard to the touch, and he wasn't sure which ones were right. It was the first time he had hurt him-self seriously since she died, and except for having to put a Band-Aid here or a corn plaster there, he hadn't needed any of the household first aid she always took care of. He almost yelled her name again before his mind jerked him back.

He fussed with several tubes and jars before losing patience and dumping them all into the trash can by the toilet. He ran more cold water over the burn, which was now red and puckering slightly, smeared some Vaseline on it, wrapped some gauze bandage around it, and tied it all up with a handkerchief.

"Have to do," he muttered. "Can't help it. Goddamn stupid old man."

When he passed through the house again, he realized that in all the years he had lived there, it was one of the few times since his childhood he had been anywhere but the kitchen or bathroom during the day. The house seemed small, tiny as he walked through the rooms. The living room appeared behind a curtain of musty sunlight streaming in from the screens and venetian blinds. The furniture looked moldy, used, and covered with dust. The front door hadn't been opened since Etta's funeral. There was probably a good half-acre of soil on every table, he thought. Lying on Etta's secretary were the brochures from the special school in Wichita Falls. Like everything else, they were dusty, brittle to the touch.

The gun case in the corner was also dirty, unused. Walker made a mental inventory—a rifle, two shotguns, and a pistol. He never went in for hunting. He suddenly remembered Dutch Cummings again. Ignored by all his family except for his wife, eat up with cancer, wheat hailed out two years running, whole place going to seed, Walker P. ticked off Cummings's problems. He wondered idly if Cummings had used a rifle or shotgun. Maybe a pistol, he thought: handier. Etta went to the house to comfort Mattie, Walker P. handled the funeral for her. He shook his head in the dusty sunlight and left the living room.

The bedrooms—two open, the rest closed off for years—were in better shape. He glanced into Mickey's neat room. The boy kept it spic and span: everything organized, in its place. At his own door he stopped. The furniture was old. Most of it belonged to Etta's folks. When they died, she had it shipped here to replace the more worn-out pieces bequeathed to Walker P. by his own parents. She shoved that into the spare bedrooms and shut the doors. The only strikingly modern piece was a console color TV—one of two sets they owned. It sat at the end of the bed, raised up on a crude platform of four-by-fours so they could watch it before they went to sleep. It had been broken for years and never picked up but two channels through the antenna mounted on top of the house. The radio in the kitchen gave Walker P. the farm and weather reports. He had never had a yen for any music he couldn't hear on the wind.

Etta's small black-and-white, which she kept in the kitchen for soap operas and game shows to keep her company while she worked, was now in Mickey's room. If he ever watched it, Walker P. didn't know it.

The house seemed strange, quiet, smaller and emptier than it ever had, and Walker P.'s odd feelings swam around him with the dust bugs he raised when he walked through the rooms.

"Need to clean this place up," he said. He vowed to set Mickey to work with mop and dust rag tomorrow.

He returned to the kitchen, cleaned up the spilled coffee, and ate his sandwich. His hand hurt, but somehow it felt like a proper retribution for how foolish he had been acting. He could hear a clock ticking somewhere, and he tried to remember where there was a clock in the house that ticked that loud. But he couldn't. He started to go and see, but he didn't. The house's interior, away from the familiar kitchen, seemed ominous suddenly. He could feel Etta there, sense her presence. It seemed a violation of something to go banging around back there during the day.

———

It was late, and he was burning the trash when Mickey came up, dirty from his face down. His arms bundled around a huge bunch of dead plants, their roots intact.

"Forgot the shovel," he said matter-of-factly. "But I'll need one to put these in up there."

Walker P. stood away from the trash fire. Boxes, cans, and bottles were visible in the flames. He used to burn trash once a week. Etta insisted that if he didn't, they'd have rats, snakes, other varmints poking around.

"Surest way to kill chickens," she said, "is to leave a bunch of trash lyin' round."

He had let it go this time for too long. But it was still early spring. No evidence of animals was about. He and Mickey didn't eat that much, anyway. Food scraps went to the hogs and Butch. It wasn't so bad to wait a while.

"It's gettin' late. You need to tend to the chickens an' hogs. I need to start supper," he said. "Them things won't grow."

Mickey looked abashed. Walker P. reminded himself that the boy had been out in the pasture all day, scraping these weeds out of the ground with his bare hands, all for the love of a dog. And Etta. He changed his tone. "Not without water, they won't. How you goin' to water them?"

Mickey looked up at the knoll. The grave sites were in deep shade now. The sun was declining rapidly. Cars and trucks whisked by on the highway. Quitting time in town, Walker P. thought with a sneer curling his lip. Get out to the goddamn lake, play a round of golf 'fore supper. Drive right through a man's land. Kill his dog.

"Well, I reckoned I could haul some up there. In a bucket." Mickey's dirty brow furrowed.

"I tell you what," Walker P. said suddenly. "There's some lengths of old hose in the barn. Don't think it leaks. Used it when we had to pump out that well few years back. More'n five hundred, maybe eight hundred feet. You take one end, put it down in the pond. Get it out to the middle, way out. Then you take the other end an' run it downhill here by the house. Ought to stretch a good ways. Then you suck real hard on it. One section at a time. Get it flowin' good, then hook up another section, and go do it again. Work your way uphill. Bet you can siphon water halfway up there. Save you a lot of hard work. Give it a try. But don't suck no water inside you. Don't drink no pond water."

Mickey looked at him, then away at the highway. "I can't—"

"Course, if you'd rather haul water in a bucket, that's your lookout."

Mickey looked at him again. "I'll go get a shovel," he said. "Plant 'em first."

"Go on, then. But remember that hose. That'll work, if you suck real hard."

"What happened to your hand?"

"Burned it. Spilled hot coffee on it. Always be careful handlin' hot stuff like that. Take a lesson, boy." Mickey nodded. "Now, go on. You got your chores. If you're goin' to water them things, you need to be quick about it."

Mickey left, and Walker P. used his rake to stir the fire. It was dying out, most of the garbage reduced to cindery ash and black coal. His face was hot from it. It made his hand burn, and he thought again of the pond. When he lifted his head and looked over toward it, he froze.

It was there, he insisted. When he told the boy about the hose, he had glanced that way, and he saw it: just as it was, shimmering in the spring twilight. He had even seen a fish jump. He was sure of it.

Now, though, he only saw the gray, flat pavement. The fence and mesquite were as they had been for almost five years. The pond was gone: plowed up by huge machines, buried under fill dirt, gravel, and asphalt. A big SUV raced by, its headlights on against the gathering shadows.

Walker P. dropped the rake and walked slowly over to the fence. His boots were heavy, and his arms hung to his sides as if they carried huge weights. From the fence line, he surveyed the old dimensions of the pond in his mind. Just for a moment, he thought he could make out in between the gaps in the crickets' songs the sounds of boys splashing in the water, the shouts of fishermen who had bent a pole over a big one. He could smell the freshness of the water, see the cattails lining the banks, hear the bullfrogs calling from the shallows.

He turned to look at the house. The trash fire still smoked from an orange flame at its center. The barn and henhouse, hog pen and corrals seemed to stand straighter than they were before. They had fresh paint, and there was grass and flowers everywhere. Etta's garden was in full bloom. The corn waved in the breeze, beans climbed trellises. The old tractor still had an intact umbrella unfurled. He saw the kitchen lights were on, golden beacons streaming from the house. A shadow moved behind a screen, and there was a figure sitting in the rocking chair on the porch: He felt his heart stop.

A doolie pulling a gooseneck horse trailer sped by, a diesel. Its noise and exhaust hung in the evening atmosphere. Walker P. turned and watched its taillights disappear, and when he looked again at the house, it was dark. No lights appeared at the windows. The shapes of the buildings showed the sway that wind and disrepair forced on them. The garden was a weedy ruin, the tractor rusty and cold. The house's exterior was gray, peeling, in need of washing and painting, and on the porch, the old rocker sat empty. But on the wind, he heard the distinct tones of a hymn being hummed.

Walker P. pulled up the top strand of barbed wire and stepped through the opening. A loud rip when his overalls caught on a sharp point didn't slow him down.

"It ain't fair," he said. "It ain't goddamn fair. I'm a old man. I don't deserve this. I always seen things clear."

His fists beat the air as he walked deliberately out to the middle of the highway. He put his boots on either side of the stripe and looked up. A cloud bank was coming in from the north. Cool front, he thought. We ain't done with winter yet. But the wind was warm on his face. He felt hot, sweaty, grimy from work he hadn't done.

He looked again at the house, and again the image transformed. The lights were on, the shapes erect and well cared for. The figure was still in the rocker, and his wife's shadow moved inside the kitchen, fixing supper, humming along with a memorized hymn. There was no fence, no ditch full of weeds and mesquite scrub between him and the farm. Instead, he seemed to be wet. He looked down and saw that his boots were awash in the blue water of Etta's Pond. He knelt, scooped up two handfuls of the clear, cold water, and splashed his face. The bandage disappeared. The moisture felt good on his burned hand. He was sinking up to his neck, floating, now swimming. His overalls fell away, and he was naked, bobbing. He filled his mouth and spouted like a whale. He felt free, clean, renewed. All around him the sights, smells, sounds of the pond and the farm lifted him up and made him buoyant. His hair matted on his forehead, and he could feel himself diving and writhing in the water.

"No bath tonight, Etta," he called. "Can't fill a tub with nothing as good as what we got right out here!" He flounced on his back and stroked away. "C'mon out! What're you scared of? Won't nobody see us way out here." The kitchen door opened.

The screaming protest of rubber on asphalt pierced the gray darkness and matched the high whine of an engine straining to wind down from highway speed to a dead stop.

"Are you crazy?" a voice shouted when the dust and dirt settled. A bright red Tahoe was in the ditch opposite the Sloan farm, and a well-dressed young man was rushing up out of the Johnson grass and onto the blacktop. "Are you nuts?" he repeated. "I damn near ran right over you!"

Walker P. Sloan sat in the middle of the highway, his hips clothed and dry and squarely on the white stripe. He blinked at the man's approach.

"Jesus Christ! Mr. Sloan, is that you? Are you all right?"

The man reached Walker P. and put hands on him.

"Are you all right? What happened? Did you fall down or something?"

"Who're you?" Walker P. allowed the young man to pull him up. He brushed away the hands. "Quit pawin' at me. Who'n hell're you an' what'd'you want?"

"I almost killed you. Almost ran right over you. What's wrong? Are you sick? What's going on here? You're in the middle of the road."

James David Leftwich. The name came to Walker P.: lawyer, smart-aleck little son of a bitch. Billed him two hundred dollars to write that letter getting me five dollars more an acre than the state originally offered.

"Must of fell down," Walker P. said, backing up from the lawyer. "Some son of a bitch run over my dog."

The lawyer looked around. It was now almost completely dark. Walker P. could see there were other people in the truck.

"James David?" a woman's voice called. "Is he all right? Do I need to call somebody?"

"Are you all right?" Leftwich asked.

"Yeah, I'm all right. Where're you goin' in such a goddamn hurry?"

"Home," Leftwich answered. "I live out here. Pumpkin Center. Go by here every day." He looked up and down the highway, remembered, then his tone softened. "I've been meaning to stop by. Say hello."

"You run over my dog?"

"Me? No! Never ran over a dog in my life. Knock wood."

"Well, somebody did. Been meaning to find out who. Owes me money. That was a good dog. Been lookin' for him."

"I think you'd do better not to do it in the middle of the highway."

Walker P. looked at him, then back at the house. It was completely dark now. The only light was in the henhouse. Mickey was about his chores.

"Yeah, well, what the hell," he said. "'Bliged to you for stoppin'.'"

"You stay out of the road, now. Hear?"

He left the lawyer in the middle of the pavement, made his way through the Johnson grass, crossed the fence, and walked up to the house. When his boots hit the porch, he heard the Tahoe start, back up, then drive off, more slowly now.

"Prissy little dipshit son of a bitch," Walker P. said. He went in to start supper.

———

It was ten o'clock, later than Walker P. had stayed up in years. Clouds covered the stars. Supper finished, dishes washed, chores done, he and Mickey sat out on the porch and watched the occasional vehicle race by. Exhaust odors mixed with noise on the night air. Walker P. was halfway through a new pint, more than he usually drank, and he had rolled his third cigarette since sitting there.

"You get all them flowers planted?"

"Water'd 'em too. Just like you said." Walker P. winced, sipped the whiskey. "I put six on Butch's grave, six on Miss Etta's." Walker P. rocked and nodded. "I put six on your mama's grave, too. Thought she'd like that."

"Likely," Walker P. said. "Mama always liked flowers. Never had none, though. Daddy said where flowers'd grow, cotton'd grow. That was that." They sat and looked at the night a while. "Chill in the air. Might sleet, maybe snow. Rain for sure. My toe aches." His hand hurt, too. But he took another sip of whiskey and ignored it.

"Good for the wheat." Mickey sat on the edge of the porch and rocked his body in imitation of the old farmer. "Walker P.," he asked finally, "if you was to die, what'd become of me?" Same question as before, Walker P. thought.

"I don't know, boy. Reckon you'd get on, somehow. You did before. You will again."

"Think?"

"Likely."

Again he rocked in silence. He heard Etta's voice—in his memory this time, not in any vision or nightmare of the past. It didn't chide or scold. It only reminded him. The time had come. He wondered what the selling price for prime field and pasture was. Tomorrow, he said to himself, he would go into town and find out.

"What'd you think 'bout moving into town, maybe goin' to school over to Wichita Falls?"

"I'd hate that. I hate school."

"Some schools is different from others. I think it's time you thought 'bout that. Seems to me like you already have."

Mickey said nothing. "I'll do what you want me to, Walker P. Whatever you say. You been good to me. You an' Miss Etta give me a place."

"Angel unawares," he heard Etta's voice say. He sipped the whiskey again. He enjoyed the way it burned going down.

"You know, Walker P., when I watered them flowers, I had to use the bucket. Made four trips." He paused, looked at Walker P. "The pond ain't there no more. You know that, don't you?"

Walker P. looked out over the blackness of the highway. Just for a moment all the sights and sounds and sensations he felt before welled up inside him. He could feel it, smell it beneath the asphalt. Just like Butch.

"Well, Mickey," he said. "That's where you're wrong. Etta's Pond is there. It'll always be there." He took a deep breath. "Now, it's time to go to bed. We got a early day tomorrow."

"We got a early day every day."

"Yeah, well, what the hell."

Out of the darkness headlights cut a path down the highway. The car zoomed past toward town, and in the quiet that settled in its wake, the two men sat in the shadows of the porch and rocked.

Acknowledgments

The author is grateful to the following publications, in which a number of the stories first appeared, sometimes in other forms and under other titles.

Concho River Review: "A Better Class of People," 1987

Current Diversions: "A Train to Catch," 1998

Inc. Magazine: "Punkin Center," 2002 (in abridged form)

South Dakota Review: "Nickleby," 1996

Sulphur River Literary Review: "Dogstar," 1994

Texas Review: "Mexico," 1991

Writers' Forum: "Etta's Pond," 1991

Writers' Forum: "Bush League," 1993

———

"The Baptism" is adapted from a chapter of *Agatite,* published originally in 1986 by St. Martin's Press.

Author photo: Judy Reynolds

Writer and critic Clay Reynolds is the author of thirteen books, including *Monuments, Franklin's Crossing,* and *Ars Poetica.* A National Endowment for the Arts fellow and member of the Texas Institute of Letters, his short fiction, novels, and essays have won a number of literary awards, and he has been recognized as a major Texas author. A native West Texan, he is Professor of Arts & Humanities at the University of Texas at Dallas and lives in Lowry Crossing with his wife, Judy, and her dog and cat.